"Teresa Medeiros is one of my all-time
favorite authors."
—SHERRILYN KENYON

"Nobody writes humor with more heart
or passion with more pleasure."
—CHRISTINA DODD

Praise for
THE DEVIL WEARS PLAID

"A sinfully sexy hero who is more than he seems; a strong-willed, intelligent heroine who is nobody's pushover; and an engaging plot richly imbued with danger and desire all come together brilliantly."

—*Chicago Tribune*

"Few authors have Medeiros's storytelling talents. From the first page to the last, she holds you enthralled with an enchanting plot, charismatic characters, and strong sensuality. It's another deep-sigh keeper from a master!"

—*RT Book Reviews* (Top Pick!)

"Medeiros is a superb storyteller. Both primary and secondary characters are vividly three-dimensional; her plot is full of tasty twists, and Medeiros can pull every last emotion from the reader with tear-inducing scenes and laugh-out-loud dialogue."

—*Booklist* (starred review)

"Charming. . . . Readers will enjoy the appealing, self-reliant heroine. . . . Quick-paced, clever dialogue lightly sprinkled with Scottish slang moves things along."

—*Publishers Weekly*

"[A] funny, gently poignant historical that revitalizes the well-worn feuding families plot with wit, sizzle, and twists that turn expectations on their heads. A delightful diversion that deserves a sequel."

—*Library Journal*

"Medeiros is a premier novelist! An entertaining historical love story which mesmerizes by keeping the surprises and humor continuously coming."

—Single Titles

"A beautifully written historical romance with all the right ingredients for a passionate, thrilling story."

—Fresh Fiction

"An exciting historical with a hero that will make your heart skip a beat and a heroine who is as smart as she is beguiling."

—Heart to Heart: The BN Romance Blog

"An adventure ride through the Scottish Highlands, with plenty of twists and turns, secrets, surprises, laughter, and sighs along the way. . . . I read it in one day, then turned around and read it all over again the next. It's Teresa Medeiros at her finest!"

—The Romance Dish

GOODNIGHT TWEETHEART

"In her latest delightfully inventive novel, Medeiros writes with effortless grace and addictive wit about the importance of love and hope in every person's life."

—*Chicago Tribune*

"A very clever love story for the technological age!"

—Fresh Fiction

"Exactly the book to warm you up on a cold winter's night. Tender, funny, and poignant, this novel will make you laugh out loud one minute and reach for the tissues the next."

—Kristin Hannah, *New York Times* bestselling author

"Measures out equal amounts of lightning-fast wit, wry intelligence, and haunting tenderness. Medeiros shows that in any era, by any means of communication, love will find a way."

—Lisa Kleypas, *New York Times* bestselling author

"Medeiros gives her well-matched Twitter couple some very funny exchanges."

—*Kirkus Reviews*

"A shrewd depiction of romance in an era of instant connection. . . . The mysteries and questions Medeiros puts into play are timeless, and they give extra depth to this cleverly crafted tale."

—*BookPage*

"Quick-witted and romantically heartwarming. *Goodnight Tweetheart* is crazy good. I loved it from its first tweet to its last one."

—Night Owl Reviews

"Exceedingly clever writing. . . . There is so much hilarity in this fun tale. . . . *Goodnight Tweetheart* is imaginatively unique and will touch the reader on a variety of levels."

—Single Titles

"This novel is unique. . . . Medeiros expertly keeps the reader entertained to the very end. . . . A winner!"

—The Romance Readers Connection

These titles are also available as eBooks

Also by Teresa Medeiros:

The Devil Wears Plaid
Goodnight Tweetheart

TERESA MEDEIROS

The Pleasure of Your Kiss

Pocket Star Books

New York   London   Toronto   Sydney   New Delhi

Pocket Star Books
A Division of Simon & Schuster, Inc.
1230 Avenue of the Americas
New York, NY 10020

This book is a work of fiction. Names, characters, places, and incidents either are products of the author's imagination or are used fictitiously. Any resemblance to actual events or locales or persons, living or dead, is entirely coincidental.

First Pocket Books paperback edition January 2012

POCKET STAR BOOKS and colophon are registered trademarks of Simon & Schuster, Inc.

For information about special discounts for bulk purchases, please contact Simon & Schuster Special Sales at 1-866-506-1949 or business@simonandschuster.com.

The Simon & Schuster Speakers Bureau can bring authors to your live event. For more information or to book an event, contact the Simon & Schuster Speakers Bureau at 1-866-248-3049 or visit our website at www.simonspeakers.com.

Manufactured in the United States of America

10 9 8 7 6 5 4 3 2 1

ISBN 978-1-4391-5789-3
ISBN 978-1-4391-7073-1 (ebook)

To Doris Medeiros. I'm so glad God sent you into my life along with your amazing son. You have always been more than a mother-in-law to me. You have been, and always will be, my friend.

For my darling Michael, whose kisses will always be the greatest pleasure in my life.

Acknowledgments

My heartfelt thanks to Lauren McKenna, Louise Burke, and Andrea Cirillo for giving me my creative wings and encouraging me to fly. Thanks to the entire amazing team at Pocket. You are simply the best!

Thanks to all of my beloved baristas at my local Starbucks. When I say I couldn't have done it without you, I mean it! And a special thanks to Ashly Wickham for always serving me smiles with my coffee and asking when she can model for the cover of my next book.

The
Pleasure
of Your
Kiss

✤ *Chapter One*

1834

*O*h, Clarinda! Have you seen the latest edition of the *Snitch*? I picked one up at the docks before we sailed and there's an absolutely delicious article about Captain Sir Ashton Burke!"

Clarinda Cardew felt her fingers tighten involuntarily, biting into the leather binding of the book she was reading. Despite the balmy warmth of the sea breeze caressing her cheeks, she could feel her face freezing into the mask of calculated disinterest it always wore whenever That Name was mentioned. She didn't require a mirror to know how effective it was. She'd had nine long years to perfect it.

"Indeed?" she murmured without lifting her eyes from the page.

Unfortunately, Poppy was too enamored of her subject matter to notice Clarinda's marked lack of encouragement. Adjusting the wire-rimmed spectacles perched on the tip of her nose, Poppy leaned forward in her deck chair. "According to this article, he's fluent in over fifteen languages, including French, Italian, Latin, Arabic, and Sanskrit, and has spent most of the last decade journeying from one corner of the globe to the other."

"Strictly speaking," Clarinda said drily, "globes don't have corners. They're round."

Undaunted, Poppy continued, "'After leading his regiment in the East India Company army to a stunning victory in the Burmese war, he was awarded a knighthood by the king. Based on his ferocious skill in single combat, the men under his command gave him the nickname Sir Savage.'"

"So much more intimidating than Sir Unfailingly Polite." Feeling rather savage herself, Clarinda flicked to the next page of her book and stared blindly down at words that might as well have been written in Sanskrit or some other ancient tongue.

"'Rumor has it that while he was in India, he rescued a beautiful Hindustani princess from the bandits who had kidnapped her from her palace. When her father offered him her hand in marriage and a fortune in gold and jewels as a reward, Burke informed him that he would be content with nothing more than a kiss.'"

"Her father must have been a most excellent kisser," Clarinda replied, lifting the book to hide her face altogether.

Poppy dragged her rapt gaze away from the *Snitch* long enough to give Clarinda an exasperated glance. "Not from her father, silly. From the princess. According to the article, Captain Burke's romantic exploits are nearly as legendary as his military ones. It says here that after requesting a discharge from the army, Burke was engaged by the African Association to lead an expedition deep into the continent's interior. His alliance with the association was severed three years ago when he returned from Africa with copious notes on the carnal habits of the primitive tribes he discovered there. Even the most sophisticated of scholars were scandalized by the attention to detail evidenced by his findings. Some of them even dared to suggest he might have participated in these rituals himself!"

Clarinda winced as Poppy's scandalized titter threatened to pierce her eardrums. The image of a man lowering himself into the sleek arms of some ebony-skinned beauty while flames leapt around them and native drums beat out an irresistible rhythm made her own temples begin to throb. She briefly considered throwing the scandal sheet overboard. Or perhaps even Poppy herself.

Normally Penelope Montmorency, known as Poppy to both Clarinda and to their former classmates from Miss Bedelia Throckmorton's Seminary for Young Ladies, was a most amiable companion. She might be overly fond of society gossip and iced tea-cakes and have a tendency to speak as if her every utterance was punctuated by an exclamation mark, but she was also good-natured and loyal, without an ounce of genuine malice in her short, plump frame.

Poppy was usually content to read to Clarinda from the sacred pages of the *Ladies' Fashionable Repository*. But Clarinda supposed the ornate plumes, stuffed birds, and clusters of ribbons the French were wearing on the brims of their bonnets that summer couldn't hope to compare to the legendary exploits—romantic or otherwise—of the dashing Captain Sir Ashton Burke.

The gentle pitch and roll of the ship's deck beneath their chairs no longer felt soothing to Clarinda's nerves. Although she'd never suffered so much as a twinge of seasickness, she was starting to feel distinctly queasy. Hoping to ease the sensation, she set aside her book, rose from the deck chair, and made her way forward to the bow of the ship. Although there was nothing but sea and sky as far as the eye could see, there was still nowhere she could go to escape Poppy's fascination with the subject of the article.

"'Since severing his ties with both the East India Company and the African Association,'" her companion read, "'the aura of mystery surrounding Burke has only deepened. There are some who speculate he now spends his time acquiring priceless archaeological treasures or that some foreign government may have even engaged his services as a spy.'"

Clarinda forced a yawn. "He must not be particularly adept at it if everyone suspects he's a spy."

"The article even includes a sketched likeness of him." There was a cheerful rustling as Poppy turned the scandal sheet this way and that, studying it from every possible angle before announcing with great conviction, "I fear the artist must have flattered him. No man could possibly be *that* good-looking, could he?"

Clarinda clutched the ship's railing, fighting the temptation to whirl around and snatch the newspaper from Poppy's hands. She didn't need a sketch to remember amber irises rimmed in black and flecked with sparks of the purest gold, a devil-may-care dimple slashed in one lean cheek, beautifully sculpted lips that always seemed to be on the verge of quirking in a teasing smile before softening to steal a kiss . . . or a defenseless heart. Perhaps Michelangelo or Raphael could have done justice to those details, but it would be impossible for a few careless strokes of a pen to capture the irresistible vitality of such a man.

"He may have been absent from England for many years, but you grew up on adjoining estates, did you not?" Poppy asked. "Surely you must have caught at least a glimpse of him."

"It's been years since I laid eyes on him and he was little more than a lad then. My recollection has grown somewhat hazy," Clarinda lied. "But I do vaguely seem to remember a long, hooked nose, a pair of spindly bowlegs, and protruding teeth like a beaver's." It took Clarinda a moment to realize she had just described their least favorite dancing master from their days at Miss Throckmorton's. Poor Mr. Tudbury had also had an unfortunate tendency to spray spittle when snapping out commands for them to pirouette or perform a *battement glissé*.

Poppy sighed wistfully. "I wonder where the captain might have disappeared to this time. Do you suppose he's gone off to rescue more princesses?"

Betrayed by the treacherous twinge of yearning her friend's mooning had stirred in her own heart, Clarinda swung around to face her. "Really, Poppy! There's no need to fawn over the man as if we were both still a pair of simpering schoolgirls! He's nothing but a greedy soldier of fortune who makes his living robbing tombs and selling his sword to the highest bidder. The press may choose to glorify him but that doesn't make him a hero." Clarinda dampened the smoldering fuse of her temper with a cool sniff. "Most men who cloak themselves in rumor and innuendo do so because there is nothing of real substance to hide. They spread these tall tales themselves simply to cover up their own . . . *shortcomings*."

"Shortcomings?" Poppy's periwinkle blue eyes widened behind the thick lenses of her spectacles. "Surely you don't mean . . ." The corkscrewed clusters of apricot-tinted curls gathered at her temples danced like the ears of a spaniel as she clapped a plump hand over her mouth to smother a shocked giggle. "Why, Clarinda, you wicked thing! You must learn to mind that naughty tongue of yours. After all, you'll be the wife of an earl in less than a fortnight!"

Poppy's chiding words reminded Clarinda of exactly what—and who—awaited her at the end of their journey through the choppy waters of the North Atlantic. She hardly needed Poppy to remind her she was the envy of every eager young debutante and scheming mama whose hopes had been crushed by the recent announcement of her engagement. She had somehow managed to snare England's most eligible bachelor—and one of its most beloved sons—at the relatively advanced age of twenty-six.

Her fiancé was a marvelous man—handsome, kind, intelligent, and noble in both name and character. He was everything a woman should want.

Which didn't explain the hollow ache in Clarinda's heart as she turned back to the sea to escape Poppy's teasing gaze. Or her desperate desire to tear off her wide-brimmed hat, pluck out her mother-of-pearl hair combs, and let the wind have its way with her long wheaten tresses.

The sun shimmered off the crest of the distant swells, its uncompromising brightness stinging her eyes. "When I am a countess," she said with determined cheer, "I shall never have to curb my tongue again. Instead, I shall expect everyone around me to curb theirs."

"Beginning with me, I suppose." Poppy tossed the scandal sheet aside and rose to join her at the rail. "I would have thought you'd be more interested in Captain Burke's adventures, especially since he is about to become your—"

"Let's talk of something else, shall we?" Clarinda interrupted before Poppy could speak the unspeakable and drive her to throw herself overboard. "Like how you're going to be the toast of the regiment once we arrive in Burma."

"Do you really think so?" A glow of pleasure suffused the ripe apples of Poppy's cheeks. "I do so fancy soldiers! It's always been my opinion that a uniform can make even the plainest of gentlemen look like a prince and a hero!"

"Just you wait and see. Handsome young officers will be engaging in fisticuffs and challenging each other to duels, all for the privilege of standing in line to fill out your dance card." Clarinda had every intention of making good on that promise. Even if her new husband had to order the men in his employ to do so upon threat of court-martial . . . or execution.

"But what if word of my"—Poppy threw a nervous glance over her shoulder and lowered her voice to a stage whisper, as if some gossip-minded old biddy could be lurking behind the oaken barrels lashed to the bulkhead—

"*indiscretion* has already reached the ears of some of the officers' wives through the post?"

It was one of the unfathomable ironies of life that a shy, mild-mannered creature like Poppy had unwittingly gotten herself embroiled in the scandal of the season. One that had set jaws to dropping and tongues to wagging from London to Surrey and effectively destroyed her last hope of landing a husband before she was placed firmly on the shelf.

Clarinda's own jaw had dropped when she had first heard Poppy had been caught in a worse-than-compromising position with a certain young gentleman from Berwickshire. She had dismissed the torrid tale as so much rubbish until she learned there had been more than a dozen witnesses to the incident. Unable to bear the thought of Poppy being condemned for a sin she had not committed, she had immediately packed a portmanteau and gone rushing to her friend's rescue, just as she had so many times at the Seminary when the wealthier, prettier girls were mocking Poppy's ill-fitting bodices and thick spectacles or calling her Piggy instead of Poppy.

Poppy, the only daughter of a humble country squire, had always been absurdly grateful for Clarinda's patronage, but Clarinda was equally grateful for Poppy's stalwart friendship. Clarinda's papa had been eager for her to get a first-rate education, but the first thing she had learned at Miss Throckmorton's establishment was that money couldn't buy the esteem of those who fancied themselves superior by birth. When the budding little "ladies" had discovered Clarinda's papa had made his fortune in trade, they had turned up their patrician noses and openly mocked her lineage . . . or lack thereof. By turning up her own nose and pretending their cruel words and petty slights didn't cut her to the quick, she had eventually earned their respect and ended up being one of the most popular girls at the school.

But she had never forgotten that Poppy had been her first and truest friend or that they had originally been drawn together because neither of them had fit in.

Clarinda was trusting the outpost at Burma would be ripe with lonely officers desperate for female companionship. Women of gentle breeding would be scarce, and past indiscretions would be more likely to be forgiven and forgotten instead of dwelled upon with malice and relish.

In their own way, she supposed she and Poppy were each fleeing England and its memories, both good and bad.

"Any officer—or gentleman—who wouldn't dismiss such idle gossip isn't worthy to polish the boots of Miss Penelope Montmorency," she assured her friend, "much less seek her hand in matrimony."

Poppy's smile reappeared, dimpling her cheeks. "I'm only hoping I can find a man half as passionate and devoted as yours. I think it's terribly romantic that he would arrange passage for you on one of his own ships so you could travel halfway around the world to become his bride."

Passion was never a word Clarinda had really equated with her fiancé. True, he had been pursuing her for a long time, but his proposal had consisted of a detailed list of all the reasons why they would suit, not an ardent declaration of love. Yet the steadfastness of his nature had finally convinced her he would never leave her to go chasing after some foolish dream.

Her shrug indicated a lightness of heart she did not feel. "The earl is both devoted and practical. His position within the Company carries with it tremendous responsibilities. I can hardly expect him to abandon his duties and return to London for something as frivolous as a wedding." Linking her arm through Poppy's, she turned her face toward the wind, relishing its promise of freedom, even if it was only an illusion. "I can't begin to tell you what a comfort it is to have you by my side on this journey. I suggest we both stop fretting over the past and the future and start savoring every moment of this voyage. It may very well be our last grand adventure before we settle down into a life of dull respectability."

Clarinda was proved wrong with her very next breath when thunder boomed down from the clear blue sky. She and Poppy barely had time to turn their bewildered glances toward its cloudless vault before something struck the water in front of the ship with a tremendous splash, drenching them both in chill salt spray.

"What in the devil . . . ?" Clarinda muttered, thankful she hadn't yet given up cursing in preparation for her new station in life.

Before she could mop the water from her eyes, another boom sounded, followed by a deafening crack from behind them. They whirled around just in time to see the towering mainmast of the ship begin to topple sideways like a felled tree, its mighty trunk splintered by the deadly weight of a cannonball. Clarinda was vaguely aware of Poppy's fingernails biting into the tender skin of her forearm, but all she could do was watch in helpless horror as what looked like acres of sail came billowing down to bury the deck in a canvas shroud.

They were forced to let go of each other and grasp the rail behind them as the ship lurched to the left, its forward momentum demolished along with its mainmast. Hoarse shouts assailed their ears, underscored by the high-pitched keening of some poor soul in agonizing pain. Sailors came pouring across the deck from every direction, some bearing buckets of water, others dropping to their knees to beat at the smoldering topsail with their bare hands.

As the vessel began to list in a stomach-churning circle, effectively crippled by that one deadly blow, a young lieutenant came racing toward them from the aftercastle of the ship. "Please, ladies, you must get belowdecks immediately! We're under attack!"

"Attack?" Clarinda echoed, his frantic words only deepening her confusion. As far as she knew, there was no one left to attack them. Since the final defeat of Napoléon's navy, most of England's enemies had been routed and subdued, if not by sword and cannon, then by various treaties. No one had dared to challenge England's supremacy on the high seas in nearly two decades.

The sailor stumbled to a halt in front of them and snatched off his bicorne hat, remembering his manners even at such a trying time. "I'm afraid it's pirates, miss." His Adam's apple bobbed in his throat as he made a valiant attempt to swallow his own terror. "Corsairs."

Poppy gasped. One had only to whisper that name to strike terror in the heart of even the most courageous of souls. Parents had been using it to chasten generations of rebellious children, whispering in their little ears that the notorious pirates would come and snatch them from their beds in the dead of night if they failed to recite their evening prayers or eat every last spoonful of their porridge.

The Corsairs had always been notorious for prowling the Mediterranean waters. They would sack every ship they encountered for its booty, none so valuable as the women they captured and sold at the barbarian slave markets in North Africa and Arabia.

And those were the lucky ones.

"I don't understand." Clarinda clenched her teeth to still their sudden chattering. "I thought the French subdued the Corsairs when they conquered Algiers."

"Most of them did surrender at that time. But that only made the ones who refused more desperate and ruthless." The lieutenant darted a glance at the growing chaos behind him. "Please, miss, we haven't much time to get you the two of you out of harm's way." His voice cracked, betraying both his youth and how near he was to succumbing to panic himself. "If they board us . . ."

There was no need for him to finish. Nor did Clarinda have the heart to point out that if the Corsairs succeeded in boarding the ship, there would be nowhere she and Poppy—or any of the other women on the ship, including the captain's wife and their own maids—could hide to escape the pirates' brutal clutches.

She closed her fingers around Poppy's trembling hand, dredging up a reassuring smile from the reserves of her faltering courage. "Come, my dear. It seems we're about to embark upon a much grander adventure than we anticipated."

The lieutenant drew his pistol and started back across the deck, gesturing for them to follow. They raced after him, hand in hand like two frightened little girls. They were halfway to the narrow passageway that would carry them deep into the tenuous safety of the hold when Clarinda stumbled to a halt.

Giving Poppy an apologetic look, she wrenched her hand free and went flying back across the deck.

"Clarinda!" Poppy screamed, terror ripening in her voice. *"What are you doing?"*

"Proving myself a sentimental fool," Clarinda muttered under her breath.

The scandal sheet still lay beside the chair where Poppy had so carelessly tossed it. As Clarinda snatched up the page with the likeness of Captain Burke sketched upon it, a round of pistol fire erupted from somewhere on the ship, followed by the ringing clash of steel against steel.

She wheeled around and went racing back to her friend's side, yanking the breathless Poppy into a dead run to make up for every step of the ground they had lost. She had no intention of letting anyone else suffer for her folly. The lieutenant had just wrenched open the hatch and was frantically waving them toward the shadowy mouth of the passageway. They had nearly reached him when his expression underwent a startling transformation.

His mouth went slack. He gave Clarinda a bewildered look, as if someone had made a joke at his expense that he didn't quite comprehend.

Then he slowly lowered his gaze to his chest.

That was when Clarinda saw the tip of the silvery blade protruding from the center of it.

Poppy let out a bloodcurdling scream. As the lieutenant pitched forward, Clarinda started toward him, instinctively trying to break his fall. But as she reached for him, that same long, curved blade was wrenched from his back and brandished in their direction. The lieutenant collapsed to the deck in a bloody heap, leaving the two of them all alone to face half a dozen men armed with pistols and scimitars. Their turbans and flowing robes were already spattered with blood, little of it their own.

Her breath shortening to terrified pants, Clarinda began to back away from them, dragging the paralyzed Poppy along with her. She gave the ill-fated young lieutenant one last look, but from the blood trickling from the corner of his mouth and the mist already claiming his eyes, clearly he was beyond anyone's help. He looked even younger in death than he had in life. Clarinda's savage regret that she hadn't at least been allowed to cradle his head in her lap as he died coalesced into a fierce urge to protect and survive.

Thrusting Poppy behind her, she reached up to the brim of her hat and whipped out the only weapon at her disposal. She thrust the pearl-tipped hatpin toward the advancing men. "Stay away from us, you miserable brigands. Or I'll run you through, I will!"

The men might not have understood her words, but there was no mistaking the murderous look in her eye. The hulking giant gripping the bloody scimitar glanced from the long, curved blade of that weapon to the slender needle gripped in Clarinda's white-knuckled hand.

His olive-skinned face split in a grin, revealing several dazzling white teeth and one gleaming gold one placed squarely in the center of his mouth. He threw back his head with a bellow of laughter. The other men were quick to join in, making it clear the joke was at Clarinda's expense.

When the man spoke, his voice was a hearty boom, but his English was as sound as her own. "'Twould be a shame to skewer a creature with such spirit. She'll fetch a pretty price at market." He looked her up and down, the assessing gleam in his eyes making her feel as if she were already standing naked and shivering on some slaver's block. "There are many men in this world who would pay a king's ransom just for the pleasure of breaking her."

At that moment a gust of wind snatched the hat from Clarinda's head. Her hair came tumbling out of its combs and around her shoulders in a spill of wheaten silk.

The Corsairs breathed an appreciative chorus of oohs and aahs. A man with the face of a malnourished weasel and two broken and blackened front teeth actually stretched out a hand as if to touch her hair, his eyes glazed and his jaw slack with longing. Before his dirt-encrusted fingertips could brush a single strand, Clarinda jabbed the hatpin deep into the tender pad between his thumb and forefinger.

Letting out a howl, the pirate drew back his wounded hand as if to backhand her. The giant gave him a casual cuff, laying him out flat on the deck with no more effort than it would have taken for an ordinary man to swat a gnat.

"Keep your filthy paws to yourself," the giant growled. "I do not want any marks on the merchandise."

The tender smile he turned on Clarinda was even more terrifying than his snarl. Deprived of her meager weapon, she began to back away from him once again with Poppy still clinging to her back like a barnacle.

The hitch of a sob in her friend's breath echoed her own growing despair. "Oh, if only Captain Sir Ashton Burke was here!" Poppy moaned. "I just know such a man could save us!"

As the half circle of pirates advanced on them, their swarthy faces still glistening with the sweat of battle and their dark eyes gleaming with a chilling combination of lust and blood-lust, an even more violent gust of wind tore

Captain Burke's likeness from Clarinda's numb fingers. The sketch went sailing over the ship's rail, borne away on the wings of the wind.

"That's the problem with heroes, Poppy," she said grimly. "There's never one around when you need one."

✣ Chapter Two

No woman was worth dying for.

That creed had kept Ashton Burke alive for more than nine years. It had inspired him to dodge the lethal points of countless bayonets when he was fighting for his men and his country in the blinding monsoons of Burma. It had strengthened his steps when he was using a machete to hack his way through the jungles of India, where the air was so heavy and thick it coiled around a man's chest like a python intent upon squeezing the last breath of air from his lungs. It had kept him in the saddle for endless hours as he drove his horse across stinging sands through the deserts of North Africa, pursued by tribes of bedouin warlords howling for his blood and for whatever priceless antiquity he had liberated from their own greedy clutches.

No woman was worth dying for.

Unfortunately, the firing squad he was facing had other notions. As did the irate husband who had ordered his execution.

He gazed down the breech-loaded barrels of a dozen muskets, assailed by a memory of midnight-black hair cascading over skin perfumed with jasmine and myrrh, inviting brown eyes lined in a kohl that accentuated their exotic tilt, lush lips that were the color of cinnamon but tasted of honey and ripe pomegranates.

Perhaps both the firing squad and the husband were right. Perhaps some women *were* worth dying for.

But strangely enough, when they came to slip the blindfold over his eyes, shielding them from the harsh desert sun, it wasn't those exotic eyes or lush lips he saw. Instead, it was green eyes the color of spring clover and a pink upper lip that was nearly as full as the lower—its delectable softness tempting a man to lean down and give it a gentle nip.

As he drew in what was sure to be one of his final breaths, it wasn't the seductive aroma of jasmine and myrrh that flooded his lungs, but a teasing hint of lily of the valley, as clean and tender as blooms nestled in the last snowfall of winter. It was the scent of all the things he hadn't allowed himself to yearn for since embracing his self-imposed exile. It was the scent of England, the scent of home . . . the scent of *her*.

He'd spent nearly a decade studiously avoiding any thought of her, but it seemed she'd been lying in wait for him all along, anticipating the moment when he'd be stripped of all his defenses.

A mocking smile curved his lips, making his executioners mutter nervously among themselves as they awaited the command to fire. His reputation for daring escapes had obviously preceded him. This wasn't exactly the first time he'd faced death. Hell, it wasn't even the first time he'd faced a firing squad.

What they could not know was that his smile did not mock them but himself. Perhaps it was only fitting she would be haunting him in these final moments of his life. Soon enough he would be haunting her. He'd be damned—and he might well be, given the alarming number of Commandments he'd broken just in the past fortnight—if he'd go to his eternal resting place without paying her one last visit.

He could almost see himself melting out of the moonlight to materialize as a misty vapor over her bed. He could see the wheaten silk of her unbound hair spilling across the pillow, the gentle rise and fall of her breasts beneath the bodice of some ridiculously virginal nightgown. He would cover her, leaning down to steal one last kiss from her parted lips as he filled all of her empty places with his essence. She would awaken in the morning, aching with longing, but remembering nothing more than the dream of a man who had once loved her not only with his body, but with his soul.

A guttural command followed by the sound of a dozen muskets being cocked in unison snapped him out of his reverie.

It seemed he wasn't even going to be offered a final smoke or a chance to make peace with his Maker. He would die here in Morocco—a stranger in a foreign land with no one to mourn him, no one to weep over his bloodied body. When word of his ignoble death reached England, as it inevitably would, he had no doubt his parents would sigh their disappointment, while his older brother shouldered the burden of the scandal with his usual stoic reserve. Chin up and all that rot.

But what about her?

Would she express shock and convey her polite condolences, then sob softly into her handkerchief when she believed no one was looking? Would she wake in the night shivering with regret over all of the opportunities lost, all of the moments squandered, all of the nights they'd never shared?

He snorted. She was far more likely to dance a merry jig on his grave than shed a single tear on his behalf.

He squared his shoulders and tossed back his head, bracing himself for what was to come. He had always known deep in his heart that he would one day die a scoundrel, not a hero. But he would at least die with the satisfaction of knowing she would never suspect her name had been the last word on his lips.

The drums began to roll out a steady beat, heralding the final seconds of his life.

He squeezed his eyes shut beneath the blindfold. Even in darkness she was there, laughing up at him with her mischievous smile and her dancing green eyes.

He held his breath, waiting to hear the command that would bring his ribald joke of a life to an end.

What he heard instead were raised voices, a brief but savage scuffle, and what sounded like an entire regiment of boots pouring into the courtyard where he was about to be shot.

He tensed. There were shouted words, the majority of them denouncing the interruption in a furious Arabic he understood only too well, but a handful in a language he hadn't heard for a long time. A language that should have been utterly impossible in this most unlikely of places—the King's English. Sensing that he was no longer the center of attention, he began to work at the ropes binding his hands behind his back. As the sounds of discord mounted, he felt a flare of something he'd surrendered long before this moment.

Hope.

The guttural Arabic erupted in a snarled curse before lapsing into the heavily accented English of an outraged husband. "And who are you that you would invade my home with your infidel dogs and dishonor me in this disgraceful manner?"

Finally responding to his desperate efforts to wiggle himself free, the ropes fell away from Ash's wrists. Just as he reached up to tug off the blindfold, he heard a voice he would have recognized anywhere. It was every bit as resolute as it had been when ordering him to surrender his toy battleships or risk having them sunk in the bathtub.

Ash snatched off the blindfold, stunned to find himself gazing into cool gray eyes that were as familiar as his own amber ones.

His savior's clipped words fell like shards of ice into the sweltering Moroccan heat. "I. Am. His. Brother."

"Lord Dravenwood will see you now."

"That's what I was afraid of," Ash murmured as he rose from where he had been lounging on a pile of sandbags to follow the pinch-cheeked young corporal. It was impossible to tell if the man's rigidly formal manner was due to military training or disapproval. Ash suspected the latter.

As he ducked beneath the open flap of the spacious tent, escaping the ruthless rays of the desert sun, it was all he could do not to let out an appreciative whistle. Leave it to his brother to create an oasis of impeccably preserved English culture in the wild heart of the Moroccan desert just outside Marrakech. If not for the billowing canvas walls and the fine layer of grit overlaying every surface, Ash might have been strolling into the elegantly appointed study of any London town house.

A Turkish rug added a rich splash of emerald and garnet to the interior of the tent. The carpet had no doubt been rolled up and transported all of the way from England when its twin might

just as easily have been purchased in a local ba-
zaar for a few pounds. A single place setting of
porcelain, crystal, and silver adorned a square
table draped in white linen. There was even
a wheeled tea cart topped by a gold-rimmed
Worcester tea service to allow his brother and
his top commanders to indulge in that most civilized of English rituals—afternoon tea.

The scrolled foot of a Grecian chaise longue
peeped out from behind the lacquered privacy
screen in the corner. The mahogany shelf next to
it held a perfectly arranged row of leatherbound
books. This time Ash couldn't quite muffle his
snort. They were probably in alphabetical order
as well. Even as a boy, his brother had preferred
weighty tomes detailing obscure military battles
and the musings of Greek philosophers, while
Ash thrilled to the derring-do exploits of the heroes springing from the fertile imaginations of
novelists such as Sir Walter Scott and Daniel
Defoe. That is, when he wasn't perusing a book
of naughty etchings slipped into the house by
one of his father's bolder footmen.

On the west wall of the tent a pastoral landscape in a gilded frame hung from a thin strand
of rope. Ash blinked at the painting, recognizing
the Romantic style of John Constable. He was
almost certain it was an original.

He shook his head in bemusement, wondering how many wagons, horses, and camels it had taken to accommodate his brother's private retinue. Ash had always prided himself on traveling light. He had learned the hard way how to beat a hasty exit with nothing but the shirt on his back. And sometimes not even that.

His brother had always preferred the comforts of home and hearth. Unfortunately, being appointed one of the chief directors in the East India Company's famed Court of Directors forced him to travel to some of the most uncivilized spots on the globe. Once he rose to the vaunted position of chairman, as he would undoubtedly do given how fast his political star was rising, he would be able to conduct most of his business without ever leaving the cozy drawing room of Dryden Hall, the family's Surrey estate.

His brother looked right at home behind the teakwood writing desk, scrawling notes in a leatherbound ledger. His handwriting had always been the only thing about him that was less than perfect. As Ash advanced, the silver tip of the pen continued to scratch its way across the paper. He didn't look up, not even when Ash halted directly in front of the desk.

Ash felt an old but all-too-familiar flare of annoyance. His brother's ability to concentrate on the task at hand was nearly legendary. But all it did was remind Ash that there had been a time in their lives when he hadn't had to settle for whatever crumb of attention Max deigned to toss his way.

Leaning down to plant both palms on the desk, he drawled, "Hello, Max."

The pen froze in midword, leaving an ugly blot of ink on the page. Max wouldn't care for that, Ash thought with a mean-spirited twinge of satisfaction. His brother had never had any tolerance for imperfection. Especially his own.

Max slowly lifted his head to give Ash the sort of frosty look that might have resulted in fisticuffs were they both still in short pants. "You know I never cared for that nickname."

He was lying. It was their father who had hated it when they addressed each other by anything other than their given names. Their father had always insisted *Max* and *Ash* were common names more suited to street urchins or chimney sweeps than the sons of a duke.

Ash straightened, confident his mocking smile would only infuriate his brother further. "Would you prefer I address you as Lord Dravenwood?"

"You may address me by my name—Maximillian." Max snapped the ledger shut and returned his pen to its inkwell.

They hadn't come face-to-face in nearly a decade. Other brothers might have shaken hands, clapped one another on the shoulders, or even exchanged a warm embrace. They simply studied one another, each taking the other's measure for a long, silent moment.

Despite their long estrangement, Ash was still caught off guard by the changes in his brother. Max was only eighteen months older than him, but the dark hair at his temples was already shot through with threads of silver. The weight of responsibility had etched deep grooves around his mouth and shallow lines at the corners of his eyes. Ash could tell by the look in those eyes that Max wasn't particularly pleased with what he was seeing.

While awaiting his brother's summons, Ash had bathed and slipped into the clean clothes provided for him. Since they were the only two men he'd seen in the makeshift camp who were both broad of shoulder and over six feet tall, he suspected the clothes belonged to Max. That might explain the mild distaste Ash had felt while donning them. He'd worn enough of his brother's castoffs as a child.

He'd modified the garments to suit himself, tossing aside the starched collar and leaving the white lawn shirt open at the throat. He'd refused to fasten the cloth-covered buttons of the coat and left off the waistcoat altogether. He ruefully stroked his freshly shaven jaw. He rather missed the close-cropped beard he usually wore. It protected his face against the harsh abrasion of the blowing sand as well as providing disguise in situations where blending into a crowd might very well decide the difference between life and death. At least there hadn't been time for Max to send in a barber to trim the shaggy mane of caramel-colored hair brushing his shoulders.

"Sit," Max said curtly, nodding toward the camp chair placed at a precise angle to the desk.

Max, of course, was sitting in a leather wing chair that probably cost nearly as much as it weighed. Ash gingerly sank into the creaky wood-and-canvas sling, hoping it wouldn't collapse beneath his weight and send him sprawling to the floor.

Stretching his long legs out in front of him, he fished a thin Turkish cigar out of his pocket. He had charmed it out of an amiable young lieutenant while waiting for Max's summons.

He struck a match on the sole of his boot and touched its flame to the tip of the cigar. It ignited with a sizzle, sending a curl of aromatic smoke into the air.

Max's slight grimace of distaste was unmistakable. "I've always believed brandy and cigars to be habits best relegated to the drawing room after supper."

Ash took a deep drag on the cigar, barely resisting the childish urge to blow a smoke ring at his brother's nose. "I don't see a drawing room and I wasn't anticipating being invited to stay for supper. Although I wouldn't turn down that brandy if you were to offer it."

Without a word, Max rose and stalked over to the cut-glass decanter resting on the table. He poured a precise three fingers of the amber liquid into a squat glass and handed it to Ash before returning to his chair.

Ash tossed back a swallow of the expensive brandy, relishing its smooth burn, then lowered the glass, sighing his satisfaction. "You have my undying gratitude. Whatever your other failings, I can't fault your taste in liquor."

Max settled back in his chair, shooting Ash a reproving look. "I should think you'd be thanking me for something a bit more substantial. Like saving your . . . hide."

Max's nearly imperceptible hesitation had come at the precise point where their father had always inserted the word *worthless*. Despite the sooty hue of his hair, Max had always been the golden boy, the son who could do no wrong, while Ash could do no right. From the moment of his birth, their father had made it clear that Max was the heir and Ash was the spare. And a poor excuse for a spare at that. Once Ash had finally realized it would be impossible for him to please their father, he had stopped trying.

He shrugged. "I just gave you my undying gratitude. I haven't much else to offer except the clothes on my back. And I strongly suspect those are already yours."

Max shook his head in disgust. "I suppose it shouldn't have surprised me that there was a woman involved in your latest little contretemps."

"Isn't there always?" Propping one boot on the opposite knee, Ash gave his brother a lazy smile.

"Would you care to explain what possessed you to seduce the wife of a powerful—and extremely hotheaded—tribal potentate in a part of the world where even the slightest perceived insult can cost a man his head? Especially if it happens to be attached to an Englishman's body?"

"*One* of his wives," Ash gently corrected. "And what usually possesses a man to seduce a woman? A sidelong glance from beneath a pair of silky lashes? Soft lips perfectly designed for kissing? An inviting swish of the hip? I doubt even a man of your legendary moral fortitude would be immune to such charms."

Ash wasn't about to waste his breath explaining to Max that Fatima had come to him. Her furtive knock had sounded on the door of his lodgings after a chance encounter in the marketplace. She had drawn aside the gossamer silk that veiled her ripe breasts not to tempt him with her nakedness but to show him the fresh bruises dealt by her husband's fists. Judging by the faded scars, those bruises were only the most recent in a long string of insults to her perfect flesh. Nor did Ash explain that his original intention in tenderly touching his lips to them was not to give pleasure but to obliterate pain. Or that after she had flung her arms around him and tumbled them both back into his bed, he had been the one to come to his senses and gently ease her out of his embrace. She had spent a restful night in his bed while he spent a sleepless night on the hard, dusty floor, cursing himself as a fool.

He didn't waste his breath telling Max any of that. He knew his brother would never believe him. Hell, he hardly believed it himself.

"As if cuckolding the man wasn't insult enough," Max said, "you had to add injury to the slight by putting her on a ship and helping her run away. Was that all part of your hare-brained scheme? To meet up with her in the next port and stay holed up in some seedy inn until you grew tired of her and went off chasing the next beauty or treasure that caught your wandering eye?"

Actually, Ash hadn't planned on ever seeing Fatima again. Before her ship had sailed, he'd shoved a purse in her hand stuffed with so much gold she need never again trust herself to the mercy of any man, including him. If one of Mustafa's men hadn't witnessed the grateful kiss she'd pressed upon his lips before boarding the ship, Ash would have ended up on the next ship bound for anywhere in the world that wasn't Morocco instead of standing in front of a firing squad in Mustafa's courtyard.

He swirled the last of the brandy around the bottom of the glass before downing it in a single swallow. "I'm surprised you didn't just let Mustafa's men shoot me."

"Don't think I wasn't tempted," Max said grimly. "I might have done just that if I didn't have a job for you myself."

Ash leaned forward and set the empty glass on the desk. "Perhaps you didn't hear the news. I resigned my commission. I don't work for the Company anymore. Or for you. I squandered several years of my youth serving king, country, and the Company. Now I serve only myself."

"I'm well aware of your mercenary exploits. As are our parents. They provide ample gossip fodder for the London papers and have been known to send our father into apoplectic fits over his kippers and coddled eggs."

"Now you're just trying to charm me."

A ghost of a smile flitted over Max's lips, and for a moment they were the same two brothers who had plotted beneath the blankets to toss an unlucky frog into their father's bathwater. Despite their father's best efforts to drive a wedge between them with his lavish praise of Max and his constant criticism of Ash, they had once been as thick as two thieves.

That had all changed after Ash had returned from Eton to find the brother he adored had vanished, only to be replaced by a man as cool and contemptuous as their father. Ash's hurt and bewilderment had slowly hardened to anger, then indifference. Since Max refused to confide in him, Ash could only assume Max no longer cared to be bothered with a younger brother whose cravat always hung crooked and who could be counted on to blurt out a sarcastic remark at just the wrong moment in every conversation.

Even now, Max's amusement at Ash's quip was short-lived. As if desperate to occupy his hands, he began to straighten an already perfectly aligned stack of papers. "This matter is in regards to my fiancée. Three months ago she was being escorted to Burma for our wedding when her ship was boarded and she and her companion were abducted." No longer able to keep up their charade of meaningful activity, his hands went still. He lifted his head to meet Ash's gaze, finally revealing the depths of his desperation. "By Corsairs."

Ash couldn't quite hide his sympathetic flinch. They both knew any woman unfortunate enough to fall into the hands of those barbarians was better off dead.

"Have they sent a ransom demand?" he asked. Her captors would be far less likely to soil the merchandise if they thought there was a handsome profit to be made from its return to its rightful owner.

Max shook his head. "I've received no word whatsoever, but I have made inquiries. According to a reliable source, she was"—he averted his eyes and swallowed, obviously having great difficulty getting out his next words—"sold. To a powerful sultan in the province of El Jadida."

For the first time Ash understood why his brother had set up camp in this godforsaken desert. El Jadida was on the coast, less than three days' ride from where they sat. "You have an army of men at your disposal. Why should this concern me?"

"Because you know the lay of the land, the history, the language, but you're not bound by the ties of convention or politics. My duties as a director of the Company put me in an extremely awkward position. I can't afford to jeopardize everything we've worked so hard to achieve in this region by storming some sultan's palace. Why, I can't even send a note to this sultan without engendering hard feelings all around, not just toward the Company but toward England herself."

"Ah! Now there's the Max I remember. More concerned about his own future than his bride's!"

"My future *is* her future! Do you think I'm enjoying sitting here on my hands while she suffers God-only-knows-what degradations at the hands of those barbarians? But I know that if I have any hope at all of giving her the life she deserves, especially after this incident, it will take every ounce of influence I've earned through decades of hard work and sacrifice. I can't afford to throw all of that away in a moment of rash desperation when there's a more viable solution sitting right in front of me."

While Max visibly struggled to contain his temper, Ash took a long drag on his cigar, pondering the novelty of being considered a solution instead of a problem. He had escaped his brother's orbit long ago with little more than his pride intact, and he had no intention of being pulled back into it. Despite what Max claimed, there were other men who were far more suited to such an undertaking. Honorable men who would consider it a privilege to risk their lives to earn the much-sought-after approval of the Earl of Dravenwood.

"How much?" Ash asked coolly.

If his brother was startled that he would demand payment after Max had just stopped a firing squad from blowing off his head, Max betrayed no sign of it. "Name your price."

Ash arched a surprised brow. Max's frugality, except when it came to his own comforts, was legendary. His management of their dwindling family fortune had saved them all from the poorhouse. His rapid rise through the ranks of the East India Company had enabled the Burke name and its accompanying titles to flourish while others of their rank were being forced to do the unthinkable to survive by selling their family estates or marrying brash American heiresses without a drop of noble blood in their veins.

Ash pretended to ponder Max's words for a moment, then named a price so ridiculously exorbitant his brother would have no choice but to refuse him.

"Done," Max said, drawing a book of cheques toward him and dipping his pen once more into the inkwell. "And this is only half of it. I'll double the amount you asked for once the job is completed to my satisfaction."

Ash's mouth fell open. The lit cigar hung on his bottom lip for a precarious moment, in imminent danger of tumbling into his lap. The very notion of his brother putting a woman before his precious profits was unthinkable.

Max signed the cheque with his customary scrawl, then slid it across the desk toward Ash. Ash took it and fingered the expensive vellum, marveling at the surfeit of zeros. "Wouldn't it be cheaper to just forget about this woman and find another bride?"

Max slammed his fist down on the desk, startling Ash. It wasn't like his brother to betray his passions. For most of their adult lives, Ash had suspected Max didn't have any. But now the cool gray smoke in Max's eyes had cleared, revealing the smoldering embers beneath. "There is no other woman who can compare to her! Her wit, her kindness, her courage, her passion for life, surpass every idle charm so prized by society. She is more than just a bride, both in my eyes and in my heart!"

The thunder of his voice faded, leaving his impassioned declaration hanging awkwardly in the air.

"So . . ." Ash drawled, "just who is this paragon of feminine virtue I'm to rescue from the clutches of the evil sultan?"

Max stiffened, dropping his gaze to the desk. "Miss Clarinda Cardew."

Without a word, Ash tossed the cheque back on the desk, rose, and went striding toward the flap of the tent.

He heard Max surge to his feet behind him. "Please, Ash," he said hoarsely. "I need you."

Ash stopped in his tracks, hearing in that plea an echo of the brother who had once been his staunchest ally.

He had never dreamed this day would come. Never dared to hope his proud, self-sufficient brother would once again confess such a thing.

Max valiantly struggled on. "I know you've never borne any particular fondness toward the young lady, but surely even you wouldn't be so heartless as to abandon her to such a cruel fate."

Ash closed his eyes briefly before wheeling around to face his brother. "Fondness? You are speaking of the same Miss Clarinda Cardew whose father's property bordered our own? The same Miss Clarinda Cardew who devoted her entire youth to making my life an utter misery? Because I'd hate to think I was tainting some other poor young woman's reputation with the venom and rancor deserved only by that . . . that . . . *creature*!"

Max sank back down in his chair with a defeated sigh. "She is one and the same."

"Well, that's a relief!" Ash exclaimed with a harsh bark of laughter. "Because for a minute there, I thought it couldn't possibly be the same Clarinda Cardew who dogged my every step from the time she was old enough to clamber over the fence between our properties. The same Clarinda Cardew who smeared the inside of my gloves and stockings with boot black, left a branch of poison sumac in my bed, and snuck into our stables to loosen the cinches on my saddle only minutes before I was to perform an important riding exhibition for Father and a handful of his most influential friends."

Max shook his head ruefully. "There's no denying she was a bit of a handful when we were lads. Especially when it came to you."

Ash felt his face harden even further. His brother didn't know the half of it. Apparently, Clarinda had never told him that the spark of animosity between them had finally flared into something so combustible it had threatened to incinerate them both.

Max continued, "It's her father who should be held accountable for her high spirits as a girl. The man always had more money than good sense. She was only eight when her mother died and he was the one who allowed her to run wild when what she needed was a firm but gentle feminine hand to guide her."

"What she needed was to be laid across someone's knee and have the working end of a coal shovel applied to her impertinent little backside." Ash closed his eyes briefly as a tantalizing image of that backside as he had last seen it flitted across his memory. "I suppose now you're going to try and convince me the nefarious little hoyden has somehow transformed herself into a genteel lady fit to be the wife of the Earl of Dravenwood . . . and a future duchess?"

Once again, Max seemed to be having great difficulty meeting Ash's eyes. "I think I can safely say she is not the same girl you knew."

Given that Clarinda had agreed to marry his brother, therefore dooming herself to a lifetime of staid respectability, Ash could find no argument for that. He turned to pace the confines of the tent as if the purposeful motion could somehow contain the turmoil mounting in his mind and heart. "I heard she was to wed that Dewey fellow years ago. Shouldn't she be long married by now and settled in the country with her own brood of brats?"

A frown clouded his brother's brow. "I'm afraid Viscount Darby perished in a horseback-riding accident before the wedding could take place. It was a terrible blow to all who knew him. Darby was such a decent chap."

"Probably rode his horse off a cliff so he wouldn't end up leg-shackled to her," Ash muttered.

Max's icy glare brought him up short. "That's a bit cold, isn't it? Even for you? Must I remind you that you're talking about my future wife?"

Ash smirked down at his brother with deliberate insolence. "What are you going to do? Call me out for insulting her?"

Ash could tell that at the moment Max would like nothing better than to do just that. But they both knew Ash was a dead shot who could drop a charging rhinoceros in its tracks at a hundred paces.

Instead, Max chose a weapon calculated to do even more damage to Ash's heart. "You're the only man I know with both the brawn and the brains to carry out this mission. I want her rescued, not killed. If I send in a regiment of men with muskets blazing, the first thing her captors will do is cut her throat. Will you help me save her?"

Ash turned away from the desk, running a hand through his already tousled hair. He was trying desperately not to imagine Clarinda at the mercy of some randy sultan with a sadistic streak and an appetite for lovely green-eyed blondes. Given her refusal to curb that sharp little tongue of hers for any man, it would be a miracle if her pretty little head wasn't already rotting on a pike in some sun-baked courtyard.

When Ash, his eyes grim and his face set in pitiless lines, turned back to his brother, few men of his acquaintance would have recognized the happy-go-lucky adventurer they knew. "Have you considered the full ramifications of what you're asking me to do? Even if I succeed in retrieving Clar—Miss Cardew, she will be considered damaged goods. She could still be as pure as the driven snow, but who's going to believe that after she's spent the last several months in a place most of society would consider little more than a brothel? Not even your vaunted reputation or your standing in the Company will be able to protect her from the wagging tongues and venomous whispers of the professional gossips. If you insist on marrying her, you'll be the laughingstock of all London. Even my exploits will pale in comparison."

Max rose from the chair and moved to stand before the Constable landscape suspended from the ceiling of the tent. For the first time, Ash realized just how closely it resembled the countryside around Dryden Hall. It was impossible to count how many times he had seen Clarinda scampering across just such a meadow, her grubby little face wreathed in a mischievous grin, her long blond braids flying out behind her.

"I'll deal with society when the time comes," Max finally said. "Just bring her home to me."

"Dear Lord," Ash breathed as his brother's words struck his already reeling heart a fresh blow. "You really do love her, don't you?"

When Max turned to face him, his eyes as unguarded as Ash had ever seen them, there was no need for him to speak.

Ash shook his head. "Then may God help you."

Feeling the inescapable weight of his brother's gaze upon him, Ash retrieved the cheque from the desk and slipped it into his pocket. He was almost to the flap of the tent when he realized their business was not yet concluded.

He glanced back over his shoulder at Max. "You're one of the most sought-after bachelors in all of England. Out of all the women in the world you might have loved, why her?"

Since that same question had been haunting him for nearly a decade, Ash was not surprised when his brother had no answer for him.

✣ Chapter Three

"What in the bloody hell is that fool doing?" Ash muttered, crouching down behind the rock and lifting the brass spyglass to his eye to get a closer look at the man he was about to abduct.

For nearly three-quarters of an hour he had been watching Zin al-Farouk, the current sultan of El Jadida, drive his mount back and forth across the valley road below as if pursued by some foe only he could see.

"Why don't you go down there and ask him yourself, Captain?" Ash's companion suggested, popping another grape in his mouth before taking a long, noisy swig from the canteen in his hand.

Ash lowered the spyglass long enough to give Luca a sideways glare. His friend and frequent comrade-in-arms was lounging behind the rock next to Ash's as if he had nothing better to do than spend the morning sunning himself beneath the relentless rays of the Moroccan sun. The product of a brief but passionate union between an Italian count and a beautiful Gypsy girl, Luca's angelic good looks were surpassed only by his talent for indolence. The negligible effort of riding their horses to the top of the bluff so they could get a clear view of the desert road below had apparently sapped what little energy he had. If they didn't act soon, he would probably curl up behind the rock for an afternoon nap.

Ash reached over to snatch the canteen from his friend's hand, discovering to his exasperation that it was nearly empty. "I hired you to help me abduct the sultan, not drink up all of our provisions before noon."

"*Hired* would imply there was actually some expectation of payment for my services," Luca drawled. "I've yet to see so much as a gold sovereign cross my palm."

Ash slipped the canteen into the leather satchel slung across his chest, avoiding his friend's knowing eyes. "I'll pay you as soon as I can get to a proper bank and cash a cheque. I told you I'd experienced a recent setback to my own finances."

"And by any chance did that *setback* have big brown eyes, long dark hair, and a most spectacular pair of—"

"Quiet!" Ash snapped, retraining his spyglass on the road as the sultan wheeled his mount around at the far end of the valley and came pounding back down its length, each strike of the horse's hooves sending up a golden plume of sand. "Here he comes again."

This time Luca actually stirred himself long enough to peek over the top of his rock. With his dark-lashed ebony eyes, flowing white robes, and the untamed mane of sooty curls tucked beneath the traditional kaffiyeh wound around his olive-skinned brow, Luca could easily have passed for a native Moroccan himself.

Since Ash's golden eyes and light brown hair made such a disguise impractical if not impossible, his own buff riding breeches, ivory lawn shirt, and loose-fitting cutaway coat were designed to blend into the endless vista of sand and sun. As he studied their quarry through the spyglass, he absently stroked his jaw, welcoming the familiar prickle of beard stubble against his palm. At least he no longer felt like a shorn lamb.

"Now, why would the man go out riding without his guard?" he murmured. "It's almost as if he's begging to be ambushed."

Even without his guard, the sultan appeared to be a formidable opponent. His crimson cloak rippled over the flanks of a massive black steed that looked to be more dragon than horse. Ash wouldn't have been surprised if puffs of smoke had come belching from the beast's flared nostrils. The man sat his ornate, silver-trimmed saddle like some emperor of old, wearing nothing but a pair of loose-fitting trousers and an open black vest beneath his cloak. The well-defined slabs of muscle in his broad chest and upper arms were clearly visible as he snapped the reins to urge the stallion into a harder gallop.

Ash's gaze followed those arms down to the powerful hands wrapped around the leather reins. An image of those sun-bronzed hands splayed against snowy flesh danced through his brain, darkening the yellow sun to the color of blood.

Luca's voice seemed to come from a great distance. "You all right, Cap? You look a trifle bit . . . well . . . insane."

"Don't be ridiculous. It must be the heat." Drawing off his wide-brimmed hat, Ash mopped at his brow as Luca continued to eye him with uncharacteristic concern. They both knew Ash had never been prone to the sun-sickness that plagued so many Englishmen in this region.

He jammed his hat back on his head. If his wayward thoughts kept drifting in such dangerous directions, he'd be less likely to kidnap the sultan than to plant a pistol ball between the man's eyes.

"Just what are we supposed to do with this fair maiden once we've rescued her?" Luca asked.

"If all goes as planned," Ash said grimly, silently praying that it would, "we'll never even have to lay eyes on her. We'll simply kidnap the sultan, then send a ransom note to his stronghold, agreeing to swap him for . . . for the girl." In England his plan would have been considered barbaric, but Ash was familiar enough with the region to know it was one both the sultan and his court would respect. Such abductions and negotiations often occurred between the powerful potentates and tribal warlords who were constantly battling for supremacy in this area. "Once they agree to our demand, we'll have her delivered to a place where my brother will be waiting to welcome her back into his loving arms."

Until he said the words aloud and heard the hint of a growl in his voice, Ash had been able to pretend Max was simply a client who had hired him to rescue a stranger. But now in his mind's eye, Ash could see his brother's hands stroking the silky softness of Clarinda's skin, his brother's lips brushing her cheek and murmuring all of the tender words Ash had been too proud — or too foolish — to say.

The sun dimmed again and the past shimmered like a mirage before his eyes. Suddenly he wasn't crouched behind a rock in the desert heat but standing beneath the spreading boughs of an old oak tree in the misty meadow where he had bid Clarinda farewell for the last time. When she had found out he was leaving, she had thrown a cloak over her nightgown and slipped out of her father's house to intercept him. She had come running across the dewy grass, her feet bare and her fair hair streaming down her back like a child's.

She had stumbled to a halt in front of him, her big green eyes darkened with accusation, and blurted out the one question that had been haunting him from the moment he had decided to go. "How can you leave me?"

He had stood there, holding his horse's lead and steeling himself against the bitter reproach in her eyes. "You know very well why I'm going. Because I have nothing to offer you."

"That's a lie!" she cried. "You have everything to offer me. Everything I could ever want!"

He shook his head helplessly. "My ancestors have been piddling away the family fortune for generations. I haven't a farthing to my name. And being the second son, I haven't even a title to offer you."

"And I haven't a drop of noble blood in my veins. Why I'm as common as Millie the milkmaid down at the village dairy!"

Knowing he would regret it in the endless days—and nights—to come but unable to stop himself, he reached down to stroke the shimmering flax of her hair, marveling at its softness beneath his hand. "There is nothing common about you." His palm glided over the downy curve of her cheek, the pad of his thumb skating dangerously near to her lips. "Once I've made my fortune, I'll come back for you. I swear it."

A breathless laugh escaped her. "But don't you see? There's no need for you to make a fortune. I already have one! Papa's shipping investments have made me one of the richest heiresses in all of England."

"All the more reason for your father to seek out a more suitable object for your affections and your hand in marriage if I don't prove myself worthy."

She lifted her stubborn little chin to an angle he recognized only too well. "If Papa won't give us his blessing, then we shall elope. You just turned one-and-twenty, and I'll be eighteen next month—old enough to decide whom I want to wed. We can run away to London or Paris and live in a garret. Why, I'll take in ironing if I have to!"

"Do you even know how to iron?"

Her smooth brow puckered in a scowl. "No, but if I can play Bach's Fantasia in A minor on the clavichord and conjugate Latin verbs in the first-person singular of the perfect indicative active, I'm certain I could learn. We shall sup on bread and cheese every night and read Byron and Molière together by candlelight." Her voice deepened a husky octave, granting him an enticing glimpse of the woman she would soon become, the woman she believed she already was. "And after the candles burn down, you can make mad, passionate love to me until dawn."

During her ardent declaration, she had clutched his arm and risen up on tiptoe until her lips were only a fragrant breath away from his. Their parted pink petals were so tempting, so tantalizing, so utterly unwavering in their idyllic—if naïve—vision of the life they could never share, that he was tempted to make mad, passionate love to her at that very moment. But if he succumbed to the temptation, if he lowered her to the damp grass and took her in the folds of her ermine-trimmed cloak, he knew he would never find the strength to tear himself away from her arms. He would spend the rest of his days despising himself for being the selfish bastard who had ruined her life.

He seized her by the shoulders, causing hope to flare in her eyes. But his next words dimmed it. "How long would it be before you would hate me? For taking you away"—he swept a hand toward the beautifully manicured grounds of her father's estate, the graceful columns and chimneys of the Greek Revival mansion peeping over the top of the hill behind her in the distance—"from all this?"

She captured his hand and pressed her warm lips fervently to the back of it. "I could never hate you. I shall always adore you!"

Gently tugging his hand from her grasp, he

took her by the shoulders once again, this time to firmly set her away from him. "I'm afraid it's too late anyway. I've already enlisted in the army of the East India Company. The Burke titles may not be worth much more than the paper they're printed on at the moment, but they still have enough influence to purchase me a commission. I'm to sail from Greenwich to Bombay on the morrow. Unless you want to make a deserter of me and see me hanged, you have to let me go."

Clarinda stood gazing up at him as if he'd struck her, at a loss for words for the first time in their long acquaintance.

Ash forced himself to take up his horse's lead, turn his back, and walk away from her.

He had never seen her shed a tear over anything, not even when she was nine and he was twelve and she had tumbled off her pony when trying to follow him over a difficult jump. Muttering an oath he wasn't supposed to know, Ash had scooped her up in his arms and carried her all the way back to her father's house. She had bitten her bottom lip bloody but had never uttered so much as a whimper. It had been Ash who had been forced to watch through stinging eyes as her distraught father ordered two footmen to sit on her so the doctor could set her broken arm.

She was crying in earnest now—great, gulping sobs that made Ash feel as if his own heart were being ripped from his chest. But when her voice finally rang out behind him, it wasn't sadness that reverberated through it, but fury. "If you go, Ashton Burke, don't bother coming back! I won't have you! I'll take your precious fortune and throw every coin of it right back in your proud, insufferable face!"

Ash hesitated, tempted to march right back and try to shake some sense into her. Or at least to kiss her more insensible than she was already being. But he squared his shoulders and forced himself to keep moving.

"I won't wait for you, either, you know. I'll marry the first man who'll have me," she vowed. "Why, I might marry the local curate or the village blacksmith or even an *American*," she added with audible relish, not wasting any time in sinking to the direst of threats. "Or maybe I'll just wed that strapping young viscount who was making calf's eyes at me last week at Marjorie Drummond's soiree."

"Dewey Darby is as dull as dishwater and you know it," Ash tossed over his shoulder. "You'd perish from boredom in a week."

When he showed no sign of slowing, her

voice broke on a fresh sob. "I hope you don't even make it out of the harbor before your ship sinks! I hope you're set upon by pirates and forced to become the cabin boy of the most corpulent sodomite to ever sail the high seas! I hope you contract cholera in India or maybe even the French pox and your manhood withers and falls right off!"

Ash kept walking, knowing that at any other time the imaginative fates she was wishing upon him would have sent them both into hearty gales of laughter.

"I might decide not to wed at all," she called after him with a haughty sniff that warned him she had decided to change tactics. "If I'm to be denied the one man I want, then why should I settle for just one man? What better way to nurse the pain of my broken heart than to devote myself to pleasure?"

Ash stopped in his tracks, his eyes narrowing.

She sighed with such dramatic gusto that Ash didn't have to turn around to see the back of her hand pressed to her creamy brow. Too late he remembered that as a small child, one of her favorite pursuits had been staging amateur theatricals to the delighted applause of her adoring parents. Even then, she had been a clever mimic, and he had been forced to suffer through more than one of her precocious performances himself. "Perhaps I shall succumb to my tragic fate by becoming one of the most practiced courtesans in London. My heart will be empty but my bed most certainly will not. Men will line up around the block and shoot one another dead in the streets just for a chance to sample the irresistible carnal delights of my—"

Dropping the horse's lead, Ash spun around on his heel and went stalking back toward her.

His approach was fraught with such lethal intent that Clarinda took a few stumbling steps backward, her eyes widening. "W-w-what are you doing?" she demanded, the question ending on an alarmed squeak.

"Giving you a reason to wait for me," he said grimly before snatching her up in his arms and sweeping his tongue through her mouth in a kiss that left little doubt as to who would be the first and *only* man to sample her carnal delights.

Her heel caught in the ermine-trimmed hem of her cloak, and then there was nothing to stop either of them from tumbling into its welcoming folds.

Ash regretted that moment the most. If he had walked away from her then, if he hadn't gone striding back into her arms, he might have been able to dismiss his obsession with her as infatuation—a young man's fancy for a pretty face. But that moment—and those that had followed—had made his feelings for her impossible to dismiss or deny.

"Captain? Ashton? *Ash?*"

Ash was jerked out of that misty dawn and back into the scorching sun to find his companion eyeing him with growing alarm.

"Perhaps you *are* suffering from the heat," Luca said, reaching over to gauge the temperature of Ash's brow with the backs of his own fingers. "I fear you might be taking a brain fever."

Ash knew it was a fever of another kind that possessed him. But he no longer had the right to moon over that memory. No matter how much it galled him, Clarinda belonged to his brother now. He had promised to return her to Max, and that was exactly what he was going to do. With any luck, Max would never find out what had transpired between Ash and Max's bride-to-be in the meadow that morning.

He impatiently brushed away Luca's hand. "There's only one cure for what ails me. And that's to finish this job and get the bloody hell out of this godforsaken country."

He was rising to retrieve their horses when Luca grabbed him by the sleeve and jerked him back down. "Look!"

Following Luca's gaze, Ash trained the spyglass on the opposite bluff. Five riders in black, flowing robes had just melted out of the desert. The men were watching the sultan canter back and forth across the valley below with the predatory patience of a flock of vultures.

Ash swore beneath his breath. "Apparently we're not the only ones waiting to have a private word with the sultan today."

He shifted the spyglass back to their prey. Even with his bulging muscles and the sunlight glinting off the wicked curve of the scimitar tucked into his belt, the sultan was still no match for five heavily armed men.

"What are we going to do?" Luca whispered.

"Well, we can't very well let them cut the fellow down in cold blood, can we? If he dies, my brother's fiancée may be lost to him forever."

Just as she had been lost to him.

He narrowed his eyes much as he had that long-ago day in the meadow when Clarinda had finally pushed him one step too far. Having fought under his command and by his side for the better part of a decade, Luca knew exactly what that look meant.

Luca sighed. "I don't suppose it would do any good to point out that there are five of them and only two of us."

"What do you want me to do? Tell them to go back to wherever they came from and get two more men to even out the odds?"

Muttering something under his breath in Italian that included the words *folle* and *insano*, Luca drew a dagger from the sheath at his waist and tucked it between his teeth in preparation for battle.

When the black-robed assassins came charging down the bluff to ambush the sultan, the last thing they expected to encounter were two riders thundering down upon them at full gallop from the opposite rise. For a moment all was chaos, punctuated by pistol fire, the clash of steel, and a guttural grunt as one of Luca's deadly daggers easily found its target.

As that man fell, one of his companions wheeled his mount around and took off into the desert at a desperate gallop. While a skinny fellow with a pockmarked face and blackened teeth grappled with Luca, the two remaining men launched themselves off their horses and onto the sultan, plainly determined to complete their mission. The three men went crashing to the sand, locked in mortal combat.

The sultan put up a valiant struggle but he was no match for two men with murder on their minds. The largest of the two had straddled him and was preparing to draw the blade of a wicked-looking dagger across his throat when two shots rang out nearly simultaneously.

Both attackers collapsed like puppets whose strings had been cut. Shaking his head to clear it, the sultan slowly ratcheted himself up on both elbows to find Ash standing at his feet, his boots planted firmly apart, his eyes narrowed to deadly slits and a smoking pistol gripped in each hand.

The sultan's handsome face broke into a grin, his short, dark beard parting to reveal a mouthful of dazzling white teeth. "Jolly good shot!" he exclaimed, his English more clipped and precise than Ash's own.

Ash squinted at him. Even with his kaffiyeh slightly askew, his lower lip swollen, and a bruise rapidly darkening one of his broad cheekbones, there was something oddly familiar about the man. Ash would have almost sworn he had seen that winning grin and those sparkling obsidian eyes before.

Throwing off one of his attacker's lifeless arms with a grimace of distaste, the man climbed to his feet, brushing sand from his voluminous black trousers. That was when Ash realized he *had* seen him before, rising from the flagstones of the courtyard at Eton, dusting himself off just so after a thorough drubbing by a rambunctious pack of his upperclassmen.

Ash's jaw dropped in disbelief. *"Frankie?"*

The sultan jerked up his head, his eyes going wide with alarm, then glanced around them and touched a finger to his lips as if the desert might be rife with eavesdroppers as well as assassins. "Frankie does not exist in this place. I am always to be known as Farouk among my people. Even though they have taken to the language I have commanded them to learn, there are those in my household who still do not approve of my father's decision to send me to England to have me educated among the infidels."

Frankie/Farouk hadn't been a well-muscled, broad-shouldered man during their years at Eton, but a plump, bespectacled lad more likely to be caught sneaking into the kitchens to pilfer a pastry than into the stables. With his swarthy skin and thick Arabic accent, he had been an easy target for anyone looking for someone weaker to torment. Ash arched one brow as he eyed the impressive span of the man's chest beneath the black silk vest. The upperclassmen might not find it so easy to best him now.

He strode forward to capture Ash's hand in his grasp, giving it a hearty pump. "I thought you looked familiar to my eyes as well. You are Burke the Younger, are you not? I remember your brother from school."

"Yes," Ash murmured, gently disengaging his hand from Farouk's grip. "Most people do."

"He was a bit of a stiff-necked ass, was he not?"

Ash felt his own lips curve into a smile as he suddenly remembered exactly why he had found Farouk's grin so winning.

A strangled cough rang out behind them. They both turned to find Luca still rolling around in the sand, locked in a life-and-death struggle with his wiry attacker.

"Hate to interrupt . . . your touching . . . reunion," he choked out, trying to pry the man's grimy hands from his throat. "But if you're . . . not too busy . . . I could use . . . a . . ." His attacker squeezed harder, reducing his last word to a gurgle.

Ash raised his pistol but Farouk stayed him with a polite "Allow me" before strolling over and applying his boot to the side of the man's head with more enthusiasm than was strictly necessary.

The man collapsed to the sand, his eyes rolling back in his head. Luca sat up, rubbing his throat and giving Ash a reproachful look.

Resting his hands on his hips, Farouk gazed down at the unconscious man. "I will have my guard deal with this mongrel." A dangerous smile curved his full lips, confirming Ash's suspicion that he was no longer an opponent with whom a man would want to trifle. "Perhaps they can use their charms to *persuade* him to expose the villain who sent him and his fellow jackals to attack me in the very shadow of my own stronghold."

While Luca staggered to his feet, still nursing his throat, Farouk turned back to Ash. "You are a long way from England, Burke the Younger. What is it that brings you here at such a fortuitous moment?"

Before Ash could waste either his time or his breath formulating some implausible explanation, Farouk raised a hand to silence him. "Forgive my rudeness. We shall discuss your business here later. I prefer to trust Allah's will in these matters. It would accomplish nothing to question his wisdom in sending you here to do his work. You have given me back my life on this day. Now you must allow me to offer you something in return. It is my sincere wish that the two of you would accompany me back to my humble home as my honored guests."

"We would be honored indeed to accept such a gracious invitation," Ash said smoothly, hoping his formal bow would hide the frantic working of his mind.

He had never dreamed such an opportunity would literally tumble into his lap. If he and Luca could infiltrate Farouk's palace, they might be able to find a way to rescue Clarinda without going to all the trouble of abducting the sultan.

Luca appeared at his shoulder. "But I thought we were planning to—" He grunted in pain as Ash jabbed an elbow into his sternum, informing him that their plans had changed.

"Excellent!" Farouk gave Luca a hearty clap on the back that nearly knocked him off his feet. "From this day forward, we will no longer be strangers or even friends, but brothers! We shall now proceed to my stronghold, where you may partake of my hospitality and the many pleasures it can provide."

As Farouk moved to retrieve his horse from where it had bolted during the attack, Ash adjusted the brim of his hat so that it would shadow his eyes.

There was only one *pleasure* the sultan possessed that was of any interest to him whatsoever.

The sultan's *humble home* was not a crude fortress or a motley collection of tents but a genuine palace nestled within a copse of swaying palm trees and topped by graceful minarets. Its walls were constructed from large rectangular stones baked to a golden hue by the sun's rays. The roof was crowned by overlapping terra-cotta tiles the color of burnished rust. Beyond the sprawling compound, wavering like a mirage in the distance, lay the cobalt waters of the Atlantic.

As they rode into the outer courtyard, Luca shot Ash a wary look. Farouk had spent the entirety of their ride pointing out the natural beauties of his native land and regaling them with tales of its rich and violent history. There had been no opportunity for so much as a whispered warning between the two of them. Luca was just going to have to trust that Ash knew what he was doing.

Ash could only pray that trust was not misplaced.

Two towering, bare-chested guards in voluminous trousers and jeweled turbans appeared to
relieve them of their mounts. Luca handed over
the reins of his horse with visible reluctance. He
knew, just as Ash did, that they were surrendering not only their horses, but their freedom.
Without some kind of mount beneath him—be
it camel or horse—a man wouldn't survive the
rigors of the desert for more than an afternoon.

Farouk had insisted on leading his captive's
horse behind his own stallion with the man's
limp form still draped over the beast's back. He
dismounted and gave the man a contemptuous
shove, sending him sliding to the flagstones in
an unceremonious heap. As Farouk barked out
a command in Arabic, two more guards materialized to drag the man away between them, ignoring his piteous groans.

There was no mistaking the look Ash gave
Luca in that moment. It was imperative they
tread with care in this place lest they also end
up in the sultan's dungeons, being *persuaded* by
his guards to reveal their original intentions and
all of their deepest, darkest secrets.

They were halfway across the courtyard
when a bearded man of middling years, bald
except for the fringe of salt-and-pepper hair

circling the crown of his head, came hurrying toward them, his long robes rustling with each step and a steady stream of Arabic pouring from his lips. Ash cultivated a blandly curious expression, pretending he couldn't understand every syllable of what the man was saying.

"English, Uncle Tarik," Farouk commanded him, nodding toward Luca and Ash. "Out of respect for our guests."

The man gave them a suspicious glance before returning his worried gaze to his nephew's face. "The guards are saying you were waylaid by bandits. Is it true, my son? Are you unharmed?"

"Not common bandits, I fear," Farouk said, gingerly touching two fingers to the burgeoning bruise on his cheekbone, "but assassins."

Tarik shot Ash and Luca another glance, this one openly hostile. "And who are these strangers you bring into our home? More assassins?"

Farouk threw back his head with a hearty laugh. "Angels of Allah, more likely. If not for their timely intervention, it would be my blood watering the desert floor right now instead of the blood of my enemies."

"Oh," Tarik said stiffly, looking even more taken aback by the revelation. "Well, in that case they have my humble gratitude for rescuing my nephew from his own foolhardiness. Have I not told you how dangerous it is to ride out from these walls with no guard to protect you?"

Farouk threw one of his massive arms around his uncle's shoulders, giving him an affectionate squeeze. "Can you blame me for seeking a few precious hours of solitude? Between you scolding me as if I were still a schoolboy in short pants and the constant chattering of my wives, how am I to hear myself think?"

Wives.

Was Clarinda now one of those wives? Ash wondered, his hands curling into fists of their own volition. He could hardly imagine the high-spirited, headstrong girl he had known being content to share the affections of a man with another woman, much less several women. That was almost as unlikely as a man craving the attentions of another woman when she belonged to him.

"Come, friends," Farouk said, abandoning his uncle to throw an arm over each of their shoulders. "I did not invite you here just to leave you standing in my courtyard like a pair of starving hounds. We will eat. We will drink. And we shall each celebrate another precious night of life in the arms of a beautiful woman!"

Luca immediately perked up, but before Ash could fully absorb Farouk's words, they were swept away from the disapproving eyes of Farouk's uncle and across the courtyard on the tide of their host's goodwill.

A pair of massive double doors inlaid with burnished bronze and decorated with carved images of twin lions swung open to welcome them into an inner courtyard redolent with the intoxicating scents of climbing jasmine and incense. A mixture of dread and anticipation quickened in Ash's veins. He had successfully been running from his past for almost ten years, and now it was about to catch up to him with a vengeance.

What would Clarinda do when she recognized him and realized he had come to bring her home? If she threw herself into his arms, sobbing with gratitude and relief, would he be able to stop himself from wrapping his arms around her and pulling her into the shelter of his body? From burying his lips in her hair and breathing deeply of the clean, fresh lily-of-the-valley scent that still haunted him every time he drew another woman into his embrace?

If she failed to temper her reaction to his unannounced arrival with caution, she might well get them all killed. He could only hope there would be time to bribe some greedy servant into slipping a message into the harem, cautioning her to pretend indifference when they first came face-to-face. Then at least he wouldn't risk catching her unawares.

A gate on the other side of the courtyard swung open. It seemed Ash's time—and his luck—had just run out.

Clarinda Cardew stood there, framed by the gilded doorway like some naughty watercolor illustration straight out of *The Lustful Turk*. Ash was shocked to realize she wasn't nearly as lovely as he remembered.

She was beautiful.

Except for the pair of jeweled combs drawing it away from her face to expose her elegant cheekbones, her hair was unbound and coursed down her back in shimmering wheaten waves. A thin line of kohl accented the feline tilt of her clover-green eyes. She was draped in diaphanous layers of multicolored silk, deliberately designed to tantalize a man by offering him teasing hints of the treasures that lay beneath every time she so much as sighed.

Ash must have made some sort of sound deep in his throat because Luca jerked his head around, his eyes widening in alarm. Fortunately,

Farouk was oblivious to Ash's distress. The sultan was gazing across the courtyard, equally entranced by the vision of feminine sensuality that had appeared in the doorway.

Oh, God, Ash thought as he saw the look in her eyes. She was going to cost them all their heads. But as he drank deeply of that look, feeling it water all of the parched places in his heart, he decided the price just might be worth it.

It was all there in her eyes. Everything that had been missing from his own life for the past nine years—longing, tenderness, passion, a desire for something more than the fleeting satisfaction of a tryst between strangers.

As she melted into motion, he took a step toward her without even realizing it.

She flew right past him, flinging herself into Farouk's open arms with a joyful exclamation. "Oh, Farouk, my darling, is it true? Were you almost killed?"

Ash stood frozen in shock as Farouk threw back his head, a booming laugh escaping him as he lifted Clarinda clear off her feet and swung her in a wide circle. "Have no fear! The villains' blades were in no danger of finding my heart since I had left it here for safekeeping in the delicate hands of my little English buttercup."

As Farouk gently set her back on her feet, she pivoted in his arms to face Ash. With a possessive hand still splayed against the broad expanse of Farouk's bare chest, she lifted her chin to a haughty angle, her smile fading and a glittering veil of frost hardening her eyes. "Speaking of villains, Your Majesty, what on earth is *he* doing here?"

❧ *Chapter Four*

He had come for her, Clarinda thought, her treacherous heart leaping with hope as she met Ashton Burke's gaze for the first time in nearly ten years.

In those dark hours after he had first left her behind while he went off to chase his dreams, her spiteful imagination had supplied her with hours of entertainment by conjuring up countless scenarios during which they might once again come face-to-face.

There was the one where she alighted from a gilded carriage drawn by six snowy white horses only to find his wasted figure huddled in the gutter outside her father's Mayfair town house. Favoring him with a pitying smile, she would pluck a farthing from her purse and toss it to him before blithely stepping over his rag-wrapped form and proceeding into the house. (If she was in a particularly mean-spirited mood, it would be snowing outside and she would *accidentally* stomp on his fingers as she swept past him.)

There was also the one where she turned in the dance only to come face-to-face with him in some glittering London ballroom. While he gazed longingly down at her, she would squint up at him as if trying to place his face. "Oh, yes! I *do* remember you," she would finally say, tapping his arm playfully with her fan. "Weren't you that horrid lad who used to dog my every step when I was a girl?" Then she would turn away to offer her arm to her next partner while he gazed helplessly after her, his heart tumbling from his chest to shatter into broken shards on the floor around his feet.

But in her most cherished scenario, she was summoned to the hospital to honor his request to see her face one last time before he succumbed to the dreaded ravages of the French pox. She would appear at his bedside garbed all in white, the lamplight haloing her face and hair. She would gently hold his hand—keeping her gloves on all the while, of course—while he poured out his regrets and begged for her forgiveness. At the precise moment he was rasping out his final breath, she would lean over and whisper tenderly in his ear, "Give the devil my regards, Captain Burke."

Those vengeful fantasies had been the product of a young girl's bruised heart, hardly befitting the mature woman Clarinda had become. A woman who had spent years mastering her more petty emotions.

Which didn't explain the malicious twinge of satisfaction she felt as she came face-to-face with Ashton Burke while she was cradled in the muscular arms of a devastatingly handsome Moroccan sultan and wearing little more than an enticing collection of veils. Even her bountiful imagination hadn't been able to whip up such an unlikely—or delicious—scenario.

As their gazes locked, Ash's familiar gold-flecked eyes narrowed in the shadows beneath the brim of his hat without betraying so much as a trace of regret or yearning. On the contrary, he looked more inclined to step over *her* body as she lay gasping her last in some filthy gutter. Or to give her the cut direct in a crowded ballroom before a throng of gawking onlookers.

She had to blink more than once to dispel the image of the beautiful boy she remembered from her youth. The jaded stranger who stood before her now was every inch a man. A man who looked as if he'd be more at home in a seedy saloon than an elegant salon. Wind, sand, and time had polished away all traces of youth and vulnerability, leaving him lean and hard and infinitely more dangerous than the boy who had walked out of her life all those years ago. Flecks of sand clung to his sun-baked skin, catching like powdered gold dust in the rakish hint of beard stubble shadowing his jaw and upper lip.

Clarinda had tried to convince Poppy the scandal-sheet artist must have flattered him, but just as she had secretly feared, the artist had failed to do him justice. A thin, diagonal scar that was new to her, yet plainly old to him, marred the perfection of a strong chin that was neither too pointed nor too squared. The bridge of his nose was no longer flawlessly aligned but canted to the right by a degree that would only be noticed by someone who had spent hours lovingly tracing every inch of his features, both with her fingertips and in her memory. The grooves bracketing his mouth had deepened, making her wonder if his devil-may-care dimple had vanished forever, left on some battlefield somewhere between England and Morocco.

Oddly enough, those fresh flaws only added to his rugged appeal. His was the face of a man who had lived hard and fought harder. That, more than anything, was what made her long to tenderly press her mouth to the scar beneath his chin so her lips might memorize it as well.

She drew in a deep breath, hoping it would calm the rushing in her ears, the mad flutter of the pulse in her throat. She had no business entertaining such scandalous thoughts when she was promised to another man. Especially when that man just happened to be his brother.

It was nearly impossible to inject the perfect note of disdain into her voice when she was fighting so hard to keep it from trembling. "Speaking of villains, Your Majesty," she inquired of Farouk, "what on earth is *he* doing here?"

"You know this man?"

Clarinda didn't dare tip back her head to steal a peek at Farouk's face in that moment, but she could hear the jealous scowl in his voice. "I know *of* him. As does every woman in England with more than a passing acquaintance with the more torrid scandal sheets."

Farouk's granite-hard muscles relaxed beneath her hand as a chuckle rumbled up from deep in his chest. "Ah, Burke the Younger, it seems your reputation precedes you!"

"So they tell me," Ash said smoothly. "Although I can assure you my exploits have been much exaggerated by men with too little adventure in their own lives and too much time—and ink—on their hands. Only the most vapid and empty-headed of creatures would give credence to what they write."

Although his tone was deliberately pleasant, Clarinda felt her eyes narrow.

Before she could form a retort, Farouk came to her defense, his voice still ripe with amusement. "I can assure you this creature's lovely head is full of clever thoughts. Much to my own detriment and the detriment of any man who would seek to match wits with her, I fear." He tugged her around to face him, giving her a scowl that would have made most men tremble in their boots. "If not, she would be safely tucked away in my harem right now instead of flitting about the palace like a naughty little butterfly."

"When the women started whispering about what had happened, I just had to make sure you were all right, so I coaxed Solomon into letting me out for a bit." Keenly aware of Ash's heavy-lidded gaze upon her, Clarinda gave Farouk a distressed look from beneath the silky length of her lashes. "You're not angry with me, are you? I couldn't bear it if I made you cross."

Farouk's scowl melted into an adoring grin. "See what I mean?" he asked Ash over her head. "This one can charm even a eunuch into doing her bidding. How could any red-blooded man hope to resist her?"

"I'm sure it would be a challenge," Ash murmured, although from his skeptical expression one might deduce he would have little difficulty doing so.

Farouk splayed his big, warm hand against Clarinda's back, urging her closer to Ash against her will. "It is my great honor to present to you Clarinda Cardew. She is my . . ." He trailed off awkwardly, as if his impeccable command of the English language had suddenly deserted him.

Was it Clarinda's imagination or was Ash holding his breath?

". . . guest," Farouk finally finished with more than a trace of regret.

"Pleased to make your acquaintance, Miss Cardew," Ash replied, dragging off the battered wide-brimmed hat that would have made a less imposing man look like a common ditchdigger. The same sun that had toasted every inch of his exposed skin to a warm honeyed hue had also woven errant strands of gold through the caramel brown of his hair.

Clarinda had hoped for nothing more unsettling from him than a polite bow, but as Ash bowed, he captured her hand and brought the back of it to his mouth. The moist heat of his parted lips against her skin dredged up a host of memories. Most of which were best left buried.

An all-too-familiar devilment sparked in his deep-set, amber eyes as his gaze met hers over their joined hands. "Or would you prefer I address you as 'Little English Buttercup'?"

Clarinda tried to wiggle her hand free from his grip but he held fast, refusing to relinquish it. "'Miss Cardew' will suffice, sir. And I can assure you the pleasure is all mine."

"That's not how I remember it," Ash murmured beneath his breath, the timbre of his voice so deep it was audible only to her ears.

This time he did not protest when she snatched her hand from his and retreated to Farouk's side. "Since your head is still firmly attached to your neck, I'm assuming you weren't among the band of cutthroats who tried to waylay the sultan, Mr. . . . Burke the Lesser, was it?"

The mocking glint in Ash's eyes hardened to

something more dangerous. She blinked innocently at him.

"I owe this man my life," Farouk proclaimed in his booming baritone. "If Burke here didn't have the bold heart of a tiger, it would be *my* head rotting in the desert heat right now."

Someone cleared his throat pointedly. Clarinda realized for the first time that Ash hadn't come alone. She had been so stunned by his miraculous appearance she had mistaken the man at his elbow in the flowing white robes and traditional kaffiyeh for one of Farouk's servants. The stranger's dark, liquid eyes had been following every nuance of their exchange with undisguised fascination.

"I would be remiss not to give equal credit to Burke's man here," Farouk amended, earning a smug smirk from Ash's companion. "He was clever enough to offer his throat to one of the villains as a distraction while his master dispatched the rest of them."

The man's smirk vanished, only to reappear on Ash's lips. "Allow me to introduce Mr. Luca D'Arcangelo," Ash interjected smoothly. "My friend and comrade-in-arms in more battles than I care to remember."

Luca had the full, sensual lips and drowsy eyes of a born lover. "Delighted to make your acquaintance, *cara mia*," he said to Clarinda. "Surely the humble buttercup does not do your beauty justice. I would be more inclined to compare your charms to those of a more rare and exotic flower, a night-blooming lily perhaps, whose scent has been known to drive even the most iron-willed of men to abandon all reason and embrace the madness of unbridled desire."

As Luca sauntered forward as if he had every intention of kissing Clarinda's hand, or perhaps even her lips, Ash caught the back of his robes and yanked him back. It was just as well because something that sounded suspiciously like a growl had begun to emanate from deep in Farouk's chest.

"You'll have to forgive my friend," Ash said, his teeth clenched in a conciliatory smile as his companion shot him a sulky look. "He learned most of his English by repeated readings of *The Bawdy Adventures of Buxom Bess*."

"How very generous of you to loan him your copy!" Clarinda said sweetly.

Farouk's growl subsided. "Although I can never hope to repay the debt I owe them, Burke the Younger and Mr. D'Arcangelo will be enjoying my hospitality for as long as they desire. I've already promised to tempt them with every manner of delicacy at my disposal tonight as we sup together."

This time there was no imagining the gaze Ash flicked her way. It danced over Clarinda's skin like living flame.

"You're very fortunate the captain is willing to settle for your hospitality as reward for his noble deeds," she said to hide the effect that look had on her. "I've heard he prefers to be paid in kisses."

"At the moment I'd settle for a hot bath to wash away the desert grit," Ash said.

"I'm sure that can be arranged," Clarinda said, then wished she hadn't as an image of Ash sinking into a steaming tub while surrounded by a bevy of giggling slave girls popped into her head.

"Followed by a long afternoon nap before supper?" Luca suggested hopefully, his leer replaced by a yawn.

Clarinda was beginning to believe disaster just might be averted—or at least delayed— when Poppy came rushing into the courtyard, a colorful swirl of veils billowing behind her. Having never quite mastered the voluminous garments, she always had the air of someone caught in a sudden windstorm.

She was so intent on not tripping over her skirts that she was paying no mind whatsoever to what was directly in front of her. "Oh, Clarinda, one of the women just told me some dastardly villains had attacked the sultan! Who would dare to do such a thing? Don't they know that he's the strongest, the most powerful, the most noble, the most courageous—"

Her breathless recitation of the sultan's apparently endless list of glowing attributes came to an abrupt end when she ran full tilt into the man. Farouk steadied her with one arm, then gave her a gentle push, placing a safe distance between them.

"Oh, there you are!" she exclaimed, blinking up at him. Her exotic dress was at direct odds with the wire-rimmed spectacles perched on the tip of her nose and the rosy blush tinting the ripe apples of her cheeks. "I'm so very happy to see you! I mean . . . I'm so very happy to see that you're unharmed," she amended, her blush deepening as she spread her skirts and bobbed him an awkward curtsy. "When I overheard two of the eunuchs discussing the attack, I feared the worst, m-m-my lord . . . and master," she added hopefully, batting her eyelashes at him.

Clarinda winced. If Poppy was hoping to hide her infatuation with the handsome sultan, she was doing a miserable job of it.

Farouk rolled his eyes, making no attempt to disguise his long-suffering sigh. His effortless charm always seemed to desert him whenever Poppy was near. "As I have told you many times before, Miss Montmorency, I am Your Majesty, not your master. It seems we have another escapee from my harem, gentlemen," he informed Ash and Luca. "Please allow me to introduce Miss Montmorency. She is Miss Cardew's . . . companion."

"And my dearest friend," Clarinda added loyally as Poppy bobbed another curtsy, this time in the direction of the new arrivals.

Poppy froze in midbob as she spotted Ash, her eyes growing even more enormous behind the thick lenses of her spectacles. "Oh! Oh my! I know who you are! You're Ashton Burke, the legendary adventurer! Why, you look exactly like the sketch that was in the *Snitch* a few months ago!" She shot Clarinda a confused glance. "I thought you said he had a long, hooked nose, a pair of spindly bowlegs, and teeth like a beaver's?"

Clarinda stiffened as Ash arched a bemused eyebrow in her direction. "You must have misheard me, dear," she said. "Or perhaps I mistook him for someone else of my acquaintance."

"Oh, no, I'm absolutely positive I heard you correctly," Poppy insisted earnestly. "I have a terrible head for sums but a frightfully good memory for conversation. I distinctly remember our exchange because it came just minutes before those nasty pirates attacked our ship. You also said men like Captain Burke cloak themselves in rumor and innuendo because there is nothing of real substance to hide. That they spread tall tales themselves simply to compensate for their own short—"

Clarinda clapped a hand over Poppy's mouth, wishing she had done so the moment Poppy came barreling into the courtyard. Luca snorted and Farouk's dark eyes sparkled with poorly concealed amusement.

Afraid to look at Ash, Clarinda gingerly removed her hand from Poppy's mouth. "I don't recall any such conversation. Perhaps your memory was simply addled by the distress of the attack."

Poppy gave Clarinda good reason to regret removing her hand when she blurted out, "Why are you here, Captain Burke? Have you come to rescue us just as you rescued that beautiful Hindustani princess?"

"Don't be ridiculous, Poppy." Clarinda laughed to hide her swelling alarm. "Rescue us from what? The lap of luxury? Being pampered like a pair of Princess Adelaide's cherished lapdogs? You know as well as I do that it was the sultan who rescued us from the horrors of the slave market. We owe him our gratitude and our loyalty . . . as well as our lives." She punctuated that declaration by returning to the protective circle of Farouk's arms and giving his chest a fond pat.

He slipped an arm around her waist and smiled down at her, his white teeth gleaming against his swarthy skin. "My little English buttercup chooses her words wisely." Although his smile lost none of its radiance, his eyes narrowed as he shifted his gaze to Ash's face. "I doubt a man of Captain Burke's reputation has survived this long by seeking to steal a woman who belongs to another man."

Even if she had first belonged to him.

The thought dawned in Clarinda's heart with shuddering clarity. For a timeless moment she was back in that misty meadow, wrapped once more in the irresistible heat of Ash's arms as they sank into the folds of her cloak.

Almost as if he could divine her wayward thoughts, Farouk tightened his possessive grip on her. "Seeking to steal a woman under such circumstances might very well cost a man not only his heart but his head." Despite his jovial tone, there was no mistaking the sharp edge of warning in his words.

Just as there was no mistaking the mocking grace in Ash's answering bow. "Then it is fortunate for the both of us that I have yet to lay eyes on the woman for whom I would be willing to sacrifice my heart—or my head."

❧ *Chapter Five*

"I sn't it a most extraordinary turn of events?" Poppy remarked as she followed Clarinda down the dimly lit corridor that led to the doors of the harem. "Captain Burke showing up here at the sultan's palace purely by happenstance? Why, when we were discussing his exploits back on the ship before those barbarians abducted us, who would have believed such an amazing coincidence was possible?"

"No one, Poppy," Clarinda replied, then muttered under her breath, "At least no one but you."

Forced to trot to keep up with Clarinda's brisk steps, Poppy continued chattering on and on about the vagaries of fortune and the whims of fate until the toe of her slipper came down firmly on the hem of Clarinda's skirts.

Clarinda was yanked to an awkward halt. Her dwindling reserves of patience exhausted, she wheeled on Poppy, snatching her hem back into her possession as she did so. "Poppy, please! It's bad enough to have to parade around in front of the whole world in this ridiculous getup. I'd rather not have to march the rest of the way back to the harem as naked as on the day I was born!"

Poppy's good-natured smile drooped; her lower lip began to tremble in a manner Clarinda recognized all too well.

Clarinda sighed, instantly contrite. "I'm sorry, dear," she said, touching two fingertips to one of her throbbing temples. "I didn't mean to snap at you. It's just that the arrival of these unexpected *visitors* has set my every nerve on edge."

At that moment all she desired was a moment of privacy to sort through the maddening whirl of her thoughts. It had taken her nearly two hours to escape Farouk's cheerful company after he had ordered a pair of servants to escort his guests to their private chambers. He had insisted upon reliving his adventure of the morning for her, poring over every detail of his rescue from his attackers while she struggled to remain dutifully doe-eyed and exclaim, "My goodness!" and, "Did he really?" at all of the pertinent moments when all she could see was Ash thundering down some sandy bluff with the reins of his horse between his teeth and a blazing pistol in each hand.

She had finally managed to excuse herself by pleading an all-too-real headache, only to find Poppy waiting to pounce on her the moment she left the courtyard.

She had no right to chide Poppy for her naïveté when her own heart was still veering wildly between shock and hope. It wasn't as if she hadn't dreamed of being rescued from this place. Her fiancé was a powerful man. It had been difficult to believe Maximillian would just shrug off her abduction and disappearance as if she were an unfortunate investment he had made at the Exchange.

But as the weeks had passed without the palace being stormed by a regiment of his men, her hopes had dimmed. When she closed her eyes on her sleeping couch at night and drifted into a fitful sleep, it was no longer Max's dear face with its strong brow and resolute chin that she saw but the face of another man—a man she had struggled to erase from both her memory and her heart.

To have him melt out of the desert like a dream after all these years made her want to pinch herself to see if she was truly awake. She supposed in some stubborn corner of her heart she had never stopped believing he would come for her someday. Never stopped hoping that the promises he had made after they had tumbled into her cloak had been more than empty words carefully crafted to seduce a foolish and innocent girl who would have done anything to make him stay.

She was no longer a foolish girl, and that corner of her heart had been walled off long ago with the jagged shards of those broken promises. She had lost so much more than just her innocence that morning and in the dark days that had followed. If she had anything to say about it, Ash would never know just how much his leaving had cost her. At least then she might be able to salvage her pride.

As difficult as it was for the woman she had become to believe Ash had come for her on his own, it was even more impossible to believe Maximillian would have sent him. Unlike his brother, Max only gambled when the odds were in his favor, and he would know better than anyone else that throwing the two of them together again was an extremely risky toss of the dice—especially for Max.

Catching Poppy's wrist to draw her closer, Clarinda cast an uneasy glance around them, half expecting to see Farouk's uncle Tarik or one of the man's many spies lurking behind some colorful tapestry or priceless urn. The ancient palace was honeycombed with trap-doors and secret passages. Tarik had made no secret of his distrust of his nephew's English *guests*, and in this place the walls really *could* have ears.

She lowered her voice. "Just as you surmised, it is quite impossible for Captain Burke's arrival to be simply a happy accident of fate."

"Aha!" Poppy exclaimed in a stage whisper so loud it could have been heard by a deaf camel. "He *has* come to rescue us, hasn't he? I just knew it!" She nervously smoothed her hair and moistened her lips with the tip of her tongue. "If he succeeds, do you suppose he'll be expecting one of us to kiss him as a reward? Or perhaps even the both of us?"

"I'd be more than happy to let you do the honors," Clarinda assured her even as an image of a much younger Ash lowering his head to gently brush his lips over hers drifted through her mind. She shook her head to clear it. "But until I have a chance to find out exactly what the captain's plan might be, it's imperative that we continue on as if nothing has changed. If we arouse suspicion in the sultan or his guard, it could put all of our lives in grave danger."

"But Farouk would never lift a hand to you," Poppy pointed out with a wistful sigh. "He adores you."

"He adores me at this specific moment in time. But I can assure you that the affections of men are far more fickle than you could ever imagine. Trust me . . . I should know. If he finds out I have a fiancé and that my fiancé's brother is residing under his roof at this very moment, there's no telling what he would do. He mustn't suspect we'd even consider running away with Captain Burke until we're far, far away from this place."

Poppy nodded her understanding. "Have no fear. I have always been known for my discretion."

As Poppy mimed locking her lips and tossing an imaginary key over her shoulder, Clarinda was reminded of a similar moment at Miss Throckmorton's when she had trusted Poppy with the news that her monthly courses had arrived for the very first time. By the next afternoon, every girl at the Seminary was pretending to scrub her hands and reenacting the "Out, damn spot!" scene from *Macbeth* every time Clarinda entered a room.

It wasn't that Poppy was deliberately malicious. She just had a tendency to blurt out the first thought that rolled onto her tongue, even if it wasn't her thought to share.

"I might as well just lop off my own head and hand it to the sultan," Clarinda muttered as she gathered her skirts and continued down the corridor.

"What will become of him after we're gone?" Poppy asked plaintively, falling into step behind her. "Aren't you afraid he'll be lonely?"

"Lonely? Are you mad? The man has at least a dozen wives and twice that many concubines."

"One doesn't have to be alone to be lonely." Poppy sounded as if she was speaking from experience. "What if you break his heart?"

"I can assure you there's absolutely no danger of that happening. The man may be infatuated with me but it's not as if he truly loves me. I'm just a shiny new bauble for his collection."

Even as she said the words, Clarinda wondered if it was possible for her to trust her own judgment when it came to matters of the heart. There was a time when she would have sworn Ash loved her more than life itself. That he would never leave her and would storm the gates of hell itself to get her back if they should ever be parted.

A pair of towering eunuchs flanked the tall, ornately carved doors that shielded the harem from the outside world, their massive arms folded over their hairless chests. Clarinda had learned most of their names, but she was particularly fond of Solomon, with his wise, dark eyes and sad smile. Although the giant Ethiopian clearly possessed the strength to crush a grown man's skull between his palms, he was as gentle as a nursemaid when it came to looking after the women entrusted to his care. He swung open the door for them and nodded to Clarinda as they passed, his well-oiled head gleaming like polished mahogany. Since she had never heard him utter a single word, she had always assumed he was mute.

She sometimes wondered if he had always been a slave and a eunuch. Or had he once had a wife of his own? A family? A voice?

As they entered the harem, a high-pitched titter assaulted their ears. Clarinda grabbed Poppy's arm and urged her closer to the opposite wall, hoping to remain undetected by the two women who were huddled in the curtained alcove closest to the door. She could just make out their silhouettes behind a translucent veil of purple silk shot through with gold threads.

"Well? Have you seen this mysterious Englishman who saved our master's life?" one of the women was asking.

"I have not," her companion replied. "But Serafina managed to steal a peek at him on her way back from the spice cellar. As you know, most of the English are pasty and soft and look as if a harsh desert wind would blow them away. But not this one, Serafina swears. He is handsome. And strong. And hard."

The first woman cupped a hand around the second woman's ear and whispered something that sent them both into lusty gales of laughter.

"Serafina claims he has the golden eyes of a tiger and moves with the grace and power of a lion." The first woman sighed. "I had hoped I would be summoned to attend him in his bath, but Solomon sent Zenobia and Salome. They returned a short while later and said he had sent them away and insisted on bathing himself. Can you imagine such a thing? A man bathing himself? The silly creatures must have displeased him in some way."

Clarinda briefly closed her eyes, a treacherous swell of relief surging through her veins. Since she no longer had any claim whatsoever on Ash, she could only attribute it to nostalgia. While the women began to discuss exactly how they would go about *pleasing* the handsome, golden-eyed Englishman in his bath, she tugged Poppy past the alcove, thankful for once that their slippers consisted of little more than scraps of colorful fabric.

As they passed beneath the gracefully arched doorway at the end of the long corridor and into the main hall of the harem, Clarinda's nostrils were overwhelmed by a choking cloud of incense and the cloying scents of dozens of women oiled and perfumed to within an inch of their lives.

The sultan's wealth was on display in every carefully chosen detail of the spacious octagonal chamber. The domed ceiling had been trimmed with genuine gold leaf while detailed murals had been painted on each panel of the ceiling, many of them erotic in nature. The top half of the walls consisted of teakwood latticework, which contributed to the airy, yet unsettling, feeling of being trapped in an oversize birdcage. Graceful columns carved from priceless marble and topped with bas-relief of papyrus leaves were scattered throughout the room. The floor had been tiled with mosaics in rich shades representing every color of the rainbow.

The chamber's opulence would have put even the most extravagant ballroom in London to shame. But to Farouk it was nothing more than a setting for his most prized jewels—the beautiful women reclining on pillows and couches throughout the room in various states of repose and undress.

Normally in the early-afternoon hours the women of the harem would be napping while eunuchs and young slave girls stirred the sultry air around them with huge fans adorned with precious gems and peacock feathers. But on this afternoon a current of excitement had swept through their ranks, leaving them wide-eyed and alert and whispering among themselves. Since they had little to occupy their idle hours but gossip and petty intrigues of their own making, Clarinda wasn't surprised the arrival of Farouk's exotic guests had generated such a stir among them.

In some ways life in the harem was no different from life at Miss Throckmorton's Seminary. Only here, instead of receiving instruction on dancing and needlework, the women learned the most effective techniques for weaving jewels into their elaborate braids and how to indulge a man's every sexual fantasy.

At first glance, it might even appear that the sultan's women enjoyed an extraordinary degree of freedom compared to their English counterparts. They rose whenever they wanted and had their every need tended to by devoted slaves. They weren't expected to lace themselves into rigid corsets or shove their feet into shoes that pinched their toes, but wore flowing robes or loose-fitting trousers that were more like pantaloons.

They didn't spend hours engaged in dutiful but dull pursuits such as doing needlework, practicing scales on the pianoforte, composing answers to endless stacks of correspondence, or learning how to pour the perfect cup of tea. Instead, they could while away a morning sunning themselves in the enclosed garden of the harem and spend the afternoon curling up with a book of poetry or having their taut muscles kneaded by the capable hands of a eunuch. It wasn't hard to understand how they had all managed to learn English at Farouk's command. With that much time on her hands, Clarinda could have mastered several languages.

She might have envied them their indolent lifestyle, but once the doors of the harem clanged shut, it quickly became evident that their freedom was only an illusion. They might be pampered and spoiled, but they were just as much captives to the sultan's whims as the slaves who served him.

Some of Farouk's women were wives, others concubines. No matter their station in life, they each had only one purpose. They existed solely to serve the sultan. To see to his needs and provide for his pleasure. To give him ease — either carnal or simply by cradling his head in their lap and stroking his brow while he poured out his cares on their sympathetic ears.

Although she had been desperately casting about for some way to escape before Ash's implausible appearance in the courtyard, Clarinda had begun to fear it was only a matter of time before she took her place among their ranks. Then she would lose what little freedom she had as Farouk's *guest* and be doomed to spend the rest of her life beating frantically against the bars of this gilded cage.

She had even wondered how long it would take her to become like the others. To end up living for the hope *she* might be the one summoned to the sultan's bed that night, if only to break up the soul-sucking monotony of the long, languid hours.

Aside from the locked doors and the towering eunuchs guarding them, one other thing was amiss in the harem — there were no children. No little feet scampered over the tiled floor, no bright bubbles of laughter floated up to the domed ceiling. If she gave Farouk a son or a daughter, the child would be wrested from her arms at birth, given to a wet nurse, and taken away so it could be raised by strangers in another part of the palace.

Clarinda felt her features harden into an expression she hardly recognized. She would never let such a thing happen. She would scale the palace walls herself and march barefoot across the scorching sands of the desert before she let anyone tear a child from her arms.

As she and Poppy began to wend their way through the chamber, several of the women cast them furtive glances beneath their lashes. Others openly stared, not bothering to hide the resentment simmering in their kohl-lined eyes.

Clarinda knew they despised everything about her, especially her pale skin, green eyes, and long blond hair, which was a constant source of both contempt and envy to them. With their luxuriant dark tresses, almond-shaped eyes, and ripe curves, most of them were more beautiful than she could ever hope to be. But they had been born knowing what she had learned only in the months since her abduction.

Men didn't crave beauty. They craved novelty.

Even more than her fair English looks, they resented her freedom to come and go as she liked without being ordered or summoned, to roam the corridors of the palace without a guard or a veil to protect her from prying male eyes. That privilege, more than any other, proclaimed her special place in their master's heart.

And earned their undying enmity.

Clarinda had survived their rancor for the past three months by telling herself that under other, less cutthroat circumstances, she might have found friends among them. That enabled her to hold her head high as she crossed the chamber, pretending just as she had during her first days at Miss Throckmorton's that their taunts and slights did not trouble her.

She might have succeeded in that ruse if a woman hadn't uncurled herself from a purple fainting couch with the sleek grace of a jungle cat and sauntered over to plant herself directly in their path. As Clarinda was forced to a halt, Poppy huddled behind her, no doubt remembering the many times Clarinda had protected her from the bullies at the Seminary.

Clarinda eyed the woman, her gaze coolly appraising. It was the sloe-eyed Yasmin, who had appointed herself Clarinda's chief adversary and tormentor.

According to what little gossip Poppy had been able to glean by eavesdropping on the other women, Yasmin had been about to take her place as one of the sultan's most honored wives when it was discovered she was not the innocent she had claimed to be. Given how proud and possessive Moroccan men were, she was lucky to have escaped with her life. Some whispered it was her extensive *talents* on the sleeping couch that had convinced Farouk to spare her life and keep her on as one of his concubines after learning of her deception.

With her pouting, plum-colored lips, her waist-length fall of glossy midnight-black hair and her dancing, dark eyes, she was truly one of the most stunning women in the harem. Her nose was a shade too large for her heart-shaped face, but that only gave her beauty a more exotic appeal. Her lush curves were covered by little more than scraps of translucent silk fashioned to draw a man's eye to the dusky circles of her areolas and the hint of shadow at the juncture of her thighs.

From the day Clarinda and Poppy had arrived at the harem, Yasmin had made no secret of her loathing for them. Clarinda suspected it was only respect for—and fear of—her beloved master that had prevented Yasmin from poisoning Clarinda's wine or slipping a jeweled dagger between her ribs while she slept. At least at Miss Throckmorton's she'd only had to worry about barbed words and venomous gossip.

The woman planted her hands on her shapely hips and lifted her chin to an even more haughty angle as she surveyed Clarinda with open contempt. Her harem sisters sat up straighter and leaned closer, like sharks scenting fresh blood in the water.

"We hear that one of your own kind has arrived at the palace," Yasmin said.

"Indeed?" Clarinda replied pleasantly, refusing to give the woman the satisfaction of confirming or denying what she already knew to be true.

"We were discussing just what might bring a strapping Englishman to our doors. We have decided that perhaps he tires of bedding bony English ice princesses and desires a taste of a real woman in his bed." Yasmin cast a glance over her shoulder, making sure her audience's avid attention had not wavered. "Or several real women."

As the women behind her collapsed on their couches in fits of giggles, Yasmin's lips curved in a triumphant smile.

Clarinda kept her face carefully impassive. "Unlike Moroccan men, Englishmen don't require a multitude of women to satisfy their desires. They only require one. As long as she is the *right* woman."

Although her sultry voice was still clearly audible throughout the chamber, Yasmin drew closer, as if to share a confidence. "Had Solomon sent me to attend this Englishman in his bath, he would not have sent me away. I would have proven myself to be the right woman to satisfy his *every* desire."

Clarinda had learned about far more than just the proper way to weave jewels into her hair in the past three months, and as an image of this woman on her knees at Ash's feet flashed through her brain with shocking clarity, she had to curl her twitching hand into a fist to keep it from slapping the smug expression from Yasmin's face.

Leaning even closer to Yasmin, Clarinda lowered her voice to an actual whisper, one intended only for Yasmin's ear. "If you were able to satisfy a man's *every* desire, you would be Farouk's wife instead of his concubine, would you not?"

Clarinda was the only one standing close enough to see the flash of hurt in Yasmin's dark eyes. She felt a reluctant twinge of remorse. It must be doubly galling to be forced to live as little more than a slave when you were plainly born to be a queen.

Knowing instinctively that the slightest inkling of sympathy would be construed as a weakness to be exploited later, she forced her feet into motion, neatly sidestepping Yasmin and sweeping the rest of the way across the chamber.

Although she couldn't afford the luxury of glancing over her shoulder to savor her triumph, Poppy was not bound by such constraints. "What on earth did you say to the hateful creature? She looks more inclined than ever to murder you in your sleep."

Clarinda tossed her head, keeping her own voice deliberately light. "I told her that the mysterious Englishman—and his desires—were absolutely no concern of mine."

Clarinda restlessly paced the curtained alcove that served as her bedchamber as she waited for her summons to join the sultan for supper. Since she was still being treated as Farouk's honored guest, she wasn't required to sleep in the main hall with the other women but had been given this tower retreat at the top of a narrow flight of stone stairs. Poppy slept in an even smaller alcove directly off the hall.

Clarinda's alcove contained little more than a luxurious sleeping couch heaped high with an array of pillows and bolsters in vibrant earth-

toned patterns, but at least it was hers. And tonight, more than any other, she was grateful for
the privacy it afforded her, even if that privilege
had also given Farouk's wives and concubines
yet another reason to resent her.

The older women who served the occupants
of the harem, many of whom had once been the
cherished concubines of Farouk's father, had already come and gone, taking their lotions and
potions with them. Although one could never accuse them of being lax in their duties, they seemed
to have taken extra care with her appearance on
this night. They must have been informed she
was about to be put on display not only for the
sultan but for his foreign guests as well.

Clarinda had lost count of the strokes as they
drew their brushes and combs through her hair
until it gleamed like spun flax beneath the smoky
kiss of the lamplight. Something about being
the center of such focused attention was undeniably seductive, especially when that attention
was devoted solely to pleasures of the flesh. It
would have been only too easy for her to close
her eyes and give herself over to the long, gliding strokes of brush and comb, to embrace the
way they made her feel as if every inch of her
body were tingling to life after a long slumber.

After tending to her hair, they had unpacked their rattling collection of vials, pots, and bottles, using the contents to dust her cheekbones with genuine gold dust, rouge the pronounced cupid's bow at the top of her upper lip, and draw a delicate line of kohl around her eyes.

One of the women had tugged the glass stopper from a costly vial of myrrh and dabbed the musky scent behind her ears and in the hollow of her throat. They would have applied the perfume in even more intimate areas if Clarinda hadn't grabbed their eager hands and shooed them from the alcove, ignoring their wounded scowls and muttered Arabic protests.

She would do well to remember that they did not perform these tasks for her pleasure but to make her more desirable to the eyes of men.

On any other night Clarinda might have found their pampering to be a pleasant distraction, but on this night her nerves were strung so tight she feared she would scream if she had to endure another pair of impersonal hands on her body. Without warning, her mind summoned up the provocative image of a pair of hands stroking her skin, their backs bronzed by the sun and lightly dusted with crisp brown hair, their touch anything but impersonal.

Cursing her unruly imagination, she made another restless circuit of the alcove, the emerald green and peacock blue of what the Moroccans considered skirts rippling around her ankles. Back in England, she had been bound in the chains of her corset and discouraged from so much as thinking about the ripe flesh that lay beneath. Here she was not only encouraged to think about it, but deliberately kept in a nearly constant state of awareness of its needs and its wants. As a woman who had struggled to keep those powerful desires in check for nearly a decade, Clarinda was beginning to fear she was more of a danger to herself than Farouk could ever be.

The gossamer silk of her skirts was so fine it might have been woven from spiderwebs and moonbeams. The only thing that kept it from being completely indecent was the care taken to drape the sheer material in multiple layers over all of her more *delicate* areas. That scant courtesy made it impossible to tell if one was actually stealing a peek at something one shouldn't be peeking at or falling prey to a teasing trick of the lamplight.

Clarinda's acute mortification at wandering around in what the English would have considered the most decadent of undergarments had begun to fade after their first few weeks in this place. Compared to what Yasmin usually wore—or didn't wear—when parading around the harem, Clarinda's own attire was positively virginal.

But tonight it would be Ash's gaze that sought to penetrate the fluttering layers of silk, his amber eyes caressing the ivory swell of her breasts revealed by her low-cut bodice. She touched a hand to her throat, the thought making her feel flushed and shaky, as if she were coming down with some sort of exotic desert fever for which there was no cure.

Despite her long-standing affection for Max, she hadn't truly felt this way since she was seventeen years old. She had wanted Ash to turn and look at her, to really *see* her, for so long that when he finally had, it had gone straight to her head. She had been giddy with triumph and drunk with power.

She could still remember delighting in the effect her slightest touch had on him. How it could make his eyes burn with hunger and his voice roughen with passion. How he would hold her so close she could feel the thick ridge of his desire pressing against the front of his trousers, pressing against her. She had savored her power over him the way a horseman might savor his control over a prize stallion. Until the morning she had discovered her power was only an illusion and that she had wanted him to lose control as badly as he had.

She gave the top of her bodice a nervous tug, wondering what gown she might have chosen from her extensive wardrobe back in England for such a momentous occasion. Her rose-colored watered silk with its shirred sleeves, tiered skirt, and off-the-shoulder lace collar? Or perhaps the bronze silk taffeta that so perfectly offset the green of her eyes? Given how erratically her heart was beating in her throat, she would have been wiser to choose something that modestly covered her from throat to toe—gray flannel perhaps or something borrowed from the nearest nunnery.

There was no denying the spark that had flared in Ash's eyes when he'd first seen her, but she would almost have sworn it was a spark of enmity, not desire. Was he even now pacing his own bedchamber and believing the very worst of her? Had he convinced himself she had willingly embraced this life? That she had surrendered herself to Farouk and spent the long, torrid nights eagerly sharing the sultan's sleeping couch?

She scowled, disturbed by the direction of her thoughts. Why should she care what Ashton Burke or any other man thought of her? She had done what she had to do to survive, and Ash could make of that whatever he would.

Sensing a presence behind her, she turned to find Solomon's shadow darkening the arched doorway. The eunuch inclined his gleaming head toward the corridor, indicating that their master's summons had come.

Clarinda wished that Poppy could be by her side on this night to bolster her courage, but for some unfathomable reason her friend made Farouk as jumpy as a cat. Squaring her shoulders, Clarinda fought to tamp down her rioting nerves. This was no different from serving as hostess for one of her papa's dinner parties, was it not? And hadn't she played that role dozens of times through the years with dazzling success?

Pasting a bright smile on her lips, she glided forward to link her arm through Solomon's, thankful once again for his solid presence. "Come, good sir. We would not want to keep the sultan and his guests waiting."

As Ash waited for Clarinda to appear, he took a carefully measured sip of the spiced wine their host had provided. The rich blend of cloves and fermented red grapes was much stronger than the spirits served in most English dining rooms. Given that Farouk did not indulge at all, Ash had no intention of letting the liquor dull his senses. If he hoped to steal Clarinda right out from under the man's nose, he would have to keep all of his wits about him.

Luca, however, appeared to have surrendered his wits without so much as a single shot being fired. "Come here, *bellezza*!" he sang out, already looking flushed and glassy-eyed as he snared one of the dancing girls by the wrist and tugged her into his lap.

She giggled as he sloshed wine into the valley between her ample breasts, then tried to steal a peek under the gauzy veil she wore over her nose and lips. As she ducked her head to nuzzle his neck, he gave Ash a delighted grin that said he wouldn't mind staying in this place forever.

Luca's antics earned him a disparaging scowl from Farouk's uncle Tarik. Apparently the man still did not approve of his nephew opening his home to the Western infidels. Although Ash knew it might not be the most diplomatic move, he could not resist lifting his jeweled goblet to the man in a mocking toast. Tarik's scowl deepened to an outraged glower and he deliberately turned his face away from Ash to confer with the hawk-nosed man seated next to him.

Seemingly oblivious to the minor dramas going on around him, Farouk sat across from Ash, a broad smile splitting his handsome face as he clapped in time to the music of drum, flute, and lyre.

Ash reclined on one elbow against the mound of cushions behind him. A casual observer would have sworn there wasn't an ounce of tension in his lean, rangy frame. The ruse was honed through years of both practice and experience. Even as he gave one of the dancing girls a lazy smile, his eyes were warily scanning the room, noting every potential threat and possible escape route.

After seeing Clarinda nestled so cozily in Farouk's arms, Ash was no longer entirely sure she wanted to be rescued. During his years with the Company in Burma, he had seen the spirits of even the strongest, most resilient men broken while in captivity. They had endured torture and unspeakable hardship only to end up becoming little more than slavering toadies to the enemy they had once despised.

Clarinda possessed one of the most stubborn and shining spirits he had ever encountered, but he still had no way of knowing what she might have endured at Farouk's hands or at the hands of the Corsairs who had abducted her.

When he had accepted Max's money, he had promised himself this would be no different from any other mission. But the thought of Clarinda suffering beneath the brutish hands of any man made him want to sweep her into his arms and carry her away to a place where no harm could ever come to her again, after destroying whoever was responsible, of course.

But that wasn't what his brother had hired him to do, he reminded himself grimly. Max had hired him to retrieve her, and it was Max who would be waiting to sweep her into his arms and tenderly nurse her spirit back to health. Ash's job was simply to get her out of this prison of a palace, and that was exactly what he intended to do—with or without her cooperation.

The banquet was being held on the top floor of one of the square towers that crowned each corner of the palace. Instead of being confined to a table and chairs, the sultan and a dozen guests, all of them men, reclined on plush nests of tasseled pillows and satin-covered bolsters in brilliant shades of emerald, sapphire, and vermilion. Low-slung benches laden with food had been arranged in a rectangle in front of them, leaving ample room for the dancing girls to use the open area in the middle of the rectangle as an impromptu stage.

Broad windows flanked each wall of the spacious chamber. Their wooden shutters had been thrown open to welcome in a balmy breeze redolent with night-blooming jasmine to mingle with the enticing aromas wafting from the platters and bowls being delivered by a steady parade of servants.

True to his word, Farouk was making every effort to tempt his guests' palates with all of the exotic delicacies at his disposal. The benches were crowded with bunches of plump grapes and platters of fresh figs and dried dates glazed with sugar. Clay bowls brimming with stewed lamb and mutton swimming in a golden sea of olive oil sat next to heaping mounds of couscous richly spiced with turmeric and cumin and steaming loaves of *khobz*—the flat, round bread Moroccans used in lieu of a fork or spoon.

Of all the delicacies on display that evening, none were more exotic or tempting than the dark-eyed beauties shimmying and twirling to the soaring song of the flute and the throbbing beat of the drums. Ash absently brought his goblet to his lips as he studied the sinuous sway of one dancer's hips, hypnotized against his will by the suggestive motion.

The dancer's skirt—if one could call it that— was precariously balanced on the graceful flare of her hip bones, giving the impression that one wrong move might send it shimmying to the floor. A high slit in the fabric exposed a flash of long, tanned leg every time she twirled. A narrow string of rubies rode low on her slender waist, matching the larger gem nestled in the tantalizing dip of her navel.

Her skintight bodice covered little more than the ripe globes of her breasts. Even those were allowed to spill over the top, as if just awaiting the casual brush of a man's hands to break completely free from their moorings. Ash took another sip of the wine, thinking wryly that most Englishmen wouldn't see that much naked flesh in the entire course of their marriage.

She danced closer to him, deliberately bringing herself within arm's reach. Her nose and mouth might be veiled, but the invitation in her sultry, dark eyes was as unmistakable as the rhythmic thrust of her hips.

Her boldness only served to remind him that he had strayed into a world of masculine privilege even greater than the one he had left behind in England all those years ago. Here a man's word literally was law, and women were considered little more than pretty playthings to be used and then discarded when a man's attention wandered to a more enticing pleasure.

Unfortunately for him, that more enticing pleasure appeared in the doorway just as the dancing girl twined one hand through his hair and leaned down to bring her veiled lips to within a heady wine-scented breath of his own.

The flute crested on a shrill note. The drumbeat swelled to a thundering crescendo, then crashed into silence, allowing Clarinda's dulcet tones to ring through the room like a bell. "Why, Captain Burke! I'm so glad to see you taking full advantage of the sultan's gracious hospitality!"

✤ *Chapter Six*

Clarinda stood in the doorway of the tower, looking less like a captive than a haughty young queen perfectly capable of ruling the heart of every man in the room, if not the kingdom. She wore a fitted bodice accented with glittering beads and flowing skirts in vivid shades of emerald and sapphire. Her garments were far more modest than the snippets of silk the dancing girls were wearing, yet somehow the illusion of uncharted territory only added to her mystique.

Her hair had been left loose to flow over her shoulders, its only adornment the thin circlet of beaten gold crowning her brow. A teardrop of an emerald a shade darker than her eyes nestled between the gentle swell of her breasts, dangling from a gold chain nearly as thick as her pinkie. Her very skin seemed to glow as if it had been massaged by countless hands whose sole purpose was to enhance its radiance. Ash found it only too easy to imagine his own hands gliding over her satiny skin, stroking oil of myrrh or sandalwood over every enticing inch of her.

He shifted, grateful Farouk had been kind enough to outfit him and Luca in native robes for the evening. Had he been wearing the skin-tight riding breeches they'd arrived in, it would have been impossible to hide the fact that Clarinda still stirred him in a way no anonymous dancing girl could ever hope to do.

Sensing the abrupt shift in his attentions, the girl who had been about to dance herself right into his lap straightened, resentment written in every line of her posture. As she backed away from him, Ash didn't have to see the pout beneath her veil to know it was there.

It seemed he had fallen out of favor with more than one woman in the room. Despite the sweetness of Clarinda's smile, her eyes held a murderous glitter Ash recognized only too well. "I do hope you gentlemen will forgive me. It was not my intent to interrupt the festivities before they reached their"—she batted her eyelashes innocently at him—"climax."

Farouk patted the tasseled cushion next to him, his adoring grin confirming he would be only too happy to indulge her every wish — including presenting her with Ash's head on a platter should she request it. "There is no need for apologies from lips as lovely as yours, my pet. Not when my heart seeks only to celebrate the radiance of your beauty."

It was all Ash could do not to roll his eyes. The devil's tongue held more silver than his treasury.

Farouk clapped his hands briskly to dismiss both the musicians and the dancing girls. They silently paraded from the room, leaving a crestfallen Luca to seek solace in a fresh goblet of wine.

As Clarinda made her way to Farouk's side, Ash almost rose to his feet out of long habit before remembering such courtesies were not afforded women here. He was forced to content himself with a wary nod, which she did not return.

She sank onto the cushion next to Farouk's, curling her shapely legs beneath her like an agile little cat. Only then did Ash notice the thick cuff of pearls encircling her slender ankle. Another priceless gift from the sultan, no doubt, but one designed as a clear sign of possession. Farouk might as well have fastened a collar around her throat and attached it to himself with an iron chain.

Ash stabbed an ivory-handled knife into a slice of honey-drizzled pear and brought it to his lips. He was still doing his damnedest not to think about Clarinda being forced to share the sultan's bed. If he did, he was afraid he might lunge across the bowl of raisins drifting in a cloud of cream sitting in front of him and plunge the knife into his host's throat.

"So, Burke," the sultan said, helping himself to a ripe fig with one hand while he absently stroked Clarinda's nape with the other, "you have traveled a great distance to reach our shores. Perhaps the time has come for you to tell us what brings you to our magnificent land."

Before Ash could reply, Clarinda snared a plump grape and popped it between her lips, her eyes sparkling with mischief. "You'd best guard your treasures well, Your Majesty. From what I hear, Captain Burke is a notorious thief."

Ash narrowed his eyes at her, wondering what she hoped to gain by deliberately casting suspicion on them. But then he realized that if Farouk believed they were trolling for gold and silver to fatten their purses, he might not suspect they'd come for a different sort of treasure altogether.

Clever girl.

"I'm not going to deny that I have been known to dabble in antiquities," he confessed.

"Someone else's antiquities, as it were," Clarinda added, making him wonder if she was trying to help him after all or get him hauled out of the room by Farouk's guards and tossed in the man's dungeon.

"In the past I have been hired to assist in the . . . um . . . *procurement* of valuable objects," Ash said. "But I didn't sneak them away in the dead of night so much as restore them to their rightful owners."

Farouk propped an elbow on one knee and leaned forward, looking genuinely intrigued. "What sort of objects are we talking about?"

Ash shrugged. "Artifacts. Ancient idols. Rare gemstones. When I heard this region was rich in such items, I thought it would do no harm to explore my opportunities."

"It has been my experience," Farouk said, "that a treasure is only worth what a man is willing to pay for it."

"Exactly," Ash agreed. "Which is why I choose my undertakings with such care. If a man is too greedy, the cost to himself may very well exceed any reward he hopes to obtain." Against his better judgment, he allowed his gaze to linger briefly on Clarinda. "Only rarely does a man stumble across a treasure so valuable it is beyond price."

"If a man is foolish enough to lose such a treasure, then perhaps he was not deserving of it in the first place," Farouk said.

As Ash watched the man's sun-bronzed fingers lay claim to the delicate curve of Clarinda's collarbone, he pried his fingers from the hilt of his knife and gently set the utensil aside. "I fear you may be right."

Shooting Ash a deliberately flirtatious glance, Clarinda ducked out from beneath Farouk's possessive caress in the guise of reaching for a bowl of dates. "If Captain Burke has yet to find this elusive treasure he is seeking, Your Majesty, then you should definitely keep your own coffers under lock and key."

"If not for Burke's boldness and bravery, I would not be here tonight," Farouk declared, spreading his hands in a magnanimous gesture. "If he desires something that belongs to me, he has only to ask and it will be his!"

Not daring to look at Clarinda for fear he would reveal his most dangerous desire, Ash hefted his goblet. "All I require on this night is fine wine, rich food, and good company."

"Here, here!" Luca echoed, holding out his own goblet so a servant could refill it.

Visibly pleased by Ash's response, Farouk

clinked goblets with Clarinda before drinking deeply of the unfermented grape nectar within.

Farouk's uncle Tarik continued to scowl at Ash, his brow a thundercloud of disapproval. "Just how long do you and your man plan to take advantage of my nephew's generosity, Captain Burke?"

"Probably no more than a few days," Ash said at the exact moment Luca said cheerfully, "Oh, at least a fortnight. Perhaps longer!"

"Captain Burke is not known for staying in one place for very long," Clarinda said. "He has the feet of a vagabond, the soul of a wanderer, and the heart of . . . " She hesitated, wrinkling her slender nose. "Well, according to the scandal sheets, I'm not sure he has a heart."

Ash reclined on one elbow, studying her boldly. "Now that we've determined what brought me and my companion to El Jadida, Miss Cardew, I'd love to hear exactly how you came to be the sultan's honored"—Ash's tongue caressed the word, imbuing it with a salaciousness it did not deserve—"*guest.*"

Farouk returned a protective hand to Clarinda's shoulder. "You do not have to speak of such matters if it troubles you, my dearest."

The sultan's tender concern immediately made Ash regret his own callousness. He should have known better than to let Clarinda goad him into doing or saying something rash. He might be desperate to find out just what she had suffered since her abduction, but not at the expense of her pride.

Although her gaze had cooled by several degrees, she waved away Farouk's concern. "One cannot fault Captain Burke for his curiosity. When he came to this place, I'm sure the last thing he expected to find were two very proper English ladies enjoying the hospitality of a powerful sultan." She arched a mocking brow at Ash. They both knew that was *exactly* what he had expected to find.

"It seems my nephew's hospitality is much in demand by the English these days," Tarik interjected. "I suppose if King William came knocking on the door with his entire army in tow, you would throw open the gates and invite him in to pillage your treasury and ravish your women."

"Hey! I had no intention of ravishing that girl," Luca protested. "I'm fairly certain she was on the verge of ravishing me."

"That is *enough*, Uncle," Farouk thundered. "We are not barbarians here, and I will not tolerate disrespectful treatment of my guests."

Tarik surged to his feet, his face darkening. "If your father were still alive, you would be whipped for daring to speak to *me* with such disrespect!"

Almost as if he had been waiting for just such an opportunity, the man went storming from the room with his robes snapping and his hawk-nosed friend in tow. The other diners observed the dramatic departure with mild interest before shrugging and going back to their own food and conversations. Apparently, such outbursts from Tarik were not unusual.

Farouk shook his head with a sigh. "Do not mind my uncle. His feet are still mired in the sands of the past instead of turning toward the future." He returned his attention to Clarinda as if the ugly incident had never happened. "Do go on, my dear."

Clarinda awkwardly cleared her throat before beginning. "Well . . . Miss Montmorency and I were traveling to India to attend the wedding of a . . . a dear friend when our ship was set upon by Corsairs. Several members of the crew were cut down in the resulting battle, but we were taken captive and confined to the hold of the pirate vessel for several days while it made its way to the coast. We were told from the beginning it was their intention to auction us off to the highest bidder at the slave market in Algiers. Our maids and the captain's wife were not so fortunate."

Oddly enough, the utter lack of passion in her voice was what told Ash what a wretched fate those poor women must have met. A fate that could just as easily have been hers if the pirates' greed had not been greater than their lust. Luca looked nearly as horrified as Ash felt.

"Once we arrived in Algiers," she continued, "they dragged us to the underground slave market in chains. They stripped us of our gowns, leaving us in nothing but our undergarments."

Although his face remained as expressionless as her own, Ash's chest had grown so tight with anguish and fury he could barely breathe. Even as a little girl, Clarinda had been stiff-necked with pride. He could hardly imagine her in chains, much less fathom the depths of humiliation she must have endured at the hands of the slavers while they tore off her clothes and exposed her to the lascivious eyes of dozens of leering men.

And there he sat, sipping wine as if watching a play from a plush box at the Theatre Royal and making her relive the degradation of that moment like the son of a bitch he was.

"Please, Miss Cardew . . ." he said gruffly, lifting a hand in the hope of staying her words. "The sultan was right. There's no need for you to dredge up such painful memories for me or any other man."

But Clarinda had never backed down from a challenge in her life, and he could tell by the stubborn glitter in her eyes that she had every intention of finishing what he had started.

She had suffered. Now it was his turn.

As she continued, he could see every miserable moment of her ordeal unfolding like a nightmare in his head. "The slaver shoved me up on the block first. When the men began to shout that they wanted to see more of his *wares*, he ordered me to remove my chemise—which was already little more than a rag by that time— and stand naked before them all. I heard him promise several of the wealthier-looking men that they could come up to the block and examine me more *thoroughly* after I had stripped. When I refused, he lifted his whip to strike me. That was when Farouk came striding out of the crowd. He jerked the whip from the man's hand and used it against him. While the man cowered at his feet, Farouk lifted me off the block and wrapped his cloak around me."

Ash briefly closed his eyes, wishing savagely that it could have been *his* hand that whipped the flesh from the slave trader's back, *his* arms that comforted a trembling Clarinda. He would have carried her away from that place and tenderly kissed away every tear from her cheek, every mark the chains had left on her delicate flesh.

When he opened his eyes, it was to regard Farouk with genuine, if reluctant, gratitude. "How very fortunate for Miss Cardew that you were there that day to intervene."

Farouk touched a hand to his heart. "I prefer to think of it as the benevolent will of Allah as well as my own good fortune."

"Farouk insisted on purchasing me right then and there," Clarinda said. "The slaver tried to convince him he should take the time to examine my hair, my teeth, all of my other . . . *assets*, but Farouk insisted he had seen everything he needed to see."

"Even with her hair hanging around her face in filthy tangles and her garments in rags, there was no mistaking the quality of this one." Farouk tenderly brushed his hand over Clarinda's head. "You should have seen her defy that miserable dog of a slaver. She was magnificent!"

As Ash watched Farouk's fingers sift through the wheaten silk of Clarinda's hair just as his own fingers were longing to do in that moment, he certainly had no argument for that.

"At first he was only going to purchase me," she explained, "but after I pleaded with him, he agreed to take Poppy as well."

"A decision I've had many opportunities to regret," Farouk confided, earning a playful swat from Clarinda.

She sobered as she returned her gaze to Ash. "So as you can see, Captain Burke, I owe the sultan more than just my gratitude. I owe him my life."

Ash trusted he was the only one in the room who knew her well enough to spot the desperation in her eyes. Until that moment, he'd tried to forget just how much time they'd once spent communicating through wordless glances. And *accidental* touches.

This was a complication he had not anticipated. Wresting her from the arms of a ruthless and rapacious despot had presented enough of a challenge. Stealing her from a decent man who had genuine feelings for her might prove to be even trickier and require a much more sophisticated plan. It was a good thing his brother had hired him for his brains as well as his brawn.

"Do not trouble your pretty little head, my gazelle," Farouk assured her. "I shall give you ample opportunity to repay that debt once your training is complete."

"Training?" Ash echoed, feeling a new prickle of foreboding dance down his spine. "What sort of training?"

Clarinda inclined her head so that her face was half veiled by the silky fall of her hair.

Farouk beamed like a proud papa. "My Clarinda has spent the last few months being tutored by some of the women who once served my father in his harem."

"Tutored?" Feeling his wariness grow, Ash glanced at Luca, who was hanging on Farouk's every word as if it would be his last. "In what subject, may I ask?"

Before Farouk could reply, Clarinda lifted her head, looked Ash dead in the eye, and said coolly, "Pleasure, Captain Burke. How to give it . . . and how to receive it."

⚜ *Chapter Seven*

*A*lthough Ash was afraid to so much as blink, there was no denying the effect simply watching Clarinda's luscious lips form the word *pleasure* had on him. His gaze lingered on those lips, shockingly graphic images of the pleasure they might give him rioting through both his brain and his body. In seconds, the temperature in the room went from mildly warm to sweltering. From the corner of his eye, Ash saw a wide-eyed Luca snatch up a silk serviette and dab at his glistening brow.

Despite making a Herculean effort to maintain his composure, Ash still had to clear his throat before speaking. "And is this a common custom of your people?" he inquired, buying himself some time by shifting his gaze to Farouk. "Do all of your female guests receive such detailed . . . instruction?"

Farouk burst out laughing. "It has been too long since we were at Eton together. I had forgotten how prudish you English were."

"From what I've read in the newspapers," Clarinda said, "shocking Captain Burke should be no easy feat. During his travels in Africa, he made an extensive study of native cultures"— she hesitated for a telling moment, her eyes looking even more green than usual—"both mundane and carnal."

"I helped him with that, you know," Luca volunteered. "I felt it was my Christian duty as his closest friend."

Ash slanted Luca a glance that warned him it was also his duty to hold his tongue or risk being skewered through the heart with a serving fork.

Farouk leaned forward, plainly warming to his subject. "This is not England. Here we do not shy away from discussing what transpires between a man and a woman, accepting it as one of Allah's greatest gifts. We feel free to speak of matters that would give even the most jaded of your libertines a fit of the vapors."

"Captain Burke does look a trifle pale at the moment, doesn't he?" Clarinda observed, blinking innocently as she tilted her head to study him.

Farouk gently folded his fingers over her hand. "Contrary to what you Westerners may believe of us, we are not barbarians. We do not enjoy forcing women to our will. It was actually Clarinda's idea that she be trained in the arts of love. When she arrived here three months ago, she expressed an eagerness to learn all there was to know about making a man happy."

"Perhaps you should allow for more time," Ash said smoothly. "Especially for her to master a skill so contrary to her nature."

Clarinda's mocking expression tightened to a glare. The fingers of her free hand closed around the stem of her goblet, making Ash wonder if he was about to get its contents hurled into his face.

Farouk brought the back of Clarinda's hand to his lips, pressing a tender kiss upon it. "She says she does not wish to disappoint me when she comes to my bed for the first time."

Ash jerked his gaze away from the sight of Clarinda's captive hand being caressed by the sultan's lips and returned it to her face, a surge of dangerous jubilation coursing through his heart. He had not come too late after all. Clarinda had yet to share the sultan's bed. It took him a moment to remember the jubilation should have belonged to his brother, just as she did.

"How very magnanimous of her," he murmured.

"I am not a patient man," Farouk said. "And

as I am sure you can imagine, I did not wish to wait to sample the delights promised by her gaze. What man in his right mind would? But how was I to deny her when she offered to willingly—and eagerly—bestow upon me the prize of her innocence?"

Ash went rigid, his breath freezing in his throat. Suddenly, it was Clarinda who could not meet *his* eyes. Clarinda who found something of such tremendous interest in the bottom of her wine goblet that she could not seem to tear her gaze away from it. The casual observer might have mistaken the flush of rose blooming over her cheekbones for a modest blush.

Studying her downturned face, the graceful curve of her cheek, Ash said quietly, "I can see why a man might be willing to make any sacrifice to win such a prize."

Her gaze flew up to meet his as Farouk nodded his approval. "Her tutors assure me she is an apt and eager pupil and will soon be ready to receive my attentions and become my wife."

While Ash was still trying to absorb that new blow on top of all the others he'd been forced to endure that night, Luca piped up to ask, "You mean one of your wives, don't you? Is it not your custom to take more than one wife, as well as many concubines?"

"That is true, but Clarinda knows she will be first, both in my harem and in my heart."

For how long? Ash wondered cynically as Farouk gave Clarinda another doting look. Until Farouk rescued some other nubile young beauty from the slave market? "Just when is this momentous occasion to take place?"

"In less than a fortnight," Farouk replied. "It was also Clarinda's idea that we postpone our nuptials until she turned one-and-twenty."

Ash sucked a mouthful of wine directly into his windpipe. As he exploded in a fit of coughing, one of the servants rushed forward to dutifully pound him on the back. Clarinda's eyes flared in warning, then narrowed to emerald slits. Ash waved the servant away, hoping Farouk would attribute the tears of mirth sparkling in Ash's eyes to the effects of the wine.

"Perhaps you and Mr. D'Arcangelo could delay your departure until after the wedding," Farouk suggested earnestly. "It would do me and my bride a great honor if you would join us in our celebration."

Ash lifted his goblet in an impromptu toast. His words might be for Farouk but his gaze was for Clarinda alone. "You honor your humble guests more than we deserve, Your Majesty. I wouldn't miss it for the world."

Chapter Eight

Farouk slipped into the gardens of his palace shortly after sunrise, hoping to escape the watchful eyes of his guards. They tended to dog his every step, even when he was safely sequestered behind the walls of the palace. After yesterday morning's attack, he'd had no choice but to heed his uncle's advice and forgo the luxury of his morning ride. At least when he was cantering back and forth across the desert with sand stinging his eyes and the hot wind whipping through his hair, he could pretend he was a free man, a man not bound by centuries of bloodshed and tradition.

Of late those moments of freedom were becoming even more rare and precious. If the women of his harem weren't clamoring for his attentions, then Tarik was hammering away at him to spend more of his gold fortifying the palace's already formidable defenses or to prove his supremacy by declaring war on some rival sultan or tribe. His uncle had always equated peace with cowardice and believed every true warrior should go to his grave with a sword in his hand and a battle cry on his lips.

His uncle's keenest shame was that his own brother—Farouk's father—had slumped over dead in the middle of a feast celebrating a truce between himself and one of El Jadida's oldest enemies. He hadn't even had the good grace to be poisoned. It had always been said among his people that Farouk's father possessed the heart of a lion, but in the end his mighty heart had failed him. His unexpected death had resulted in Farouk being summoned back to Morocco to assume the weighty mantel of sultan after completing only one year at Cambridge.

Sometimes Farouk felt as much a prisoner of these walls as the slaves who had served his family for generations. He was grateful for the distraction Captain Burke's arrival had provided and could only pray wedding and bedding Clarinda would ease the terrible restlessness that seemed to plague his every step these days.

He followed the wending flagstones that led to his favorite haven.

The small garden sat on a slight rise, the sheer drop at its far end making a wall unnecessary for defense and allowing for an unobstructed view of the rambling coastline. On gusty days like this, the briny scent of the sea was borne on the wings of the wind, allowing a man to dream of other shores, other lives he might have lived.

A sharp stab of disappointment waylaid Farouk at the mouth of the garden. It seemed he should have risen even earlier on this fine morning. Someone had already laid claim to his refuge. At moments like this he feared he had been cursed with his uncle's temperament after all because suddenly all he wanted to do was roar with rage and demand the head of the unfortunate interloper.

But when he realized who it was, he made an abrupt about-face, hoping to slink out of the garden before she could spot him.

"Oh, Your Majesty, is that you?" she called out. "You mustn't rush off! Why don't you come and tarry for a while?"

Farouk halted in his tracks, cringing at the unabashed delight in that voice. He'd rather face a horde of bloodthirsty marauders scaling the palace walls with daggers clenched between their teeth than spend a moment in Miss Penelope Montmorency's company.

He couldn't have said what he found so grating about Clarinda's companion. There was something about the way she looked at him, those earnest blue eyes of hers magnified by the thick lenses of her spectacles.

He was certainly no stranger to the demands of women. But he had learned early on that most of them could be placated by pretty words complimenting their charms, priceless baubles that matched the shade of their eyes, or the promise of an extra night in his bed. The problem with Miss Montmorency was that he could never quite figure out what she wanted from him, which left him feeling utterly helpless to provide it. And he'd spent enough time feeling helpless when at the mercy of the bullies at Eton.

He slowly pivoted on his heel, his usual affable smile failing him. All he had to offer was a curt nod. "Miss Montmorency."

Undaunted by his lack of enthusiasm, she gave the space next to her on the stone bench a cheerful pat. "Won't you join me? It's such a lovely morning! I simply adore taking the air before the heat of the day sets in. I discovered this corner of the garden just yesterday, and I do believe it's fast becoming my favorite place in all the world!"

Wonderful, Farouk thought, scowling as he watched a gust of wind tease a peach-colored tendril from the knot of curls clustered at the crown of her head. Despite being garbed in what appeared to be a dozen layers of diaphanous silk, she still looked like a plump English rose that had inexplicably bloomed in the desert.

He lowered himself stiffly to the stone bench, managing a grunt of assent. The charming banalities that normally tripped from his tongue seemed to have deserted him along with his smile.

His failure to uphold his end of the conversation did not seem to dampen Miss Montmorency's irrepressible spirits. She retrieved the wicker basket sitting on the ground by her feet and placed it on her lap. "One of your cooks was kind enough to pack this basket for me so I could break my fast while gazing out over the sea." She peeled back a scrap of crimson satin to reveal a nest of freshly fried *ktefa*. The traditional pastries were dusted with sugar and drizzled with warm honey. "Would you care to join me?"

To Farouk's keen humiliation, his stomach rumbled a reply before he could. He gazed down at her offering as if it were a basket of cobras, holding his breath so as not to be seduced by the heavenly aroma of the pastries wafting to his nose. When he had returned from Cambridge, it had taken him nearly a year of constant training—all conducted beneath the ruthless tutelage of his uncle—to hone away the softness around his middle and carve what remained into rock-solid muscle.

He had accomplished that feat only by denying himself such indulgences. Although a feast was spread before him nearly every night, he took great pride in choosing only the freshest fruits and the leanest cuts of meat to take the edge off his hunger. He supposed that a part of him believed if he allowed himself so much as a taste of something sweet, he might not stop eating until he had gorged himself right back into being the pudgy poltroon his classmates at Eton had mocked so mercilessly.

As his uncle had reminded him hundreds of times since his return to Morocco, such a man could never be fit for the title of sultan.

"I have already broken my fast," he said gruffly, although the handful of pomegranates, nuts, and dates he'd gulped down upon arising had only whetted his appetite for something more substantial.

"Suit yourself," she sang out like the most shameless of temptresses, her full cheeks dimpling into a teasing smile. "But I wager you'll be sorry."

As he watched her sink her teeth into one of the flaky pastries, he already was. She ate with the unabashed relish of a woman who truly enjoyed food and wasn't afraid to show it. There was something undeniably sensual about her enthusiasm for such a basic pleasure. It transformed the simple fare into a feast for the senses. Her pink tongue darted out to lick a creamy dollop of custard from the corner of her lips, and Farouk realized with a jolt of shock that beneath his loose trousers his body had begun to stir with another sort of hunger altogether.

He was accustomed to being courted, seduced, and pleasured by breathtakingly beautiful women who had been taught erotic tricks unknown even to the authors of the *Kama Sutra*. Unless her lips were wrapped around him, he had never become aroused simply by watching a woman dine.

Deeply troubled, he touched a hand to his brow. Perhaps hunger was simply making him light-headed. That was a far more comforting thought than admitting that all the blood that was supposed to be circling through his head was now rushing to some other, less discriminating part of his anatomy.

Hoping to hide his consternation, he asked, "Have you been made comfortable during your stay at my palace, Miss Montmorency?"

"Most assuredly. But we mustn't stand on ceremony!" Returning the basket to its place at her feet, she licked the last of the sugary crumbs from her lips. "Everyone has always called me Poppy. Well," she added apologetically, "everyone except for those nasty girls at Miss Throckmorton's Seminary for Young Ladies who insisted upon calling me Piggy."

"The lads at Eton used to call me Frankie," he blurted out, much to his own surprise. "Or worse," he added in a mutter. "They were all Jameses and Edwards and Charleses just like their fathers before them. No one there had ever heard a name like Farouk before." He shrugged. "After a while, I just let everyone believe Frankie was my name. It was easier. Once they tied two sacks of potatoes to a pony's back to make them look like the humps of a camel, then dragged the poor beast into my room and left it there for me to find when I returned from class. When the headmaster heard me trying to wrestle it back out the door and came to investigate, I was the one who was caned in front of the entire class."

He half expected her to laugh at the absurd tale, but instead she reached over to give his hand a pat, sympathy clouding the misty lavender-blue of her eyes. "Sometimes people can be very unkind, can't they? Especially when dealing with something they don't understand and instinctively fear. It must have been difficult for you. How is it that you ended up being educated halfway across the world at Eton?"

She had left her hand resting gently on top of his. He gazed down at it, fascinated by the contrast between his coarse, sun-baked skin and her pale, plump fingers.

"Your Majesty?" she said softly.

Snapping out of his reverie, he jerked his hand out from underneath hers. "My father was a forward-thinking man. He was determined his only son was going to be educated in the ways of both the East and the West."

"So you had no brothers at all?"

"No. Just seventeen sisters." He sighed. "There are times when I wish my father had been blessed with a dozen sons. Although if he had, they would have probably slaughtered each other while fighting over which one of them was going to live long enough to be sultan."

"What happened to your sisters?"

"I found them all fine husbands. They're all wed now with their own homes . . . their own children."

"You have children, too, do you not? I mean with all those wives, I just assumed . . ." Poppy trailed off and gazed into her lap, her cheeks blushing to an even deeper rose.

"I do."

"How many are there?"

Farouk blinked, doing a quick mental tally. "Twelve girls and seven boys. Or is it seven girls and twelve boys? Or four boys and fifteen girls?" He shook his head hopelessly. "I can never remember. They are kept in another part of the palace, just as I was until my father decided to send me off to school in England."

"I adore children," she confessed. "I had always hoped to have at least a dozen of them myself."

"That is not possible. They will require a father."

Although Farouk failed to see the humor in the observation, she burst out laughing. When he eyed her askance, she laughed even harder, her merriment so infectious he felt the corners of his own lips begin to twitch.

"I may be something of a naïve nelly, but even *I* know that much," she assured him. "I thought I had found the perfect candidate for the position in Mr. Huntington-Smythe of Berwickshire. But as it turned out, the gentleman's intentions were less than honorable."

Farouk frowned. "He tried to seduce you without first making you his wife or his concubine?"

A rueful laugh escaped her. "I'm afraid all he was interested in making of me was sport. It seems he had made a wager among his friends that he could coax me into climbing down the trellis outside my bedchamber at Lady Ellerbee's house party to meet him for a moonlight rendezvous."

"And did he win his wager?"

"I'm afraid so. But the trellis was not so lucky. It gave way when I was only halfway down."

"Were you harmed?"

"Not in the least. Mr. Huntington-Smythe broke my fall, and I broke his leg. Unfortunately, when the rest of the guests came rushing out of the house, drawn by his screams—which, I should add, were rather high-pitched and unmanly for a fellow of his virile reputation—there I was, lying atop him in my dressing gown. As I'm sure you can imagine, it caused quite the scandal among Lady Ellerbee's houseguests, as well as putting an end to any hope of my snaring a husband . . . or a father for my children."

A shadow of wistful sadness passed over her face, and in that moment all Farouk wanted to do was lay waste to the scoundrel responsible for making her merry dimples disappear. "This Huntington-Smythe was a faithless dog! Only a man with no honor would treat a woman so.

Had I been there, I would have given the devil a reason to scream by running him through with my sword."

Poppy clapped her hands, clearly delighted by Farouk's bloodlust. "How very gallant of you! Although I daresay that would have created an even greater scandal, not to mention a dreadful mess on Lady Ellerbee's lawn. I'm not exactly the sort of woman who incites violence in men. No man has ever challenged another to a duel on my account." She was doing it again, gazing up at him as if she had a question poised on the tip of her tongue that only he could answer.

He was seized by a ridiculous desire to reach down and draw off her spectacles. To see if her eyes would be even bluer without them. "Why do you always look at me like that?" he asked, his voice coming out more harshly than he intended.

He expected her to blush and stammer and deny that she had a habit of staring at him but she surprised him by continuing to boldly meet his gaze. "I would think you'd be accustomed to women staring at you. You are a very handsome man."

"Yes. I am."

Her smile softened. "I have dimples here." She touched one of her cheeks, then reached up to gently press one fingertip into the bearded cleft in his chin. "And you have a dimple there."

"Yes. I do," he whispered as her finger lingered against his jaw.

She was very close to him in that moment. Close enough for him to see his own reflection in the lenses of her spectacles. He was shocked to realize his gaze was a mirror of her own. His dark eyes must look exactly as they had when she had offered him a peek at the forbidden pastries nestled in the bottom of her basket.

He couldn't even have said what he was hungry for in that moment. All he knew was that he was drawn to the fullness of this woman — her full laughter . . . her full cheeks . . . her full lips . . .

As he leaned toward her, those lips parted ever so slightly. He inhaled the breath of her sigh, which was somehow even sweeter than honey and sugar. Oddly enough, that tender little sigh of surrender yanked him to his senses.

He sprang to his feet. "You do not have to give up on your dream of having children. Once Clarinda becomes my wife, I will find a husband for you among the men of my guard. One who will give you many strong sons and half a dozen daughters as lovely as yourself." Farouk felt a curious twinge as the gracious words spilled from his lips. He had always prided himself on being a man of his word, but this was one promise he would take no pleasure in keeping.

He had finally succeeded in freeing himself from the burden of her regard. She was gazing into her lap, refusing to look at him at all. Her dimples had vanished along with her forthright gaze. "As I said before, Your Majesty, you are ever so gallant."

If that was true, Farouk thought as he turned on his heel and left Miss Montmorency gazing out over the sea with her unruly curls blowing in the breeze, then why did he feel like the worst sort of villain?

Worse even than the despicable Mr. Huntington-Smythe.

✣ *Chapter Nine*

The last thing Clarinda felt like doing the morning after Farouk's banquet in Captain Burke's honor was lounging by a pool in the courtyard of the harem gardens with a dozen chattering, giggling women. But she was afraid any deviation in her normal routine might be noted and reported to the eunuchs or even to Farouk himself. Yasmin was holding court next to the burbling fountain at the opposite end of the pool, and Clarinda was only too aware that the concubine and her cronies were watching her every move in the hope she would slip up and commit some unforgivable transgression that would cost her the sultan's favor.

And perhaps her head.

She rolled to her stomach on the sun-warmed tile, resting her cheek on her folded arms. Although she had spent most of the night pacing the confines of her alcove instead of sleeping, she was still too tense to steal a nap. She had dared a single glance back at Ash as she had left the banquet only to find his gaze following her, his face as inscrutable as it had been the first time he had laid eyes on her upon her return from Miss Throckmorton's. She must have imagined the raw exhilaration that had leapt in them when it was revealed she hadn't yet gone to the sultan's bed.

As long as they had to conduct their every exchange beneath Farouk's watchful eye, it was going to be difficult for her to find out whether Maximillian had sent him or if he had come for her on his own. Not that it should matter one whit, she told herself sternly. Even if he had come for her without any prompting from Max, he was more than nine years too late.

She restlessly rolled back over. A round moon of a face slathered with a thin mask of mud hovered over her, blocking out the sun. She let out a strangled yelp.

The spectacles perched on the tip of Poppy's mud-caked nose looked even more incongruous than usual. Little else of her face was visible except for her big blue eyes and her pink rosebud of a mouth. "I didn't mean to startle you," she said. "The nice woman said the mud would make my skin glow like the rump of a newborn babe."

Pressing a hand to her still racing heart, Clarinda sat up. "It's not your fault. My nerves are so on edge I was expecting to find Farouk standing over me with a scimitar. But what are you doing here?" Clarinda stole a quick glance around them to find several of the other women eyeing them with a combination of contempt and amusement. "It was part of my deal with Farouk that you not be subjected to these lessons or ridiculous beauty treatments."

Poppy plopped down next to her, plunging her bare feet into the cool water of the pool. Not even the mask of mud could hide her wistful expression. "Don't you think I want to be beautiful, too?"

"You already are. And this is no place for a proper English lady." Clarinda leaned closer to her friend, lowering her voice to a whisper. "I'd like for one of us to be able to go back and take her place in society with her innocence intact."

Poppy sighed dramatically. "Then I'm afraid it will have to be you because, in case you've forgotten, *I'm* the one who left England a fallen woman."

Clarinda shook her head, marveling anew at the injustice of that. Swiping a fingerful of mud from the bridge of her friend's nose, she laughed ruefully. "You look exactly like I did when I tumbled down the coal chute at the curate's house when I was eight."

"How on earth did you manage that?"

"I was balancing on the open door while I tried to steal a mincemeat pie that was cooling on his windowsill. His wife was a *very* good cook." Clarinda's smile faded as she remembered it had been an exasperated Ash who had heard her frightened howls and come to pull her out of the coal chute by her ankles. Come to think of it, he had always been around to rescue her when she required it.

Except for the one time when she had needed him the most.

She was almost grateful when a bloodcurdling shriek distracted her from her thoughts. A short while earlier, one of Farouk's concubines had disappeared behind a lacquered screen at the far end of the garden with two of the older women.

Poppy shot the screen an alarmed look, the whites of her eyes growing even larger against their mud backdrop. "The poor creature! Are they torturing her?"

"In a manner of speaking," Clarinda replied darkly.

While she didn't mind having the hair on her head brushed a thousand strokes every day, she had no intention of letting Farouk's handmaidens touch a hair anywhere else on her body. Whenever the old women started circling her with their hopeful expressions and pots full of boiling wax, Clarinda would cross her legs and give them an evil look. In England, only women of the loosest moral character would allow the fine down to be removed from their legs, much less anywhere else.

She had already gathered from the stares and whispers of the concubines that her nether curls were a source of unending fascination to the women here. She supposed it had never occurred to them that they would so perfectly match the hue of the hair on her head.

Biting her lip, Poppy peered around the courtyard in reluctant fascination. "So is this where they teach you how to . . . please a man?"

Clarinda understood her friend's curiosity and chagrin all too well. Clarinda had never considered herself a shrinking violet or a bashful bluebell, but when she had first begun her lessons with the older women who had once served—and serviced—Farouk's father, she had wondered if it was possible to actually die of embarrassment.

After a few days of being taught both the English and the Arabic terms for parts of the body a woman wasn't even supposed to acknowledge she possessed, and poring over erotic etchings whose mere possession would have gotten a man tossed into jail in England, Clarinda had found herself warming to the women's matter-of-fact instruction. She had always respected common sense, and what could make more sense than explaining to a woman *exactly* what she was going to face on her wedding night . . . and on all the nights to follow?

"Considering how sheltered women are kept at home, I know this must all seem terribly shocking," she said. "But if you want to know the truth, I think it's a shame every blushing bride doesn't receive such a thorough education. If they did, there would certainly be more happy marriages. And happy husbands. The bawdy houses would also see a decline in business as wives gave their husbands a reason to stay home at night. And I have little doubt prospective husbands would benefit from such instruction as well."

Clarinda could only imagine how scandalized Maximillian would be if on their wedding night she performed some of the more exotic tricks she had been taught in this place. He had always been so courteous and proper where she was concerned, treating her with the utmost decorum even when they escaped the prying eyes of their family and friends. It was almost as if he were seeking to atone for a sin he had never committed.

Ash had been just the opposite. When they were beneath the watchful eyes of others, he had found every excuse he could to touch her, even if it was only to brush her fingertips with his own as she handed him a cup of tea or to politely correct the angle of a crooked ribbon on her bonnet. And in those rare moments when they managed to sneak away to be alone . . .

Alarmed by the wayward direction of her thoughts, Clarinda jerked them back to her fiancé. Maximillian would be scandalized by what she had learned, but might he not also be pleased? She closed her eyes and tried to imagine such a scene, but it wasn't Max's face she saw looming above hers but his brother's.

And he was most definitely pleased.

Clarinda's eyes flew open with a guilty start.

"Where do they keep the men?" Poppy asked, as if she expected a dozen muscular male slaves girded only in loincloths to be paraded into the courtyard at any minute.

"Oh, Poppy, they don't use actual men! Except for the sultan and his eunuchs, any man who dared to breach the walls of the harem would be instantly put to death."

"Well, then how do they teach you . . . oh, goody, it must be lunchtime!" Poppy exclaimed, mercifully distracted by the sight of Solomon swinging open the towering iron gate that separated the harem courtyard from the rest of the sultan's rambling gardens, a bronze platter balanced in one of his enormous hands.

A stooped, old woman rushed forward to take the platter, and the eunuch retreated to guard the gate, planting his feet in an imposing stance and staring straight ahead. He could have easily been mistaken for a magnificent statue carved from ebony marble.

"Ah, fresh cucumbers!" Poppy said as the woman rested the tray on top of a low pillar next to the pool. "What a delicacy!"

Clarinda sighed. "They're not to eat, Poppy. Well, not precisely."

"No man would be safe with the English cow." Yasmin made sure her husky voice carried to every corner of the courtyard. "To her, *everything* is to eat." Spurred on by the laughter that rippled through the ranks of the women, she added, "They should teach that one how to pleasure herself since I doubt any man will ever lend his hand to the task."

Poppy inclined her head. She had probably forgotten the mask of mud was hiding her mortified blush.

"Don't mind Yasmin, Poppy," Clarinda said loudly, her temper flaring on behalf of her friend "From what I've heard, all she requires is a fish head and a saucer of cream every morning."

Was it her imagination or did Solomon's intractable lips twitch just a fraction?

The other women subsided into respectful silence as the wrinkled crone chose an impressive specimen of a cucumber from the tray and held it up, her eyes twinkling merrily in their sunken folds of flesh. "The tradition of our forefathers tells us that men are strong and women are weak. But if a woman wants to bring even the most powerful of men to his knees, she need only learn what to do when she is on hers."

Clarinda shot Poppy a worried glance. If Poppy's eyes got any larger, they were going to spring right out of her head.

"Would anyone care to demonstrate?" the woman asked, raking her hopeful gaze over the women.

"Allow me." Yasmin rose and sauntered forward, shaking back her mane of glossy, midnight-black hair.

She took the cucumber from the woman's hand and slid one rounded end of it between her pouting lips.

Clarinda could only gape right along with the rest of the women as it disappeared inch by inch. For a minute she thought Yasmin was going to swallow the thing whole, the way a python might swallow a rat. But after letting out a moan that made it sound as if she were partaking of the most delicious chocolate syllabub in the world, she finally withdrew the glistening cucumber from her mouth, holding it aloft with a flourish and a smile.

Clarinda cocked an eyebrow, impressed against her will. No wonder Farouk was willing to put up with the woman's spiteful temperament and churlish behavior.

Returning the cucumber to the tray, Yasmin slanted Clarinda a triumphant look. "That is just a taste of what awaits the handsome Englishman when *I* am summoned to attend him in his bath."

While the women broke into giggling groups to see if any of them could duplicate Yasmin's impressive performance, Clarinda was forced to pretend an indifference she was far from feeling. She had absolutely no right to be jealous. Especially not while betrothed to both the sultan and the *handsome Englishman*'s equally handsome brother.

She turned back to the pool to discover that Poppy had disappeared. Puzzled, Clarinda looked around until she found her hovering near the pillar. After making sure none of the other women were paying any mind to her, Poppy plucked a rather puny-looking cucumber from the tray and gingerly slid the tip of it between her lips.

"Poppy!" Clarinda exclaimed, both shocked and amused by her friend's unexpected boldness.

Poppy gagged. Offering Clarinda a rueful shrug, she tucked the cucumber back into her mouth and cheerfully chomped off the end of it.

This time there was no mistaking Solomon's wince.

Ash spent the entire day exploring Farouk's palace, feigning interest in its beauty and opulence while he sketched a map in his head of every wall, every door, every corridor where an armed guard might be stationed. He was searching for any weaknesses in its fortifications, any chink in Farouk's formidable armor that might allow him to smuggle Clarinda to safety once he figured out a way to get her out of the harem.

Unfortunately, he didn't find a single one. His frustration was only compounded when Clarinda failed to appear at supper and he was forced to endure Farouk's jovial company while smiling through gritted teeth.

When his restless prowling led him into one of the sultan's walled gardens late that night, he wasn't surprised to find Luca soaking in a manmade pool. Fragrant lotus petals floated on the surface of the water, drifting like clouds across the misty reflection of the moon. A doe-eyed, dusky-haired beauty knelt on the flagstones behind Luca, massaging his broad shoulders. He sat with the back of his head propped against the stone lip of the pool, groaning with pleasure every time the slave girl's delicate thumbs dug deep into the tender muscles on each side of his shoulder blades.

He opened his eyes to give Ash a drowsy look. "Would you care to join us? I'm sure she has a sister—or perhaps even a twin—somewhere around here."

"No, thank you." Luca's languor was at direct odds with the tension coursing through every inch of Ash's own body. "And it might be best if she left so we could speak privately."

Ash jerked his head toward the palace to dismiss the woman, but before she could rise to go, Luca caught her slender wrist in his grip. "There's no need. Farouk's mandatory language lessons don't extend to his slaves. She doesn't speak a word of English or Italian. It's part of her charm." He brought the woman's hand to his lips and kissed each fingertip in turn, eliciting a delighted giggle before she went back to rubbing his shoulders.

Ash began to pace around the pool, rubbing the back of his neck. It seemed he had only traded one set of walls for another. Everywhere he turned in this place, there were walls.

Walls keeping him from the woman he had come to save.

To a less jaded eye, the sultan's gardens might not seem like a prison, but a sensual paradise. Swaying palm trees stood guard over the end of the garden overlooking the moonlit sea. Flowering bougainvillea twined its way up the stone walls, while a staggering variety of tropical plants set in fat clay pots flourished in every available bit of space. Their glossy green leaves were splashed with the dramatic colors of dozens of exotic blooms emitting a blend of heady fragrances designed by God for the sole purpose of intoxicating a man's senses. Broad, flat stones had been laid in the sand to create narrow, winding paths perfect for enticing a man and woman to seek an even more shadowy—and private—corner of the garden.

At any other time Ash might have appreciated the effort it must have taken to create this heavenly oasis at the very edge of hell. But on this night, the sultry breeze whispering through the palm fronds failed to soothe him, and the melodic spill of a fountain over stone only grated against his already raw temper.

After watching him pace for several minutes, Luca cautiously cleared his throat. "Your brother's fiancée is quite the beauty. I can see why he's willing to pay so handsomely to get her back."

Ash wheeled around to face him. "A task that's going to prove difficult—if not impossible—if I can't find a way to get to her so we can work out a plan for her rescue."

Luca seemed to be choosing his words with great care. "Are you absolutely certain Miss Cardew wants to be rescued? From what I observed, she seemed perfectly content to play the role of the sultan's pampered consort. Not that I could blame her for that, of course." He let out a fresh groan as the slave girl's nimble hands slid over his shoulders and down his chest, her long fingernails raking through the curling black hair she found there. "If Farouk invited me, I'd be tempted to move into the harem myself."

"I'm fairly certain you'd have to be a eunuch first," Ash said pleasantly, resuming his pacing. "But given how many guards he has standing around with incredibly sharp scimitars, that could probably be arranged."

Wincing, Luca sank even lower in the water. "All I'm suggesting is that perhaps she's truly fallen in love with the man."

Ash froze in his tracks. If he was going to be honest, he hadn't even allowed himself to entertain such a notion. But then he remembered the quiet desperation in Clarinda's eyes when she had talked about owing Farouk her life as well as her gratitude.

"No," he said with absolute certainty as he swung around to face Luca again. "Such a thing would be quite impossible. Which is exactly why she's in even more danger than we originally feared."

Luca's brow furrowed. "What are you talking about? The sultan clearly adores her."

"Of course he adores her! What man in his right mind wouldn't? But don't you see? It's his regard for her that makes him so dangerous. His pride will be shattered when he takes her to his bed on their wedding night and discovers she's been leading him on a merry chase for all these months."

"What are you saying? That her whole 'I must spend a thousand and one nights learning how to pleasure a man' is all a ruse?"

"Precisely." Ash shook his head with reluctant admiration. "I should have known she'd find a way to use her mind instead of her body to survive. She's always been a clever girl, as quick-witted as she is quick-tempered. It would be a bloody brilliant plan if her time wasn't running out. Once the sultan realizes he's been duped and she's no innocent, he'll kill her."

Luca sat straight up in the pool, water streaming from the sleek, dark ends of his hair. "Wait a minute. How do you know she's no innocent? Did your brother confide in you?"

Ash just looked at him.

Luca wasn't an easy man to shock, but Ash had finally succeeded. "*You?* With your own brother's betrothed?"

"She wasn't his then. She was mine." Ash knew it was wrong, but he still felt a savage rush of satisfaction as he said the words. He'd had to bite them back for too damn long.

"But if you dallied with her before you signed on with the Company, she must have been only . . ." Luca trailed off, horror dawning in his eyes.

"Good God, man, how depraved do you think I am?"

Luca opened his mouth, but before he could incriminate himself, Ash held up a warning hand. "Miss Cardew is six-and-twenty, not twenty. She fibbed about her age to make the ruse of her innocence seem more convincing to the sultan."

Luca cocked an admiring eyebrow. "Impressive. She's nearly as skilled a liar as you are. Perhaps it's your brother I should be lecturing on his morals—or lack thereof. Even among the members of my mother's Romany tribe, it was considered ill-mannered to poach your kinsman's lover."

"Max never knew about the two of us. No one did." Ash sank down on a stone bench, running a hand through his hair. "I've known Clarinda since I was just a lad in short pants. Her father's estate bordered our lands. She was three years younger than me and always underfoot, seemingly hell-bent on embarrassing and tormenting me at every turn."

"And like any young lad puffed up with a sense of his own self-importance, I'm guessing you ignored the poor child's every attempt to win your attention . . . and your affection."

"Of course I did." As Ash remembered being a randy fourteen-year-old trying to steal his first kiss from a buxom goose girl only to have Clarinda chase the entire flock of geese into the barn before their lips could meet, Ash's tone darkened. "Although there were times when I would have liked nothing better than to throttle her scrawny little neck. But then I went away to Eton and she went away to Miss Throckmorton's Seminary for Young Ladies. By the time we both returned home, she wasn't the same girl."

"She'd developed bosoms?" Luca suggested helpfully.

"No!" Ash exclaimed, before sheepishly admitting, "Well, yes, she had. Rather impressive ones, if you must know. But it was more than that. She no longer seemed to have any use for me. Whenever I entered a room, she would turn up her haughty little nose and find some excuse to leave, usually on the arm of the nearest eligible bachelor."

"Aha! And naturally, you found her contempt for you utterly irresistible." Luca sighed, his dark eyes going misty with remembered longing. "There's nothing more enthralling than a woman who despises the very sight of you."

"You would know, wouldn't you?" Ash's jibe earned a reproachful look from his friend. "But perhaps you're right. Once she made it clear she wanted nothing whatsoever to do with me, I discovered I couldn't stop thinking about her. She haunted my every waking thought. And most of my dreams." A wry smile curled one corner of his mouth as he remembered waking tangled in his sheets, his sweat-drenched body as hard as a rock and aching with the need for release. "One sweltering June night my father decided to throw yet another ball we couldn't afford. I was stalking morosely about the grounds, puffing on a cheroot I'd pilfered from my father's study, when I heard the sound of someone weeping inside the stables. I pushed open the door to find Clarinda huddled in one of the empty stalls, crying as if her heart had been broken.

"Her ball gown was torn, her hair tousled, her beautiful face streaked with tears. At first I believed the worst." Ash's hands curled into fists at the memory. "I was shocked by the depths of my rage. All I wanted in that moment was to do violence to whoever had dared to harm her.

"Then she looked up at me, her big green eyes still filled with tears, and said, 'What are you gawking at? Have you come to make sport of me, too?' That's how I found out she had overheard some of the other girls at the ball talking about her behind her back, girls she had believed to be her friends. They were all from noble families and they were laughing at her because she was nothing but an heiress with a vulgar father in trade. They even intimated that she was hanging around my family because she had designs on my brother, but that a Burke wouldn't look twice at such a common bit of baggage. Before they could catch her eavesdropping, she slipped out through a French window and ran away from the house. That's when she tripped and tore her dress."

"And is that how your romance began?" Luca had gone all starry-eyed, as he always did when talk of love arose. "Did you take her into your arms, tenderly dry her tears with your handkerchief, and comfort her with your kisses?"

"I took another puff on the cheroot and asked her why she didn't tell them all to go straight to the devil because that's what she would have done if it were me."

"What did she do then?"

"She threw a horseshoe at my head and told me to go straight to the devil." Ash grinned. "And that, my friend, is how our romance began."

"No one in your family, including your brother, ever knew about it?"

"Not a soul." Ash felt his grin fade. "Her papa wouldn't have approved because I was the second son and he was richer than Midas and still had every hope of snagging a title for his darling little princess. My parents, who, ironically enough, were always one enraged creditor away from debtors' prison in those days, would have thought her beneath me simply because some king had never awarded her ancestors a worthless scrap of paper for licking his boots or sacking a pile of rubble on the Scottish border. So in public we continued the charade of loathing each other, eluding the suspicion of both of our families, while in private . . ."

Ash trailed off, remembering how he would stay hard for hours after Clarinda slanted him a sideways glance from beneath her silky lashes or teased his calf with the toe of her slipper under the supper table. Remembering the mischievous smile that would crinkle her nose whenever she managed to slip away and meet him in the woods. They would spend the entire afternoon lying on their backs on a bed of moss, holding hands and arguing over the best name for the firstborn of the dozen children they were going to have after they were wed. He had favored Clarence, while she had insisted Ashtina was a perfectly sound name since their first child would doubtlessly be a girl. After squabbling for a while and then making up with several deep, passionate kisses that left him even harder than before, they had finally settled on Charlotte for a girl and Charlie for a boy.

It all seemed so innocent now. They had been children playing at love, contenting themselves with longing glances and stolen caresses even as a more dangerous and combustible spark began to flare between them every time their hands brushed or their lips touched.

"I suppose we thought it was all some sort of silly, clever game," Ash said, "never realizing it was one we could never hope to win."

"What happened?"

"I left her." Ash spread his empty hands and met his friend's gaze, a wealth of regret expressed in those three simple words. "Despite what everyone believes, it wasn't a thirst for adventure that drove me out of England and into the service of the East India Company but a hunger of another sort altogether." He shook his head, unable to resist mocking his own stubborn romanticism. "I wanted to prove myself worthy of the girl I loved. I wanted to be able to return and lay not only my heart, but the world, at her feet."

"Then why didn't you?"

If Ash had any intention of answering that question, he would have done so long ago.

As he rose from the bench, making it clear the formal portion of the inquiry was over, Luca slapped his open palm against the water. "Damn it all, Cap! You can't just leave me hanging like that! Your tale has everything I adore in a story. Perilous secrets, a grand passion, star-crossed young lovers separated by fate. All it lacks is a happy ending."

"The only happy ending to this story will occur on the day I deliver Miss Cardew safely back into my brother's arms."

Luca looked crestfallen. "You still intend to hand her over to your brother?"

"Of course I do. That's what we were hired for, isn't it?"

"I don't know the man, but I suspect he's not going to be any happier than the sultan when he discovers his bride's . . . um . . . bloom has already been . . . plucked. And by no less than his little brother."

"That's not my problem, is it?" Ash said grimly. "My problem is figuring out a way to scale these walls and get to Clarinda."

"Clar-Inda?" Giving Ash a questioning glance over Luca's shoulder, the slave girl touched her hair, then pointed at the glowing orb hanging low in the night sky.

Strangely enough, Ash knew immediately what she meant—the girl with hair as bright as the moon.

He nodded before echoing softly, "Clarinda."

As a glimmer of possibility dawned in his heart, he smiled with every ounce of charm he possessed and crooked an inviting finger at the girl. She rose without hesitation and padded over to him.

Luca rolled his eyes in exasperation. "I offered to find you your own slave girl. There's no need for you to steal mine. Besides, I told you— she doesn't speak a word of English."

"She may not speak my language but I do speak hers." Slipping a brotherly arm around the girl's shoulders, Ash gently guided her to the bench, the Arabic words tripping from his tongue like music.

✤ *Chapter Ten*

*C*larinda lay belly down on the high, padded couch with her cheek cradled on her folded arms. If someone had told her a few months ago that one day she would be lying all alone in a room, wearing nothing but a silk towel draped over her rump, and waiting for a eunuch to come in and rub oil all over her body, she would have called a constable and had them consigned to Bedlam.

She had to admit her daily massage was one of the less onerous duties expected of her as the sultan's bride-to-be. Back in England, such a sensual indulgence would have been unheard of, except perhaps behind the locked doors of certain notorious gentlemen's clubs. And while she might whisper and giggle about such places with her closest companions, no lady would ever publicly confess to knowing of their existence.

The room was as dim as a cavern, lit only by a single oil lamp set in a latticed alcove in the wall. Some exotic incense that reminded Clarinda of Christmas morning smoldered in a brass brazier set on a teakwood table. Curlicues of fragrant smoke drifted past her nose, making her feel more than a little light-headed. Seduced by the cozy atmosphere, she felt her eyes begin to drift shut. She had spent another night sleeping only in restless dribs and drabs, her dreams haunted by images from the past. Failing to receive a summons to supper the night before had only increased her tension.

She was just beginning to relax into a drowsy stupor when she heard the muted creak of a door opening and closing, followed by the soft pad of bare feet approaching across the tiled floor.

Already anticipating the ease the eunuch's touch would give her, she breathed out a contented sigh. "Oh, Solomon, I'm so glad you're here. I don't think I've ever had greater need of you."

Something about just being in the presence of the mute eunuch was soothing. He provided much needed relief from Farouk's courteous yet exhausting attentions, Poppy's prattling, and the constant chatter of the women in the harem.

The footsteps ceased and she felt him standing over her, his presence itself nearly as tangible as a touch.

"Feel free to tug down the towel a bit more if you need to," she informed him.

She thought she heard a sharply indrawn breath but quickly dismissed it as a trick of the silence and her overwrought nerves.

She felt the towel drift an inch or two lower, as if guided by invisible hands. A stray draft teased the dimpled cleft just above the swell of her buttocks, sending a shiver of gooseflesh dancing over her exposed skin.

She was still amazed by how quickly modesty deserted one in this place, especially around the other women and the eunuchs who guarded them. Back home an accidental flash of a petticoat hem was enough to cause a scandal and condemn a woman to a loveless marriage. Here the women often paraded around the harem in little but their sandals and a smile.

A smile curved her lips as Solomon poured a stream of warm oil over her back, beginning just below her nape and following the delicate curve of her spine all the way down to the hollow at the base of it. She wriggled her hips a little as a wayward stream of oil trickled beneath the towel, ending up in places it had no business being. The intoxicating aroma of sandalwood flooded her nostrils.

Just when she thought she might be on the verge of perishing from anticipation, he put his hands on her.

Although she wouldn't have believed it possible, his hands were even warmer than the oil. His fingertips glided over the smooth skin of her back in a motion more akin to a caress than a massage.

"Mmmm . . ." she moaned, tantalized even more by that sly pressure. "There's no need to treat me like a piece of fine porcelain, Solomon. You know I like it hard and I like it deep."

Those hands froze for a long moment, then resumed their exquisite torture, kneading the muscles of her shoulders and upper back with such skill she felt in imminent danger of melting into a puddle of bliss. To have those probing fingers seek out every taut sinew, every tender muscle that had secretly been aching for attention, was an indescribable luxury.

She had pinned up her hair in a loose topknot to allow him free access to her shoulders. A fresh shiver rocked her as his hand slipped beneath the wispy tendrils that had escaped the topknot to take masterful possession of her neck. Trusting something so fragile to the brute power of those hands was oddly compelling. Especially when their one intent was to bring pleasure, not pain.

He slid his other hand around the graceful column of her throat until his fingertips rested against the pulse at its base while his thumbs gently probed the tendons on each side of it. His attentions made everything in her body relax, including her tongue.

With her face still buried in the crook of her folded arm, she said, "I don't suppose you've had the privilege of meeting the sultan's esteemed guests, have you?" After all those years of directing her every errant thought away from Ashton Burke, it was a relief to finally be able to talk about him. Especially to someone who could never repeat what she said. "Captain Burke may be considered something of a dashing hero these days, but he was a most odious and arrogant boy."

For a nearly imperceptible moment, Solomon's hands seemed to tighten around her throat.

She chuckled. "Or at least that's what he wanted everyone to believe."

Those hands relaxed and glided higher, raking through the silky strands of her hair until the hairpins she'd used to secure it went tumbling to the tiles with a musical tinkle. His fingertips massaged her scalp in concentric circles, sending a decadent rush of pleasure through her and stirring long-buried memories of her mother brushing her hair when she was a little girl. The impersonal hands of the nannies and maids her papa had hired to replace her mother after a wasting illness had taken her away from them had never been able to duplicate that loving touch.

A fresh moan escaped Clarinda. "My compliments, Solomon. You seem to be especially diligent in your duties today."

As if to prove her point, his clever hands began to work their way down her back again. She stretched like a satisfied cat, surrendering to a shameless sensuality that was not only discouraged where she came from but openly denounced. Each languorous stroke of his hands warmed the oil another degree until she began to feel flushed all over, which oddly enough make her think of Ash again.

"Captain Burke and I grew up on neighboring estates, and after my mother died when I was eight, I spent more time at his home than my own. My father doted upon me, but the demands of his business required frequent trips to London so I was often left to my own devices.

Sometimes I would even climb out my window after my governess believed me safely tucked in bed and scale the tree overlooking the Burkes' drawing room." She sighed. "I suppose I just wanted to be part of a family again.

"One night when I was up in the tree, I leaned out too far and the branch I was sitting on broke, dumping me in the rosebush right outside the French windows of the drawing room. The duke and duchess were deep in discussion about this or that, and Captain Burke's brother, Max, had his nose buried in a book. Max was always so serious, even then.

"But Ash was lounging in a chair near the window, one of his long legs thrown over the arm. He turned and looked right into my eyes through the glass, and I knew I was done for. I was already dreading the lecture I was going to get from my papa when he returned from London. While he indulged me shamelessly, he was also consumed by the idea that I learn how to behave with the proper decorum so that some day I could take what he considered to be my rightful place in society. It would have horrified him to learn I'd not only been caught trespassing, but spying on our illustrious neighbors.

"I held my breath and I waited for Ash to laugh, to point, to set the dogs on me, to do anything at all that would draw his family's attention to my predicament. But he simply rose, gave me a nod, and drew the drapes over the window, hiding my disgrace from his family's view and giving me a chance to make a less-than-graceful retreat.

"The very next day a footman came knocking at our door with a note penned by the duchess inviting me to join the family for supper. I think that's when I knew . . ."

She trailed off. Knew what? That her life would never be the same? That she would never know another moment without longing?

Despite the deft ministrations of Solomon's hands, she stiffened, deliberately steeling her heart against the wistful ache the memory had evoked.

"That was probably his last official act of chivalry," she said crisply. "Captain Burke may be a knight now, but it's going to take more than a tap on the shoulder from the king to make that man a hero . . . or a gentleman. Why, his brother has more honor in his little finger than Captain Burke has in his entire—*ow!*" she wailed as Solomon's hand came down on her right buttock in a stinging swat. "What on earth are you—"

Before she could finish, he gave her other buttock a slightly less vigorous smack. Then both of his hands settled into a brisk but more gentle rhythm, their steady tattoo strangely soothing.

She relaxed again, and by the time he had stopped smacking and started massaging again, his powerful thumbs working their own brand of magic as they dug into the softness of her silk-covered rump, she was ready to forgive him anything.

She could feel the heat of his hands even through the silk, almost as if he was imparting a soaring fever from his skin to hers. As his thumbs traced the inner curves of her buttocks, straying dangerously near to the cleft between them, a different sort of tension began to coil deep within her. She had been receiving these massages for months, but she had never been so aware that a few inches were all that separated those clever hands from what lay beneath the silk.

As the beguiling friction of Solomon's thumbs sent a delicious little throb through the most vulnerable and tender part of her, she resisted the temptation to wriggle her thighs even farther apart and instead curled her arm closer around her face to shield her burning cheeks. Was she losing her mind? The man was a eunuch, for God's sake! Had she finally been too long in this den of iniquity or was it Ash's reappearance that had stirred such ridiculously wicked feelings in her?

Hoping to distract herself from her mortifying descent into debauchery, Clarinda let out a prim sniff. Unfortunately, since her face was still buried in her folded arms, it sounded more like a snort. "I wonder if Captain Burke considers this simply another one of his fine adventures. Do you think he intends to write a paper for the Geographical Society of London on the carnal habits of the Moroccan harem girl?"

She breathed a sigh of relief as those hands ceased their exquisite torment and began to glide up her back. They finally came to rest against her shoulders, gently imprisoning her against the table. The eunuch leaned over her, so close she could feel the heat radiating from his body.

His warm, cinnamon-scented breath stirred the baby-fine tendrils of hair at her nape as he said in a husky whisper she would have recognized anywhere, "I don't know, my little gazelle. Why don't you ask him yourself?"

❖ *Chapter Eleven*

*C*larinda's eyes flew open in shock. She rolled off the couch and leapt to her feet while snatching up the length of silk towel and wrapping it around her to shield her nakedness.

Ashton Burke stood there, smirking at her in the rosy glow of the lamplight. He'd retrieved the freshly laundered ivory shirt and buff riding breeches he'd been wearing when he arrived at the palace, and all it took was the briefest flick of a downward gaze at the snug-fitting fabric of those breeches to prove he wasn't nearly as unaffected by their situation as he was pretending to be.

She jerked her gaze back to his face, clutching the bunched-up fabric between her breasts in a white-knuckled grip. "You, sir, are no eunuch!"

His smirk deepened until an all-too-familiar devil-may-care dimple appeared in his left cheek. "And you, miss, are no twenty-year-old virgin."

"And whose fault is that, I might ask you?"

"Yours, I suppose, since you were the one who seduced me."

She gasped, outraged anew. "*I* seduced *you?*"

"As I recall it, my choice was between you and a corpulent sodomite." He lifted one shoulder in a negligent shrug, his expression as innocent as a choirboy's. "What was a fellow to do?"

Clarinda didn't know whether to be flattered or alarmed that he remembered every word and nuance of their last exchange as clearly as she did. "You may recall it that way if it pleases you, but I most certainly did *not* seduce you."

"You're right." Disarming her with his congenial tone, he leaned down and whispered, "You practically ravished me."

With an incoherent sputter of rage, Clarinda spun around and paced away from him, determined to put some distance between them. She was nearly undone by her ire when her toe caught in the trailing hem of the towel, bringing her up short and offering him the briefest flash of her naked bottom. She snatched the slippery silk back around her, her cheeks burning with mortification and some other emotion too unsettling to name.

Whenever she had allowed herself the wicked luxury of picturing this moment, she was usually wearing more than a towel. (Although not always, if she was being completely truthful with herself.) There was something dangerously stirring about being in the presence of a man as virile as Ash while he was fully clothed and she . . . well . . . wasn't.

She stopped in front of the teakwood table, gazing down at the wisps of smoke drifting up from the incense brazier as if they could divine both the future and the past. How could she ever have mistaken him for Solomon? How could she have allowed herself to forget the power of those hands against her flesh?

"If you were any sort of gentleman," she said, "you wouldn't speak of such things."

"Weren't you the one who just said it would take more than a tap on the shoulder from the king to make me a hero . . . or a gentleman?"

Clarinda winced, struggling to remember exactly what other incriminating things she might have revealed while under the influence of those devilish hands. "I wasn't talking to you. I was talking to Solomon." She swung back around to face him, seized by an even more terrible thought. "Oh, dear Lord, what have you done with Solomon? Have you killed him?"

Ash tilted his head to give her a reproachful look. "Despite the stories you may have read about me in the scandal sheets you're so fond of quoting, I'm not given to bashing eunuchs over the head with rocks. I figure the poor devils have already suffered enough. Have no fear. Your trusty Solomon has simply been sent to the market on a fool's errand." A troubled frown furrowed Ash's brow. "Although from what I've been able to gather, the man is no fool."

"What about the other harem guards? Did you send them to the market as well?"

"No, I poisoned them." When her mouth fell open in dismay, he rolled his eyes. "There was no need for such dire measures. Thanks to the dubious romantic charms of a certain Italian Gypsy of my acquaintance, I was able to coax a lovely young miss into revealing the location of a secret passage into the harem."

As their eyes met, Clarinda realized this was the first time they had been alone together since that fateful morning in the meadow. She had done her best to vanquish him from her thoughts, but not a single day had gone by since then when he hadn't flitted through her heart like a phantom. Now he stood before her once again—in the flesh yet somehow still larger-than-life.

As that reality began to sink in, her outrage shifted to alarm. Casting the door a desperate look, she strode back over to him. "Do you realize what sort of risk you're taking? If any man besides the sultan or one of his eunuchs is discovered in the harem, the penalty is death. You could lose your head!"

Ash's gaze took a leisurely stroll up her body, drinking in the well-toned length of milky-white thigh exposed by the uncooperative towel, the uneven rise and fall of her breasts with each shuddering breath, the disheveled tumble of her hair, the traitorous flush riding high in her cheeks.

By the time his eyes reached hers once again, there wasn't a trace of mockery in them. "I think it's too late. I may have already lost it."

For a painful moment, Clarinda stopped breathing altogether. She had forgotten how it made her feel when he looked at her like that. Or had she? That look made her wonder what he might do if she loosened her panicked grip on the towel and let the sleek silk slip right through her fingers to ripple into a puddle at her feet.

She dug her fingernails into the fabric as if it contained the only remaining thread of her sanity. Hadn't she learned the hard way that a moment of such folly could lead to a lifetime of regret? If she let him melt her resolve with one look, how was she ever going to prove to him she was no longer the love-struck girl he had left behind but a woman grown?

How was she ever going to prove it to herself? Or to Max?

Pretending she was wearing her most severe morning gown instead of a thin scrap of silk, Clarinda lifted her chin. "If you've come to execute one of those daring rescues you're so famous for, Captain Burke, we'd best make haste. I may be the sultan's favorite pet at the moment, but he still keeps me on a fairly short leash."

The wicked gleam had returned to his eyes. "Why the sudden urgency? From what I understand, you're not scheduled to get married until the sixth anniversary of your twenty-first birthday."

She narrowed her eyes at him. "They weren't paying any attention to my age when I arrived at the palace. They were all too busy gawking at my hair."

He reached down to capture a strand of it from her naked shoulder. As he sifted the silvery-blond skein through his fingers, his reverent touch sent an unbidden shiver of longing through her. "You have to admit, it is your most striking feature." He let his gaze glide down her once again. "Or at least *one* of them."

She smacked his hand away. "I can't believe I let myself forget how insufferable you always were."

He leaned closer to her. "I've certainly never forgotten how much you always enjoyed making me suffer. Do you remember the time you shoved me over the cliff into the thicket of thistles while we were playing blindman's bluff?"

"I should have found a higher cliff."

Just like that they were nose to nose, glaring at each other as if he were twelve and she nine. It was exactly that crackling cord of tension that had finally yanked them into each other's arms that long-ago night in his father's stables when he had kissed her for the first time.

Clarinda didn't know whether to be disappointed or relieved when Ash was the first to snap that cord. He moved away from her to lean against the scrolled end of the couch, crossing his booted feet at the ankle and folding his arms over his heart like a shield. "After watching the sultan make moon eyes at you, Luca isn't entirely convinced you require rescuing. Given how cozy the two of you seemed, he thought that perhaps you'd fallen in love with the man." Judging by the dryness of Ash's tone, one would have guessed her reply was of no particular import to him.

"Farouk is a genuinely nice man with a kind heart. He has an unfortunate tendency to think of women as possessions, but I don't really see how that makes him any different from most men of my acquaintance. Don't our English laws presume the very same thing—especially after a man takes *possession* of a woman by wedding her? Once she agrees to take his name, she has no more rights than a prize hunting hound or a broodmare."

"If you're trying to convince me you'd be content being any man's broodmare, I'm not buying it. I know you haven't changed *that* much from the girl I knew."

"You're right," she admitted with a sigh. Tossing the trailing hem of the towel over her arm as if it were the train of some extravagant ball gown, she began to pace back and forth in front of him, her words coming out in a relieved rush. "Everything I've done since the day Farouk purchased me, every word I've spoken, every promise I've made, has been a desperate attempt to postpone the inevitable. I've coaxed. I've cajoled. I've sung. I've danced. I've batted my eyelashes and licked my lips and twirled my hair around my finger and told every silly joke and witty story I could remember. I've agreed with Farouk when it pleased him and argued with him when it pleased him more. I've pranced about in front of strangers in little more than my unmentionables. I've been combed and brushed and prodded and poked and massaged and bathed and oiled and perfumed until I wanted to scream. And I've lied through my freshly polished teeth with every breath!" She stopped directly in front of Ash, throwing up her hands in exasperation. "Do you know how utterly exhausting it is to be charming every infernal second of every day?"

Though Ash remained as straight-faced as an undertaker, a muscle in his cheek twitched. "For you, I'm sure it's a tremendous challenge."

Giving him an evil look, she slumped against the wall, still clutching the towel in front of her. "Your friend was wrong. I have no desire to stay here and spend the rest of my days as the sultan's pet, no matter how pampered or cherished."

"I'm sure my brother will be relieved to hear that."

Clarinda slowly raised her head. "You've spoken to Maximillian?"

"Of course I have. Why else would I be here?"

His words were so casually cruel that they took her breath away. To hide their effect, she choked out a brittle laugh. "So Maximillian doesn't care enough to come for me himself but he cares enough to send you? What am I to make of that?"

"You can make of it whatever you like. My brother has never been one to let his heart rule his head. And his head knows I'm the man most likely to get you out of here alive. Besides, from what I witnessed during our short time together, my brother's devotion to you was not in question. Let me see . . . how did he phrase it? After effusively praising your kindness, your courage, and your passion for life, he exclaimed, 'She is more than just a bride, both in my eyes and in my heart!' His passion was really quite touching, if a bit overwrought."

Clarinda lowered her eyes, hoping to hide her bewilderment at Max's impassioned declaration. He had never said anything remotely that romantic to her. He'd been trying to talk her into marrying him for years, but he had always couched his intentions in the most practical of terms—how well they would suit, how advantageous their match would be to both their families, how she deserved a second chance at happiness while there was still time for her to have children, a family of her own.

He had to have known that would be the most compelling argument of all.

Perhaps Max was still trying to protect her. If Ash believed her and Max's union was one of passion rather than deep, abiding friendship and mutual respect, then Ash might not suspect just how much his leaving had devastated her.

"I'm not surprised you would mock him for that," she said, lifting her head to give Ash a cool gaze. "The difference between you and your brother is that Maximillian doesn't just use pretty words to coax a woman into his bed. He speaks from the heart."

"Fascinating. I wasn't aware he still had one." Ash studied her face through narrowed eyes. "You really care for him, don't you?"

"Of course I do." Although the words didn't sound as convincing as Clarinda would have liked, they were true. In his own steadfast, taciturn way, Maximillian had saved her life as surely as Farouk had. Ash might never know it, but when Ash had broken her heart, Max had been there to sweep up the pieces. "I agreed to marry him, didn't I?"

"You agreed to marry Dewey Darby as well though, didn't you?"

She drew in an uneven breath, shocked that Ash did know about her brief, ill-fated engagement. "How did you hear about that?"

He shrugged, his expression revealing nothing. "People talk. From what I understand, I barely made it up the gangplank of the ship before you accepted his suit."

"Well, the blacksmith wouldn't have me and I couldn't find an American," she retorted, stung by the unfairness of his words.

"So you had to settle for a viscount. Not that I blame you, of course. I'm sure you would have made a stunning viscountess."

"We'll never know, will we?"

"I'm sorry," Ash said softly, looking as if he meant it. "Max told me about Darby's accident. It must have been very difficult for you."

Already regretting her outburst, Clarinda briefly closed her eyes. If she had anything to say about it, he would never know just how difficult. "I survived."

"That doesn't surprise me. Not many women would have survived being abducted by Corsairs and sold in a slave market." This time there was no mistaking the note of reluctant admiration in his voice. "Yet here you are, matching wits with a sultan like some modern-day Scheherazade straight out of *Arabian Nights*. Perhaps it's no mystery why my brother is willing to pay so handsomely to get you back."

Jolted by a fresh shock of disbelief, Clarinda

straightened. "Maximillian is *paying* you? You accepted money from your own brother to rescue me?"

Ash's shrug was even more negligent than usual. "If he's fool enough to offer, I'm certainly not fool enough to turn him down. You really shouldn't be too hard on him. Ever since he managed to make back the family fortune, his answer to every problem—including me—has been to throw money at it."

For a minute Clarinda felt as if she were right back on the slaver's block, her fate snatched from her own hands only to be balanced precariously in the hands of men. "How much? How much is he paying you?"

"Judging by the look in your eye right now, not nearly enough." Ash pointed a finger at her. "I know that look. You're about to tell me to go to the devil again, aren't you?"

"Don't flatter yourself, Captain Burke. I doubt the devil would have you." She took one step toward him and then another, not even caring that the towel had slipped down to expose the creamy white swell of her breasts. "But what you can do is march right back to your brother and tell him to go straight to the devil for me. I'll find a way out of here without your help, thank you very much. Perhaps I'll even decide to take my chances with Farouk. At least when he buys and pays for a woman, he does it openly, without couching the entire transaction in worthless sentiment!"

She whirled around with every intention of storming from the room, but Ash caught her forearm, bringing her up short. "I thought you wanted to be rescued."

"I do. Just not by you!" Gritting her teeth in frustration, she twisted her wrist around in a vain attempt to escape his intractable grasp.

He stilled her struggles by pinning her arm against the broad plane of his chest, a move that brought their lips into dangerous proximity. "What are you going to do? Scream for a guard?"

"Don't tempt me!"

It had been a long time since she had been this close to him. Close enough to watch the darkness of his pupils swallow the golden light in his eyes. Close enough to count each bristle of the beard stubble on his jaw. Close enough to recognize the precise moment when his gaze drifted downward to her parted lips.

Although it was taking negligible effort on his part to restrain her, his breathing was as patchy as her own. She could feel his chest hitch beneath her captive arm with each breath, could feel the irregular hammering of his heart in his chest.

With visible effort he dragged his gaze away from her lips and back to her eyes. "I could care less how you feel about me." Every ounce of passion had been stripped from his voice, leaving it as cold and ruthless as a stranger's. "Or, for that matter, about my brother. The only thing that matters is getting you out of here before Farouk finds out you've been lying to him all along about being an innocent and decides to strangle you in his bed."

"I had no choice but to lie! If Farouk had realized I was no innocent, he would have made me his concubine the first night I arrived in this place. I'd be imprisoned in his harem right now, never to be seen outside its walls except on those nights when I was summoned to his bed. But you needn't worry that Farouk would harm me. He worships the ground I walk on. He would never—"

"I know these men," Ash said, cutting her off without a trace of mercy. "I've been living among them for years now. They live in a world where nothing is more important than their honor and their pride and no one is more dispensable than a woman. If Farouk finds out you lied, he'll kill you. It might even pain him to do so, but he would feel he had no choice." Ash lifted his other hand to cup her face. Despite the harshness of his tone, the callused pad of his thumb stroked the downy softness of her cheek with irresistible tenderness. "I'm the one who put you in this position. And, by God, I'm the one who's going to get you out."

As Clarinda gazed into the determined depths of his eyes, it was almost possible to believe his concern for her was motivated by something much more complicated—and more dangerous to her heart—than simple avarice. "Why, Captain Burke, you almost sound as if you care about what happens to me."

"If I don't bring you back alive," he said, the silky note returning to his voice, "I won't get the rest of what my brother owes me."

This time when she tried to jerk her wrist out of his grasp, he made no attempt to stop her. Although it galled her to admit it, she knew he was right. She might be tired of being used as a pawn in the games of men, but she couldn't afford to underestimate Farouk or refuse Ash's help in a fit of childish temper.

She glared up at him, massaging her wrist with her other hand even though he had left no mark upon it. "I can't tell you how relieved I am to know Maximillian will be footing the bill for my rescue. At least I won't be expected to pay you with a kiss."

"That's a fee I'd be only too happy to forgo in your case." Clearly recognizing that he had won this hand, Ash said, "Now that I know about the secret passage into the harem, all I have to do is find a way out of the palace. It may take a few days for me to coax Farouk into relaxing his guard. In the meantime, you'll have to continue to play the role of doting fiancée. We must take great care not to arouse his suspicions. When I come for you, you'll have to be ready to travel and you'll have to be ready to travel fast. Without looking back." He paused as if weighing his next words with great care. "And you'll have to trust me."

She shook her head, a rueful smile touching her lips. "You always did have a habit of asking the impossible."

He was halfway to the door when she said, "I won't leave here without Poppy, you know."

He acknowledged her words with a brisk nod. "I assumed as much."

He turned at the door, eyeing her thoughtfully. "Do you have any more fiancés lurking in the wings that I should know about? You seem to have amassed quite a collection since I saw you last."

"I'm sure it surprises you to learn that there are men who aren't driven to flee to the ends of the earth by the mere prospect of marrying me."

He shook his head in mock pity, the devilish dimple returning to his cheek. "God help the poor bastards."

She narrowed her eyes at him. "If I had a horseshoe right now, Captain Burke, I'd throw it at your head. And I wouldn't miss this time."

"You don't have to throw a horseshoe at my head to get my attention, Miss Cardew. You never did." With that, he slipped out of the door, easing it shut soundlessly behind him.

⚜ *Chapter Twelve*

*C*larinda reclined in a meadow of fragrant wild-flowers beneath the sheltering boughs of an old oak tree. She closed her eyes, exulting in the warmth of the shade-dappled sunlight bathing her face, and didn't open them again until she sensed a presence standing over her. Although the face of the boy gazing down at her was in shadow, she would know his long, lean silhouette anywhere. She lifted her arms to him, a drowsy smile of invitation curving her lips.

He came into them without hesitation, dropping to one knee between her legs and gathering her into his embrace. As his mouth melted into hers, their clothes seemed to melt away as well. She had thought the sun was warm, but its radiance dimmed in comparison to the fevered heat of his skin against hers. He devoured her with his mouth and pressed her to his heart as if he were trying to drink her in through his pores, to obliter-

ate every bit of space between them so they could become one not just in body but in soul.

One minute he was over her and the next he was inside her, filling her with a single smooth thrust that made her gasp aloud. As she arched her hips off the ground, responding to the primal urge to take him even deeper inside her, Clarinda knew she would never truly belong to herself again. She would forever belong to this beautiful boy who groaned her name deep in his throat as if she were the answer to his every prayer.

Her womb began to pulse with pleasure, straining toward fulfillment. Her eyes flew open. It was no longer Ash the boy moving above her but Ash the man. His jaw was shadowed with beard stubble and his shoulders were broad enough to block out the sun. His eyes were pressed shut, his rugged face strained with passion. He reached beneath her and dragged her thighs even farther apart as his hips settled into a relentless rhythm, pounding into her with a force that drove every breath from her body and every thought from her mind.

As those pulses of pleasure began to swell into a torrent of rapture, she dug her fingernails into his back and opened her mouth to scream her delight . . .

Clarinda sat bolt upright on her sleeping couch, still tangled in her sweat-dampened sheets. She clapped a hand over her mouth, fearing she might have actually screamed aloud.

She held her breath, her gaze locked on the thin curtain that shielded her alcove from the women sleeping in the harem at the bottom of the steps. When she didn't hear footsteps come pounding up the stairs, she let out a shaky sigh. If she *had* screamed, one of Farouk's guards would have already come running, scimitar in hand.

She raked her tousled hair out of her face with an unsteady hand. Since she hadn't been invited to join the men for supper for the second night in a row, she had hoped to banish all thoughts of Ash from her mind before resting her head on her pillow and closing her eyes. She might have succeeded if her dreams hadn't betrayed her.

Such a scandalous dream should have left her feeling limp with satisfaction. Instead, she felt frustrated and out of sorts, her pleasure just as much a phantom as the man who had given it to her. Her breasts felt heavy, and there was a haunting ache between her thighs that made her want to press her hand there in what she knew would be a vain attempt to soothe it.

Even before she had been abducted, she had dreaded the thought of waking next to her husband after such a dream. How would she ever explain to Max why she had cried out in her sleep? Or worse yet, she probably wouldn't have to explain. Given how well Max had always been able to read her thoughts, he would simply look into her eyes and know she had been dreaming of another man. A man who just happened to be his brother.

Kicking away the sheets, she slid off the couch and padded over to the window set deep in the sun-baked stone. Most of the women of the harem slept completely nude, but she insisted on wearing a short silk shift. The wisp of a garment was so insubstantial she might as well have been naked, but it made her feel slightly less vulnerable in this place where women were expected to be available to fulfill a man's every need at any hour of the day or night.

A sultry breeze drifted across her heated skin as she curled her hands around the delicate iron latticework that separated her from the night. Farouk liked to call her his buttercup, while Luca had branded her a night-blooming lily. But she felt more like a hothouse orchid trapped in some sweltering greenhouse. All she longed to do was escape into the wild, where she would finally be free to bloom.

She had been trying to escape that night in the stables of Dryden Hall when Ash had caught her weeping over the petty cruelty of the girls she had believed to be her friends. After she had hurled the horseshoe at him, she had scrambled to her feet in a panic, fearing her fit of temper might have killed him.

Not until he had slowly straightened, letting out a low-pitched whistle of admiration, had she realized she had missed him. "Those girls were right about you, you know. No lady could throw like that. If I didn't have quick reflexes, you'd have brained me."

She sniffed. "I do believe that would require possessing a brain on your part."

"I can't argue with you there. If I had even half a brain, I'd be up at the house right now dancing with one of those simpering vipers you call friends instead of risking life and limb out here with you."

Clarinda swiped at the tip of her nose with the back of her hand, wishing the moonlight streaming down from the loft wasn't quite so revealing. She must look a fright. She had never been a particularly pretty crier.

It was the first time she and Ash had been alone since his return from Eton. He was still lean, but his shoulders were so much more intimidating now, his chest beneath his striped waistcoat and the starched white frills of his shirt so much broader. It made a girl wonder just how it might feel to rest her cheek against it and listen for the true, steady beat of his . . .

She jerked her gaze back to his face to find him taking another puff on his cheroot and eyeing her as if she were a puzzle he had yet to solve.

"You should probably go," she said. "They already think I'm trying to snare your brother, and if they find me here with you, they'll probably accuse me of trying to trap you into marriage as well." She smoothed the tattered and mud-stained skirts of her lavish ball gown, wondering how she was going to explain them to her papa. "Or something worse."

"Don't worry," Ash said cheerfully. "If we're discovered, I'll just tell them we snuck out here to smoke a cheroot together."

Clarinda felt her lips curl in a reluctant smile. "Then they'll know for sure I'm nothing but a bourgeois little hoyden."

He extinguished the cheroot on a post and flicked the butt away. "I could have told them that a long time ago."

She wouldn't have thought it possible but his words stung even more than the slights she had already endured that night. Tossing back her hair, which had spilled halfway out of its pins during her mad dash from the house, she said, "Then why don't you just leave me be and go back to where you belong?"

"Because I happen to like bourgeois little hoydens." He came sauntering toward her, his lazy gait belied by the intensity in his golden gaze. "They're so much more interesting than ladies."

Since Clarinda had all but given up hoping this moment would ever come, she could only gaze up at him in wide-eyed wonder as he took her into his arms and lowered his head toward hers.

To her surprise, it wasn't her mouth he sought in that moment but the softness of her cheek. He brushed his lips over each tearstain in turn, soothing away her hurt with an eloquence words could never express.

When his lips finally did close over hers, it seemed the most natural thing in the world. Clarinda had already fended off any number of young men intent upon stealing a kiss or two from her ripe lips. But Ash wasn't stealing. He was laying claim to what was rightfully his.

His mouth played over hers with an almost reverent tenderness, tasting of tobacco laced with a hint of brandy. Apparently the cheroot wasn't the only thing he'd pilfered from his father's study. In that moment it was as if everything about them became one—their mouths, their breaths, the rhythm of their hearts. Her own heart was pounding so loudly in her ears Clarinda barely registered the creak of the stable door swinging open until Ash's arms tightened around her and he pulled her against the wall and into a pool of shadow.

"Who is it?" she whispered, her arms slipping instinctively around his waist.

Ash scowled. "Probably just one of my father's grooms."

"Clarinda? Are you out here, poppet? One of the footmen said they thought they saw you come this way. The Earl of Cheatham's son has just arrived, and he's eager for introductions to be made."

Clarinda buried her groan in the front of Ash's waistcoat. "Oh, no! It's Papa! He's been parading a steady stream of suitors with titles in front of me ever since I returned from Miss Throckmorton's in the hopes I'll take a fancy to one of them."

Ash tipped up her chin with one finger, forcing her to meet his gaze. "You'd still the flapping tongues of those harpies forever if they were forced to address you as 'Lady Cheatham' one day."

She bit her lip before giving him a mischievous smile. "What if I prefer to be addressed as 'Lady Hoyden'?"

"Then I'll be only too happy to oblige." Pressing another brief but fierce kiss to her lips, he seized her hand in his and tugged her toward the rear of the barn.

He held open a loose board on the back wall and urged her through the narrow gap, ripping the hem of her skirt free when it caught on a nail. The next thing she knew, they were racing through the warm, windy night hand in hand, their giddy laughter floating behind them.

That memory of perfect freedom only made the tower feel more like a cage. Clarinda could just make out the indigo shadow of the sea over the tops of the swaying palms, its serene swells brushed with silvery fronds of moonlight. How could Fate have been so cruel as to have carried her all the way across that sea only to deliver her right back into the arms of Ashton Burke?

She rested her brow against the latticework. She'd do well to remember it was only in her dreams that she was likely to find herself in those arms. It wasn't the first time she had visited that sunlit meadow in the dark and lonely watches of the night, and she feared it wouldn't be the last.

Her willful imagination always seemed to forget the cold, the damp, the clammy fingers of mist that had enveloped them as Ash had borne her back into the folds of her cloak that long-ago morning. Perhaps it was simply too painful to remember the way his hands had trembled with raw emotion everywhere they touched her. How she had bitten his shoulder to keep from crying out when he had breached her maidenhead and filled her with his thickness. His inexpressible tenderness as he had used his monogrammed handkerchief to mop up the mess they'd made.

She had known even then that she was supposed to feel shame at what they'd done, but any shame she might have felt had been eclipsed by the wonder of what they had shared. The shame had come later, after he was gone and she was left all alone to face the consequences of that all-too-brief idyll.

As the weeks had passed without so much as a letter from him, it had almost given her aching heart comfort to imagine him dead or imprisoned in some foreign cell where he spent his days dreaming of sunlight and his nights dreaming of her. She had still been young and naïve enough to believe that surely only chains or death could have kept him from her arms.

But as the weeks had turned into months and word of his daring exploits with the East India Company had begun to pop up in both the reputable newspapers and the scandal sheets, she had realized he had no intention of returning to her.

And perhaps he never had.

For all she knew, she had never been anything more to him than some foolish girl he had once seduced—the first in a long line of conquests to come. And now she was simply a job—a business transaction conducted between two men that would end with her being exchanged for a large sum of money, like some sort of thoroughbred filly.

She supposed she ought to be grateful to Maximillian for finally disabusing her of any lingering notion that Ash was going to come charging up on a white horse someday and declare his undying love for her. Max might be more likely to have a coachman drive him around in a sensible barouche than to ride a white horse, but he had proved himself to be her hero in every way that mattered. He deserved better than to have his bride-to-be pining over another man.

She was turning away from the window to return to the dubious comfort of her sleeping couch when a flash of movement in the gardens below caught her eye. At first she thought it was just the shadow of a cloud flitting across the moon. But as she squinted into the darkness, her eyes picked out the shape of a man restlessly prowling the winding garden paths below. As she watched, the tip of his thin cigar flared, illuminating the lean planes of his face.

She had to admit it gave her a perverse pleasure to see Ash stalking through the garden, deprived of sleep just as she was. Perhaps he had been driven from his own couch by some equally vexing dream, his body aching for a fulfillment that would never come.

Her smile abruptly vanished when he stopped at the mouth of the path directly below her and lifted his gaze to the tower, homing in on the window as if he knew exactly where to find her.

She took a hasty step backward, seeking shelter in the shadows. Although it should have been impossible, she could not shake the sensation that he could still see her. That he was aware of the hungry look in her eye, the ragged rise and fall of her breasts, even the way her nipples tightened to rosy little buds beneath the smoldering heat of his gaze.

It wasn't until he leaned one shoulder against the scaly trunk of a palm tree and took a long drag on the cigar that she realized he wasn't going anywhere.

She slowly backed away from the window, a treacherous flush of triumph coursing through her. Ash's mouth might lie, but his eyes never could.

He might not love her, but he still wanted her.

Oddly enough, Clarinda slept deeply and dreamlessly for the rest of the night. Somehow knowing Ash was watching over her made her feel more protected than being guarded by an entire army of scimitar-wielding eunuchs.

As she emerged from her sleeping alcove and descended the stairs the next morning, her step was lighter than it had been in a long time. She even caught herself humming a lively tune under her breath.

She had exchanged her multilayered skirts for a pair of the exotic trousers worn by so many of the women in the palace. They hugged the ripe curve of her derriere, then ballooned out to flow over her long legs, only to be gathered once more at the ankle. The gauzy silk had been dyed in sumptuous hues of coral and sapphire. It was a bit like strutting about in one's pantaloons, but there was no denying how comfortable they were.

The trousers were complemented by a fitted bodice cut low enough on the top to reveal a healthy portion of cleavage and high enough at the bottom to expose a narrow strip of her abdomen. Clarinda smiled to imagine the hackney wrecks she would cause if she paraded down any street in London wearing such outrageous garb.

It was early enough that most of the women of the harem were still sprawled on their sleeping couches in the main hall. Clarinda picked her way through them, stealing a few fresh dates and a handful of nuts from a tray as she passed. She was relieved not to find Poppy among their ranks. Given her friend's propensity for blurting out the first thing that came into her head, Clarinda didn't dare mention Ash's sneaking into the harem yesterday or reveal so much as a word of their exchange. When the time came for them to make their escape, she would have no choice but to take Poppy into her confidence.

Until that day, Clarinda wasn't going to give her any secrets to keep.

What she was going to do was seek out Farouk so she could charm an invitation to supper out of him. She didn't think she would survive another restless night of pacing her alcove while she trusted her fate to the fickle hands of men.

She was relieved to discover Solomon was one of the eunuchs guarding the main door of the harem. When she explained that she wished to have a word with the sultan, he simply nodded and swung the door open for her.

She was strolling down a long, arched corridor that was open to the spectacular vista of the gardens on one side when Yasmin came barreling toward her from the opposite direction, her arms piled high with towels. Clarinda wanted to groan, but she lifted her chin a notch instead, determined not to let a contemptuous glance or a spiteful remark daunt her high spirits.

Yasmin did not disappoint. "Out of my way, you clumsy cow," she snapped when they were almost upon each other.

Clarinda was opening her mouth to form a retort when she noticed that beneath Yasmin's sheer purple veil, the woman's usual sneer had been replaced by a smug smile. The hair on the back of Clarinda's neck prickled with unease. "What are you doing up and out of the harem at this hour? The eunuchs usually have to drag you out of the bed by your hair."

Yasmin neatly sidestepped her without even slowing. "Solomon has ordered me to tend the Englishman in his bath."

Clarinda froze in her tracks, paralyzed by an unwelcome image of Yasmin all but swallowing the cucumber whole. She spun around and set off after the woman, doubling the pace of her steps so she could intercept Yasmin before Yasmin reached the door that led to the baths.

"I'm afraid there's been a change of plans," she said, forcing Yasmin to stop by darting in front of her and blocking her path. "*I'll* be the one attending Captain Burke in his bath this morning."

Beneath the veil, Yasmin's smile vanished. "I do not believe you. If this were so, Solomon would have told me."

"Solomon was not made aware of the change." Well, that much at least was true. "It was the sultan who decided the captain might take comfort in being tended by someone from his homeland."

Yasmin's eyes narrowed to glittering slits. "I do not believe you. His Majesty would never send a *virgin* to tend a man in his bath." She spat the word *virgin* the way some women might say *whore*. "I am going to request an audience with him right now, and then I will prove you are nothing but a miserable, lying little—"

"I wouldn't do that if I were you." Although it made her wince inwardly, Clarinda knew she had no choice but to channel every ruthless skill required to survive seven years living among adolescent girls in an English boarding school. "*You* are a concubine. *I* am the one who will be Farouk's wife very soon. And once I am, I will also be the one who decides which concubines will continue to enjoy his favor." Praying Yasmin wouldn't call her bluff, Clarinda leaned closer to the woman. "And which ones are to be banished from his presence forever."

Yasmin continued to glare daggers at her, but when her tongue darted out to moisten her rouged lips, Clarinda knew she had won. Biting off a guttural Arabic curse, Yasmin shoved the towels at her and spun around to stalk off into the gardens, where she would no doubt spend the rest of the morning looking for a poisonous asp to put in Clarinda's bed.

Clarinda gazed stupidly down at the towels in her arms, wondering what she was supposed to do now. But then she remembered just how smug Ash had looked when she had sprang up off the couch after he had allowed her to believe he was Solomon.

A wicked smile slowly curved her lips. Captain Burke had been kind enough to attend her in her massage, so why shouldn't she return the favor? Perhaps revenge wasn't a dish best served cold after all but one that should be savored while it was still steaming.

Clarinda eased open the heavy bronze door and slipped inside the hammam, the sultan's lavish private version of the public baths one might find in any great city in Morocco. The harem had its own separate hammam, but it was always full of giggling women. Every time Clarinda disrobed in front of them, they would point and gawk at her as if she were some sort of albino monkey. She had finally taken to bathing in her alcove or only visiting the women's hammam early in the morning when most of the women were still sprawled out on their sleeping couches.

Praying that Ash was currently the only occupant of the spacious domed chamber, Clarinda padded soundlessly across the damp mosaic tiles.

At least she thought she was being soundless until Ash's smoky baritone came drifting out of the clouds of fragrant steam hanging over the room. "I'm a grown man. I don't need a nanny to bathe me. I appreciate your master's hospitality but you're free to go."

Clarinda felt her lips tighten in exasperation. Even as a child, she had never been able to sneak up him. The trait had probably served him well in battle but was quite infuriating to an eight-year-old girl trying to drop a live cricket down the collar of his shirt.

She called upon the acting skills she had perfected while staging theatricals, both for her doting parents and at Miss Throckmorton's, to duplicate Yasmin's heavily accented English. Allowing a husky note to creep into her voice, she said, "Oh, please, kind sir, will you not at least allow me to bring you some towels? If you send me away, I'm afraid my master will be displeased with me and will punish me most severely."

There was the briefest hesitation, followed by, "I don't suppose that would do any harm. I certainly wouldn't want to be responsible for you being . . . punished."

"You are far too generous to this humble maid-servant," Clarinda replied, her voice dripping with just the right amount of obsequious charm.

Before seeking him out in the hammam, she had returned to the harem just long enough to retrieve a pair of diaphanous veils. She had fastened one over her nose and mouth, then had twisted her hair into a tight knot at the top of her head and covered it with the second veil. She was counting on the balsam-scented steam to provide the rest of her disguise.

She slowly approached the crowning jewel of the hammam—an octagonal pool recessed into the floor directly below the dome. Diamond-shaped panes of cut glass had been set in the dome, inviting in pale shafts of misty morning light. Since Farouk's ancestors had possessed the foresight to build their palace on top of a natural hot spring, there was no need for the traditional Roman wood furnace and hypocaust system to heat the water and the air. The spring provided a constant flow of fresh, hot water to soothe the weary bather.

The pool was large enough to seat two dozen men, but fortunately for Clarinda, its sole occupant this morning was one exasperating Englishman.

Her steps faltered as Ash came into view. He

was seated in the pool with the water lapping at the well-defined planes of his abdomen. His arms were stretched out on either side of him, relaxing against the tiled wall supporting his back, a posture that only emphasized the corded muscles in his forearms and the impressive breadth of his shoulders. Clarinda was reminded all over again that he was no longer the boy she remembered, but some other sort of creature altogether, wildly masculine and possibly dangerous.

There were those who believed the devil himself lived in the hammam, and in that moment Clarinda was tempted to believe them.

With the fingers of steam swirling around him, Ash looked like some overlord of the underworld, idly biding his time while he waited for a hapless female soul to devour.

That was all it took to convince Clarinda she had made a serious miscalculation. She had hoped to repay him for the trick he'd played on her the day before, but with so much at stake, this was no time for games. Especially one she had little chance of winning. Fortunately, no harm had yet been done.

"You may leave the towels on the bench," he said, following her every move through narrowed eyes.

"As you wish, my lord." She kept her own eyes demurely downcast as she crossed to one of the marble benches flanking the pool. If he caught a clear glimpse of her eyes, she would lose all hope of escaping with her disguise — and her pride — intact.

Practically tossing the towels on the bench, she spun around to flee.

"Wait." Ash's deep, commanding tone sent a tingle down her spine. "I've decided I could use some assistance with my bath after all."

❖ Chapter Thirteen

*C*larinda froze. Swallowing the knot of trepidation in her throat, she said, "If it is your
desire to enjoy your bath in solitude, sir, I do not
wish to intrude."

"There are very few men who wouldn't welcome such an *intrusion*. Perhaps you could begin
by washing my back."

Clarinda scowled as an image of a wet, naked
Yasmin twined around him like a pit viper
flashed through her mind.

"Very well, my lord," she replied stiffly, returning to the pool.

Even with her eyes downcast, she could still
feel Ash's gaze stalking her as she reluctantly
circled the pool until she arrived at the spot
where he was sitting. She hovered awkwardly
behind him, absurdly grateful that the lazy bubbling of the water shielded her eyes from what

lay beneath it. She was embarrassed to discover that she might not be a virgin but she was still perfectly capable of blushing like one.

She retrieved a cake of the brown olive-oil soap from the shallow lip of the pool. "Is there no sponge?"

"There is no need for one. You may use your hands on me." Bracing his hands on his powerful thighs, Ash leaned forward, leaving her with no choice but to accept his unspoken invitation and go down on her knees behind him.

As she got her first clear look at his naked back, she barely managed to suppress a gasp of shock.

The back she remembered had been as smooth as marble beneath the curious caress of her hands. Now it was a rugged map of the life he had lived for the past nine years. Judging by the number of scars it boasted, he had been stabbed and perhaps even shot more than once.

"You seem to be a man who has earned more enemies than friends in this world," she said softly, unable to resist using her fingertip to trace the puckered edges of the jagged bayonet scar that ran from the top of his spine to his right shoulder blade.

"Does that surprise you? Not every man

can command his own army to protect him as your master does. Some have to fight their own battles."

Reminded by his words that he wasn't talking to her but to Yasmin or some other anonymous concubine, Clarinda dragged her hand away from the scar. She dipped the bar of soap into the heated water, then smoothed it over his back, lathering up his skin until it was as sleek as silk beneath her hands.

The steam swirling around them was already beginning to have its way with her. As Clarinda worked the lather into the taut muscles of Ash's upper back, droplets of sweat began to trickle between the fullness of her breasts. A limp strand of her hair slipped out from beneath the veil and plastered itself to her damp cheek. She could feel her own muscles relaxing, growing looser and more languid with every stroke of the soap.

"Mmmmm . . ." Ash's rumbling groan of pleasure seemed to reverberate through her entire being. She could feel the leonine ripple of his muscles beneath her hands as he shrugged his shoulders to stretch them. "Moroccan women are so attuned to the needs of a man. They're completely unlike those English harpies we're accustomed to."

Clarinda's hand tensed, sending the soap shooting straight up into the air.

Ash's hand shot out to catch it before it could hit the water. "What is it? Is something wrong?"

"No, my lord," she replied, finding it much harder to maintain her fake accent while speaking through clenched teeth. "I simply need to rinse your back."

As she retrieved the clay pitcher designed for that task and dipped it into the pool to fill it, he cheerfully continued, "Take that Miss Cardew, for instance. I can't imagine why the sultan would even consider marrying a shrew like her when he has a stable of beautiful, biddable women such as yourself at his beck and call."

Clarinda slowly lifted the pitcher in a white-knuckled grip, using every ounce of her self-control to pour a stream of water over the sleek planes of his back instead of breaking the pitcher over his arrogant head.

"Perhaps you are being too harsh on this Miss Cardew. I have heard it said a strong woman can be the very backbone of a man."

"Ha! Not this woman. She's much more likely to be a pain in his backside. If Farouk goes through with his harebrained plan to marry her, I can promise you he'll have nothing to look forward to but a lifetime of misery. And nagging.

Why, that woman could flay the skin off a man's back with her tongue!" Ash shook his head. "I shudder when I think of how close I came to being leg-shackled to just such a— *What the hell?!*" he exclaimed as the empty pitcher went bouncing off his skull and into the water.

Rubbing his head, he shot her a wounded look over his shoulder.

"Forgive me, my lord." Clarinda lowered her eyes, hoping he would attribute the trembling of her hands to shame, not rage. "The soap must have made my hands more slippery than I realized. Your back is clean now. May I go?"

"I should say not." He settled back against the edge of the pool with a sulky sniff. "I'm afraid my front is feeling quite neglected."

All of her plans for revenge forgotten, Clarinda jerked her head up to give him a shocked stare, but his eyes had already drifted shut.

According to the older women who had been instructing Clarinda in the arts of love, women were interchangeable in the eyes of a man. All men desired was a warm, slick place to spill their seed, and as far as they were concerned, one womb would do as well as another. That was why a woman must strive to make herself more attractive, more charming, more irresistible, than all of the other women around her if she hoped to catch the sultan's attention and be summoned to his bed for more than just one night.

Despite the warning words of her teachers, Clarinda supposed some part of her had still wanted to believe Ash was different from other men. That he wouldn't be as quick to slake his lust with some nameless — and even faceless — harem girl.

She lowered her head again, despising the tightness in her throat almost as much as she despised him in that moment. "Perhaps it would be best if you minded your own front."

She was halfway to her feet when his hand shot out to capture her wrist, imprisoning her. Although she kept her face turned away from him, she could still feel the steady weight of his gaze. "Your master assured me that any woman he sent to tend me in my bath was mine to command." His voice was no longer congenial but rumbling with sensual menace. "Is it your intention to make a liar of him?"

Clarinda hung there in his grip, poised between escape and surrender. Her every instinct was urging her to flee, but she had never backed down from a challenge, especially if it came from him. Perhaps it was not too late for her to exact her revenge against him after all.

"Of course not," she said softly. "It is my sole desire to please my master . . . and you."

With that promise still on her lips, she returned to her knees and accepted the soap from his hand. As Ash settled back against the edge of the pool, breathing out a lusty sigh of anticipation, she reached around him with both arms, wrapping him in her embrace.

For a long moment, he didn't breathe at all. Then she felt his chest heave beneath her hands as he dragged in a shuddering breath. She slid her fingernails through the damp whorls of his chest hair, then began to rub the soap in lazy circles over his torso, lingering over the rigid nubs of his nipples.

Bringing her mouth close to his ear, she whispered, "Does this please you, my lord?"

"More than you could ever know," he replied, his voice little more than a growl.

The soap slid from her hand, disappearing beneath the water. She used the flat of her palms to work the slick film of soap into a creamy lather, her hands straying deeper into the far more dangerous territory of his abdomen with each languid stroke.

To keep her balance, she was forced to lean forward until the very tips of her breasts brushed his back. Given how hot his skin was, she wouldn't have been surprised to hear a sizzle or see fresh tendrils of steam rise from those points of contact. The water sleeking his skin melted through the silk of her bodice as if it were butter, making it impossible to hide the fact that her own nipples had tightened into turgid little buds.

As one of her hands drifted even lower, slipping beneath the surface of the water, she felt the rock-hard muscles of his upper abdomen twitch in reaction.

His hand dove beneath the water to close around her wrist, snaring her in a trap of her own making. The motion threw her off-balance and she tumbled forward, plastering the softness of both of her breasts against his back.

He is going to send me away, she thought, torn between exultation and disappointment, both emotions that were best left unexamined. She had been right about him after all. He was not a man to be satisfied with the seductive charms of a woman who would go down on her knees for any man just to please her master.

But instead of pushing her away, he covered her hand with his much larger one, flattening her palm against his abdomen. Turning his head so that the warmth of *his* lips was pressed to *her* ear, he whispered, "You have extremely nimble little hands, my dear. If we set both of our minds to the task, we should be able to devise an even more clever use for them."

She gasped aloud as he captured her earlobe between his teeth and gave it a gentle tug even as his hand began to exert a subtle pressure, urging her hand down . . . down . . . down . . .

She was on the verge of forgetting all about her own plan to work him into a frenzy of desire and leave him wanting when she remembered that it wasn't her hand he was holding.

It was Yasmin's.

She reared back on her haunches, jerking her hand out of his grip. "Oh, I already have a use for my hands," she said sweetly. "I think they would be just perfect for washing your hair."

"But I've already—"

Before he could finish, she planted both hands on his shoulders and shoved with all her strength. If he had known what was coming, she wouldn't have been able to budge him. But her unexpected attack caught him off guard and he disappeared beneath the water without a struggle.

He came up sputtering and cursing, water streaming from his hair. Reaching behind him, he closed his hands around her waist and flipped her neatly over his shoulder and into the pool, the resulting splash swamping them both.

Everything happened so fast. One minute Clarinda was kneeling at the edge of the pool, savoring her triumph; the next she was *in* the pool, lying across Ash's lap.

She was still struggling to catch her breath when he yanked off the veil covering her nose and mouth, sending it fluttering to the surface of the water like a flag of surrender.

"Now there's my darling little English harpy!" A wolfish grin spread over his face, making his teeth look dazzlingly white in contrast to the sun-toasted copper of his skin. "I was wondering just how long it was going to take you to show your claws."

❧ *Chapter Fourteen*

Clarinda glared up into Ash's laughing face. "Why, you miserable wretch! You were just toying with me, weren't you?" Infuriated to find herself once again the butt of his joke, she slapped both palms against his chest. "Just how far were you going to let me go before you stopped me from making an even bigger fool of myself?"

"Oh, far be it from me to stand in the way of your desire to—how did you so eloquently put it?"—he wagged his eyebrows at her—"please your master . . . and me."

She swiped a sodden strand of hair out of her eyes. "How long have you known it was me?"

"From the moment you opened the door. And your mouth."

"So that's why you said all of those horrid things about me! To torment me!"

"Oh, no. I meant every word of it," he said cheerfully. "You have a sharp tongue, a shrewish temper, and I've never met a woman more likely to be a pain in a man's back—"

"I know I was a horrid pest when I was a little girl, but all I wanted was for you to look at me. To really see me."

"Oh, I saw you," he said, his voice softening. The way he was looking at her in that moment made her feel as if she were the only woman in the world. "I saw how brave you tried to be when you lost your mother, how you slipped your hand into your father's at the gravesite and tried to comfort him. I saw how badly you wanted to please him, even when it was such a challenge for you to play the part of the perfect little lady. I saw how you hated injustice and were always the first to champion anyone who was weaker or less clever than you." He tucked a sodden strand of hair behind her ear, his touch playing havoc with her pulse. "I always saw you. It just took me a while to figure out what to do with you."

Hoping to hide just how breathless both his confession and his touch had made her, she sniffed and said primly, "Well, I still think I did a very creditable impersonation of a harem girl."

"You'll get no argument from me on that. Aside from the part where you almost bashed in my skull with the pitcher, I was on the edge of my seat waiting to see what the next act of your performance would bring."

"Then how? How could you have known it was me?"

"How could I *not* know? Have you forgotten that I've known you since you were barely old enough to toddle after me on your fat little legs? The first time I saw you, you were riding on your papa's shoulders and using the poor man's ears as a pair of reins! I know the timbre of your voice, the way you swing your hips when you walk." The mirthful glitter faded from his eyes, leaving them oddly somber. "I know the feel of your hands against my skin, the rhythm of your breath . . ." She stopped breathing altogether as he lowered his head and ran his nose along the damp column of her throat, inhaling deeply. "I know the scent of you, even beneath all of that ridiculous perfume and oil."

Her tumble into the pool had left her in an even more precarious position than before. The warm water had done nothing to dampen the brazen enthusiasm of her nipples. On the contrary, it had molded the silk of her bodice into a second skin that was even more provocative than bare flesh. All it took was the briefest downward flick of Ash's heavy-lidded gaze for her to imagine his teeth tugging on her through the sheer silk just as they had tugged at her earlobe.

He lifted his head, bringing their mouths back into dangerous proximity. "And I know the taste of you . . ."

As if to prove his point, he brushed his lips over hers in a feather-light caress, sending her already shaky senses reeling. It was as if their lips had never been parted. As if time had stopped and all the moments between their last kiss and this one had only been grains of glittering sand suspended in some frozen hourglass.

Clarinda had no defenses against such shattering tenderness. As he deepened the kiss, sweeping his tongue through her mouth in a velvety caress, she was forced to curl a hand around the broad expanse of his nape and tangle her fingers in the wet silk of his hair just to keep from sliding back into the water. If she went under this time, she didn't think there would be any saving herself.

Her tongue welcomed his caress with a wanton flick of its own, eager to sample all of the delights she had been denied for far too long. No exotic spice or dish could compare to the flavor of him. Not the richest, darkest Arabian coffee or the flakiest *ktefa* drizzled with thick, golden honey. He was indulgence itself, and all she wanted was to gorge her starving senses, even though she knew from harsh experience that it wasn't possible for her to ever get enough of him.

The steam swirled around them just as the mist had swirled around them that morning in the meadow, making it even easier to believe they were the only two lovers in the world. With their bodies slicked with water and sweat and nothing but the thin layer of her silk trousers separating her softness from the hard, hungry heat of his lap, it would have been so easy for her to melt into him.

And even easier for him to melt into her.

He wrapped his arms around her and cupped the back of her head in his palm, tilting her head back to give him even fuller access to the forbidden delights of her mouth.

His tongue grew bolder with each foray, making her more his own with each possessive thrust, carrying her back to a time and place when there was no Maximillian, no Dewey, no Farouk, no man in the world except for him.

Which was why it took so long for the muted thud of a heavy door's opening and closing followed by the sound of a man's off-key singing to jerk her back to the present.

I loved me darling Jenny
She was a maiden fair and true
At least 'tis what I believed
Till I caught her dallying with you

Turned out she was no maiden
But a cheating, lying whore
But when she showed me what you taught her
I loved her all the more!

Clarinda and Ash sprang apart, gazing at each other in wide-eyed horror. There was no mistaking that booming basso profundo.

"Dear Lord, it's Farouk!" Clarinda whispered, paralyzed in place by the disaster that was about to unfold.

"We used to sing that ditty at Eton." Ash scowled. "Damn it all. If we had to be caught in flagrante delicto by one of your fiancés, why did it have to be the one with the biggest sword? At least my brother would have only discharged me. Or challenged me to a duel, during which I could have winged him and then apologized profusely."

"We are not in flagrante delicto!" she protested.

His deft fingers stroked the sensitive spot on her nape just below her hairline, the one that had always made her shiver with some unspeakable longing and tempted her to allow him far more than just stolen kisses. His smoky whisper filled the delicate shell of her ear: "Yet."

She shuddered, her breath catching in her throat. Was he right? After years of playing the role of proper lady with great success, had she actually been on the verge of surrendering herself to him after only a few well-timed caresses and a handful of kisses?

There was no more time to contemplate her moral fortitude—or distressing lack thereof. Farouk was rapidly approaching through the veil of steam, his heavy footfalls slapping the damp tiles.

"Go!" Ash commanded, reluctantly lifting her from his lap and giving her a frantic shove toward the curtained apse on the nearest wall. Despite their desperation, he was unable to resist giving her wet rump a fond pat as she scrambled out of the pool.

Tossing him an outraged glare over her shoulder, Clarinda darted across the floor and ducked behind the curtain. She hunkered down on the floor, wrapping her arms around her knees to make herself as small as possible, and prayed Farouk wouldn't notice the trail of water that would lead him directly to her hiding place.

"Your Majesty," Ash said smoothly, warning her that Farouk had reached the pool.

"Good day, Burke," Farouk replied with his usual impeccable courtesy. "I am glad to see you taking advantage of the pleasures of my hammam."

Clarinda doubted Farouk would have been so gracious had he realized just exactly what pleasure his guest had been about to take advantage of. She inched the edge of the curtain away from the rounded wall so she could keep an eye on the two men. Unfortunately, she did so just in time to see Farouk peel away the white cloth girding his loins in preparation for stepping into the pool. He did so without so much as a trace of self-consciousness, tossing the cloth aside and rearing back for a thorough stretch that left nothing to the imagination and little doubt as to how he managed to keep so many women satisfied.

Clarinda didn't realize she had gasped aloud until Ash aimed a murderous scowl in her direction. She ducked back behind the curtain and clapped a hand over her mouth, barely resisting the urge to giggle like a schoolgirl. Perhaps it would be wiser to remain where she could hear but not see.

Water splashed as Farouk settled himself into the pool, his heavy sigh audible even to her ears.

"You seem troubled on this fine day, my friend," Ash said. "Is there any counsel I can offer to ease the burden on your heart?"

Clarinda sobered, reminded anew that Ash's aim was to earn Farouk's trust so they could both betray him.

"My heart is plagued by the same ailment that has troubled man since the beginning of time. Women! They are the most maddening of creatures, are they not?"

"Indeed!" Ash agreed heartily. "Maddening. Infuriating. Exasperating. Stubborn. Untrustworthy. Fickle. Faithless. Easily impressed," he added pointedly.

Clarinda pressed her lips together, knowing that his recitation was for her ears, not for Farouk's. She should have held his head under the water for a little longer. Perhaps for an hour or two.

Ash's enthusiasm for the topic showed no sign of waning. "Flighty. Vindictive. Mercurial. Vain. Illogical—"

"Exactly!" Farouk exclaimed before Ash could come up with several more unflattering adjectives. "They are utterly without logic and impossible to understand, and yet we allow them to dictate our moods, our hopes, our desires."

"That we do," Ash admitted ruefully. "It is our one failing as the stronger, more intelligent, and far superior sex."

This time Clarinda didn't even try to muffle her disdainful snort.

"I suddenly find myself questioning the wisdom of my forefathers in these matters," Farouk admitted. "Perhaps you can shed some light on the darkness of my thoughts."

"It would be my honor to try."

Farouk seemed to be considering his next words carefully. "Here we are taught from the cradle that one man can be the husband of more than one woman, a belief that makes us little more than savages in the eyes of many in your own culture."

"You'd be amazed by how many men in London ascribe to exactly that same philosophy," Ash said with a cynical laugh. "They just don't call the women wives or concubines, but mistresses."

"But in your world, are there not also those who believe there is only one true mate for every man? That for a man to embrace her is to embrace his destiny?"

"There are," Ash replied. "We have a name for them as well—'pitiable fools.'"

"So you do not ascribe to this notion yourself?"

Ash did not reply for a long moment. Long enough for Clarinda to realize she was holding her breath. When he finally spoke, it was with great reluctance. "It has been my experience that there are many women who can stir a man's shaft."

Clarinda closed her eyes, thankful that he couldn't see the disappointment in them.

"But only one who can stir his heart."

Her eyes flew open. Now it was his face she longed to see. For all she knew, he was simply trying to torment her again. He might not even be talking about her but about some other woman he had encountered in his many travels.

"You are a wise man, Burke," Farouk proclaimed. But this time his voice was a shade too hearty. "And if I am to be equally wise, then I can only conclude Clarinda must be that woman for me. *She* is the destiny I must embrace."

Ash was silent for so long Clarinda feared he was going to betray them both and destroy any chance of escape. When he finally spoke, his voice was as soft as velvet but with a steely edge only she would recognize. "It is a wise man indeed who is not afraid to embrace his destiny. Only a fool would let it slip through his fingers."

✢ *Chapter Fifteen*

*H*e wasn't coming back.

Poppy drew off her spectacles and gazed out over the sea, a plaintive sigh escaping her lips. Sometimes the world was more pleasing to her eyes when it was slightly out of focus. It seemed to soften the sharp edges that could be so bruising to a tender heart.

Five days had passed since Farouk had stumbled upon her garden retreat. Even though there had been no sign of him there since then, she had returned faithfully to the bench each morning, taking great care to always arrive at the exact same time with a basket of freshly baked *ktefa* hooked on her arm. The sultan's behavior toward her might be a mystery, but there could be no mistaking the way he had looked at those pastries.

A gentle breeze sifted through the clusters of curls pinned over her ears, but the merciless golden orb of the sun was already climbing in the eastern sky. Soon the heat would begin to rise over the desert in shimmering waves, making even the most heavily shaded corners of the garden unbearable until nightfall, especially to a woman with Poppy's generous curves.

Despite the oppressive heat in this place, she was growing increasingly fond of her attire. There were no corsets with their biting whalebone stays, no endless layers of petticoats, no too-tight slippers to ruthlessly pinch her toes. Without the ribbons, buttons, and hooks, she no longer felt trussed up like a Christmas turkey. She was free to draw a deep breath, to stretch her legs and wiggle her toes, to entertain silly, girlish notions such as believing the sultan had been on the brink of kissing her.

She should have known that was just another of her foolish fancies, like believing Mr. Huntington-Smythe was infatuated with her just because he had retrieved her parasol when a gust of wind had turned it inside out and whisked it from her hand. Why would such a magnificent man as Farouk ever look twice at a plain, plump girl like her, much less kiss her, when he had a bevy of exotic beauties fawning all over him? Why, he was probably languishing in his bed with one of them at that very moment!

Swallowing her disappointment, she pushed her spectacles back up the bridge of her nose and opened the book in her lap. There was no point in letting her melancholy musings spoil a perfectly fine morning.

She had just begun to read when a forbidding shadow fell over the pages of the book.

She glanced up to find Farouk scowling down at her, his stern visage blocking the sun as surely as a thundercloud.

She could not stop a delighted smile from spreading over her own face. "Why, good morning, Your Majesty! What a wonderful surprise to see you here!"

"It is my garden, you know."

"Of course I do. The entire palace is yours. Why, one might even venture that the entire province belongs to you!"

He continued to glower down at her from beneath the thick, raven wings of his brows, not even bothering to blink. Poppy knew the man could smile. He positively oozed charm every time he looked at Clarinda. Or at any woman, for that matter.

Any woman except her.

The awkward silence stretched until he said, "This has always been one of my favorite spots in the garden."

"Mine, too," she replied eagerly.

"I like to come here early in the morning. To be alone," he added pointedly.

"Oh!" Suddenly it became much more of an effort for Poppy to keep the smile pasted on her lips. She reached for the handle of the basket resting next to her on the bench. "I didn't mean to intrude. Perhaps I should go."

"No!" Farouk snapped with such ferocity that she jumped a little. The book slid off her lap and tumbled to the ground. "What are you reading?" he demanded as she scrambled to retrieve it.

Her confusion growing, she turned the volume toward him so he could read the gilt lettering embossed into its leatherbound cover. As he squinted down at it, looking even more fierce than before, a flush slowly made its way up the corded tendons of his throat.

"Oh, dear!" Poppy exclaimed, her own cheeks coloring as realization dawned. "You can't read English! I'm so terribly sorry. I just assumed since you'd spent all those years at Eton . . ."

"I can read. I just can't see."

"Pardon?"

To her surprise, he reached out and gently tapped the nosepiece of her wire-rimmed spectacles with his forefinger. "When I was in England, I was fitted with a pair of those so I could complete my lessons. But when I returned to El Jadida to become sultan, my uncle insisted that being seen in them would be considered a sign of weakness by my enemies."

Poppy couldn't imagine being deprived of her beloved books and scandal sheets because she couldn't see to read. She would never have survived Miss Throckmorton's if she hadn't been able to escape between their pages for a few precious hours each evening after the other girls had fallen asleep. She'd come close to burning down the school more than once by sneaking a lamp beneath her sheets.

"It sounds to me as if your uncle is the shortsighted one. I should think not being able to see your enemies when they're creeping up on you would be a far greater sign of weakness." Growing ever more indignant on his behalf, she whipped off her spectacles and held them out to him.

He gazed down at them for a long moment before reluctantly reaching for them. Their fingers brushed as he did so, the heat of his skin a marked contrast to the cool wire rims of the spectacles.

As he hooked the earpieces over his ears, Poppy bit back a smile. He was far too handsome to resemble any professor she had ever seen, but there was no denying the spectacles gave him a dignified air more suited to a barrister or a member of Parliament than a lusty Moroccan sultan.

She knew it was wrong to gawk but she couldn't resist letting her eyes drink their fill of him. If Captain Burke had his way, they would be gone from this place soon enough and she would never see him again.

"Here," she said, absently holding out the book.

But he wasn't looking at the book. He was looking at her.

"What is it?" she asked softly, afraid his newly restored eyesight had revealed some dreadful flaw in her. Had she forgotten to apply rice powder to her nose that morning? Was her native garment on backward? Or was he just now realizing she was no slender sylph like Clarinda but a woman who had always had a difficult time turning down an extra portion of chocolate syllabub at supper?

"Your eyes."

She blinked up at him. "Yes?"

"They are lavender."

Relieved to discover there wasn't a bit of pastry stuck between her two front teeth after all, she waved away his observation. "Don't be silly. They're a perfectly ordinary shade of periwinkle. My granny in the Cotswolds used to grow periwinkles in her garden. That's how I know."

This time when she offered him the book, he took it, perusing the cover with unabashed interest. "Coleridge, eh?"

She nodded. "I do love *Christabel*, but somehow 'Kubla Khan' seems far more suited to this place. Your garden reminds me of Xanadu. And one could certainly call your palace a 'pleasure-dome' of sorts," she added, unable to resist giving him a mischievous smile.

He arched one eyebrow, warning her that he wasn't completely oblivious to her mockery. "So tell me, Miss Montmorency—do you fancy yourself a 'damsel with a dulcimer' or a 'woman wailing for her demon-lover'?"

Just hearing the word *lover* on lips as beautifully sculpted as his was somehow dangerously provocative. She laughed to hide its effect on her. "I am naught but the daughter of a humble country squire and I'm afraid I haven't any lovers at all, neither demon nor mortal."

Farouk drew off the spectacles with painstaking care, handling them as if they were made of gold instead of wire and common glass, and handed both them and the book back to her. "Read to me."

"Oh, that won't be necessary! If you'd like to borrow the spectacles for a while, you can read to yourself."

"I prefer the sound of your voice."

Poppy was taken aback by his words. Given her tendency to prattle on about nothing at all, especially when she was trying to hide her innate shyness, she was more accustomed to people excusing themselves from her company while feigning a headache. Or the Black Plague.

She was even more shocked when Farouk reclined on the seat of the bench, stretched out his long legs in their loose trousers, crossing them at the ankle, and rested his head in her lap. For a moment, she couldn't even breathe, much less remember how to read.

"You may proceed," he commanded with a haughty wave of his hand.

She cleared her throat. Perhaps this was the customary position in which one read to a sultàn. She dug her fingers into the cover of the book, terrified one of her hands would accidentally stray down to gently stroke the thick, ebony curls away from his brow.

For some reason the book fell open to the last lines of Coleridge's poem:

For he on honey-dew hath fed
And drunk the milk of Paradise.

Her nervous gaze darted to the basket of pastries sitting on the other side of her. "Would you care to try a *ktefa* while I'm reading, Your Majesty? I believe they're still a trifle bit warm."

Farouk frowned, pondering the question as if she had asked him to solve some impossibly complicated mathematical equation upon which the entire fate of the universe rested. "I do believe I would."

Delving beneath the crimson kerchief covering the basket, she broke off a generous piece of one of the flaky pastries and offered it to him. He took it from her sugary fingers and popped it into his mouth, chewing with great relish. Then he did something she never thought she would see him do.

He smiled at her.

❋　　❋　　❋

The next afternoon Clarinda was reclining on a chaise longue in one of the spacious chambers off the main hall of the harem, having her toe-nails buffed to a pearly sheen by an old woman with more hair on her chin than Farouk, when Poppy came wandering in.

Rather than circumventing the low-slung table in her path, Poppy barked her shin on it with enough force to make Clarinda wince in sympathy. Still rubbing her shin, Poppy limped over to the brightly brocaded ottoman next to the chaise. Instead of sitting in the middle of it, she plopped down on its edge, nearly upending both herself and the ottoman.

Clarinda might have attributed her friend's odd behavior to her dazed expression if she hadn't noticed something else was amiss. "Poppy, where on earth are your spectacles?"

Looking even more self-conscious than usual, Poppy touched a forefinger to the bridge of her nose as if expecting to find them there. "I'm not sure. I must have mislaid them. You know what an addlepated goose I can be. Why, only this morning I nearly set my box of rice powder afire when I mistook it for a lamp."

"Probably because you weren't wearing your spectacles." Ignoring the old woman's chattered protest, Clarinda started to swing her legs over the edge of the chaise. "I'm on the verge of perishing from boredom. Why don't you let me help you find them?"

"No!"

Startled by Poppy's violent response, Clarinda gave her friend a puzzled look.

Poppy's wide-eyed panic was quickly replaced by a conciliatory smile. "There's no need for you to trouble yourself. I'm sure they'll turn up in time. They always do." As if eager to cast about for another topic, Poppy leaned forward on the ottoman. "So tell me — have you had any word from Captain Burke about his plan for our rescue?"

Clarinda settled back on the chaise, earning a toothless grin of approval from the old woman. Since Farouk did not require his slaves to learn English, Clarinda knew it was safe to speak freely in front of her.

While the woman went back to buffing her toenails, Clarinda shook her head. "I've managed to coax Farouk into letting me join them for supper every night, but we're under constant scrutiny from that vulture of an uncle of his. There hasn't been a single opportunity for him to slip me a note, much less for us to exchange anything more than the vaguest of pleasantries."

She and Ash hadn't been alone since that morning in the hammam. Given what had transpired there, perhaps that was just as well. Clarinda was still dismayed that it had only taken one kiss to dismantle all of the defenses she had spent the last nine years constructing around her heart. One very long, very wet, very hot . . .

She shook her head, snapping herself out of her reverie. Her passions had betrayed her once before with grave consequences. She had no intention of letting it happen again. "I'm afraid our time is running out, Poppy. We only have a few more days before Farouk intends to make me his wife." A despairing little laugh escaped her. "Or at least one of them."

Poppy looked positively stricken. Clarinda should have known better than to confess her fears to Poppy. Poppy had always been more tender of heart than those around her. She was probably sick with worry on Clarinda's behalf.

"Don't abandon hope, darling." Clarinda reached over and gave Poppy's hand a comforting squeeze. "Regardless of my personal feelings toward him, Captain Burke is a man of tremendous resources. He won't give up until he finds a way to rescue us. Then we shall leave this place and never think of it again."

And Ash would return her to Maximillian, collect what was owed him, and vanish back into the mists of her past, a bittersweet reminder of everything that might have been.

Poppy didn't appear to be any more consoled by Clarinda's words than Clarinda was. Without the spectacles to shield her eyes, the sudden shimmer of tears in them was impossible for her to hide.

Before Clarinda could ask her what was wrong, Solomon came padding into the chamber, a large woven basket cradled in his massive arms. A mouthwatering aroma quickly filled the room.

He rested the basket on the table, then plucked a scroll of parchment from the crimson kerchief draped over the top of it and handed it to Clarinda, inclining his head in a gracious bow as he did so.

The note was penned in the precise hand of a man who had learned English as a second language. "Farouk thought we might enjoy an afternoon repast so he sent us some freshly baked *ktefa* from the kitchens." Bemused by the extravagant size of the basket, Clarinda shook her head. "It's no wonder the man has a dozen wives and twice that many concubines. He may never give his own heart to just one woman, but he certainly knows how to woo a woman's heart."

Farouk's fanciful offering seemed to have accomplished what Clarinda could not. She should have known that all it would take to banish Poppy's worried tears and bring a smile to her face was a basket of pastries.

Ash leaned against a post in the outer courtyard of the palace, waiting for his host to appear. Farouk had promised him a tour of his stables, and Ash was eager for any diversion that did not make him want to strangle the sultan with his own kaffiyeh. Especially when that diversion would include working out a plan to steal some horses so they'd have a way across the desert when the right moment came to make their escape.

Ash's casual posture did nothing to betray the dangerous tension roiling through him. He was beginning to wish he'd let the assassins finish Farouk off in the desert. If he had to spend one more interminable evening watching the sultan paw Clarinda right in front of him, Ash was afraid he was going to strangle the man with his bare hands.

Only last night he had been forced to calmly sip his wine while the sultan tugged Clarinda into his lap and fed her plump, juicy grapes, popping each one between her luscious lips with a languid care that made the hair on the back of Ash's neck bristle. When she had giggled and given Farouk's finger a teasing nip with her little white teeth, Ash had risen halfway to his feet without realizing it before being jerked back to reason—and into his seat—by Luca's hand tugging on the back of his robes.

"Take care, my friend," Luca had whispered. "There is more at stake here than just your pride."

Farouk's attentions to Clarinda might be more tolerable if she wasn't such a consummate little actress herself. Based on how skillfully she batted her lashes and twirled her hair while hanging breathlessly on the sultan's every word, even the most astute observer would have sworn she was a woman in love, desperately devoted to the man who would soon become her husband.

As he watched her wrap Farouk around her graceful pinkie, Ash couldn't help but wonder if he hadn't been every bit as gullible as the sultan when it came to being deceived by her charms. Despite the swaggering bravado affected by all young males desperate to impress the girls they desire, he had been little more than a callow lad before that morning with Clarinda in the meadow. What if his passion for her had been so all-consuming he had fooled himself into believing she felt the same way about him? Perhaps that's why she had been so quick to accept Darby's suit after he had left.

It hardly soothed his temper to know he had no more right to his jealousy than he'd had to Clarinda's kiss that morning in the hammam. He no longer had any claim on her at all. She belonged to Max now, and he was nothing but a hired gun whose only mission was to get her out of this place and back into his brother's arms so she could become the countess she was born to be. The sooner they both escaped this palace of sensual delights and the temptations it provided, the better off they would be.

Ash's grim musings were interrupted when Farouk came striding into the courtyard. The sultan was always in a jovial mood but seemed to have an extra spring to his step on this sweltering afternoon. A pair of wire-rimmed spectacles was perched incongruously on the tip of his strong Roman nose.

Ash squinted at them. "Aren't those—"

"No!" Farouk yanked them off and shoved them into the pocket of his loose-fitting trousers. "They most certainly are not."

Mystified by the man's curious behavior, Ash fell into step beside him, matching his long strides easily. It would be so much easier to despise Farouk if he weren't so damnably likable. He might be outwardly unrecognizable from the plump, awkward lad Ash remembered from Eton, but inwardly he was much the same — amiable, generous, eager to like and be liked. If Farouk had been wooing any other woman besides Clarinda, Ash would eagerly have given the sultan his blessing. After being wed to such a bully as Mustafa, poor battered Fatima would have probably considered herself blessed to be counted among the wives of such a man.

Ash didn't have to be pretend to be impressed during their tour of the royal stables. The stable itself was more lavish than his own family's town house in Belgrave Square, and Farouk's taste in horseflesh was nearly as impeccable as his taste in both jewels and women. A king's ransom was on display in nearly every spacious stall. While some men would have given their birthright just to be seen riding one of the equine beauties down Rotten Row in Hyde Park on a Sunday afternoon, Ash would have wagered every penny he had to his name to see one of them race at Newmarket.

By declaring himself an enthusiastic horseman, Ash was able to learn a great deal of useful information about the strengths and weaknesses of the various mounts, the layout of the stables, and the habits and schedules of the sultan's numerous grooms.

Their visit culminated with a stop by the outdoor pen where a young boy was brushing the magnificent black stallion Farouk had been riding when Ash and Luca had first encountered him in the desert. As Ash watched Farouk run a loving hand down the beast's sleek neck while murmuring tender Arabic words into its ear, all he could see was Farouk murmuring those same words in Clarinda's ear, running his loving hands all over the sleek curves of her body.

"Forgive me, Your Majesty, but I must beg your permission to return to the palace." Although every drop of sweat had already been sucked away by the parched air, Ash made a great show of drawing a handkerchief from his pocket and mopping his brow. "I fear I'm not as immune to the ravages of the afternoon heat as His Majesty."

"One more stop and we shall return to the palace for some cool libations," Farouk promised. "As a former military man, I thought you might enjoy taking a look at the improvements we are making to the fortifications."

Although the last two words Ash wanted to hear in the same breath were *improvements* and *fortifications*, he couldn't afford to refuse a chance to search for any chink in the palace's defenses. Not with Clarinda's wedding day—and night—only a few days away.

"It would be my honor," he said with a slight bow.

The walls of the palace were already more than three feet thick, but their height was being augmented with four more rows of stones to increase their height to well over fifteen feet. Dozens of shirtless men were swarming all over the top of the wall, their bodies caked with copper-colored dust. Shading his eyes against the sun, Farouk pointed out the complicated system of ropes and pulleys they were using to lift and then lower the massive stones into place.

"Impressive," Ash murmured, although all he saw was one more wall they might have to scale when it came time to get Clarinda out of this place.

As soon as he spotted them, a skinny overseer came running over, bowing so low the top of his snowy white turban nearly brushed the ground.

Farouk greeted him warmly, then said in Arabic in a booming voice loud enough to be heard even over the labors of the workers, "Make sure the men receive an extra portion of water and rations immediately. They have been working like dogs to bring glory to this palace and the name of Zin al-Farouk. I will not have them being starved or mistreated as their reward."

The workers broke into a rousing cheer as the overseer bowed again, then rushed away to do his master's bidding. Ash sighed. If Farouk had snatched up a whip and flayed a few stripes of flesh from the workers' backs, Ash would finally have had a good excuse to draw his pistol and shoot him.

The laborers came scampering down the crude wooden ladders propped against the wall to cluster around the overseer and claim their extra rations, leaving the top of the wall deserted. Ash and Farouk resumed their stroll in the scant shade provided by its shadow.

"The improvements to the fortifications were Tarik's idea," Farouk admitted, his hands locked at the small of his back. "Thanks to my father's negotiating skills, we are enjoying an era of unprecedented peace and prosperity in El Jadida.

But I am afraid my uncle still sees enemies lurking behind every palm tree and sand dune."

"It is a wise man who does not underestimate his foes," Ash replied, feeling like the lowest of traitors.

"But does there never come a time when a foe might not choose to lay down his arms and become a friend?" Farouk asked, his dark eyes looking genuinely troubled. "Just because their ancestors drew arms against one another, does it follow that men must be forever enemies? If the two of us had met on a battlefield, we might have never broken bread together, and both of us would be poorer for the loss."

Now Ash wanted to draw his pistol and shoot himself. Unable to meet Farouk's earnest gaze, he studied his boots as they walked. "Unfortunately, there are more things in this world to cause strife between men than there are those that foster peace. Disagreements over religion, squabbles over territory, water, wealth . . . women," he added with a sidelong glance at Farouk.

Farouk threw back his head with a laugh. "There are very few women in this world worth going to war over, my friend." His smile slowly faded. "Although perhaps there are one or two who might be worth dying for."

As he waited for Farouk to pronounce Clarinda just such a woman, Ash slowed his steps and rolled his eyes heavenward, praying for a lightning bolt to shoot out of the cloudless, white vault of the heavens and put him out of his misery.

A flicker of movement on the top of the wall caught his attention. Another man might have hesitated, but Ash's instincts had been honed by years in battle when the slightest hesitation might mean the difference between living the rest of one's life whole or as a legless cripple forced to beg on street corners for a crust of bread. He darted forward, shoving Farouk out of the way only seconds before an enormous stone block came tumbling out of the sky.

✣ *Chapter Sixteen*

*A*sh's momentum carried both him and Farouk to the ground. They lay there for a moment, dazed and breathless from the near miss, before lifting their heads in unison to eye the rubble littering the cobblestones only a pace or two away from the exact spot where Farouk had been standing seconds before.

For a moment all was silence in the courtyard except for a telltale creak. Ash's gaze slowly traveled from the rubble up to the frayed end of the rope dangling from a pulley far above their heads. The rope swayed back and forth in the hot wind like a hangman's noose.

While the stunned workers looked on, the overseer rushed over to them, wringing his hands and chattering frantically in Arabic. Ash understood every syllable of what the man was saying, but even the most casual observer would have been able to tell from the man's wild eyes and hysterical tone that he was afraid he was about to be relieved of both his position and his head.

Farouk lumbered to his feet, brushing the dust from his trousers and waving away the man's desperate apologies and explanations. "You need not shoulder the blame. I was the one who encouraged the workers to leave their posts before the stones could be secured."

While the overseer returned to his men, walking backward and bowing to Farouk the whole way, Ash slowly rose, studying the top of the wall through narrowed eyes. He wasn't entirely convinced the incident could be dismissed as the result of a worker's carelessness. In that split second before his brain had registered the threat, he would have almost sworn he'd seen a ray of sun glint off something shiny.

Something like the blade of a dagger.

He was beginning to suspect Farouk's enemies didn't lie outside the castle walls, but within them.

Before he could follow that thought to its grim conclusion, Farouk clapped a hand firmly on Ash's shoulder. He reluctantly turned to face the sultan, biting back a groan as he realized exactly what he had done.

If he had let the block crush the man to a

pulp, Ash would never again have been forced to watch Farouk caress Clarinda's nape in that infuriatingly proprietary manner of his while Ash choked down supper through a throat constricted with rage.

"Thanks to the merciful grace of Allah, you have twice given me back my life." Farouk gave Ash's shoulder a painful squeeze with his ham of a hand, the affectionate glow in his eyes more terrifying than any assassin. "From this day forward, Burke the Younger, you are no longer my friend, but my brother!"

"Oh, Clarinda, the most extraordinary thing just happened! Have you heard—"

Poppy broke off her gushing announcement in midbreath as she burst into one of the private chambers of the harem and caught sight of the watercolor illustration propped up on the easel sitting in the corner.

Clarinda was lounging on a plush fainting couch, her face slathered with a bright green beauty mask that smelled as if it had been concocted from a mixture of brussels sprouts and eye of newt. She lowered the scroll she was studying as Poppy wandered over to the easel to squint at the detailed illustration.

"Dear heavens, what is that?"

"What do you think it is?"

Poppy turned her head first one way, then the other, stopping just shy of standing on her head. "I'm not sure. A vegetable of some sort? A rutabaga perhaps?"

Clarinda rolled her eyes before leveling a mischievous look at her friend. "Well, I've never heard it called a rutabaga before, but the women who have been teaching me all about its many charms do occasionally call it"—she lowered her voice to a conspiratorial whisper—"a *manroot*."

Poppy looked even more bewildered. "A man—oh! Oh my!" She clapped a hand over her eyes, then ruined the effect by peeping through her fingers. "If such things as they teach here were taught in England, I fear the cradles would soon be overflowing. Every noble family would have an heir and at least a dozen spares."

Thankful Poppy was still peeping at the illustration instead of looking at her so she wouldn't see the shadow of sadness in her eyes, Clarinda said softly, "The women here have ways to prevent that as well."

"Well, all I know is that our art instructor at Miss Throckmorton's certainly never had us paint anything like *that*."

"Miss Throckmorton used to blush if the stamen of a watercolor lily was too rigid. This would have given the prune-faced old spinster a fatal apoplexy."

"It nearly gave me one," Poppy said, finally daring to lower her hand.

"What were you saying before you were distracted by the . . . um . . . rutabaga?"

Dragging her gaze away from the easel, Poppy plopped down on the end of the couch, her eyes sparkling as they always did when she had gleaned a particularly delicious snippet of gossip. "Have you heard what Captain Burke did?"

"That depends," Clarinda replied, blowing a strand of hair out of her eyes. "Are you talking about wrestling a full-grown lion, warding off a horde of black-robed assassins who scaled the palace walls and stormed the courtyard, or dispatching an angry crocodile with his bare hands? Because according to the women in the harem, he's done all of that and more in the course of a single afternoon."

Clarinda hated to admit it, but it was even more grating to have every woman in the harem gushing over Ash's latest feats of derring-do than it was to read about them between the pages of some silly scandal sheet.

Poppy's face fell. "So you've already heard?"

"Oh, Poppy, surely you don't believe such ridiculous drivel. Why, it's utterly absurd to think—" Clarinda paused in midsentence, noting for the first time that Poppy's spectacles had returned to their usual perch on the tip of her nose. "Where did you find your spectacles?"

"Right where I lost them." Poppy nervously nudged the spectacles back up to the bridge of her nose, avoiding Clarinda's eyes. "And you may scoff if you like, but I heard Captain Burke risked both life and limb to save the sultan from being crushed to death by a stone as big as a camel."

"Given how exaggerated the tales of his exploits always are, isn't it more likely that he simply removed a piece of gravel from the sultan's boot before it could bruise his heel?"

"I have it on the *highest* authority that this particular tale is true. One of the workers left his stone unsecured when he climbed down from the wall. When I think what might have happened to the sultan had Captain Burke not been there . . ." Poppy shuddered, the color draining from her usually rosy cheeks.

"I'm glad Farouk was spared," Clarinda admitted. "I might not want to spend the rest of my life imprisoned in his harem, but I don't wish him any harm, either. And I'm sure the captain was only too eager for another chance to play the hero."

Ash always seemed to be around when someone needed him, Clarinda thought. Unless that someone happened to be her.

Both Poppy's color and her smile returned. "Tonight Farouk—I mean *His Majesty*—is throwing an extravagant celebration in the captain's honor. There will be dancing girls, jugglers, acrobats, snake charmers, magicians . . . even a full-grown tiger!"

"Which Captain Burke will no doubt wrestle into submission in front of all the guests. If he's not too busy wrestling with the dancing girls, that is," Clarinda added under her breath.

It had not escaped her notice that Ash's efforts to resist the considerable charms of the sultan's women had only made him more irresistible in their eyes. Each night at supper the dancing girls would wind their scarves around his neck like silky nooses and thrust their jiggling breasts into his face while Clarinda was forced to calmly sip her wine and feign interest in what Farouk was saying.

Just yesterday she had wandered through the hall of the harem to find several of the concubines wagering their favorite baubles and hair combs over which of them would be the first to lure the handsome Englishman into her bed. At the moment Yasmin seemed to be the favorite.

"I hadn't realized how late it was getting!" Poppy exclaimed, eyeing the deepening slant of the sun through the latticed window. "I must go and find something suitable to wear to the party."

"Farouk invited *you*?" Clarinda blurted out before she realized how rude it sounded.

Usually Farouk avoided Poppy's company like the proverbial plague. Clarinda had been begging him to let her friend join them for supper from her first day at the palace, but it was the one boon he had refused to grant her.

A fresh blush tinted Poppy's cheeks. "Perhaps the sultan's close brush with death has put him in a magnanimous mood."

"Perhaps," Clarinda murmured, eyeing her friend thoughtfully. Poppy was usually as transparent as a pane of glass, but she had been behaving in an increasingly odd manner for the past week.

Clarinda retrieved the scroll she had been reading and lifted it to hide her expression, already feeling less than magnanimous herself at the prospect of spending yet another evening hailing the dashing and debonair Captain Burke as a hero.

✤ *Chapter Seventeen*

Poppy might be given to flights of fancy when it came to many things, but her description of the sultan's upcoming celebration in Captain Burke's honor had failed to do the reality justice.

The fete was being held in a hall twice as spacious as the one they had occupied on the night Farouk had first welcomed Ash and Luca to the palace. Towering marble columns supported the lofty ceiling of the long, rectangular chamber. The walls had been festooned with flowing drapes of crimson and purple silk shot through with threads of silver and gold. Jasmine and jacaranda blooms had been scattered across the colorful squares of the tiled floor, flooding the room with their intoxicating scent. Plush cushions and tasseled bolsters had been artfully arranged in a smaller rectangle as seating for the sultan's guests, leaving the open area in the center of the floor to serve as a stage for his after-supper entertainments.

And what magnificent entertainments they were! Acrobats flipped and tumbled across the tiled floor, while contortionists flexed their rubbery limbs into positions that should have been impossible for the human body to attain. A man in a silver half mask elicited gasps from the crowd when he doused a sword in oil and set it afire, then appeared to swallow the entire blade. The guests watched in breathless anticipation as a magician in a towering turban wheeled a large, painted box into their midst, secured one of the dancing girls inside it, then drove a scimitar right through the center of the box with lusty glee. Several of the guests screamed, but their horror rapidly shifted to relieved applause when the woman emerged unscathed from the opposite end of the box to take her bow alongside the magician.

Four soldiers of Farouk's guard flanked each of the massive bronze doors at opposite ends of the hall, while others were stationed at precise intervals around the outskirts of the walls. Even their impassive faces softened as they fought to hide their smiles.

The only sour face in the hall belonged to Farouk's uncle. Tarik kept muttering to anyone who would listen that his nephew was going to bankrupt his treasury with his extravagance and cast disgrace upon the very throne of El Jadida—and all to honor an infidel.

Poppy had been misinformed about only one thing. Farouk's feline guest wasn't a full-grown tiger but a litter of tiger cubs. Each of the charming little cats wore a gold collar adorned with a priceless fortune in sapphires, rubies, and emeralds to set off their dramatic black markings. They frolicked and bounded among the guests, earning the loudest shouts of delight whenever they engaged in mock battle with one another, hissing savagely and rearing back on their hind legs to bare their razor-sharp little claws.

Clarinda sat at Farouk's side, cradling the smallest of the tiger cubs in her lap. The little fellow showed no desire to romp with his littermates but seemed perfectly content to loll across her legs while she gently raked her fingers through his thick fur.

Caressing her nape as if she, too, were a wild feline to be tamed, Farouk leaned closer to her, his voice a deep rumble in her ear. "If he pleases you, you may keep him for your own."

"As always, you are far too generous, Your

Majesty." Clarinda's fond smile was beginning to feel like a mask that no longer fit her face.

She stole a glance across the hall at Ash, only to discover his mask had slipped away entirely. Through narrowed eyes he was giving Farouk a look that could only be described as murderous. Fortunately, Farouk's attention had already been recaptured by the magician, who had just made one of the tiger cubs vanish in a puff of smoke. The sorcerer whipped off his immense turban with a flourish, thrust his hand into it, and fished around until his hand reemerged clutching the squirming tiger cub by the loose skin at its nape. Farouk's booming laughter nearly drowned out the delighted oohs and aahs of his guests.

When Clarinda risked another look at Ash, he was leaning over to converse with Luca, the flash of his easy grin leaving her to wonder if she had imagined the whole thing. He looked as at home in the native robes of El Jadida as any tribal warlord. Their dazzling white folds deepened the bronze tones in his skin and sharpened the glitter of gold in his amber eyes. A hint of razor stubble a shade darker than his hair shadowed the clearly defined planes of his lean jaw, making Clarinda wonder how it would feel beneath the caress of her lips.

"Oh, Clarinda, isn't it just about the most marvelous thing you've ever seen?" Poppy, seated on the other side of her, burst into wild applause as the magician drew a seemingly endless array of colorful scarves out of his own ear before taking another bow.

"Indeed it is, Poppy," Clarinda replied absently, her gaze still locked on Ash.

"I've been reading about such wonders my entire life but never dreamed they truly existed! Why, Lady Ellerbee would be green with envy! I doubt even she has ever thrown a house party that could compare to *this*!"

Poppy's blue eyes sparkled behind the thick lenses of her spectacles, and her full cheeks were positively aglow. Clarinda had never really noticed how pretty Poppy could be when she wasn't trying to cram her voluptuous figure into a rigid corset or bodice so tight it pinched all the color from her face. The flowing garments the women wore in this place actually seemed to suit her. Instead of pinning the springy clusters of corkscrew curls up over her ears, she had let one of the older women from the harem dress her hair into loose curls that spilled down her back in glossy waves.

"Your friend flatters me, Clarinda," Farouk

said, leaning around Clarinda to pin Poppy with a teasing stare. "Perhaps she is implying that there are those who might even call my palace a 'stately pleasure-dome.'"

Poppy giggled. "I prefer to think of it as a 'savage place, holy and enchanted.' And what is the next entertainment you have planned for us, Your Majesty? A 'damsel with a dulcimer' perhaps?"

Farouk wagged his eyebrows at her in a forbidding manner. "Cease your wailing, woman, lest I summon a 'demon-lover' to carry you away."

They both broke into hearty gales of laughter. Clarinda gave her wine a sniff, wondering if perhaps someone had drugged it and she was beginning to hallucinate. She'd never seen Poppy quite so animated, not even when in the company of that dreadful windbag Mr. Huntington-Smythe. And she'd certainly never heard Farouk quote Coleridge or seen him directly address Poppy without being browbeaten into it.

As the magician rounded up the rest of the tiger cubs, including the one in Clarinda's lap, and took his leave, the musicians seated in the corner between two columns struck up a sinuous melody on flute, lyre, and drum. This was the moment Clarinda had been secretly dreading. The moment when Farouk would clap his hands to summon the dancing girls.

But it seemed on this night Farouk had other plans.

He rose to his feet, silencing both the musicians and his guests with nothing more than a masterful wave of one hand. His flowing robes were even more ornate than usual, adorned with embroidered stars and crescent moons. "As most of you know, I have summoned you here tonight to honor a man with the soul of a warrior and the heart of a tiger. Not once, but twice, he has risked his own life so that mine might be spared." Farouk turned his grave smile on Ash before lifting his golden goblet. "To Burke the Younger! You came to this place as a stranger, but on this night I am honored to call you both friend . . . and brother."

The other guests lifted their goblets in unison while Tarik made a great show of *not* lifting his.

Ash acknowledged the tribute with a wary smile and a gracious nod, while Luca tossed back the contents of his goblet in a single swallow.

Lowering his own goblet, Farouk said, "It is not within my nature to let such bravery go unrewarded. Every great warrior deserves a weapon equal to his skills, so tonight I would like to present to you a dagger used by my father, the Lion of El Jadida, to dispatch one of his most worthy enemies."

One of Farouk's guards came marching across the floor, bearing a tasseled pillow with a dagger resting on top of it. The rubies and emeralds encrusted in its gold hilt sparkled in the warm glow of the lamplight.

Luca's low-pitched whistle of appreciation perfectly echoed Clarinda's amazement. The thing must be worth a small fortune.

The guard paused briefly in the middle of the floor so the rapt guests could admire the sultan's offering before proceeding to where Ash was sitting. The man extended the cushion and Ash accepted the dagger, handling it with the reverence such an exquisite piece of craftsmanship deserved.

"You are far too generous, Your Majesty," Ash said, modestly inclining his head.

Luca inched his hand toward the dagger, but Ash slipped the weapon into the far side of his belt before Luca could touch it, ignoring his friend's pout.

"There is one other gift I would seek to bestow upon you," Farouk said. "I am sure it has not escaped your notice that I am a man who possesses many priceless treasures."

Luca perked up, his dark eyes glinting with avarice.

"But I have discovered there is a treasure worth far more than silver or gold."

Rolling his eyes, Luca slumped back down on his cushion.

"And tonight it is my great honor to share that treasure with you."

Farouk clapped his hands, just as he did every night to summon the dancing girls.

The bronze doors at the west end of the hall came swinging open. As the guests craned their necks to see what new wonder might appear, an odd little frisson of foreboding danced down Clarinda's spine. She stole a glance at Ash to find him looking equally wary.

But it was only Solomon's towering form that filled the doorway.

Clarinda frowned, wondering why the eunuch would have been summoned from his duties in the harem for such an occasion.

That question was answered a moment later when Solomon stepped to the side, ushering in a line of women who marched single file to the far end of the room before turning to face the guests. Although the women wore silken veils to cover their noses and mouths, their low-cut bodices and clinging Turkish trousers ensured that all of their other charms were on full display.

Farouk's voice seemed to echo even more than usual. "In gratitude for your bravery, Burke the Younger, I bring before you a dozen of my most beautiful concubines. For a man to spend even one night in the arms of such a woman is to create a memory that will forever warm him. Tonight I offer you that memory . . . and a woman of your choosing to help you create it."

Farouk beamed at Ash, his white teeth gleaming in his swarthy face; Clarinda's bloodless fingers froze around the stem of her goblet.

She didn't realize she had ceased to breathe until Ash shook his head, smiling ruefully. "There is no need for such an extravagant reward, Your Majesty. While I appreciate your generosity more than you will ever know, I can assure you that your hospitality and goodwill are reward enough for one humble man."

While Clarinda breathed out a sigh of relief she did not care to examine, Luca's hand shot up as if he'd just been called on in class. "Pardon me, Your Majesty, but if the captain doesn't want—"

Ash grabbed the sleeve of Luca's robe and yanked his hand back down.

Farouk's smile slowly faded. A stunned silence descended over the hall.

"What did you expect, you naïve fool?" Seizing both the opportunity and the stage, Tarik surged to his feet, tossing a contemptuous look in Ash's direction. "The man is an infidel dog. He has no manners, no breeding, no respect for the traditions of our forefathers. He is little more than a savage!"

Spurred on by Tarik's snarled words, the guests began muttering among themselves, their glances toward Ash and Luca growing increasingly hostile.

"Silence!" Farouk thundered, cowing even the boldest of his guests. When he turned back to Ash, he spoke softly, but the warning edge in his voice was as sharp as the blade of the jeweled dagger. "Burke may not be familiar with our ways but he is no savage. I am sure he did not realize that to turn down such a gift would be considered a grave insult, both to me and to my ancestors."

Farouk's words left little doubt that if not corrected, Ash's insult might not only be grave, but fatal.

Ash did not shy away from the sultan's challenging gaze. "I humbly beg your forgiveness, Your Majesty. Your uncle, wise man that he is"—this said with a respectful nod toward the still-fuming Tarik—"is right. I am undeserving of such an extraordinary tribute, which is why I made the misguided effort to reject it. I swear upon the graves of my own ancestors that I have no desire to cast shame upon the exalted name of His Majesty. Or his ancestors." Ash rose to his feet and spread his arms wide, flashing the devil-may-care dimple Clarinda had never been able to resist. "I can assure you that I am only too eager to embrace your gift."

Unable to resist Ash's teasing leer, the guests relaxed, sending a ripple of laughter through the hall. Grinding his teeth in thwarted rage, Tarik sank back down to his cushion.

"Come, my brother," Farouk commanded Ash, his own relief palpable. "You will choose from among my women."

Ash offered him a bow more suited to a London ballroom. "It will be my pleasure."

As the two men approached the row of waiting women, the concubines' shameless preening made it clear that being the one chosen to warm the Englishman's bed for a night would not be considered something to be dreaded or feared but a coup to be much desired.

"They're all so beautiful," Poppy whispered in Clarinda's ear, the wistful note in her voice echoing the ache in Clarinda's heart.

Clarinda told herself she had no reason to be jealous. She had a man waiting for her once she escaped from this place. An honest man. A dependable man. A man who had patiently bided his time for almost ten years. A man who would never turn his back on her and walk away when she needed him the most.

Ash was welcome to spend the night in the arms of the woman of his choice. He did not belong to Clarinda. He never would and perhaps he never had.

As he took his own sweet time strolling along the line of women, favoring each one of them with an encouraging word and a tender smile, that litany played over and over in Clarinda's mind, accompanied by vivid images of one woman drawing him down on top of her, another raking her nails down the smooth, muscled planes of his back, a third licking her lush lips and shooting him a coy glance as she dropped to her knees before him.

Farouk trailed after him, his hands locked at the small of his back. He looked as proud as a

benevolent papa every time Ash paused to remark on the lustrous sheen of a woman's hair,
the graceful curve of her hip, the irresistible
charm of a flawless dimple of a navel set in a
slender waist. The guests followed their prog-
ress with equal fascination until they came to
the last woman in the row.

Luminous dark eyes glittered above the
deep purple silk of her veil, their kohl-lined
depths promising pleasures no man could resist. A proud toss of her head sent her glossy
midnight-black hair spilling down her back
until the feathery tips of it brushed the shapely
curve of her rump. Her rouged nipples jutted
proudly against the deliberately dampened
fabric of her bodice, as if to tempt every man
in the room to lean down and give them a lick
or a nibble.

Yasmin.

He was going to choose Yasmin.

And why not? With her exotic looks and
queenly bearing, Yasmin was by far the most
beautiful woman in the harem. And probably
the most beautiful woman in all of El Jadida.
According to the other women in the harem,
she possessed the skills to drive a man mad with
pleasure, to make him howl her name and forget
his own.

Clarinda closed her eyes, knowing she wouldn't be able to bear seeing the triumphant look on the woman's face when Ash took her by the hand and led her from the hall.

But, no, Clarinda thought. She was done with hiding. She'd spent the last nine years of her life shielding her heart from every blow, and what had she gained for her trouble? Nothing but a numb heart and a cold, lonely bed. If Ash was going to do this thing, then she was going to force herself to witness every second of it. If she had to watch him walk out of this room with Yasmin, had to imagine him doing to Yasmin what he had once done to her with such haunting tenderness and raw passion, then when the time came to stand before the altar with his brother, perhaps she would finally be able to give her heart to Max without reservations or regrets.

She opened her eyes just in time to see Ash lift a hand to gently brush the back of his knuckles against the smoothness of Yasmin's olive-skinned cheek. He had once caressed *her* cheek with identical tenderness. Had once gazed down at *her*, his eyes sparkling with the same seductive charm. Her determination nearly faltered but she forced herself to keep watching, her eyes as dry and hot as the desert air.

Almost as if sensing her regard, Ash turned away from Yasmin and the other women and looked directly at her. Their eyes met, his gaze as cool and calculating as any stranger's.

With the absolute confidence of Salome asking for the head of John the Baptist on a platter, he pointed directly at Clarinda and said, "I want her."

✢ Chapter Eighteen

The hall erupted in chaos.

One minute Ash was standing next to Farouk. The next he was shoved up against one of the marble columns with Farouk's powerful forearm pinning him to the column and the blade of the jeweled dagger Farouk had just given him pressed to his Adam's apple. Farouk had moved so quickly no one had even seen him snatch the weapon from the belt of Ash's robes. The sultan's upper lip was curled in a snarl. His broad chest heaved with rage.

As the guests leapt to their feet and scrambled to get out of the way, their alarmed cries mingling with the startled screams of the concubines, Farouk's guard rushed forward to surround the two men, scimitars drawn. Their master appeared to be in no danger of losing this particular skirmish, but they had obviously been trained not to take any chances.

"Get back!" Farouk roared through his clenched teeth. If Ashton Burke was going to die by anyone's hand on this night, it was clearly going to be his.

The guards reluctantly retreated while Farouk's uncle drew nearer, plainly delighted by this unexpected turn of events. Tarik jerked his head toward Luca. Two of the guards roughly seized Luca by the arms and yanked him to his feet, thankful to have something destructive to do.

Clarinda was halfway across the hall before she even realized her feet had moved. Solomon intercepted her, wrapping one of his massive ebony arms around her waist and scooping her clear off the floor.

"Let me go, damn you!" She twisted in his grip and clawed at his arm with her fingernails, desperate to stop Farouk from slitting Ash's throat right before her eyes.

"Compose yourself, woman. If the sultan sees your face right now, both you and your captain will taste the bite of his blade before this night is done."

As that mellifluous voice poured into her ear, Clarinda went limp, stunned to realize the eunuch not only wasn't mute but spoke the King's English as well as she did. Solomon gently lowered her feet to the floor, rewarding the wide-eyed look she cast him over her shoulder with an encouraging nod. He withdrew his arm from her waist but she could still feel his presence behind her, as solid and immovable as a boulder.

Poppy crept up next to them. All of the color had drained from her plump cheeks, leaving her as pale as a Dresden figurine.

"I don't see what the problem is," Ash said coolly, as if a thin trickle of blood weren't already easing its way out from under the deadly tip of Farouk's blade. "You told me I could have the woman of my choice. I choose Miss Cardew."

"Miss Cardew is not mine to give. She is my guest!"

"No, she's not. That's just a pretty lie you've been telling each other for the past three months. She belongs to you just as surely as any concubine. You bought her from a slaver. You paid for her with your own gold. And you have every intention of getting back the pound of flesh she owes you when you take her to your bed. You may choose to call her your 'guest' or even your 'wife' if it pleases you, but we both know she'll never be anything more than your whore."

As the fragile illusion Farouk and Clarinda had so carefully maintained crumbled to dust beneath the ruthless flick of Ash's tongue, Farouk looked stricken. "Why?" he asked hoarsely, his anguished gaze searching Ash's impassive face. "Why are you doing this? I thought you were my friend. My brother . . ."

"And I thought you were a man of honor. You promised me a night with one of your women. The woman of *my* choice. Are you going to insult the memory of your ancestors by going back on your word now? By breaking your oath before all of these witnesses and Allah himself?"

Dear God, thought Clarinda, pressing her fingertips to her lips in a vain attempt to still their trembling. What was the fool trying to do? Goad Farouk into killing him? Even Luca, still hanging helplessly in the grip of Farouk's guards, had gone as pale as parchment beneath his olive tan.

Tarik circled the two men like a rabid jackal. "Do you not see? This is what happens when you are foolish enough to welcome a hungry dog into your home. He bides his time until he finds an opportunity to help himself to what is yours." Stopping directly in Farouk's line of sight, Tarik shrugged. "But the infidel is right. You cannot break your oath. The woman is his. At least for this night."

Farouk slowly turned his head to look at Clarinda, his white-knuckled grip on the hilt of the dagger unwavering. "Give me the word," he rasped out. "One word and I will cut him down where he stands."

Ignoring the blade biting into his throat, Ash also turned his head to look at her. If he was worried about having his fate balanced in her delicate hands, he showed no sign of it. His was the face of a man who had his finger poised on the trigger of a gun and absolutely no compunction about pulling it. The steely resolve in his eyes had probably been the last sight many of his opponents had seen on the battlefield.

You'll have to trust me, he had told her on the day he had snuck into the harem.

You always did have a habit of asking the impossible, she had replied, without fully realizing just how impossible.

She turned her sorrowful gaze back to Farouk before saying softly, "I cannot ask you to do that. You are a man of honor who has treated me with nothing but courtesy. I cannot be the one to bring shame to your name by asking you to break your oath or murder a man in cold blood."

Farouk slowly lowered his arm. The dagger slid from his limp fingers to clatter on the tiles. Dropping his head as if he could no longer bear to look at her, he said, "Take her, Solomon. Have the women prepare her."

As the eunuch's hands closed around Clarinda's forearms from behind, Tarik clapped a hand on his nephew's shoulder, a conciliatory smile thinning his lips. "Perhaps this is all for the best, my son. Virgins can be so tiresome. After being mounted by this mongrel, the English bitch will no doubt be panting for the more civilized attentions of a real man."

Both Ash and Farouk lunged forward, but it was Farouk's enormous fist that connected with his uncle's jaw first, laying the man out cold on the tiles.

As Solomon gently urged Clarinda past an ashen-faced Poppy and toward the door, Clarinda dared one last glance over her shoulder at Ash. She didn't know what she expected to find, but the look he gave her wasn't the relieved look of someone who had just pulled off a carefully calculated bluff, but the triumphant look of a man who was finally about to take full possession of what was rightfully his.

Poppy slipped out from behind the marble column to find Farouk standing all alone in the ruins of his celebration. His guests had fled, his guards had been dismissed, and his concubines had been ushered back to the confines of the harem.

The tiled floor was littered with scattered cushions and crushed blooms, their fragile edges already beginning to curl and turn brown. The guttering flames of the oil lamps mounted on the wall sent shadows creeping slowly across the floor to swallow every drop of light in their path.

Poppy drifted nearer to Farouk. If she had been an assassin, it would have been only too easy for her to slide a dagger between his ribs. He had the look of a man who had already taken a blade to the heart.

Aching to comfort him in some way, she drew close enough to reach out and touch the sleeve of his robe. "I'm so sorry," she whispered. "I know you loved her."

Jerking away from her touch, he turned on her, his dark eyes blazing with fury. "What do you know of love? You are nothing but a silly virgin who hides from the world behind your spectacles and the skirts of your friend! The only thing you will ever know of love will come from mooning over some ridiculous story or poem where a man finds the one woman who can forever satisfy the yearning in his heart."

Although his cruel words dealt a painful blow to her heart, she stood her ground. "I'd rather believe in those stories than waste my life searching for love in the arms of one lover after another but never finding it."

He seized her by the shoulders, jerking her up until their faces were only a scant few inches apart. "Between the pages of a book, there may only be one woman for every man, but between the sheets of his sleeping couch, any woman can satisfy a man's lust."

"Any woman?" she whispered. "Even a woman like me?"

His gaze dropped to her trembling lips for a dangerous moment, then he bit off a guttural Arabic oath and shoved her away from him. He turned and stormed from the hall, his robes rippling around his ankles with each of his long, angry strides.

As Poppy watched him go, a rush of warm tears fogged up the lenses of her spectacles. She reached up to tug them off, thinking that the world was indeed a much kinder place when one couldn't see so clearly.

⚜ Chapter Nineteen

For the first time since arriving at the sultan's palace, Clarinda felt like a prisoner. Solomon marched her past the expressionless guards and through the doors of the harem, his grip on her upper arm gentle but as unyielding as an iron cuff. The doors swung shut behind them with a hollow clang, the sound echoing with chilling finality.

Clarinda had been dying to pepper the eunuch with questions about his timely warning ever since they had left the hall. But knowing the palace walls were riddled with secret passages and peepholes, she hadn't dared to do more than shoot him a quizzical glance.

His sad, wise eyes had stared straight ahead, and his broad, placid face had betrayed nothing, leaving her to doubt her own senses.

As Solomon led her through the main hall of

the harem, the women silently parted ranks as if a condemned criminal were passing among them. The other concubines hadn't even made their way back to the harem yet, but as always in this place, word of what had happened had traveled to the ears of the harem's occupants as if on wings. Clarinda could feel their knowing gazes on her, some envious, some pitying, some gloating with satisfaction. No doubt some among them believed she was about to get exactly what she deserved for stealing their master's attention away from them.

We both know she'll never be anything more than your whore.

Ash's heartless words seemed to echo what they all must be thinking—that this night would mark the end of her special status in Farouk's eyes. After being used by the Englishman, she would be forever sullied and unfit to be the sultan's wife. She would be no better than Yasmin or any of the other concubines who had been paraded before the guests at the celebration and put on display like a stable of prize fillies. The next time Farouk entertained an honored visitor to the palace, she could be the one offered up to tend him in his bath or warm his bed.

Clarinda cast the stairs leading up to the haven of her alcove a longing glance as they passed, but Solomon's resolute steps did not slow.

It seemed he had other plans for her on this night.

He led her down a long, narrow passageway she'd never traveled before. As they approached the door at the end of the hall, it swung open as if guided by invisible hands. Two women garbed all in black stood in the flickering lamplight of the chamber, waiting to receive her. If Ash had chosen Yasmin, would they have been waiting for her as well?

Solomon gave her a somber bow before backing into the shadows of the passageway, his dark eyes as unreadable as chips of polished obsidian. One of the women reached past Clarinda and gently closed the door in his face.

Although Farouk had commanded Solomon to have his women prepare her, Clarinda knew that nothing in this world could prepare her to spend an entire night in Ashton Burke's company.

She stood as still as a marble statue as the women descended upon her, their gnarled hands efficiently stripping her of her garments until she stood naked before them. Lifting her chin, she stared straight ahead, refusing to quail with fright or shame. She had no choice but to go along with this charade if she didn't want to cast suspicion on Ash or herself.

One of the women removed the circlet of beaten gold from her brow and began to run a pearl-handled brush through her hair in long, languorous strokes, while the other poured warm rivers of sandalwood oil over her skin and massaged it into her frozen muscles. Their touch was kind but impersonal, as if they were preparing a sacrifice for the god of some pagan altar.

Clarinda tried not to flinch as one of them brought out an earthenware pot and dabbed a spot of crimson rouge on each of her nipples. It hadn't occurred to her until that moment that the rouge Yasmin used with such a free hand had been spiked with some sort of abrasive herb. Clarinda's nipples tingled and puckered beneath its kiss, the unfamiliar sting disconcerting but not entirely unpleasant.

She had to close her eyes when one of the women knelt in front of her and drew a jeweled comb through the silvery blond nest of curls at the V of her thighs. She opened them to find the woman trading the comb for a fresh vial of oil. The old woman poured some of the oil in her withered palm, then smeared it on her fingers.

As she reached to part Clarinda's curls with those bony fingers, Clarinda's hand shot out to capture her wrist.

"No," she said firmly. Some indignities she would not submit to, no matter the cost.

The woman's wrinkled face fell. "We have heard the English can be quite savage in their attentions. The oil will ease his passage and make it easier for you."

Her companion held out the pot of rouge. "And this will show him exactly where to touch to please you the most."

A little shudder ran through Clarinda as she imagined the sting of that concoction against her most sensitive flesh. As she gazed into the hopeful dark eyes of her attendants, she had to fight an absurd desire to burst out laughing. She sincerely doubted a man with Ash's experience required a road map to find his way around the female body. If half of what the scandal sheets said was true, he could give these women a guided tour.

When she continued to shake her head and firmly push their hands away, the women sighed and clucked their disappointment but quickly moved on to their next duty, which was to drape Clarinda in a shift so sheer it made what Yasmin usually wore when strutting around the harem look like something Miss Throckmorton would have worn to a dignitary's funeral.

Clarinda's courage did not begin to falter until the women each took one of her icy hands in theirs and led her toward the piece of furniture that dominated the chamber. The plush sleeping couch with its silken sheets and scattering of pillows and bolsters in all shapes, sizes, and colors was twice the size of her own and was so decadent and sumptuous it could have been designed for only one purpose.

And that purpose was not sleep.

Clarinda hesitated, her knees betraying her. When confronted with the reality of what everyone expected to happen on that couch, it was far too easy to forget that this was all for show, the first act in Ash's daring plan to rescue her.

Wasn't it?

In that moment before Solomon had led her from the hall, Ash's face had been the face of a stranger, its rugged planes set in ruthless lines she barely recognized. How well did she truly know the man he had become? What if their years apart had changed him more than she had ever suspected? He and his brother had been at odds for a very long time. Just how badly did he hate Maximillian? Or even her?

If he had even the slightest inclination to take advantage of the situation in which they now found themselves, there was no one to stop him. Here in this place where women existed solely to satisfy the needs and hungers of a man, she was as much at his mercy as she had been at Farouk's.

A dark shiver of mingled fear and longing raked her.

The women tugged her numb feet back into motion, urging her to turn and sit on the edge of the couch. When one of them poured a stream of liquid from an earthenware flask into a golden goblet, then tipped the goblet to her lips, she did not protest. Perhaps a little wine would take the edge off her nerves and make her less inclined toward flights of fancy.

But the instant the liquid in the goblet touched her tongue, she knew she had made a grave error. The thick brew was both sickly sweet and sharply bitter. She tried to push the goblet away, but one of the women grabbed her wrists, her wiry hands possessing surprising strength, while the other turned the goblet up, forcing her to drink deeply or choke.

By the time she finally managed to knock the goblet away, sending it flying from the woman's hand to roll across the floor, it was nearly empty.

She glared at them. "What are you trying to do? Kill me? What in the devil was that foul stuff?" Resisting the unladylike urge to spit out the last mouthful, she swiped her lips with the back of her hand, her throat burning and her eyes watering.

She blinked away the tears only to find the four women still swimming in front of her eyes. *That's odd*, she thought. Just a minute ago, she would have sworn there were only two of them. Or was it three?

One of the women tenderly stroked her hair. "Do not fight the effects of the elixir, my child. It is an ancient recipe, handed down to us from our mothers and their mothers before them. It will dull any pain you might feel." The woman's voice had begun to echo as if it were coming from the bottom of a deep well, and Clarinda had to strain to make sense of what she was saying.

One of the other women gave her a sly smile. "It will also make you crave his touch. You will be like a wild creature, begging him to do whatever he likes with you. And you will be begging to do whatever pleases him."

"No," Clarinda whispered, dismay swelling within her. Didn't they know that no elixir in the world was powerful enough to dull the pain

Ash was capable of causing her? And she certainly didn't need any ancient potion to make her crave his touch.

"It is a very rare and costly elixir. That is why we save it for the virgins," one of them whispered.

Clarinda opened her mouth to tell them she was no virgin but was shocked when nothing but a shrill giggle came out. She tried to clap a hand over her mouth to contain it, but her hand felt as heavy as an anvil. It only made it as far as her waist before falling uselessly back into her lap as if no longer attached to her wrist, which only made her giggle harder.

Exchanging knowing looks, the women (all six of them) eased her back on the nest of pillows as if she were a lifeless doll designed solely for their amusement. She thought about protesting their high-handed treatment of her, but it was so much more pleasant to lie in dreamy contentment gazing up at the erotic frescoes painted on the plaster ceiling.

In the mural directly over Clarinda's head, it was not a woman on her knees before a man but a man on his knees before a woman. A dark-eyed beauty with a flowing mane of sable hair reclined before a turbaned warrior, her hips propped high on a nest of ruby red pillows, her plump thighs splayed in wanton abandon. Her eyes were closed and her round face was a study in sensual indolence, as if her entire being were concentrated on the gratification his mouth was bringing her in that moment. As if that wasn't shocking enough, the next mural in the fresco revealed a second man watching the two lovers and holding his exaggerated manhood in his clenched hand as he patiently awaited his turn to pleasure her.

"My goodness," Clarinda murmured, blinking up at the scandalous, yet oddly stirring, vision with frank fascination. "Do you think she knows he's watching?"

"Oh, she knows, my lamb," one of the women said with an earthy chuckle. "She knows."

The sheer fabric of Clarinda's shift offered meager protection against the night breeze drifting through the open window. Her flesh was becoming so attuned to even the slightest stimulus that she found herself writhing beneath its sultry caress as if beneath the touch of a living hand.

"Rest, my child," the other woman whispered. "You will have need of all your strength on this night."

Heeding her wise words, Clarinda sighed and returned to contemplating the mural, not realizing that her own face was already beginning to mirror the blissful expression of the woman in the painting.

The last time Ash had been blindfolded he had been facing a firing squad.

I suppose it shouldn't have surprised me that there was a woman involved in your latest little contretemps.

Isn't there always?

Max's contemptuous words and his own cavalier reply echoed through his memory, causing a grim smile to flirt with Ash's lips. Perhaps his brother wouldn't be so quick to condemn him now that it wasn't just any woman involved, but Max's own bride-to-be.

As two of the sultan's hulking harem guards marched him deeper into the belly of the palace, their impersonal hands gripping his arms just above the elbow, all he could do was trust that his host truly was a man of his word and a black-hooded executioner wasn't waiting for Ash at the end of his trek.

If he had been sitting on Farouk's throne, he might have been tempted to arrange just such a nasty little surprise for himself. Claiming Clarinda so boldly and so publicly had been a carefully calculated wager on Ash's part, more dangerous than any he had ever made at the faro table or on the battlefield. He could just as easily have lost his head and his life along with Farouk's regard.

He was still haunted by the look of raw anguish he had glimpsed on Farouk's face when the sultan had found himself cruelly betrayed by a man he had believed to be his friend. He hoped like hell that Clarinda was worth the price he had paid for her.

Each measured step brought him closer to his destiny, whatever that might be. He would have tried to refuse the blindfold but knew no man besides the sultan or his eunuchs was allowed to pass through the harem and live. Even with the blindfold securely in place, he was still only allowed to approach that sacred bastion of feminine charms through a series of complicated detours, backtracks, and secret passageways. Neither Farouk nor his guards had any reason to suspect he had already visited it once.

The eunuchs also had no way of knowing he was counting every step they took and committing each turn to memory, a talent that had always served him well when a hasty retreat or escape became necessary. With any luck, he and Clarinda would be retracing his steps together before this night was done.

The cloying smell of incense grew more over-powering with each breath he took, adding to the sense of disorientation caused by being led forward by invisible hands into absolute dark-ness. Ash didn't know whether to be relieved or alarmed when the eunuchs finally brought him to a stumbling halt and released his arms. The blindfold was whisked away. He blinked rap-idly, his eyes adjusting with surprising ease to the hazy light.

They were standing at the end of a corridor that ended in a single bronze-banded door. A guttering oil lamp mounted high on the wall cast flickering shadows everywhere he looked.

Instead of a black-hooded executioner wield-ing a freshly sharpened scimitar, a pair of stooped old women were waiting to greet him. Ash eyed them warily as they beamed up at him, baring their toothless gums. Their gazes raked him from head to toe, their beady little eyes glowing with an unabashed appreciation that made him regret shedding the native robes and donning his own riding breeches and lawn shirt.

He stole a glance behind him only to discover his escorts had soundlessly melted back into the shadows.

Perhaps Farouk was more diabolical than he'd anticipated. Perhaps the sultan planned to take his revenge by turning him over to these two randy little crones instead of allowing him to spend the night in Clarinda's bed. A faint shudder traveled through him as he imagined them climbing atop him to gum his shrinking flesh.

One of the women captured his hand, drawing him toward the door. "Come, good sir. She is waiting for you."

Ash blew out a silent sigh of relief. Apparently the women were only there to steer him to Clarinda.

Eyeing him coyly, her companion patted his other arm. "Be gentle with her. She is a tender blossom."

Ash barely resisted the urge to laugh. Clarinda had never been a tender blossom but always a rose in full bloom, her soft, velvety petals hiding dangerous thorns. God knew his heart had been pricked by them often enough.

He pressed an open palm to his heart. "I promise to be the perfect gentleman," he vowed, hearing his brother's skeptical bark of laughter in his head as he did so.

Exchanging a glance, the women bobbed their heads in approval, then tugged open the door and ushered him through it.

Without giving him time to get a clear look at what was waiting for him in the chamber, the more withered of the two women caught his forearm in her bony claw. Drawing him down to the level of her mouth, she croaked, "Have no fear. She will not resist you. We made sure of that."

Before he could ask her what her cryptic words meant, both of the women withdrew, gently drawing the door shut behind them. He heard the decisive clink of a key turning in a lock, sealing his fate.

"Damn it all!" he swore, whirling around to face the door.

He waited until he heard the women's shuffling footsteps move away from the door before seizing the handle and testing the strength of the lock.

He hadn't anticipated being treated as a prisoner himself. With every window in the harem covered by an impenetrable web of iron latticework, he and Clarinda might as well have been locked away in the deepest dungeon of the fortress. He rested his clenched fist against the thick wood of the door and lowered his head, breathing harder than he should have been.

A throaty little moan came out of the shadows behind him. His nape prickled with foreboding.

He slowly turned. The corners of the octagonal chamber were draped in mysterious shad-

ows, which only made the spill of moonlight
through the latticework that much more dramatic. Its gentle glow poured over the sleeping couch in the center of the room, creating a
pattern as delicate as Brussels lace against the
flawless ivory skin of the woman reclining on its
lavender sheets.

No, not a woman but a goddess—silvery,
ethereal, irresistible—the embodiment of man's
eternal fascination with the moon. She lay cross-
wise, the shimmering ribbons of her unbound
hair spilling over the edge of the couch. A couch
that could just as easily have been some sort of
enchanted bower.

"Clarinda?" he whispered, the passion-
roughened timbre of his voice nearly unrecognizable, even to himself.

When she didn't respond, he took one step
toward her, then another. If he had been born
with even one iota of his brother's prudence, he
would be pounding on the door, demanding to
be let out. But it was too late to stop the forward
momentum of his steps.

Perhaps it had always been too late.

As he drew nearer to the couch, he saw that
Clarinda was wearing nothing but a diaphanous
scrap of silk that clung to every curve and hollow of her exquisite body, leaving little to the

imagination. Especially the imagination of a man who had been exploring every inch of her flesh in his dreams for nearly a decade.

Some shortsighted fool had decided her pert nipples weren't enticing enough without enhancement, so they had been darkened with crimson rouge and left to thrust boldly against the sheer silk. As if that sight wasn't enough to make a man's mouth water with unbridled hunger, one of her knees was cocked to the side, inviting the silk to pool between her thighs and offering even the most causal observer a teasing peek at the silvery blond nest of curls beneath. Every exposed inch of her skin had been oiled to a satiny sheen, making a man dream of how easily his hands might glide over her . . . and into her.

Ash's burning gaze drifted back to her face. Her plump lips were moist and slightly parted, perfectly poised for kissing and other even more forbidden pleasures. She was gazing up at the ceiling, her eyes dreamy and unfocused, her arms flung wide as if to embrace an invisible lover.

As if sensing his presence with an instinct deeper than hearing or sight, she slowly turned her head and looked directly at him. She had the sleepy, sloe-eyed look of a temptress who knew exactly what she wanted and would do whatever was needed to make sure she got it. She was Delilah, Bathsheba, and Eve all rolled into one. She was woman, distilled down to its most primal essence. Drawing a man's rigid cock to her like a moth to a flame.

Ash closed the last of the distance between them in two long strides. Bracing his weight on one knee between her splayed thighs, he seized her by the shoulders and yanked her up to face him. Her head lolled to the side, a fetching little scowl puckering her brow as she struggled to focus on his face.

"Oh, sweetheart," he whispered hoarsely, mesmerized by the tiny pinpoints of her pupils swimming in the clover-green seas of her eyes, "what in the name of God have they done to you?"

She leaned forward to press the softness of her lips to his throat, her husky giggle igniting a dizzying rush of lust low in his belly. "Never mind that. The question, Ashton Burke, is what are *you* going to do to me?"

Chapter Twenty

During his military career and in the years following, Ash had been bayoneted through the shoulder twice, shot three times, and gored in the calf by a charging boar. He had contracted a tropical fever that had soared so high he hadn't remembered his own name for a fortnight and had narrowly escaped being roasted in a Pygmy's cook pot. But all of those trials were just a stroll in Hyde Park on a lazy Saturday afternoon compared to the fresh hell that was Clarinda's hot little mouth nibbling its way down the broad column of his throat.

He groaned aloud as her clever tongue darted out to flick his skin.

"Mmm . . ." She was practically purring with satisfaction. "You taste so good. Salty and sweet and spicy all at the same time." Her mouth drifted lower, teasing the crisp whorls of hair peeping out from the open throat of his shirt. "Why, I could just gobble you right up!"

Ash gazed helplessly down at the top of her head, paralyzed by a staggeringly detailed mental image of her doing just that. Taking advantage of his immobility, her greedy hands seized both sides of his shirt at the throat, jerking the thin lawn apart with such unbridled enthusiasm he could hear the stitching give way. As she ducked her head to sample the swath of golden skin she had exposed, he bit off an oath that described exactly what he was aching to do to her.

Recapturing her shoulders, he drew her upright, giving her a slight shake as he did so. "Look at me, Clarinda. I need you to concentrate on what I'm saying."

Unfortunately, she tried to achieve that aim by lowering her hungry gaze to his mouth. Which made it nearly impossible for him to concentrate on what he was saying.

"When Farouk offered me one of his women for the night, I had no choice but to seize the opportunity. I thought if I could get into the harem with an entire night at our disposal, then I could find a way to get you and Poppy out. But I'm afraid I've made a grave miscalculation. They've locked us in here together." Wrapping one arm around her shoulders to balance her weight, he cradled her chin in his other hand and gently tipped her head back, forcing her to meet his gaze. "I'm trying to make you understand. You're not yourself right now."

She blinked up at him, looking genuinely perplexed. "Then who am I?"

The woman my brother is going to marry.

As that damning reminder echoed through his mind, Ash sighed. "The women who were here before me . . . they gave you some sort of drug. From the condition of your pupils, I'm guessing it contained opium and some manner of aphrodisiac."

Ash had heard about the dangerous effects of such concoctions before, deep in the jungles of Africa. He had been told tales of decent, morally upstanding women being stripped of their every inhibition, behaving like cats in heat, literally backing up and lifting their skirts to offer their wares to any man who passed by.

Clarinda didn't seem the least bit concerned about the urgency of their situation. "Ah, yes!" she exclaimed, her eyes lighting up. "That must have been the nasty brew they forced me to drink! They said it would make me crave your touch. That it would turn me into a wild creature, begging you to do whatever you liked with me. And that I'd be begging to do whatever would please you the most. Is all of that true?"

Ash had to clear his throat twice before he could answer her. "Yes, sweeting, it's true. The drug they gave you is going to make you feel things . . . want things . . . do things you wouldn't normally do."

Her eyes widened. "Do you mean you could . . ."

He nodded grimly.

"And I would . . ."

He nodded again.

She looked fascinated instead of horrified. "So you could do anything you wanted to me?"

"Anything at all." Despite his best efforts to restrain it, his gaze flicked downward, drinking in the saucy thrust of her nipples against the sheer fabric, the teasing shadows where the silk was draped at the juncture of her thighs. He jerked his gaze back to her face, the hint of a growl deepening his voice. *"Everything."*

"Would I remember any of it in the morning?"

"I don't know. It depends on the nature and potency of what they gave you."

She pondered his words for a moment, then lifted one shoulder in an airy shrug. "Then what's stopping you?"

Before Ash had time to ask himself that question or catch his breath, she was on him again, clutching at his shirt and rubbing her face against his throat like a needy little kitten, peppering the rigid jut of his jaw with a tantalizing line of tender, openmouthed kisses.

He closed his eyes, his chest heaving with a ragged breath as he allowed himself a moment to savor the wonder that was Clarinda in full bloom with nary a thorn in sight.

He had faced many temptations in his life and had discovered few worth resisting. In most cases, the rewards of surrender far outweighed the consequences. He had certainly never faced a temptation with a more enticing reward. Even if the consequence was his mortal soul, he couldn't be entirely sure it wasn't too steep of a price to pay.

Clarinda's pebbled nipples grazed the muscled planes of his chest through the thin lawn of his shirt, forcing him to grit his teeth against a shudder of pure lust. Here in this place so far from any civilization they knew, it would be all too easy for him to throw off the chains of convention. To abandon centuries of restraint and revert back to the primal state that allowed a man to ravish a woman simply because he possessed the will and the physical strength to do so.

He already knew exactly what Max would expect him to do under these circumstances. He could almost see the look of disgust on his brother's face, the contempt in his cool gray eyes.

Clarinda twined her lithe arms around his neck, her beguiling kisses skating dangerously near the corner of his mouth. If he allowed her seeking lips to find his, there would be no saving either of them.

Using every ounce of the meager self-control God had given him, Ash reached behind him to unhook Clarinda's clinging arms from his neck. Striving to keep his motions brisk and efficient — no easy feat when he was already as hard as a rock — he pushed her down on the pillows, pinning her wrists on either side of her head in the improbable hope of keeping her hands off him long enough to allow the blood to start flowing to his brain again.

Visibly delighted to find herself on her back with him looming over her, she wiggled her hips and bit her bottom lip in brazen invitation, her eyes sparkling with mischief.

It was no struggle for Ash to keep his expression stern. "You might not remember any of this in the morning, but I would. Once you regained your senses, you would hate me. And I would hate myself even more."

"Don't be ridiculous! I could never hate you!"

"What you're feeling right now has absolutely nothing to do with me. Trust me. When it comes to assuaging the hungers you're suffering right now, any man would do."

Her smile faded. Her lower lip began to tremble ever so slightly, making him feel like the meanest ogre in the world. "Is that what you believe? That any man would do? That's simply not true. It's always been you, Ash. Only you."

Ash had already committed himself to enduring whatever physical torture she might dole out, but he had no defenses against the unabashed adoration in her big green eyes. He ought to be impressed that she could still lie so convincingly while under the influence of opium and God knew what else.

"What about Max?" he asked grimly.

She gazed up at him blankly.

"You do remember Max, don't you? *My* brother? *Your* fiancé?"

"Oh, Maximillian!" A fond smile lit up her face. "Your brother is such a dear. Have I ever told you what a dear he was?"

"No," Ash growled. "And I'd rather you didn't."

Knowing it wasn't going to be possible for him to maintain his stern demeanor for long with her flat on her back beneath him, he tugged her to a sitting position. "What I want you to remember in the morning are all of the things I *didn't* do to you so that you can tell my brother about every one of them in great detail."

"Then what will we do tonight to pass the time?" She sat up on her knees to face him in the moonlight, all eagerness and big, dewy eyes.

"Wait for the effects of whatever they gave you to wear off."

"How long will that take?"

"An eternity," he muttered, propping his back against a plush purple bolster. He'd had enough experience with the more potent aphrodisiacs himself to know things were likely to get much worse before they got better.

For the both of them.

Despite his concerted effort to keep Clarinda at arm's length, she couldn't seem to keep her hands off him. When he folded his arms over his chest and tried to hold her at bay with a forbidding glower, she began to pet the front of his shirt as if he were some sort of faithful hound. Even that innocent touch was enough to send shock waves of heat shooting straight to his groin.

She leaned forward, swaying slightly on her knees, and whispered loudly in his ear, "Did you know it was possible for a woman to pleasure herself?"

The corner of his mouth curved in a reluctant smile. "I've heard rumors to that effect."

Clarinda sank back on her heels and stole a look over her shoulder, as if to make sure no one was eavesdropping on their conversation. "They taught me how to do it. Would you care to see?"

"God, yes," he breathed. She reached for herself, but he grabbed her wrist before her hand could arrive at its destination. "I mean, hell no!"

If she touched herself in front of him, he was going to explode right then and there.

His refusal earned him a brief pout, but Clarinda's disappointment was short-lived. "When the women of the harem were teaching me all of the ways a woman can pleasure a man," she said softly, inclining her head so that the fall of her hair veiled the flushed curve of her cheek, "I tried to think of Max, honestly I did. But it was always you I saw in my mind. Doing all of the things we never had a chance to try before. Me touching you. Kissing you." She lifted her wistful gaze to his face, her wayward hand drifting over his folded arms and down to the tightly clenched muscles of his abdomen. "Putting my mouth on you."

Ash stopped breathing altogether, mesmerized by her confession. He made a valiant effort but could not stop his gaze from dropping to the parted pink petals of her lips, from imagining what they would look like—and feel like—wrapped around him.

"If it would make things more . . . bearable for you, I could show you what they taught us," she offered earnestly. "Would you believe they used a cucumber?" Another one of those adorably sly glances over her shoulder. "I pretended to be disinterested but I smuggled one out when no one was looking and took it to my alcove so I could practice. I might not be as adept at it as Yasmin, but I'm sure you could talk me through it. After all, don't they always say practice makes perfect?" A husky little giggle escaped her. "I used to spend all of those hours practicing my scales on the pianoforte just to please Papa. There's no reason I can't practice to please you, is there?"

"Yes. No. Yes," he blurted out, tearing his gaze away from her mouth. Her oh-so-soft, oh-so-luscious, oh-so-tempting mouth. "There are any number of reasons why you can't *practice* on me." Oddly enough, even as he said the words, he couldn't think of a single one. He couldn't think at all.

As if sensing his mounting distress, she reached up to caress his face, her expression tender and her eyes darkened with sympathy.

"This is all so unfair. I can only imagine how difficult this must be for you." He didn't even realize her other hand had escaped his grip until she brushed her fingertips over the part of him already straining to escape the front placket of his trousers.

Ash had somehow managed to stop her from touching herself, but no force in heaven or on earth could have given him the strength to stop her from touching him. He couldn't have moved in that moment if a stone block had been about to tumble from the sky and crush him to death. Not that there was any need for a stone block. As Clarinda curled her fingers around him, stroking his rigid length through the snug fabric of his trousers with bewitching boldness, he thought he was going to die right then and there.

"Please, Ash," she whispered, the wild look in her eye warning him the effects of the aphrodisiac were just beginning to make themselves fully known. "I can't wait anymore. It's been so long . . . too long. I want you . . . I need you . . ."

How many nights had he lain awake and dreamed of her whispering those very words? It was so hard to deny her anything when she was looking at him like that. He had only done it once, and he had spent every moment since then keenly regretting it.

He sat as still as a marble statue as she slid into his lap, neatly straddling him. Now it wasn't her hand pressed against him but the damp heat between her thighs. She wasn't wearing any undergarments beneath the shift, and he could smell her desire. It was more powerful and beguiling than any exotic perfume or oil — Musk of Clarinda, its sole intent to drive a man wild with lust. To turn him into a ravening beast with only one thing on his mind. If Ash could have found a way to bottle it, he could have made a fortune.

Tugging up the hem of his shirt with her other hand, she writhed against him, making helpless little sounds deep in her throat. "It's so very hot in here. Aren't you hot?"

As she rubbed the fulsome weight of her breasts against his chest, Ash had never been so hot, not even when the tropical fever had raged through his body, robbing him of both his senses and his name.

"I know you don't care for me anymore, but there's no need for you to be so cruel. Oh, please, Ash . . . won't you help me? I'm on fire down there . . . burning . . . burning . . ." Clarinda was shivering and crying now, nearly incoherent with need. "I want . . . I need . . ." A ragged moan tore from her throat, the piteous sound arrowing straight through his heart.

Her shaking hands reached between them, fumbling clumsily with the fastenings of his trousers. All he had to do was lean back on his elbows and let her have her way.

In this state there would be nothing she wouldn't let him do to her, nothing she wouldn't do to him. He would be able to use her nubile body to fulfill his darkest and most erotic fantasies, including the ones she had already fulfilled in his dreams a hundred times before.

It was no longer possible for him to pretend she wouldn't know what he had done to her. If he unleashed himself on her now, there wouldn't be a muscle anywhere in her body that wouldn't know she had been loved . . . and loved in every way that a man could love a woman. If she tried to swear she didn't remember a moment of it, they would both know she was lying.

Ash could still remember chasing her through the meadow on a beautiful spring day while she teasingly made him beg for the simple favor of a kiss. It was his turn now. He could tease her, make her beg, shatter her pride. He could bring the high-and-mighty Miss Clarinda Cardew to her knees and punish her with pleasure for every transgression she had ever committed against him.

As the irresistible temptation of Clarinda's

mouth descended on his, turning his face away from her kiss was one of the most difficult things Ash had ever made himself do.

"Shhh," he murmured, wrapping his arms tightly around her and rocking her like a baby. "It's all right, angel. Everything will be all right."

He knew what he had to do. Knew there was only one way to take the edge off of her need. Even if doing so might kill him.

Perhaps if he thought of it as some sort of scientific experiment, something to be dissected with clinical precision in a paper delivered before the Geographical Society of London, he might survive. Perhaps then he could remove his own emotions, his own desires, his own savage need to possess her—to bury himself in the softness she was still grinding against him—from the equation.

Ignoring her whimpered protest, he urged her around in his lap until she was sitting between his splayed legs with her back pressed to his chest. He slid one arm around her waist, gently but firmly imprisoning her in place.

She dug her fingernails into his muscled forearm. Her breath hitched in a shuddering sob. "W-w-what are you doing?"

As one of her helpless tears splashed on his arm, he knew beyond the shadow of any doubt that he was making the right decision. For her. For himself. Perhaps even for Max. "Taking care of you," he whispered, sweeping aside the moonlit fall of her hair and pressing his mouth to the graceful column of her throat. He might deny himself a taste of her lips, but he could not resist sampling her sweet-smelling skin.

She settled back against him, her unspoken trust in him more touching than anything that had come before.

Forcing himself to ignore the enticing weight of her breasts resting against his forearm, he slipped a hand between her legs. He didn't have to coax her into spreading her thighs for him. They fell apart of their own volition as she let out a sharp cry and arched off the couch, pressing herself into the cup of his hand. He gently squeezed, molding the sheer silk of the shift to that enticing mound and acclimating her to the shock of his touch.

Her flesh felt feverish beneath his hand, hot enough to scorch. He didn't dare let his hand slip beneath the shift. He was too desperate to get any part of himself inside her again, even if it was only his finger. Or fingers. She was already so wet for him that the silk was clinging to her like a second skin.

Even the most callow of lads could easily have located the hooded little bud tucked between the delicate petals of her womanhood. And Ash was no callow lad.

He brushed the pad of his longest finger over that bud only to find it as hard and swollen as a ripe cherry just begging to be plucked by a man's finger . . . or his tongue. He had hoped to bring the fires that were burning her alive under control, but the stroke of his fingertip against that exquisitely sensitive bundle of nerve endings was more like striking steel to tinder, igniting a conflagration of lust that threatened to burn them both to ash.

Clarinda bucked against him like a wild thing, gasping for breath. He cinched his arm tighter around her waist to hold her fast, gritting his teeth against a groan and fighting to steady his own breathing. He could feel the taut rope of his control already beginning to fray.

"Just relax, sweetheart," he bit off through his clenched teeth, wishing he could do the same. "Give yourself over to the pleasure."

Determined to do everything he could to make that possible for her, he began to rub the very tip of his middle finger over her in taut little circles. Her hips arched off the couch, rotating in a sinuous counterrhythm as her body instinctively responded to the silent but glorious music of that ancient dance.

Ash took that as his cue to expand his attentions, petting her, stroking her, deftly fingering her through the silk until it was all but dripping with the proof of her desire for him. His entire being was focused on one thing and one thing only—lifting her to the peak of pleasure so he could send her soaring. He might not be able to accompany her, but he would be waiting with open arms to catch her when she came crashing back down to earth.

"Oh, Ash . . ." she moaned, her head lolling back against his shoulder, then twisting around to give him a fierce look through eyes glazed with passion. "Promise me . . ."

"Yes?" In that moment he would have promised her anything.

"Promise me . . ." Her moan deepened to a groan as the callused pad of his thumb flicked back and forth over that engorged bud, mimicking the precise motion of what he was longing to do to her with his tongue. "Promise me . . . you won't stop."

She had always been able to make him laugh, even in the most unlikely circumstances. Ash buried his lips and his chuckle in her tousled hair. "I promise you I won't stop. I'll never stop."

The rocking motion of her hips and the shuddering twitch of the silky flesh beneath his fingers warned him that she would make a liar of him soon enough. Finally encountering a temptation he was helpless to withstand, he lifted his face from her hair and stole a glance over her shoulder. The sight of his strong, masculine hand cupped around all of that delectable womanly softness made him want to growl like a savage.

He used his thumb and forefinger together to deepen that delicious friction. Clarinda whipped her head back and forth, the silken strands of her hair catching on his own moist lips. "Oh, Ash . . . oh, my . . . *oh, God!*"

Her hand shot downward to cover his much larger one. Gripping him with surprising strength, she rode his fingers over the edge of pleasure and into ecstasy, a broken wail spilling from her lips like the sweetest of songs.

Ash was prepared for her release, but not for how close he came to following her over that dangerous precipice. He hadn't unintentionally spilled his seed outside a woman since he'd been a love-struck lad waking up with wet sheets from dreams of a certain saucy-tongued, green-eyed minx. But it took every ounce of will he possessed to stave off the rapture that threatened to come rolling through him like a tidal wave, obliterating everything in its path.

Still cradling a trembling Clarinda, he collapsed against the bolster, his chest heaving as if he had been running for a long time. And perhaps he had. Running away from the woman in his arms, although in that moment, he could barely remember why.

Blissfully oblivious to the havoc she was wreaking by rubbing her bottom against his unabated arousal, Clarinda sighed with contentment and wiggled around until she could twine her arms around his neck and rest her cheek against his chest. Her eyes were already fluttering shut. She yawned like a sleepy little lion, the unself-conscious gesture making her look exactly like the little girl who had stolen his clothes while he and Max had been swimming in one of the ponds on their father's estate.

Now that she no longer had to battle the effects of the aphrodisiac, she was free to surrender to the more pleasant influences of the opium. With any luck, she would sleep until morning, her dreams unfettered by regrets from the past or fear of the future.

Ash was to be allowed no such luxury.

He had come here planning on escape only to end up trapped in a web of his own making. Wrapping his arms around her even more tightly, he pressed a kiss to her sweat-dampened brow and settled back for what he knew would be the longest night of his life.

❧ Chapter Twenty-one

Clarinda awoke from the most satisfying sleep of her life with the morning sun slanting across her face and a smile on her lips. Still too deliciously drowsy to actually pry open her eyelids, she balled up her fists and stretched her tingling muscles from head to toe, indulging in a yawn so fulfilling she was tempted to roll to her other side and go right back to sleep.

She reluctantly opened her eyes to find Ash sprawled in a chair a few feet away, glowering at her with what appeared to be thinly disguised hostility. His warm caramel locks were tousled, his jaw unshaven, his shirt laid open at the throat. Clarinda frowned in bewilderment. Actually, it was laid open all the way to the middle of his chest, exposing the well-muscled planes of his chest with their delicious dusting of crisp, golden-brown hair.

He didn't look nearly as well rested as she felt. Judging by the brooding shadows beneath his eyes, he didn't look as if he had slept a wink all night. Despite his rumpled appearance — or perhaps because of it — he looked absolutely irresistible.

And more than a little dangerous.

She gave him a quizzical look, wondering what on earth he was doing in her bedchamber at that time of the morning.

He nodded toward her body, his eyes heavy-lidded and his jaw set in a harsh line. "You might want to cover yourself."

Growing even more confused, Clarinda glanced down to discover she was draped in a scrap of sheer fabric that would have been considered indecent as a nightdress back in England. Spotting red smears on the front of it, she felt a brief moment of panic. But a closer inspection revealed that what she had mistaken for blood was only rouge.

Glancing back at Ash to discover his smoldering gaze was still lingering below her neck, she reached down to the end of the unfamiliar couch and snatched the silk sheet she found there all the way up to her chin.

She cast him a wide-eyed look, her heart beginning to pound in an erratic rhythm. "Did you . . . did we . . . ?" His face was so forbidding she couldn't bring herself to finish.

His black chuckle contained little humor. "If we had, you would have remembered. I would have damn well made sure of it."

Unsettled even more by that provocative promise, she touched a hand to her brow, struggling to sift through the drifting fog in her head. Despite her debauched appearance and a faint throbbing in her temples, she seemed none the worse for wear. The last thing she remembered with perfect clarity was the two old women urging her to sit on the side of the couch so they could pour their bitter brew down her throat.

Everything became fuzzy after that. She remembered the sultry caress of the night breeze against her skin, being enthralled by the lurid mural painted on the ceiling above the couch, one of the women urging her to rest for what was to come. Then Ash had been there, his handsome face looming over her in the moonlight.

Other, more unsettling images came to her in flashes—her hands desperately tearing at his shirt, her fingertips boldly tracing the impressive outline of his arousal through his trousers, her mouth kissing . . . tasting . . . pleading . . .

As those images and a host of others came flooding back in excruciating detail, Clarinda snatched the sheet up over her head. Wondering if it was actually possible to die from mortification, she moaned aloud. "Dear God, what was I thinking? I can't believe I told you about the cucumbers and begged you to let me put my mouth on you."

"And I can't believe I was fool enough to turn you down."

She heard the resolute click of his bootheels crossing the tiled floor.

He tugged the sheet from her tightly clenched fingers, peeling it back to survey her burning face. "There's no need for you to be embarrassed. I warned you that the elixir the women gave you would make you do things you wouldn't normally do, want things you wouldn't normally want."

She could hardly tell him that wasn't why she was embarrassed. She was embarrassed because she *had* wanted those things. Because she still wanted them.

Realizing she had little hope of reclaiming her dignity while lying flat on her back and cowering beneath a sheet, she slowly sat up. "Why? Why would those women have given me such a thing?"

Ash settled one lean hip on the edge of the couch, taking care to keep a safe distance between them. "Sometimes in a place like this where men appear to have all the power, women have spent centuries developing clever little secrets their men know nothing about. I'm sure the women genuinely believed they were helping you . . . making what you were about to endure more . . . *agreeable* for you."

Clarinda was horrified to realize they probably would have given her the same elixir if it had been Farouk coming to her bed. Or any other man, for that matter. And how many men, no matter how well-intentioned or noble in character, would have been able to restrain themselves when faced with the overpowering temptation of a woman half out of her mind with lust begging them to make love to her?

"Well, it certainly made *me* more agreeable," she said glumly. "Had I been any more agreeable, you would have had to beat me off with a stick."

"Don't think I didn't consider it." Suddenly Ash was the one having difficulty meeting her eyes. "Just how much do you remember?"

Clarinda desperately wanted to lie. Wanted to tell him she remembered nothing beyond her pathetic pleas for him to make love to her and to allow her to do any number of deliciously wicked things to him. But she had long ago learned the terrible price of keeping secrets from him.

"Everything," she whispered, pushing her tangled hair out of her eyes to meet his wary gaze. "I remember everything."

She remembered every deft stroke of his fingertips, every deep-throated moan he had wrenched from her lips, every shudder of pleasure she had experienced all the way up to that soul-shattering moment when her entire world had exploded into indescribable bliss beneath the skilled caress of his hand.

The only recollection that made no sense was a hazy memory of him cradling her in his arms, brushing his lips over her hair with the helpless tenderness of a man in love, which she knew he hadn't been for a very long time. If ever.

"You must be wondering why I took such shameless advantage of you," he said.

Clarinda also remembered how her pride had been in ruins, how her flesh had burned as if it were being consumed from within, until he had offered her release—and sweet relief—with his touch. And all while denying himself his own release.

"You didn't take advantage of me. You took care of me. Just as you promised you would do." Since she no longer had any excuse to climb all over him like a wisteria vine, Clarinda had to content herself with softly touching the back of his hand. "Thank you. I realize it must have cost you."

The look he gave her warned her it was still costing him.

She quickly withdrew her hand, fresh heat flooding her cheeks. "You'll have to forgive me," she said with an awkward laugh, "but I'm not sure what the appropriate response should be in these circumstances. Would it be more fitting if I sent a note expressing my gratitude? Or perhaps some flowers?"

"I've always been partial to lilies of the valley," he said cryptically, his voice rough but his hand gentle as he reached to tuck a strand of hair behind her ear.

His fingertips lingered against that tingling swath of skin, reminding her just how persuasive they could be, just how much pleasure they were capable of coaxing from her flesh.

Would he be able to resist her now that she was in full possession of her faculties? Or at least in as full a possession of them as she could be with his lips so close to hers and his mink-colored lashes sweeping down to veil the glittering gold of his eyes.

A key rattled in the lock, but apparently someone thought better of barging in with no warning so that was followed by a tentative rap on the door.

Ash swore, but Clarinda couldn't tell if it was out of disappointment or relief that the timely interruption had kept him from making a terrible mistake neither of them would have regretted.

"One moment, please," he called out, touching a finger to his lips in warning.

He reached into his boot and withdrew a dagger. It wasn't the ornate weapon Farouk had given him but an elegant little misericord, perfect for delivering the coup de grâce to an enemy on the battlefield.

"That won't be necessary," she whispered, raising both hands in the air. "I've learned my lesson. I promise I won't try to ravish you again."

Shooting her a dark look from beneath his lashes, he shoved up the sleeve of his shirt. "You were supposed to be a virgin, remember? They'll expect to see blood."

Clarinda was the one who flinched as he made a fist and drew the blade neatly across the inside of his forearm. He tossed back a fold of the sheet next to her hip and squeezed several drops of blood from the shallow slice onto the couch, creating a convincing pattern on the lavender sheets.

"We don't want it to look like the scene of a murder," he explained. "We just want to convince Farouk you've been telling him the truth from the beginning."

"So that when he takes me to his bed, he won't strangle me to death?" she asked glumly.

Ash jerked his sleeve back down to hide the cut and slipped the dagger back into his boot. "I have no intention of letting him do either one of those things. Locking us in may have ruined my original plan, but if I've learned anything in the past few years, it's that a man has to be ready to think on his feet. Now that you've been *despoiled*—at least in Farouk's eyes—I believe he'll be much more likely to let you leave this place. Especially when I graciously offer to purchase you from him."

"With what?" she asked disbelievingly.

"The money Max paid me to rescue you. I'll have to send Luca to cash the cheque and it's not as if Farouk has any need of more gold for his treasury, but it might just be enough of a gesture to soothe his wounded pride. Especially once I explain to him how falling desperately in love with you drove me insane with lust and impaired my judgment."

Despite his mocking tone, his words still made Clarinda's treacherous heart leap in her breast.

"I do tend to have that effect on men," she said drily. "It's my curse. But why would you give up your precious reward? Despite your noble act of self-sacrifice last night, I didn't think you were inclined toward charity work."

Ash rose, crooking an eyebrow at her. "I'm sure Max will reimburse me for my trouble. As we both know, my brother is a man who always keeps his promises and pays his debts."

He turned and strode to the door, leaving her as numb as if he had used the misericord to administer the coup de grâce to her heart. A heart that was even more defenseless than before after the night she had spent in his arms.

He swung open the door to reveal two of the harem guards waiting in the corridor. One of them was Solomon, his placid face and ebony eyes as unreadable as ever, and the other a stern-faced older eunuch Clarinda did not recognize.

"The sultan has commanded that you join him in breaking his fast," the older man informed Ash. He glanced past Ash to where Clarinda was still huddled on the couch, his broad nostrils flaring in definite disdain. "And the woman as well."

Although Poppy suspected she would probably do just as well languishing beneath the sheets of her sleeping couch feeling sorry for herself, she dutifully picked up a basket of *ktefa* from the palace kitchens and went trudging up the hillside to the garden overlooking the sea where she and Farouk had met every morning for the past week.

The gentle breeze had been replaced by a hot, dry wind that burned her sleepless eyes and whipped the normally serene sea into a witches' brew as choppy and tumultuous as her thoughts.

She plopped down on the bench and set the basket beside her, sighing heavily. She hadn't yet broken her fast, but not even the delectable aroma of the freshly fried pastries could tempt her on this morning. Had it been only yesterday that Farouk had ignored her giggled protests and insisted upon breaking off sugary bits of the treat and feeding them to her from his fingertips?

She desperately wanted to believe he would come strolling down the garden path any minute, his robes rippling around his ankles, his dazzling smile breaking through his beard. But hope had always been an indulgence a woman like her could ill afford. Learning to live without it made it so much easier to carry on and keep smiling when there was no hope to be had.

Despite what she had wanted to believe, it

seemed Farouk was no different from any other man in the world. He would rather waste his time pining over a woman who would never love him than take a second look at the woman who did. She had been dismissed as a silly fool more than once in her life, but this was the first time she had truly felt like one.

She drew out the leatherbound volume of Coleridge's poetry she had tucked into a corner of the basket and opened it to the page marked by one of her faded hair ribbons. She and Farouk had finished discussing "Kubla Khan" a few days ago only to plunge directly into the giddy pleasure that was *Christabel*. They had traded her spectacles back and forth, taking turns reading each stanza aloud.

As Poppy's eyes drifted over the page to the last few lines of Coleridge's uncompleted masterpiece, it wasn't her own voice she heard in her head but Farouk's, its deep and compelling resonance bringing fresh meaning to the timeless beauty of the poet's vision.

> *And pleasures flow in so thick and fast*
> *Upon his heart, that he at last*
> *Must needs express his love's excess*
> *With words of unmeant bitterness.*
> *Perhaps 'tis pretty to force together*

Thoughts so all unlike each other;
To mutter and mock a broken charm,
To dally with wrong that does no harm.
Perhaps 'tis tender too and pretty
At each wild word to feel within
A sweet recoil of love and pity.

A solitary tear splashed on the page, blurring the words. Poppy gently closed the book and set it aside, knowing she would never open it again. She peeled back the satin napkin covering the *ktefa*, seeking refuge in the most reliable comfort she had ever known. She crammed a large bite of pastry into her mouth, but it seemed to crumble to sawdust on her tongue, its honeyed sweetness as bitter as persimmon juice. It was all she could do choke it past the lump in her throat.

She rose from the bench and headed back down the garden path, turning away from the sea and leaving the book, the basket, and all of her ridiculous dreams behind.

Since arriving at the palace of El Jadida, Clarinda had been invited, wooed, persuaded, sweet-talked, cajoled, coaxed, and had the pleasure of her company humbly requested, but Farouk had never lorded his authority over her by *command-ing* her to appear before him. His high-handed summons to break her fast with him must be the first sign of her lowered status in his eyes. She feared that if Ash wasn't successful in his bid to purchase her, many more signs would come.

After the other eunuch had escorted a blind-folded Ash away, ostensibly to prepare him for his appearance before the sultan, Solomon had patiently waited outside the door of the chamber where she and Ash had passed the night while she bathed and donned the garments he had provided for her.

She glanced down at the flowing layers of multicolored silk as Solomon ushered her from the room, wondering if they were to be her shroud.

She could feel the curious gazes of Farouk's wives and concubines upon her as Solomon led her through the main hall of the harem. Was it her imagination or did even Yasmin's narrowed eyes hold a glimmer of knowing pity? Long-ing to see a truly sympathetic face, she looked around for Poppy, but her friend was nowhere to be found. She could only hope it wouldn't be their last chance to say good-bye. If she was walking into a trap that might prove fatal, leav-ing tenderhearted Poppy to fend for herself in this ruthless place would be one of her keenest regrets.

Farouk had honored his word by allowing Ash to spend the night in her bed. But what if he had simply been biding his time until morning came so he could avenge the terrible blow Ash had dealt his pride? For all she knew, she and Ash could both be marching to their deaths. She flinched as the doors of the harem clanged shut behind her and Solomon with jarring finality.

A long, empty corridor stretched before them. Now that she had the inscrutable eunuch all to herself, she had every intention of trying to pry some answers out of him.

"Do you know what the sultan has planned for us?" she asked.

He continued to march a few steps ahead of her, as if each of his long strides were measured by the beat of an invisible drum.

She sighed. "I know you can hear me, Solomon. There's no need to pretend otherwise."

She might as well have been talking to the wall. Her panic and frustration were swelling with each step. The door at the far end of the corridor loomed before them. Once they passed through it, they would be back in the public areas of the palace without even the illusion of privacy.

"Damn it all, Solomon, I'm tired of being ignored!" Taking two extra steps to catch up with him, she grabbed the back of his vest and held on, refusing to budge until he acknowledged her.

He could just as easily have kept walking, dragging her behind him like a tenacious terrier with its teeth dug into his trousers. But it seemed she had finally managed to get his attention. He slowly turned, his expression so thunderous she let go of the vest and began to back away from him. Since he always seemed to be standing in the shadows, as stolid and dependable as a battered armoire, she had forgotten how very large he was. As she continued to retreat, he stalked her step for step until her shoulder blades came up against the wall, making escape impossible.

Perhaps Farouk wasn't going to kill her, she thought, fighting an insane desire to giggle. Perhaps he had ordered Solomon to do it. The eunuch could probably snap her fragile neck in one of his massive hands without so much as breaking a sweat.

As if still not completely trusting they were alone, Solomon stole a glance over his shoulder before leaning down and saying sternly, "If a man learns to hold his tongue, there are many around him who will forget to hold theirs."

Clarinda had learned that lesson only too well when she had mistaken Ash for Solomon during her massage and spilled out all of those embarrassing confessions.

"Is that why you let everyone believe you are a mute?"

"People believe what they want to believe," he replied, his voice every bit as musical as it had been the first time she had heard it. "They see what they want to see and hear what they want to hear."

"Have you by any chance heard what the sultan has in store for us?"

"I have not. But I do know it would be wise for you to tread with great care. Even the most gentle of beasts can lash out when wounded."

Clarinda touched his arm. "This is not the first time you have offered me your counsel . . . or your kindness. Why is that?"

"You remind me of someone I knew when I was very young."

She searched his stoic face but his shaven head and unlined visage made it impossible to determine his age. He could have been any age from thirty to sixty.

He lifted a strand of her hair from her shoulder, sifting its brightness through his ebony fingers. "She was dark everywhere you are light.

But she had the same proud set to her shoulders, the same unyielding spirit."

"You loved her?" Clarinda ventured softly.

He straightened, folding his arms over his chest. "On the night before we were to be wed, the slavers came to our village and carried me away. I was young and strong and my only thought was to make my way back to her, so I tried to escape more than once but they always caught me. They finally decided there was only one way to stop me. After they had at me with their knives, I knew there was no reason to ever go back to her."

The eunuch's simple words made Clarinda's heart clench with sympathetic anguish. "You never saw her again?"

"She was young and beautiful. I would imagine she married another man from our village and had many fine children."

Children that should have been his.

"How you must hate them," she said, her voice low and passionate. "How you must hate them all! The ones who enslaved you and the ones who keep you enslaved."

"Out of all the masters I have had, Farouk is the best. He no longer follows the barbaric practice of creating eunuchs for his service. He simply puts to good use the ones who were created by his father and his father before him. He was the one who taught me Arabic and English so that I could be his eyes and his ears in the harem and elsewhere. You are the only secret I have ever kept from him."

"Me?" she whispered, gazing up at him in bewilderment.

"You and your Englishman."

Clarinda felt the color drain from her face. "I don't know what you're talking about."

"You may have believed I was mute but I have never pretended to be blind. I have spent most of my life since my capture in the company of women. It is not so easy for them to hide their hearts from me."

"I have no idea what you think you see," Clarinda said stiffly to hide how flustered she was feeling, "but I can assure you that Captain Burke is not *my* Englishman. We did enjoy a brief dalliance once, but whatever was between us was over many, *many* years ago. As soon as I'm free of this place, I plan to marry his brother."

Although not a single muscle in Solomon's face twitched, she would have sworn he was laughing at her.

She glared up at him. "You know, I think I may have liked you better when you were pretending to be mute."

"Come." His massive hand closed around her elbow. "It would not be wise on this day for either one of us to keep the sultan waiting."

The chamber where Farouk was waiting for them would have been called a conservatory at home. One wall sported a row of tall windows overlooking a spacious courtyard. They had been thrown open to welcome in the morning breeze. The walls were lined with brightly colored clay pots overflowing with glossy green foliage and fronds that made it look as if a corner of his garden had been brought indoors. Splashes of red, orange, and yellow nested among them, the exotic blooms sending invisible tendrils of fragrance curling through the room. Golden shafts of morning light spilled through the expansive skylights set in the ceiling.

The floor was tiled in terra-cotta with nary a carpet in sight. The rusty hue would be simply perfect for hiding unsightly bloodstains, Clarinda thought with a slight edge of hysteria.

When she and Solomon had arrived, Farouk and Ash weren't breaking bread together while propped up on cushions on the floor but were seated European-style in chairs at opposite ends of a long teakwood table. Normally, Clarinda would have been seated right next to Farouk where he could easily reach over to stroke her hair or feed her a particularly plump date or morsel of lamb, but today only one other chair was in the room, placed with strategic precision at the center of the far side of the table between the two men. Farouk's guard was glaringly absent, as if he didn't wish to have a single witness to this occasion.

As Solomon escorted her around the table, Clarinda did a double take. While Ash had a single golden plate and goblet in front of him, the table in front of Farouk was littered with bowls and platters, many of them already half-empty. One of them contained what looked like the picked-over carcass of an entire goat.

The only platter that hadn't been touched contained a towering stack of *ktefa* drizzled with golden honey. As she watched, Farouk dipped a piece of *khobz* in a bowl of mutton stew, using the flat bread to mop up every lingering drop of the stew's savory juices before cramming it into his mouth and chewing with relish.

Clarinda's own mouth fell open in astonishment. In the three months since she had been dining by his side, she had never seen Farouk attack a meal with such ferocious gusto. Something about his single-minded concentration made the tiny hairs on her nape prickle to life. As Solomon settled her in the chair and turned to go, it was all she could do not to latch onto the eunuch's leg and beg him to stay.

After Solomon bowed his way from the room, the awkward silence deepened until Farouk glanced up from fishing the last handful of dates out of a wooden bowl to give Clarinda a jovial smile. "Good morning, my little buttercup. I trust that you passed a pleasant night?"

Ash choked on whatever he was drinking.

Tossing another date in his mouth, Farouk gave him a bemused glance.

Ash dabbed at his lips with his napkin before rasping out, "Forgive me, Your Majesty. I'm not accustomed to partaking of such strong spirits so early in the morning."

Clarinda picked up her own goblet and stole a peek at the ruby red wine within, wondering if it was laced with poison.

She lowered the goblet to discover that Farouk's questioning gaze had once again returned to her face. "I did indeed pass the night . . . um . . . pleasantly, Your Majesty."

All it took was the briefest glance from beneath her lashes at Ash's guarded face to make her remember just how pleasantly. As heat crept into her cheeks, she tipped the goblet to her lips, draining it nearly dry in one swallow.

Considering that she and Ash had once coupled on a cloak beneath a tree in the middle of a meadow, it was ridiculous that she should feel so shy about what had transpired between them last night. Perhaps it was Farouk's knowing smile that was making her so skittish.

The sultan picked up a knife and stabbed a slice of lamb with it, which she supposed was preferable to his burying it in one of their throats. As the sun glittered off the plump emerald set into the weapon's hilt, Clarinda realized it was not just any knife, but the jeweled dagger he had given to Ash the previous night as a reward for Ash's bravery and a token of his own friendship.

After making short work of the lamb, he waved the knife in her general direction. "You need not blush so prettily, my little gazelle. As I have explained before, we are not so provincial here as they are in your homeland. We do not believe there is any shame in a woman learning all there is to know of pleasure in a man's bed."

While Clarinda briefly considered crawling beneath the table, Ash said cautiously, "You'll have to forgive our confusion, Your Majesty. After my rather rash actions in the hall last night, I was left with the impression that you might be . . . displeased."

Clarinda lifted her empty goblet in a silent toast to what must surely be the understatement of the century.

Farouk chuckled. "I will forgive your confusion if you will forgive my outburst. Despite my best attempts to embrace restraint and reason, I am still my father's son, and sometimes my temper gets the best of me. But after a night spent in prayerful contemplation, I realized I should be thanking you." He lifted his shoulders in a mock shudder. "After all, the last thing I needed was another wife."

Clarinda exchanged a startled glance with Ash. She could tell from his wary expression that he, like her, could hardly dare to believe events were turning so swiftly in their favor.

"Your Majesty is, as always, the voice of restraint and reason," Ash said, visibly warming to their discussion. "Which is exactly why I had hoped you would allow me to—"

"I have decided that Miss Cardew will make a much more enticing concubine than a wife," Farouk said, cutting off Ash as if he hadn't even opened his mouth. "With such a rare and exotic jewel in my harem, I will be the envy of every warlord in the region. And now that I have fulfilled my vow to you, Burke the Younger, and she is virgin no more, there will be no need for me to delay taking her to my bed." Farouk turned his dark eyes on Clarinda, their possessive gleam impossible to misinterpret. "On this very night, I will make her my own."

❖ Chapter Twenty-two

Although Clarinda was paralyzed with shock, she still expected Ash to say something, do something. Anything at all. But he sat in stony silence as Farouk turned that calculating gaze on him.

"Since there will be no wedding," the sultan said, "there is no further reason for you and Mr. D'Arcangelo to delay your journey. I shall see you on your way before nightfall."

Just like that, Farouk's trap snapped shut on their throats with the delicacy and precision of a French guillotine. Clarinda had allowed herself to foolishly forget that a man who wielded his degree of power had no need of poison or blade to vanquish his enemies. His every smile was as sharp and lethal as a blade, his every honeyed word laced with poison.

Ignoring Ash's fierce gaze and the desperate shake of his head, Clarinda rose halfway out of her chair, determined to tell the overgrown bully just what he could do with his jeweled dagger and all of his high-handed plans for her.

It would be wise for you to tread with great care. Even the most gentle of beasts can lash out when wounded.

Solomon's gentle words of warning echoed through her head. If she dared to defy Farouk, it would be Ash who paid the price. She might already be doomed, but he still had a chance to escape this place with his life . . . and his head.

Swallowing her fury with an effort that nearly choked her, she rose the rest of the way and spread the flowing skirts of her gown in a stiff parody of a curtsy. "You honor me with your attentions, Your Majesty. I shall look forward to having the opportunity to fully express my gratitude for the kindness and generosity you have shown me."

Farouk's eyes took her measure, the thoughtful gleam in them deepening. "And I shall look forward to it even more." She flinched as his fist came down, driving the blade of the dagger deep into the table.

❃   ❃   ❃

He was leaving her again.

Clarinda stood atop one of the highest minarets of the palace, the hot, dry wind whipping
the hair around her face and searing the tears
from her eyes before they could fall. The cool
blue sea behind her might as well have been a
million leagues away because there was nothing
before her but desert as far as the eye could see.

She had no way of knowing if Farouk had allowed Solomon to escort her to this place so she
could watch Ash and Luca depart the palace for
good as a boon or a punishment. She only knew
she hated him all the more for it.

Up until the moment she had watched them
ride through the outer gates of the fortress, she
had allowed herself to believe Ash would never
leave without her. Had clutched at the stone
parapet ringing the tower and held her breath,
just waiting for the moment when he would
whip out a pair of pistols and stage some sort
of dramatic rescue, creating a new legend that
would live forever between the pages of the
scandal sheets.

But the wind that carried the distant jingle of
their harnesses to her ears had scattered the last
of those dreams.

Ash was wearing the same coat and battered
hat he had worn when she had come running

into Farouk's courtyard to find him standing there like a ghost from her past. Even from this distance with his back to her, she would have known the deceptively relaxed slouch of his shoulders, the lazy grace in the way he sat the horse. There was no mistaking him for any other man on this earth.

Clarinda wondered how many other women throughout the centuries had stood on this very tower and watched their men ride away. To other lands. To war. Perhaps even to the arms of other women. But at least they had been allowed to hold on to the hope, however meager, that their men might someday return.

At least this time Ash had left without saying good-bye. She had been spared his tender caresses, his pretty promises, the lies he told with each kiss and every breath. This time he had never even looked back.

What would he do now? she wondered. Where would he go? Would he return to Maximillian to tell his brother he had failed in his mission and that his bride was lost to him forever? Or would he take the money Max had paid him to rescue her and escape to some other foreign shore? Perhaps he was already dreaming of new lands, new adventures, new lips to kiss and hearts to steal.

She watched the two men grow smaller in the distance, her own heart growing so dry and brittle she feared she might turn into a pillar of sand that could be scattered by nothing more than a careless nudge of the wind.

At least then she would be free. Free to soar away from this place in the arms of the wind.

She let go of the parapet and stepped closer to the edge of the tower. Ash and Luca were almost out of sight now. A few more leagues and they would be swallowed by the billowing sea of sand. The distant wail of the muezzin calling the faithful to prayer drifted to her ears like an echo from her own heart. She spread her arms wide and closed her eyes, no longer fighting the wind but embracing it.

Her eyes flew open. She was not about to let Ash's desertion destroy her. She had survived his leaving and its devastating aftermath once before and she would survive it now. If loving him had taught her anything, it was that her heart was strong enough to bear even the cruelest blow. She wouldn't give any man, whether it be Ash or Farouk, the power to destroy her. If no one was willing to save her, then she would save herself, even if that meant biding her time for months or even years while she waited for another opportunity for escape to present itself.

She turned away from the parapet only to find Solomon standing within arm's reach of her and realized he had been waiting all along to pull her back from the brink.

Clarinda sat on the edge of the sleeping couch in her darkened alcove and waited for the women to come and escort her to the sultan's bed. The lavender shadows of twilight had descended over the garden below well over an hour ago, but she hadn't bothered to light her lamp. There was no longer anything—or anyone—in this place she cared to see.

Tonight she would be begging the women for another dose of their magical elixir. Perhaps if she willingly succumbed to its dark enchantment, she would be able to close her eyes and pretend it was Ash's lips claiming her own, Ash's hands caressing her naked flesh, Ash's body moving over hers. Her lips thinned into a taut line. She would drink any manner of poison to blot out the bearded face of the man she had once believed to be her friend.

A draft danced across her skin, warning her that she was no longer alone. While she had been brooding, someone had silently slipped through the curtain shielding the door.

The woman they had sent for her was a forbidding figure, cloaked and hooded in a long black robe. Clarinda slowly came to her feet. After watching Ash ride out of her life for the last time, she had believed she would never feel anything again except for a desperate determination to survive. Yet still she found herself quailing with dread before this grim specter of her future.

Not sure she had any desire to see what lay beneath, Clarinda dragged in a shuddering breath as the woman reached up to tug back the hood.

Her breath froze in her throat. She must have already fallen beneath the spell of some powerful potion because it wasn't one of Farouk's handmaidens who stood before her but Ash, his golden eyes gleaming like a tiger's in the darkness.

✣ Chapter Twenty-three

$\mathcal{R}$efusing to trust that Ash wasn't the product of some sort of fever dream or delirium, Clarinda drifted closer to him.

His hair was windblown and the stubble on his jaw was already threatening to bloom into a full-fledged beard. A fine layer of sand coated his skin, making him look as if he'd been dipped in powdered gold. She reached up and ran her trembling fingertips over the thin, diagonal scar marring his otherwise perfect chin. That scar—that beautiful, beautiful scar—convinced her he was real.

Her pride dissolving beneath the force of her relief, she threw her arms around his neck with a muffled cry. He gathered her into his arms, holding her so tightly she could barely breathe.

"Thank God you're all right." He rubbed his face against her hair, his voice hoarse with raw emotion. "I was afraid I'd be too late."

"I thought you were gone for good," she mumbled into his throat, savoring the warm, masculine spice of his scent.

He drew back and grinned down at her, his devil-may-care dimple making him look every inch the rogue he was. "Don't you read the scandal sheets? Captain Sir Ashton Burke never leaves a job unfinished."

She clutched at his shoulders, afraid to let him go for fear he would vanish all over again. "But how? How can you be here? I saw you ride away with my own eyes."

"As soon as we were out of sight of the fortress, we doubled back and slipped up on the palace from the sea side."

"How did you get back into the fortress? Past the harem guards?"

He wagged his eyebrows at her. "I've always prided myself on having friends in unusual places."

"Solomon," she whispered, knowing the answer to her question before she even asked it.

"We don't have a minute to spare," he said, dragging a second cloak out from under his own and whisking it around her shoulders. "Our *friend* can only keep the guards away from the outer gates for so long or someone will get suspicious. Remember how I told you the day might come when you'd have to be ready to travel and travel fast? Well, that day has officially arrived."

Although she wanted to ask him a thousand other questions, some of which she'd been biting back for nearly a decade, she knew now was not the time. He tugged up the hood of his cloak to veil his features and she followed suit. Slipping an arm around her waist, he urged her through the curtain and down the stairs.

When they reached the bottom of the stairs, he paused in the shadow of the wall, touching a warning finger to his lips.

They could hear the muffled voices and low-pitched laughter of Farouk's wives and concubines drifting out of the hall of the harem. At least her mysterious disappearance would give them something new to chatter about.

After looking both ways to make sure no one was watching, Ash tripped a hidden switch and slid open a panel to reveal a secret passageway lit by a single torch. He ushered Clarinda inside, then slid the panel shut behind them. They were halfway to the end of the passageway when Clarinda heard an indistinct moan coming from behind a nondescript cedar door set in the wall. She slowed her steps, giving Ash a questioning glance.

He eased open the door to reveal the two old women who had prepared her for his own possession, writhing about on the floor of the small chamber with their eyes closed.

"They were on their way to take you to the sultan's bed," he explained. "I had no choice but to *delay* them."

Clarinda watched the women squirm and moan, baffled by their strange behavior. "What on earth did you do to them?"

He nodded toward the empty earthenware flask lying on the floor between them. "Let's just say I gave them a taste of their own medicine."

Judging by the blissful smiles curving the women's toothless mouths, they were both enjoying decadent dreams of lovers from days gone by.

Drawing the door quietly shut, Ash sighed with regret. "I was tempted to lock Luca in there with them, but we had to leave our horses behind so I sent him to the stables to steal us some fresh mounts. He's half-Gypsy, you know. They enjoy that sort of thing. We should probably hurry before he tries to make off with half the horses in Farouk's stables."

They had barely taken two steps when Clarinda once again jerked to a halt, clapping a hand over her mouth in horror.

"Good God, what is it now?" Ash snapped, his patience plainly beginning to fray.

"It's Poppy! I can't believe I almost forgot her!"

Ash turned, cupping her elbows in his desperate grip. "The sultan has absolutely no interest in Miss Montmorency. Couldn't we send for her later?"

"She's right off the main hall. It will only take me a minute to fetch her. You said you wouldn't make me leave without her. You promised," she reminded him sternly, although she had certainly learned not to put much faith in his promises.

Swearing softly but effectively, he bent and yanked from his boot the same small dagger he had used to slice his forearm. He pressed the weapon into her hand, folding her fingers around its hilt. "Don't hesitate to use it if you have to." She was already turning away when he yanked her back into his arms and pressed a brief but fierce kiss to her lips, much as he had in his father's stables so long ago. "And don't get your fool self caught and make me rescue you again. That will cost you far more than a kiss."

With the dagger hidden in an inner pocket of her robe and her hood drawn up to cover the brightness of her hair, Clarinda slipped through the hall of the harem like a wraith, thankful the eunuchs had already dimmed the lamps so the women could prepare for sleep. She had left Ash pacing the secret passageway, running a hand through his hair and muttering something beneath his breath about the folly of trying to reason with a woman. She could still taste his kiss on her lips.

She slipped through the curtain veiling Poppy's alcove, sighing with relief to find her friend propped up on a cozy nest of pillows on her sleeping couch, her wire-rimmed spectacles perched on the tip of her nose. A nose buried in a yellowing scandal sheet.

The sight was so familiar and so dear that it brought a rush of warm tears to Clarinda's eyes. She still couldn't believe she had been so consumed with her own misery at Ash's desertion and joy at his return that she had allowed herself to forget her friend. Vowing she would find some way to make it up to her, Clarinda soundlessly crossed the chamber and sank down on the edge of the couch.

Poppy gave her a mild glance, then returned to perusing the scandal sheet. Given how insatiably curious Poppy was, she didn't seem the least bit intrigued by Clarinda's odd attire.

"We have to go, Poppy," she informed her friend, stealing a nervous glance back at the curtain. "Captain Burke has returned to rescue us. We may have only a few minutes before the sultan's guards sound the alarm."

Poppy turned the page, her gaze still fixed on the scandal sheet. "You go on, dear. I've had the entire day to think about it and I've decided I'm not going."

Clarinda leaned back, utterly bumfuzzled by her friend's response. "Pardon?"

Poppy finally looked up from the scandal sheet to survey Clarinda over the top of her spectacles. "You heard me. I'm not going."

"Have you lost your wits? You can't stay here. Farouk is going to be even more livid than he already is when he discovers I've run away with the captain. What if he decides to take his revenge out on you?"

Poppy gave Clarinda a look Clarinda had probably given her hundreds of times during their years of friendship. "Don't be such a silly goose. Farouk wouldn't hurt me. He would never hurt me. And just so you know, he wouldn't have hurt you, either. He's not that sort of man."

"If you'd have seen him waving his enormous dagger around this morning at breakfast, you might not be so quick to defend him. And besides, how on earth do you know what sort of man he is?"

Poppy laid aside the tabloid, her nostrils flaring in a superior sniff. "Trust me. I know."

Clarinda stared at the composed stranger who had taken her friend's place, comprehension slowly dawning. "Oh, dear Lord, it's Mr. Huntington-Smythe all over again! You're fancying yourself in love with the man, aren't you?" She seized Poppy's hands in hers, giving them a tender squeeze. "Listen to me, darling. I know it's hard for you to accept this since you and Farouk have barely exchanged two words since we came to this place, but he isn't some dashing, romantic figure from one of your scandal sheets or Gothic novels. He is a very dangerous and powerful man, and the sooner we're free of his influence, the better. What do you think he's going to do if you stay? Ask you to become his wife?"

"You did bring me along on this journey to find me a husband, didn't you?"

"Yes. Preferably one who doesn't have an entire stable of wives already. And concubines."

A wicked little smile played around Poppy's lips. "Perhaps I could coax him into making me his concubine instead of his wife. Then you could go back to England and tell all of our old classmates from Miss Throckmorton's—and that nasty Mr. Huntington-Smythe—that plump little Penelope Montmorency has become the cherished concubine of a handsome and powerful Moroccan sultan. Wouldn't that just make them pea green with envy?"

Clarinda gaped at her friend, on the verge of tearing at her own hair in frustration. She knew from experience just how stubborn Poppy could be once she got an idea into her head.

She stole another desperate glance over her shoulder. Every second she lingered put Ash and his hiding place in more danger of being discovered by the harem guard.

It was Poppy's turn to squeeze Clarinda's hands. She smiled tenderly, her spectacles magnifying her fine periwinkle eyes and making the sheen of tears in them look even more brilliant. "There's no point in arguing with me. I've already made up my mind. I'm not going with you. Now go!" she urged. "I'm afraid you're going to have to kiss Captain Burke for the both of us."

A helpless sob escaped Clarinda as she threw her arms around her friend, treasuring her solid and dependable warmth, perhaps for the last time. "I don't care what you say. I'm coming back for you," she vowed fiercely. "Even if I have to lead a regiment of East India Company soldiers myself. And if Farouk harms so much as a hair on your head—or breaks your heart—I'll kill him. I swear I will."

Poppy squeezed her back. "Don't you worry about me, Clarinda Cardew. I do believe I'm finally ready to embark upon that grand adventure you promised me."

As Clarinda reluctantly drew away and rose, Poppy thrust the scandal sheet into her hands. "Here. You might need something to read on your journey."

Clarinda tucked the tabloid inside her robe and started for the door. She turned in the doorway. "The desert sun is very fierce. Don't forget to always wear your bonnet or a veil when you go outdoors. You know how absentminded you can be and how fair your complexion is." She started to go, then turned back again. "Take care not to leave your spectacles someplace where you're likely to sit on them. And don't you let those other women bully you. You stand right up to them and tell them Penelope Montmorency is not a woman to be trifled with!"

Poppy made a shooing motion with her hands. "Go! Captain Burke won't wait forever."

Dashing a tear from her cheek, Clarinda said, "You're the best friend I ever had."

Poppy beamed at her. "I know."

Smiling through her tears, Clarinda touched two fingers to her lips, then lifted them to Poppy in silent tribute before ducking through the curtain.

Several of the women were already curled up on their sleeping couches fast asleep, allowing Clarinda to tiptoe back through the hall of the harem without incident. She broke into a trot as she reached the torchlit corridor that would lead her back to where Ash was waiting.

Her heart was already reeling with relief at the thought of seeing him again when she darted around a shadowy corner only to find her path blocked by a raven-haired beauty wearing little more than a diaphanous silk shift and a triumphant smile.

❧ *Chapter Twenty-four*

*O*ne scream from Yasmin's beautiful damson lips and all was lost.

When the hood of Clarinda's robe slid from her hair, Clarinda made no effort to stop it. There would have been no point. "Good evening, Yasmin," she said pleasantly. "I was just on my way to the hammam for a bath."

Yasmin tossed her head, sending her own glossy midnight-black tresses spilling down her back. "Do not waste your breath on foolish lies, ice princess. I know you are running away with your lover."

"Captain Burke is not my lover," Clarinda snapped, not realizing her mistake until Yasmin's smug smile deepened.

"Not now perhaps. But he has been before and he will be again."

It was utterly absurd that those words still had the power to make Clarinda's heart leap with hope. Especially when she would never again be any man's lover if Yasmin summoned the harem guards. Neither she nor Ash would leave this place alive.

She slipped a hand inside her robe, her fingers inching toward the pocket where she'd secreted the dagger. "You've been locked away too long in this hotbed of lust and intrigue, Yasmin. You're imagining trysts and conspiracies where none exist."

"It takes little imagination to expose the truth."

Clarinda wrapped her fingers around the cool metal of the dagger's hilt, her hand steadied by an image of a blindfolded Ash being led up the steps of a scaffold where a black-hooded executioner awaited him, the shiny blade of his scimitar glinting in the desert sun. She had briefly stood off a pack of rapacious Corsairs with a hatpin. If one catty little concubine thought she was going to get the best of this English ice princess, she had another think coming.

"Do not do anything foolish," Yasmin said, plainly alarmed by the look in Clarinda's eye. "I will not rouse the guards."

Clarinda cocked her head to the side, refusing to relax her own guard. She had seen that cunning look on the woman's face too many times before. Yasmin granted no favor without a price. It just remained to be seen whether that price would be too steep to pay.

"I will not rouse the guards," Yasmin repeated, drawing close enough to whisper, "*if* you take me with you."

Clarinda gaped at Yasmin in astonishment, the dagger sliding from her limp fingers and back into its hiding place. "You want to go with us? Why would you even contemplate such a thing? I thought you were madly in love with the sultan."

"I am. But I will never be his wife. And as long as I stay here, I will never be the wife of any man. No man will ever look at me the way your captain looks at you."

"He's not my . . ." As Yasmin arched one raven eyebrow in blatant skepticism, Clarinda trailed off. She was still trying to absorb the unexpected shock of the concubine's request. "What makes you think I'd even consider taking you along? You've done nothing but torment Poppy and me since the day we arrived here. Instead of ridiculing and undermining us at every turn, you could have extended a hand of friendship, which might have encouraged the other women of the harem to do the same. Give me one good reason why I should help you now."

"Because if you do not, I will scream at the top of my lungs and everyone you love will die."

"That's a very good reason." Yet still Clarinda hesitated, torn between her desperate need to rejoin Ash and her hatred of this woman.

"Please." Yasmin choked out the word as if it were poison in her throat. She stared at a spot just over Clarinda's right shoulder. "I am begging you."

Given that the concubine was even more stiff-necked with pride than she was, Clarinda knew exactly how much those words must have cost Yasmin.

Clarinda held within her hands the power to rescue this woman from a half life that could just as easily have been hers. She could have been the one growing older and less desirable by the day, watching younger and more beautiful women take her place in the sultan's heart and his bed. She could have ended up a toothless old woman, relegated to pouring opium and aphrodisiacs down the throats of terrified virgins, just so they could bear what she had once desired more than life itself.

Clarinda blew out an exasperated sigh. "Oh, for heaven's sake, you're embarrassing yourself. Stop groveling and come on!" She grabbed the startled Yasmin by the hand, nearly yanking her off her feet, and took off down the corridor. "We can't keep the captain waiting forever."

"That is *not* Poppy," Ash said when Clarinda and Yasmin ducked into the hidden passageway where he was waiting.

Despite making a noble effort, he could not stop his gaze from darting ever so briefly down to the magnificent sight that was Yasmin's ample breasts heaving with exertion beneath the diaphanous silk of her shift. A man would have to be a eunuch to ignore them, and Clarinda knew only too well that Ash was no eunuch.

She rolled her eyes. "Poppy refused to come because she thinks she's in love with Farouk, and Yasmin insisted on coming because Farouk will never love her. If I hadn't agreed to bring her, she was going to wake up the entire harem with her screams."

"I could just knock her out," Ash offered, the ruthless glint in his eye giving her a glimpse of what a dangerous adversary he must be on the battlefield.

Crowding Clarinda aside, Yasmin twined one arm around his neck and offered up her parted lips as if they were ripe, juicy pomegranates picked just for his pleasure. "You could kiss me insensible instead."

Clarinda grabbed a fistful of Yasmin's shift and yanked her off Ash. "Try that again and I'll knock you out myself."

Ignoring Yasmin's pout, Ash gave Clarinda an arch look. "For a woman with two fiancés, you have quite the jealous streak, Miss Cardew."

"Haven't you heard, Captain?" she asked, smirking at him. "I'm down to only one fiancé now."

Ash's lips thinned into a grim line. "And if either one of us ever hopes to see him again, we'd best catch up with Luca before he takes off without us. Unless, of course, there's someone else you'd like me to rescue while I'm here. Two or three more concubines? A half-dozen eunuchs? A litter of tiger cubs perhaps?"

"You didn't tell me I could bring the tiger cubs!" Clarinda acted as if she were going to go darting back toward the harem, prompting Ash to snare her by the elbow and pull her into his arms.

Despite their dire circumstances, he looked so much like the boy who had caught her sneaking a baby hedgehog into his favorite beaver hat she could not resist laughing up at him.

"Mind your tongue, you incorrigible little minx," he warned, "before I'm forced to mind it for you."

After lingering just long enough to filch a third robe from the harem for Yasmin, Ash, Clarinda, and the concubine slunk through the moonlit gardens, picking their way through the shadows cast by the swaying palms. Their every step, no matter how careful, seemed to echo with the force of a gunshot. Clarinda caught herself holding her breath, waiting for someone to sound the alarm that would spell their doom.

But the peaceful hush of the night was broken only by the distant murmur of the sea and the whisper of the wind through the feathery palm fronds. After what seemed like an eternity but was in actuality only a few minutes, they finally reached the unguarded gate where Ash had arranged to meet Luca.

At first there was no sign of him, but then he came springing up from behind a lush hibiscus plant like a grinning jack-in-the-box, giving them all a terrible fright. "What took you so long?" he asked. "I nearly fell asleep."

"We had to go back for Poppy," Clarinda explained.

Yasmin, of course, had let the robe Clarinda had stolen for her gape open all the way down the front, exposing her voluptuous form to the kiss of the moonlight and Luca's lascivious gaze.

Luca let out a low-pitched whistle. "That is most definitely *not* Poppy."

"We've already established that," Ash said, rubbing a weary hand over his jaw.

Although she couldn't quite stop herself from preening beneath Luca's appreciative gaze, Yasmin gave him a contemptuous look, her dark eyes spitting fire. "Keep your eyes in your head, you English dog, lest I claw them out."

"I hate to disappoint a lady, but I am an Italian dog. Well, half-Romany actually."

Yasmin's upper lip curled in a sneer. "A loathsome cur by any name."

Luca grinned at Ash. "Did you hear that? She hates me already. I told you I've always found that to be an irresistible quality in a woman."

"Have I mentioned she's looking for a husband?" Clarinda asked sweetly.

Luca paled beneath his tan. "A husband?"

"And if Clarinda wasn't hogging up all the fiancés for herself, she might have found one by now. Did you get the mounts?" Ash asked Luca, enunciating each word as if he were talking to the village idiot.

Luca gave him a reproachful look. "What sort of Gypsy would I be if I couldn't manage to rob a stable?"

He beckoned and they followed him through the gate and into the alley that bordered the curve of the garden wall.

"You can't be serious," Clarinda said when she saw what was waiting for them.

"That is not a horse," Yasmin said needlessly.

"Of course it is not a horse. It is a camel. And quite the beauty he is, too." Luca rubbed a hand over the animal's mangy haunches, beaming proudly. "Or she. Based on the length of those eyelashes, I can't be sure."

The beast lifted its head and gave them a placid look, its rubbery lips still chewing on a fat bougainvillea bloom. It definitely didn't look like the sort of beast one might ride when making a dramatic escape that would be forever immortalized between the pages of a scandal sheet.

"There are three of us," Ash pointed out with excruciating patience.

"Four," Clarinda corrected, giving Yasmin a baleful look.

"And only one camel," Ash said.

Holding up a finger in a plea for their continued forbearance, Luca disappeared into the bushes on the far side of the alley. Much rustling ensued and then he reappeared, holding a leather lead studded with rubies and emeralds. "Fortunately, while I was searching for a second camel, I stumbled over this fellow."

They all went slack-jawed with shock as a magnificent black stallion came prancing into the alley behind Luca. Moonlight poured over the creature's powerful haunches, making them gleam like polished ebony. As Luca brought the beast to a halt, the stallion tossed its head much as Yasmin was given to do, as if to show off its flowing black mane to its best advantage.

"Now that," Yasmin purred, "is not a camel."

"Oh, this is just marvelous!" Ash reached up as if to snatch off a hat that wasn't there just so he could crumple it up in disgust. "We're already making off with two of the sultan's most beautiful women, so why not take his most valuable horse as well? Because if you steal a woman in Morocco, they only cut off your head. If you steal a horse, do you know what they do?"

Despite the urgency of their situation, Clarinda had to bite back a smile. She had forgotten how adorable Ash was when he flew into a towering rage. There was a reason she had spent so much of her youth mercilessly goading him.

"*They cut off your head and piss down your neck!* It's a pity there's no time to break into the sultan's treasury so we can stuff our pockets with a fortune in his gold before we leave."

Luca visibly brightened at the idea.

"Oh, but wait! That won't be necessary." Ash snatched the stallion's lead from Luca's hand, thrusting it into his face. "Because I'm sure there are enough gems on this bridle and saddle to ensure that the sultan and his guard will chase us to the ends of the earth!"

"The horse alone is probably worth a hundred of me in Farouk's eyes," Clarinda pointed out. "Especially now."

"Then he's a bloody idiot," Ash said grimly. "But once you're safe, I'll make sure and send it back to him. With Luca's head and a note thanking him for his generosity."

Still muttering under his breath, Ash swung himself astride the stallion and offered Clarinda his hand. She took it without hesitation, swinging herself up behind him.

Luca's face fell. "No fair! Since I was the one who risked my neck stealing him, I thought I would get to ride the—"

"You thought wrong," Ash said flatly. "We'll follow the coastline until we're certain there's no one following us, then cut back to the desert."

He gave the reins an authoritative yank, wheeling the horse around so that they faced the sea. Clarinda glanced over her shoulder to find both the camel and Yasmin giving Luca the evil eye.

"Don't mind Yasmin, Luca," Clarinda called out softly. "She's just jealous because the camel has longer eyelashes than she does."

At that moment a panicked cry went up, not from the palace but from the stables. Torches began to flare in the darkness, followed by the sound of running feet.

As Luca and Yasmin scrambled to mount the camel, Ash reached one arm around to make sure Clarinda was secure. "Hold on to me," he ordered, his voice low and urgent. "And don't let go no matter what."

As he drove his heels into the stallion's flanks, sending them plunging down the alley and into the night, Clarinda wrapped her arms around his waist and pressed her cheek to his back, finding that one command she had no desire to disobey.

Farouk sat all alone in the darkness of his throne room.

He had dismissed his guard, something he found himself doing with increasing frequency lately, preferring the solitude of his thoughts.

But on this night his thoughts were as black as the shadows gathering around the throne that had once been his father's and his father's father's before him. Why should he concern himself with an anonymous assassin's blade when he was already surrounded by enemies?

By now one of those enemies would be waiting for him on his sleeping couch, her silvery blond tresses rippling across his pillow in the moonlight. He had longed for this moment for so long. All he had to do was go to her and claim what was rightfully his, what he had paid for with a fortune in gold that day in the slaver's market.

Yet there he sat, brooding all alone in the dark.

He could still clearly see the outrage on her face when she had risen out of her chair after he had informed her she would be sharing his bed that night. He had been spoiling for a fight in that moment and had halfway hoped she was going to give it to him. But instead she had swallowed her pride and offered him a mocking curtsy.

That was when he had finally seen what had been right before his eyes all along. There could be only one reason for her reluctant surrender—she was willing to sacrifice herself to save the man she loved.

And that man was not him.

She had never truly loved him. Her heart was not hers to give because it already belonged to another. It belonged to the man Farouk had welcomed into his home with open arms, the man who had saved his life not once, but twice, the man who had pretended to be his friend while plotting all the while to steal Clarinda right out from under his unsuspecting nose.

The two of them had played him for a fool. Had made him feel like the fat, clumsy boy the English had called Frankie, the boy who had cowered on the ground while his classmates rained blows down on him with their fists and kicked him with the hard, polished toes of their boots.

When he had returned from England to assume his father's throne, he had vowed he would never again be that boy.

If he failed to exert his mastery over Clarinda now, to punish her for her lies and her betrayal, he would prove himself to be everything his uncle believed him to be—weak, foolish, unfit to rule a province as magnificent as El Jadida.

He had a harem full of women fighting over the privilege of being summoned to his bed, women who would do anything to please him.

Yet tonight he would force himself on a woman who would be counting the seconds until he was through with her. She would submit, of course. What choice did she have? Her champion had fled, leaving her at his mercy. But as he gave her even more of a reason to despise him, her face would be turned away from him, her eyes squeezed shut as she dreamed of the man she wished were touching her, taking her.

Farouk might possess her body but he would never possess her heart or her soul.

When he wearily closed his own eyes, it wasn't Clarinda he saw but another woman, good-hearted and true. Her laughter was a merry ripple that did not humor him or mock him but soothed his restless soul. Her smile was always welcoming, her eyes always hungry for the sight of him. She did not look at him like that because he was Zin al-Farouk, the Exalted Sultan of El Jadida, but simply because she enjoyed his company. He had the strangest feeling she might have liked Frankie as well. That she might have helped him sneak into the kitchens at Eton to pilfer pastries so they might enjoy them together beneath the light of the pale English moon.

Someone sharply cleared his throat, interrupting his reverie.

He opened his eyes, expecting to find Solomon waiting in the torchlit corridor to escort him to the bed of his new concubine.

It wasn't the hulking eunuch who stood in the doorway of the throne room but Tarik. There was no disguising the look of gloating satisfaction on his uncle's face. Not even the nasty bruise on his jaw could dim the radiance of his wolfish smile.

"You should have never let the English infidel escape with his life," his uncle said, a triumphant sneer curling his upper lip, "because now he has returned to take what is yours."

"The sultan is coming! The sultan is coming!" The frantic whisper rippled through the harem, generating hope and panic in the heart of every women who heard it.

Some shot straight to their feet, frantically snatching up their robes, while others, still half-asleep, rolled off their sleeping couches, groaning and blindly fumbling for brushes and combs. After living with so many women day in and day out, very little ruffled the eunuchs who guarded them, but even they were stumbling over one another in their haste as they rushed about to light the lamps and rouse the more sluggish women.

When one of the concubines burrowed deeper beneath the sheets, dragging a colorful pillow over her head, the wife next to her gave her rump a sharp swat. "Get up! Do you want His Majesty to see you looking like the lazy cow you are?"

The concubine popped out from beneath the pillow just long enough to spit a curse at her. The wife beckoned to a younger wife, and together the two women yanked the sheets clear off the couch, dumping the sputtering concubine onto the floor.

It was rare indeed for the sultan to appear in the harem. He was far more likely to summon one of his wives or concubines to his sleeping quarters or even allow the eunuchs to choose a suitable bedmate for him. But tonight was different. Tonight he had decided to choose his companion for himself.

The women scrambled to the foot of their couches to stand at attention, desperately raking their fingers through their tangled hair, licking their lips and struggling to look sloe-eyed and seductive with eyes still dazed and puffy from sleep.

As the sultan's towering figure appeared in the doorway, they lowered their heads, bowing as one. Farouk stalked through their ranks as if they weren't even there, his long robes whipping around his ankles with each resolute stride. The women exchanged apprehensive looks beneath their lashes as he passed, and those who dared to steal a peek at the forbidding thundercloud of his face almost wished they hadn't.

It wasn't romance the sultan appeared to have on his mind that night but murder.

⚜ *Chapter Twenty-five*

When Farouk came barging into Poppy's alcove, tearing the curtain clean off its hooks with one furious swipe, the look on his face made her wonder if she had made a terrible miscalculation, perhaps even a fatal one.

The book of sonnets she was reading slid from her numb fingers as he stopped just inside the door, breathing hard and gazing at her with the oddest mixture of relief and fury. It was almost as if he had expected to find her alcove — and her couch — empty.

When he lunged back into motion, she scrambled off the other side of the couch, her every instinct warning her that if she cared one jot about her survival, she needed to get as far away as possible from this man.

But it was a very small alcove.

And he was a very large man.

He walked right over the couch, leaving an impressive bootprint in the middle of her silk sheets. Capturing her shoulders in his hands, he drove her back against the wall, pinning her as handily as a collector might pin a captive butterfly. Poppy had always felt like a big, clumsy ox standing next to Clarinda, but being handled in such a masterful way made her feel positively delicate and slightly light-headed. Thinking about all the wicked things he might do to her if she swooned only made her head swim faster.

"Where are they?" he demanded.

She blinked innocently at him through her spectacles. "Who?"

He lowered his head to give her a baleful look.

"Oh! You must mean Clarinda and Captain Burke. If I'm not mistaken, I do believe they're on their way back to England."

Although she wouldn't have thought it possible, her confession only enraged him further. He spat out a stream of guttural Arabic before remembering to switch to English. "Then what in the name of Allah are you still doing here? Why did the fools not take you with them?"

Poppy lifted her chin. Did no one in this world believe she was capable of deciding her own fate? "Because I didn't wish to go. I like it here. I can read as much as I like and I never have to wear a corset or slippers that pinch my toes." Her courage faltered as his heavy-lidded gaze danced down the front of her satin dressing gown, almost as if he could see the unrestrained softness beneath. "And besides, I've become very fond of *ktefa*. I sincerely doubt you could get a decent *ktefa* in any coffeehouse or bakery in London."

Farouk gave her a little shake, his bared teeth looking incredibly white against the darkness of his beard. "Did it not occur to you that you were taking a terrible risk? What if I had decided to take my revenge on them by throwing you in my dungeons or turning you over to my guard so they could use you for sport?"

Poppy knew she was supposed to quail with maidenly horror before such vile threats. But before she could stop it, a bubble of laughter welled up in her throat. "I was more worried about you jabbing hot spikes beneath my fingernails or cutting me up into tasty little morsels with one of your very large swords and feeding me to your crocodiles." She was laughing so hard now that his hands on her shoulders were all that was keeping her from doubling over. "You do have crocodiles, don't you? If you don't, you could always feed me to your tiger cubs, although I daresay it would take them a

very long time to finish me off since I'm a rather
hearty girl and they really are only overgrown
kittens."

Farouk glowered down at her, looking as if he
were on the verge of wolfing her down himself.
Instead, he seized her by the hand and started
for the door.

"Where are we going?" she gasped, wondering if she had spoken too soon and he was going
to fetch his sword and personally cut her up and
feed her to his crocodiles.

"To find your treacherous little friend and her
lover."

"But Captain Burke isn't—"

"And when I do, I am going to give them a
piece of my mind for being so foolish as to leave
a woman like you with a man like me." Farouk
dragged her right over the top of the bed with
him, making it clear that any more protests
would fall on deaf ears.

As he strode through the hall of the harem,
giving her no choice but to stumble after him,
the women ceased their whispering and gaped
at the two of them in slack-jawed astonishment.

Amused by their disbelieving faces, which
reminded her so much of the faces of the girls
at Miss Throckmorton's, Poppy could not resist
dragging her feet just long enough to give them

a smug smile and a cheery wag of her fingers before Farouk jerked her out the door.

The stallion went plunging down the rocky path that led to the sea, leaving the shadow of Farouk's fortress behind them. Clarinda knew she should have been terrified, but all she felt was exhilaration. She would gladly have raced through the night forever, her arms wrapped around Ash's waist, the fullness of her breasts pressed to the warmth of his back.

She felt liberated at last. This freedom had nothing to do with escaping the gilded bars of Farouk's cage. She had always felt free when Ash was in her arms. He had never expected her to be anything more than what she was. She could be mischievous, charming, or as ill-tempered as a wet cat and still trust that he would adore her. At least that's what she had believed up until the moment he had walked out of her life.

She linked her hands together over the shifting muscles of his abdomen and turned her face to the wind, finally ready to leave that moment behind forever, just like Farouk's fortress, and embrace this one. She had lived long enough now to know it might be the only one they would ever share. The wind whipped away the hood of her robe, setting her hair free to stream behind them in silvery ribbons.

As they ran out of road, Ash guided the stallion in a wide arc and sent them racing along the shoreline. Moonlight frosted the curl of the waves spilling onto the sandy shore. The stallion thundered down the beach, his flashing hooves sending up a fine mist of sand and spray. The scent of the sea filled Clarinda's lungs, its clean, salty tang washing away every lingering trace of sandalwood and jasmine.

They were going to make it. They were going to be free.

At least that's what she allowed herself to believe until the first shot rang out. Her heart leapt into her throat. She twisted around in the saddle. All she could see behind them were Luca and Yasmin, their camel making a valiant effort to keep pace with the stallion.

A second pistol ball whizzed past her ear, sending up a plume of sand a few feet in front of them.

To Clarinda's shock, Ash began to tug on the reins, slowing the stallion from a gallop to a canter.

"They're shooting at us!" she shouted. "You need to go faster, not slower!"

"Those were only warning shots," he called back to her. "If they had meant to hit us, we'd be dead right now."

"So what's your plan? Making it easier for them to hit us when they decide to stop firing warning shots?"

As they slowed even further, Luca pulled the camel abreast of them, a disgruntled Yasmin hanging on to him for dear life. "What in the bloody hell are you doing, Cap?" he yelled. They could hear the thunder of hoofbeats behind them now, growing louder with every second they squandered. "We'll never be able to outrun them at this pace."

Ash twisted around to face his friend, his profile as grim as Clarinda had ever seen it. "I can't risk them firing on her. I won't risk it. Even if they take us, at least she'll be alive."

"For how long?" Luca's panicked shout echoed Clarinda's own bleak thoughts.

Plainly in no mood for argument, Ash sawed on the reins, wheeling the stallion around so they could face their pursuers. The spirited beast reared up on its hind legs and pawed at the air, forcing Clarinda to cling even more tightly to Ash or risk being dumped on her bottom. Ash easily brought the creature under control, using little more than a masterful squeeze of his thighs.

Swearing in both Italian and Romany, Luca followed Ash's example, guiding the camel in a clumsy circle that nearly unseated Yasmin, who proved she needed only one language in which to swear.

Then all they could do was sit and wait for Farouk and his riders to descend upon them.

❖ *Chapter Twenty-six*

Farouk had brought only a dozen soldiers of his guard with him. Clarinda couldn't decide if that was a measure of his confidence in himself or of his contempt for his adversaries.

As the riders approached, Ash surprised her once again by dismounting and then reaching up to lift her to her feet. "I'd rather be on my feet to face an enemy than have my horse shot out from under me," he murmured, his hands lingering against her waist. "Although I have a feeling Farouk would shoot me before he'd shoot this particular horse."

Ash was right, Clarinda thought. There was something bracing about standing on one's feet to face an adversary. At least there was until Ash firmly tucked her behind him, forcing her to crane her neck to see around one of his broad shoulders.

The riders swooped down upon them like vultures, their black robes rippling behind them. Beneath the kaffiyehs wound around their brows, their faces were dark and forbidding. When Clarinda saw that Farouk's uncle Tarik was among them, her heart plunged all the way to her toes.

Farouk was riding a towering chestnut that could have held its own during any race at Newmarket. It wasn't until he reined in the horse that Clarinda saw the cloak-wrapped bundle in his arms. A pale hand appeared to push back the hood of the cloak, and a pair of spectacles emerged, moonlight winking off their wire frames.

"Poppy?" Clarinda whispered disbelievingly. She started forward instinctively, thinking only to make sure her friend was unharmed. Ash's arm shot out to block her path.

Before anyone else could speak, Yasmin heaved a dramatic sigh from atop the camel. "I was a fool to run away. I should have known he would never let me go."

Farouk squinted at her. "Yasmin, is that you? What are you doing here?"

Yasmin gaped at him, her tragic resignation turning to outrage. "You did not even notice I was missing?"

"Forgive me," Farouk said, sarcasm ripening in his tone, "but I did not have time to count my concubines before riding out. My stable had just been robbed and I was too busy counting my horses!"

"Pshaw! This is why I can no longer be this man's concubine. He cares more for his horses than his women!" Yasmin twined her arms around Luca's waist, rubbing against him like a hungry cat. "Today is a good day for you, Gypsy. I have decided I will marry you after all."

"That's odd," Luca said, "since I don't recall asking you. But if you keep doing what you're doing, I just might."

Farouk slid off his mount, putting himself on equal footing with Ash and leaving Poppy sitting astride the horse. His contemptuous gaze encompassed both Clarinda and the stallion before shifting to Ash. "I finally recognized you for the scoundrel you are, Burke, but I did not take you for a thief as well."

"Didn't you once tell me if I desired anything that belonged to you, I had only to ask?"

Farouk's eyes narrowed, the gleam in them reminding them all just how dangerous he could be. "You did not ask."

Tarik flung himself off his own horse and strode forward. "You are wasting your breath arguing with these infidels. Why do you not just kill them all and have done with it?"

"Silence!" Farouk roared. "If I require your counsel, I will seek it! Until I do, it would be wise for you to stop wasting *your* breath."

Although he was still visibly seething, Tarik was not so foolish as to ignore his nephew's warning.

Farouk nodded toward Clarinda. "You have risked everything for this woman. Do you believe she is worth it?"

Ash lifted one shoulder in a careless shrug. "She's worth far more to me than you know. If I don't return her to the man who hired me to retrieve her, I don't get paid the rest of what he owes me."

Even though Clarinda suspected Ash was bluffing, the words still stung.

"So now you are a scoundrel, a thief, *and* a liar," Farouk said.

"Captain Burke is telling the truth." Clarinda stepped out from behind Ash. "He is not my lover. I am betrothed to his brother—Maximillian Burke, the Earl of Dravenwood."

"She was on her way to marry him when

those nasty Corsairs attacked our ship," Poppy added helpfully.

With Poppy's words adding weight to their own, Farouk appeared to be on the verge of believing them. Unfortunately, it did nothing to improve his temper. "You might have mentioned you belonged to another when I asked you to be my bride," he told Clarinda.

"As I recall," she replied with withering scorn, "you did not ask me. You *told* me. And since I knew the only other path open to me was to become one of your concubines, I decided it was safer to play along. If I had told you I was already betrothed, would you have let me go?"

Farouk pondered the question for a moment, but in the end his silence was answer enough. He studied them both, the calculating gleam in his eye deepening.

"Very well, Burke," he finally said. "If the woman is nothing to you, then it shouldn't trouble you if I take her back to my palace. I will pay you double the gold her fiancé owes you and you will be free to go on your way. Since I am in a generous mood, I will even let you keep the horse."

"What about the camel?" Luca asked. "Can I keep the camel?" Yasmin grabbed a fold of his flesh just below his ribs and gave it a vicious pinch, prompting him to wheeze out, "And the concubine."

Ignoring him, Farouk turned to his guards. "Seize her."

Two of the guards dismounted, but before they could take more than a step toward Clarinda, Ash wrapped an arm around her waist and snatched her against him. A pistol magically appeared in his hand, pointed straight at Farouk's heart. "If they lay so much as one finger on her, you're a dead man."

An array of weapons materialized with equal ease in the hands of Farouk's guards, including pistols, scimitars, and even a short-handled ax. The two men coolly surveyed each other. They both knew Ash was badly outnumbered. If he fired on Farouk, Clarinda would die anyway.

"Take me," Ash said grimly. "If it's a pound of flesh you want, then you can lash it from my back. Or even get it by relieving my head from my body. I don't care what you do to me. But let her go."

"No!" Clarinda shouted, trying to wrench herself from Ash's arms. "I'll go back with you! I'll do whatever you want! Just don't hurt him!"

The last response either of them expected from Farouk was for him to throw back his head with a booming laugh. "I cannot decide which one of you is the greater fool. She is willing to sacrifice her body for you even as you offer your life for her. What a touching—and somewhat stomach-churning—display." He shook his head scornfully at Clarinda. "May your God help this poor fiancé of yours if he loves you as I did."

"You never loved me!" No longer willing to hide behind any man, Clarinda finally managed to jerk herself free of Ash's arms. "Oh, you wanted me and you may even have been fond of me. But you never loved me."

Farouk nostrils flared with outrage, much like his stallion's. "How can you—a mere woman—presume to know how I—the Exalted Sultan of El Jadida—feel?"

"How do you feel right now, Farouk?" Clarinda took a step toward him, forcing Ash to lower the pistol. "Do you feel as if someone has taken one of those big daggers of yours and jammed it right through your heart? Do you weep into your pillow until you finally fall asleep from exhaustion only to wake the next morning and start weeping all over again?" She took another step, keenly aware that Ash was listening to her every word as she described the darkest hours of her life. "Do you dream of a day when you'll be able to draw breath again without feeling as if you've swallowed a bag of ground glass?" She came to a halt directly in front of Farouk, stabbing a finger at his massive chest. "Because *that's* what love is. And *that's* how it feels when everything you love the most is torn from your arms." She shook her head with genuine regret as she gazed up at him, remembering all of the kindnesses he had shown her. "I didn't break your heart, Farouk. I simply bruised your pride."

Farouk scowled down at her for a moment, then threw up his hands in frustration. "What am I to do with the both of you? Am I supposed to let your insult to my pride and to the honor of my forefathers go unavenged? If I set you free now, how will I ever be able to hold up my head among my own people?"

No one even noticed Poppy had slid off the chestnut until she tugged on the sleeve of Farouk's robe. "I believe I might have a solution for your quandary, Your Majesty. You can take me instead of her."

"Poppy, no!" Clarinda cried, horrified that her defiance had led to this.

Ignoring Clarinda, Poppy continued talking to Farouk as if they were the only two people on the beach. "Weren't you the one who told me one woman in your bed was as good as the next?

And just think how deliciously vengeful you'll appear when everyone believes you ripped Clarinda's dearest friend from her arms and forced her to become your concubine to punish Clarinda for running away with Captain Burke." Poppy's eyes sparkled behind her spectacles as she lowered her voice to a stage whisper. "You can even chain me in the dungeon for a few nights if it will make you look more dastardly."

Farouk gazed down at Poppy for a long moment with no expression whatsoever before taking a threatening step toward her. "Your attempt to spare your friend my wrath is a noble one, Miss Montmorency. But if you think you are going to get off that lightly, you are mistaken."

Visibly alarmed by the look in his eye, Poppy began to back away from him. He followed her step for step, towering over her. "You underestimate my thirst for vengeance. I am not going to make you my concubine. I am going to make you my wife." Clarinda's mouth fell open in shock as he continued stalking Poppy. "That way I will have a lifetime in which to make you pay for your friend's misdeeds."

Poppy stopped retreating and stood her ground, resting her hands on her generous hips. "Contrary to what most people believe, I do have my pride. What makes you think I would stoop to accepting such a romantic and heartfelt proposal?"

"This." Farouk hauled her into his arms and kissed her without an ounce of the polite restraint he had always shown Clarinda. Clarinda and Ash exchanged a stupefied glance, and for once even Luca was speechless.

Yasmin rolled her eyes. "It sounds like a fair trade to me. The silly cow is large enough to make two of us."

The kiss went on for so long that Farouk's guards began to awkwardly shuffle their feet and look at the ground. Everyone knew Farouk wasn't worried about them revealing anything they had witnessed on this night. They were too attached to their tongues.

Farouk finally drew away from Poppy, lifting a hand to smooth back her hair as he gazed into her eyes with the utmost tenderness. "I have a responsibility to the women already under my protection. I may not be able to make you my only wife in the tradition of your people, but I swear to you on the blood of my forefathers that you will be my last wife."

Poppy sniffed. "Well, in that case, my answer is yes."

Clarinda might have suspected she was losing her mind if several puzzle pieces hadn't suddenly fallen into place. "Wait just one minute," she said.

Farouk and Poppy faced her, looking like two children who had just been caught with their hands in the biscuit jar.

Clarinda pointed an accusing finger at Farouk. "When you were going on and on in the hammam that morning about there being only 'one true mate for every man' and that to 'embrace her was to embrace your destiny,' you weren't talking about me, were you?"

Farouk's brow furrowed in a puzzled frown. "How did you know about that?"

"Never mind that." Clarinda shifted her attention to Poppy. "And that big basket of *ktefa* Farouk sent to the harem wasn't for me, either, was it? It was for you. He was courting you behind my back, wasn't he?" Clarinda wagged a finger at Farouk. "You sly dog! You should be ashamed of yourself!"

He gave her an arch look.

"But I can certainly see why you're not. And, Poppy, you're nothing but a sneaky little tart!" Clarinda exclaimed, no longer able to hide her delight at this unexpected turn of events. "You finally managed to find a secret you could keep, didn't you?"

In response, Poppy mimed turning a key at her beaming lips and tossing it over her shoulder.

Slipping an arm around Poppy's shoulders as if it had always belonged there, Farouk swept his stern gaze over Clarinda and Ash. "Since Miss Montmorency has so nobly agreed to pay your debt, you are free to go. But I want my horse back." He signaled to one of his guards. "You may take the chestnut instead."

"Have you gone mad?" Tarik rushed forward, all but foaming at the mouth. "I cannot believe you are just going to let him go! Why, he may even be the one behind the attempts on your life! Did he not appear on the very day you were first attacked by the assassins? And was he not in the courtyard on the day the stone nearly crushed you to death?"

"He was the one who saved me," Farouk patiently pointed out.

Tarik spun around and pointed an accusing finger at Luca. "What of him then? Where was the Romany jackal when the stone fell? Does anyone know?"

"There is a certain lovely slave girl who might be able to attest as to my whereabouts that afternoon," Luca offered.

Ash stepped forward and said calmly, "Perhaps you should ask your uncle where he was on that day."

Tarik gaped at Ash for a minute before barking, "Do not listen to him! Why would you even think about believing this infidel or his whore? They have already proven there is no truth in them. Nothing but poison and lies spew from their lips!"

Farouk eyed Ash warily. "What are you trying to say?"

Ash shrugged. "Sometimes a man has no need to look outside his walls for his enemies."

Farouk slowly turned to study his uncle, the disbelief on his face rapidly turning to appalled fury. "You? You would seek to kill the only son of your own brother? Your own blood?"

Tarik lifted a hand as if to ward off a blow. "The assassins were not supposed to kill you." Too late, he realized his mistake. The color drained from his rage-mottled cheeks. "They were only supposed to wound you. To make you angry."

Judging by the murderous glitter in Farouk's obsidian eyes, Tarik had succeeded beyond his wildest dreams.

"And what of the stone? Was that supposed to *wound* me as well?"

"A simple miscalculation. You were closer to the wall than I realized. Do you not see?" Tarik pleaded, taking a step away from his nephew. "I did it for your own good. For the good of all El Jadida. I had to wake you up to the dangers that surround us on all sides. I had to make you see that you cannot afford to relax your guard or negotiate with those who seek to do you harm and take what is yours. The only way for a man to prove himself a true lion of El Jadida is not through treaties or by inviting his enemies to break bread with him but on the battlefield with a sword in his hand and a battle cry on his lips."

"So you would have had me attack our innocent neighbors while my true enemy sat at my own table and broke bread with me?" Gently setting Poppy aside, Farouk swept a scimitar from one of his guard's hands and advanced on his uncle, his upper lip curled in disgust.

Tarik scrambled backward but there was nowhere he could go to escape his nephew's towering shadow. "Please, my son! I beg of you . . . mercy . . ."

"I am not your son."

Farouk drew back the weapon, its blade glinting in the moonlight. Ash pulled Clarinda back into his arms, pressing her face into his chest. She clutched at the front of his robe and squeezed her eyes shut, wishing she could close her ears as well to spare them the sound that would come next.

Instead, she heard Poppy's cheerful voice. "It occurs to me, Your Majesty, that if I am not to be chained in your dungeon on this night, you just might have a vacancy. And what better way to usher in a new era for El Jadida than to show your subjects that mercy is not a sign of weakness but a measure of a ruler's strength."

Clarinda dared to steal a peek at Farouk, waiting for him to chide Poppy—a mere woman—for daring to interfere in his business.

Farouk slowly lowered the sword, his furious snarl turning into a contemptuous sneer. "Get the traitor out of my sight."

Tarik collapsed on the sand, gibbering in Arabic. As two of the guards hauled him to his feet and dragged him to one of their mounts, Farouk turned to face Ash and Clarinda once again.

"Before you go," he told Ash, "I would like to have a word with Miss Cardew. In private."

Ash's arms tightened around her but Clarinda said, "It's all right," and gently eased herself from them.

Ash folded his arms over his chest and watched them walk to the edge of the water, never once taking his eyes off her.

Farouk rested his hands gently on her shoulders, gazing down at her face with a bittersweet mix of tenderness and regret. "I wanted to tell you that you were right. I never loved you. But I did like you very, *very* much. Until you came along, I had never entertained the notion that a woman could be more than just a body to warm my bed. That she could be my friend. But you were."

She smiled up at him. "If you harm Poppy in any way—including breaking her heart—I shall no longer be your friend. And I can promise you that I would make a most formidable enemy."

The look he gave Poppy in that moment proved there was little danger of that. "I will consider her heart my greatest treasure and guard it with my life. I swear it upon the honor of my forefathers."

Rising up on her tiptoes, Clarinda threw her arms around his neck and gave him a brief but fierce hug. "Thank you," she whispered, surprised to find her throat so tight she could barely speak. "For everything."

Farouk returned to Poppy's side while Clarinda strolled back to Ash, finally able to enjoy the gentle breeze and the murmur of the surf against the sand. One of the guards had swapped the chestnut for the stallion while she and Farouk said their good-byes.

Holding the horse's reins, Ash watched her approach, his amber eyes as opaque as the desert sands. "For a minute there, I thought you were going to change your mind and beg Farouk to take you back to his harem."

"Why, Captain Burke," she said, unable to resist giving him a mocking smile, "for a man who is only doing his job, you certainly have a jealous streak."

✤ Chapter Twenty-seven

Clarinda sat on a rock near the gently burbling spring, gazing up at the sky. After her months in captivity, the vast sweep of stars was almost too much for her eye to embrace. When they had first seen the oasis wink into view in the moonlight after plodding across the shifting sands of the desert for over three hours, she had thought it must be a mirage, a trick being played on her mind by her weary body. But as they had drawn closer, the oasis hadn't vanished but grown even larger and more enticing. One side of the pool was fringed with swaying palms, the other open to the glittering vista of sand and sky.

With Farouk's blessing they had turned their backs on the coast and headed inland across the desert. If any of them had found it odd that the sultan had set off in pursuit of them with his guard carrying extra water and supplies, in-

cluding a small tent, they had been wise enough
not to mention it. They had simply thanked him
for his generosity and patiently waited while
Clarinda bid Poppy a second tearful farewell.

Tucking her hands in the sleeves of her robe,
Clarinda rubbed her arms to ward off the night
chill. She was going to miss her loyal friend more
than she could say. Poppy had promised she
would coax Farouk into returning to England
for a visit as soon as possible. Given the openly
adoring glances the sultan had been casting at
her friend, Clarinda had no reason to doubt Poppy's words. She shook her head, marveling once
again at the mysterious workings of the heart.

Her own heart thudded heavily in her breast
as she heard a footstep in the sand behind her.
Ash dropped the robe he had been wearing during their flight from the palace over her shoulders, enfolding her in the warm, masculine musk
of his scent. "Most people don't realize how cold
the desert can be at night," he said, propping
one foot on the rock where she sat.

He tipped back his head to study the sky, his
profile as inscrutable as its glittering face. He
had stripped down to his breeches and shirt-
sleeves and pushed those sleeves up to reveal
powerful forearms lightly dusted with fawn-
colored hair.

Although the tent had been set up at the far end of the pool, beneath the sheltering fronds of the palms, Yasmin's shrill voice still carried easily through the hush of the desert night. "You are a pig dog. Your mother was a pig and your father was a dog!"

"Ah, *cara mia*! How I adore it when you talk so sweetly to me!"

Luca's tender reply elicited an outraged shriek from Yasmin, followed by the sound of shattering pottery.

Then all was ominous silence.

"They've been bickering since we left the coast. Do you think they've finally killed one another?" Clarinda asked, more worried about Luca than Yasmin.

"I daresay they'll die in one another's arms before this night is done," Ash replied cryptically. "Or at least before we reach Max's encampment."

"Max?" Clarinda echoed, reeling with shock. "Maximillian is *here*? In Morocco?"

Ash nodded. "He's set up camp with his men just outside of Marrakech. It shouldn't take us more than three days to get there."

Three days, Clarinda thought, the very words making her heart go numb.

All this time she had pictured her fiancé sitting safely behind some desk at his outpost in Burma, not camped three days away from where she was being held captive in Farouk's harem. She had assumed Ash would have to transport her to Burma by ship. That they would spend long, lazy days—and nights—together at sea before he sauntered back out of her life for good.

Three days was nothing but a wink of time after a decade of waiting. Until he had materialized in Farouk's courtyard like a mirage, Clarinda hadn't even realized she had still been waiting. She had genuinely believed she had been moving forward toward the future. A future with Max. A future without Ash.

Which, it seemed, was exactly what she was going to have.

Still studying the sky, Ash said, "Max and I haven't always seen eye to eye, but he'll make you a good husband. Steady and true."

"I know," she said, unable to deny his words, no matter how deeply they cut.

"You won't have to hurl things at his head just to get his attention or worry about him running off to the far ends of the world to chase some ridiculous dream."

"Was that why you left me?" She strove to keep her voice light to disguise the hurt that still lingered in her heart. "To see places like this?

Wondrous places you might have missed if we had settled down to live in that garret together?"

"I've seen creatures in the Indian rain forest so wondrous and rare they haven't had names since the Garden of Eden. I've ridden an elephant across the African veldt with nothing but grass as far as the eye could see. I've watched the sun rise and set over the ancient pyramids of Giza. I've traveled the world over and seen sights so incredible most men would never even dare to dream of them." He turned to look at her, his eyes smoldering like smoky topazes in the starlight. "But I've never seen anything that could compare to you."

Clarinda rose to face him, his robe slipping from her shoulders. In that moment, there was no ghost of the past or specter of the future. No questions and no regrets. There was only this night, this place—an oasis paradise in the shifting sands of time.

"Is it true what the scandal sheets say about you, Captain Burke? That when you rescued the Hindustani princess, you turned down a fortune in gold and precious gems?"

"I did." His gaze dropped to her lips. "And all for the pleasure of a kiss."

"Then who am I to deny you such a reward?" Clarinda said softly. After a heartbeat of hesita-

tion, Ash framed her face in the warmth of his
hands and brought his mouth down on hers.
The second their lips touched, she knew neither
of them would ever be content with a mere kiss.

Yet still he strove to be a man of his word,
not stealing kisses he hadn't earned but lavish-
ing her lips with one long kiss that went on and
on. Each feathery brush of his mouth over hers
poured water on the parched desert her heart
had become without him and sent lush tendrils
of desire coiling through her. The tip of his
tongue flirted with the seam of her lips, teasing her, toying with her, making it impossible to
resist or protest when he parted those lips and
took her with his tongue in exactly the same
way he had once taken her with his body.

As her tongue responded to that unspoken
challenge by exploring his mouth with equal
abandon, he wrapped his arms around her, fitting her to his body as if she had always belonged there.

She was grateful for that support because her
knees threatened to fail her the minute he bent
his head and touched his warm, moist lips to
her throat, seeking the pulse that had begun to
beat madly just beneath the silken skein of her
skin. It was beating for him and him alone, responding to every velvety caress of his lips like

a primitive drumbeat. She was forced to cling to him even more tightly as his lips formed a seal over that tender spot, gently sucking even as his teeth came together to give her a sharp little nip, branding her as his own in the most primal way imaginable.

She turned her head, helplessly seeking any taste of him she could find. Her lips hungrily traced the strong curve of his jaw, exulting in the scrape of his razor stubble beneath their softness. But that enticing sample of him only made her crave more. She tore open the front of his shirt with both hands, not caring that it was the only one he had. Her lips flowered against that spectacular meshing of muscle and sinew, her tongue flicking through the crisp curls of his chest hair to savor the salt and spice of the skin beneath.

Cupping her bottom in his hands, he lifted her, molding her to him so tightly she could feel the full measure of his desire for her pressed against the softness of her belly. She gasped, having allowed herself to forget both its power and its magnitude.

His warm chuckle filled her ear. "You needn't pretend to be impressed, darling. Weren't you the one who told Poppy I was spreading tall tales about my exploits to compensate for my own short—"

This time it was his lips she silenced with her two fingers before whispering, "I lied."

He watched, his golden eyes wary, yet glowing with desire as her other hand began a sinuous slide down the front of his shirt to the muscled planes of his abdomen. Her fingertips glided even lower, finally brushing the broad tip of him through the straining buckskin of his trousers.

He threw back his head with a ragged groan. "I'm not sure what sort of elixir you've been drinking now," he gritted out from between his clenched teeth, "but I hope you brought a whole barrel of it."

As Clarinda traced every hard, throbbing inch of what he had in store for her and watched his high cheekbones grow taut and flushed with hunger, she felt drunk all right. Drunk with need. Drunk with power. Drunk with desire.

Ash took his revenge by cupping the plump weight of one breast in his palm through her robe, squeezing softly even as his thumb flicked back and forth over the turgid bud of her nipple, sending tongues of flame racing through her blood that threatened to consume her where she stood.

Then his hands were at her shoulders, gently easing her robe from them so that it rippled to the sand behind her. Beneath it she wore only the diaphanous layers of silk she had been expected to wear to Farouk's bed.

"By God, woman," he growled as he cupped the back of her head in his hand and gently lowered her into the soft linen folds of the robe, "the things I would do if I could ever get you into a proper bed."

As his mouth descended upon hers once more, Clarinda could think of no bed more fitting for the two of them than a shifting bed of sand next to a gently bubbling pool with a glittering canopy of stars above it.

Still ravishing her mouth with deep, drugging kisses, Ash covered her with his weight, pressing one knee to the aching mound between her thighs with deliberate care. She tangled her hands in the coarse silk of his hair and reared off the robe to ride that knee, seeking any relief at all from the delicious ache that was beginning to spread out in waves from that gentle but relentless pressure.

When he rolled off her after a few minutes of that exquisite torture, she moaned in protest at his heartless cruelty. She opened her eyes to scowl at him only to find him lying on his side next to her, his head propped on one hand.

"Do you realize I've never seen you completely naked? Well, at least only in my dreams."

Clarinda frowned, thinking back to that morning in the meadow. They had both been so young, so fevered, so desperate to carry out what they had begun before they lost their nerve. She remembered Ash's hands impatiently tugging up her nightdress, her own trembling fingers awkwardly struggling with the unfamiliar fastenings of his trousers until he had captured both of her hands in one of his and finished the task for her. She was so lost in that memory it took a moment for the second part of Ash's statement to sink in.

When it did, her nose crinkled in a delighted smile. "Did you really dream about me?"

"Every night," he confessed solemnly. "Without fail."

"Was I naked in most of them?"

He nodded. "Except for the ones where you were wearing nothing but lace garters, silk stockings, and high-heeled, red velvet slippers with jeweled buckles. Those were some of my favorites."

"I dreamed about you, too," she admitted, lowering her eyes.

"I trust I wasn't wearing garters, stockings, and high-heeled slippers?"

"Of course not. Although occasionally you were wearing shackles. And sometimes a noose."

"Vengeful little minx." The look in his narrowed eyes sent a fresh thrill down her spine. "Don't you think it's time we made those dreams come true?"

She slowly nodded, giving him her leave to gently strip her of the layers of silk until she lay naked before him in the starlight, utterly exposed, utterly vulnerable.

Clarinda had to resist the urge to cover herself with her hands like the shyest of virgins as his heavy-lidded gaze drifted down her, lingering at the pink-tipped fullness of her breasts, the gentle curve of her waist, the silvery blond nest of curls between her pale thighs, before finally returning to her face.

"Sweet Christ, Clarinda," he whispered hoarsely. "You almost make me wish I were a sultan. That I could carry you away and keep you locked in my harem away from the eyes of other men. I wouldn't be as generous as Farouk. I'd chain you to my couch and keep you just like this so I could come to you at any time, day or night, and pleasure you until you abandoned all thoughts of escape and begged me to never let you go."

Clarinda drew in a shuddering breath, stirred more deeply than she would ever have admitted by the power of that dark fantasy.

His gaze drifted downward again. "Is it true that the women of the harem taught you exactly where to touch to give yourself the most pleasure?"

"They did," she cautiously admitted.

"Where?"

Clarinda gave him a chiding look, embarrassed that he could still make her blush after everything she had been through, everything they had done. "You know perfectly well where."

His lips curved in a slow, wicked smile. "Show me."

They both knew she was helpless to resist such a blatant challenge. Slanting him a provocative glance, she slid her hand down over her belly to the pale curls between her legs. As her longest finger disappeared into them, Ash's smile faded, making his face look as hard and dangerous as some desert marauder's.

His hand shot out to capture her wrist in a velvety vise, much as it had done that night in the harem. "There's no need for a lady to see to her own pleasure when there's a gentleman eager to set his hand to the task."

"You, sir," she murmured, pressing her lips to the irresistible swath of skin just below his ear, "are no gentleman."

His devil-may-care dimple reappeared. "And I'll make you glad of it before this night is done. See if I don't."

As if to prove his boast, he threaded his own fingers through the gossamer silk of those curls, an indulgence he had denied himself while she was under the influence of the elixir. He brushed one fingertip over the rigid little bud he found nestled beneath them, setting off a shuddering tremor of delight.

Having already learned the dark and wondrous power of his hands, Clarinda was shocked to realize her pleasure was not dulled but intensified now that she was in her right mind. Of course, if Ash kept touching her that way, she wouldn't be in her right mind for long. He was going to drive her mad with longing.

Each deft stroke of his fingertip only deepened her torment, stripping her of her pride and bringing her one step closer to abandoning reason and pleading with him just as she had in the harem to take her. This time she couldn't even blame her wanton behavior on some ancient potion. She was intoxicated by his touch, her senses staggered by the pleasure his skillful hands were delivering to her throbbing flesh.

Her thighs fell apart as his finger glided downward to part the silky petals below that bud. She could feel herself beginning to swell and open like one of the exotic blooms from Farouk's garden, her body offering an invitation Ash was helpless to resist. She gasped as his finger slid right into her, gently pressing against the resistance it met there.

It had been so long. Too long . . .

When a second finger joined the first, Clarinda could only pant and squirm in helpless delight, and when a third joined those two, she had to sink her teeth into Ash's broad shoulder to muffle a moan of raw need. He took advantage of the slick nectar his touch had coaxed from her yearning body to work his fingers even deeper inside her, filling her, spreading her, preparing her for some wonder that was yet to come. As his fingers ravished her with breathtaking thoroughness, the callused pad of his thumb began to circle the bud at the crux of her curls once more, leaving her helpless to do anything but lie there writhing and twitching beneath his hand, a slave to the mastery of his touch.

She was so lost in her bliss that Ash kissed a tingling path all the way down to the quivering plane of her belly before she even realized it.

"What are you doing?" she demanded breathlessly as his tongue had its way with the shallow little dimple of her navel.

He lifted his head, eyeing her with deliberate intent. "I realize you've been enjoying the tutelage of Farouk's women, but I like to think I've also learned a thing or two since the last time we were together this way." His rakish grin sent a delicious shiver down her spine. "Or three."

After the things Clarinda had learned in the harem, she would have sworn nothing could surprise her, but as Ash wrapped his big, warm hands around her thighs, ensuring that she couldn't bring them together even if she wanted to, she found herself trembling all over with a giddy mixture of shock and anticipation. He was going to do to her what the man in the harem fresco had been doing to the sloe-eyed beauty. He was going to put his mouth on her. *There.*

Before she had time to fully grasp what was about to happen, Ash used his clever tongue to lick into the very heart of her. She gasped and arched off the robe, nearly undone by the illicit pleasure of it all. She had spent the last nine years building a wall around her heart to protect it from him but she had no defenses against the tender lash of his tongue against the very heart of her womanhood.

The desert and the stars vanished in a blinding flash. Clarinda's entire world narrowed to Ash's mouth and the pleasure it was giving her. She understood then the mindless wonder she had glimpsed on the face of the woman in the mural. She knew why the woman's mouth had been slack, her eyes glazed, her thighs splayed wide to welcome whatever pleasure her lover chose to give her, no matter how scandalous or forbidden.

Then all rational thought deserted her as Ash flicked his tongue over that swollen nubbin of flesh at the exact same moment he dipped his fingers into her, setting off a quaking explosion of ecstasy that rocked her to her core. Clarinda cried out his name, feeling as if everything between her legs were melting with pleasure.

Ash took advantage of all that softness, all that heat, all that wetness, by unfastening his trousers and driving his rigid shaft deep into her. Clarinda shuddered and bucked, taking him even deeper without meaning to. He had tried to prepare her with his fingers, but there was no preparing her for the glorious thickness of him, the way he filled her to the brim, driving out all doubts, all fears, all regrets.

When he went completely still, she might have protested if he hadn't done it while buried so deep within her she could feel each shuddering beat of her heart in the place where their bodies were joined.

Bracing his weight on his hands, he gazed down into her face, his savage expression betraying the cost of his control. "When Max found me, I was facing a firing squad. If I had died that day, I was going to come back and haunt you."

"You already were," she said softly, cupping her hand around his nape and dragging his lips back down to hers for a fierce kiss.

This time Ash didn't kiss her so much as consume her. It was as if he could no longer be content with feasting on her mouth and body but would devour her heart as well. And in that moment she would have willingly fed it to him, along with her soul.

As he began to move within her, the proper English lady she had striven to become disappeared, leaving behind the wild child he had once adored. She dug her fingernails into the shifting muscles of his back, no longer able to lie to herself or to him. She could never belong to any other man because she had always belonged to him.

And she always would.

They were just as desperate for one another as they had been all those years ago. In so many ways it was even better now than it had been then. There was no shyness, no fear of discovery, no awkwardness, no pain. There was only the wonder of their breaths mingling with each kiss and gasp of pleasure, the dizzying joy of their hearts pounding as one, the graceful dance of their bodies moving in perfect rhythm.

Clarinda wanted it to go on forever but she had waited too long, suffered through too many endless nights dreaming of this moment. When Ash would have held back to prolong her pleasure, she wrapped her legs around him and squeezed him even tighter.

"Remember what I told you during the massage?" she whispered in his ear. "That I didn't want to be treated like a piece of porcelain? That I liked it hard and I liked it deep?"

She didn't have to remind him again. He quickened the pace and urgency of his strokes, only too happy to oblige her. She succumbed to that irresistible rhythm until a broken wail escaped her lips, heralding an indescribable bliss that rolled through her like thunder.

As her inner muscles convulsed around him, she felt him grow even harder and thicker within her. It turned out he *had* learned a thing or two since the last time they'd been together. For at the exact moment a guttural groan escaped his lips, he withdrew from her, spilling his seed against the softness of her belly.

✣   ✣   ✣

Clarinda lay naked in the warm cradle of Ash's arms, listening to the wind whisper through the palms and gazing up in wonder at the shimmering swath of stars strewn across the indigo sky. "I don't remember there ever being so many stars back in England. They look as if you could just reach up and pluck one out of the sky."

"I suspect they were the exact same stars, just obscured by soot and fog and mist. But I can't say for sure." Ash drew her even closer to him, pressing a reverent kiss to the softness of her hair. "I never saw them because I never looked up. I was too busy looking at you."

She toyed lazily with the crisp whorls of his chest hair, tilting her face up to give him a dreamy smile. "As I recall, you weren't quite so complimentary when we were children. I seem to remember names like 'hellacious little hoyden' and 'sneaky little shrew' being bandied about more than once."

"That's because you were a hellacious little hoyden and a sneaky little shrew." He cocked an eyebrow at her. "Did you ever once consider just telling me you liked me instead of doing all of those wicked things to me?"

She recoiled in mock horror. "Of course not! What fun would that have been? I mean, what if you hadn't reciprocated my feelings? I would have looked like a fool. Besides, if you weren't so pigheaded, you would have been able to see that I adored you. Everyone else knew. Even Maximillian."

Ash blinked at her. "What did you say?"

"Max always knew I was infatuated with you. He was the one who caught me blubbering out behind the dovecote after I found out you were besotted with that silly goose girl."

Ash scowled, clearly chalking up another mark against his brother. "He might have told me."

"Perhaps he thought it best that you figure it out in your own time. Plus I swore him to secrecy."

Ash snorted. "If there's anything Max excels at, it's keeping secrets."

Clarinda lowered her eyes, hoping to distract him from that dangerous topic with a pretty little pout. "I was only twelve at the time and it broke my heart because the goose girl's bosoms were so much more impressive than my own."

Ash closed a possessive hand over one of her breasts, testing its generous heft in his palm. "Something you clearly no longer have to fear."

She bit her lip, looking every bit as mischievous as she had at twelve. "Now that I'm not drunk on some ancient potion, I was hoping you might let me show you some of the tricks I learned in the harem."

Ash gave her a wary look. "I'm afraid I don't have a cucumber handy."

"I know," she whispered, closing her hand around him only to discover he was already fully aroused.

His hips jerked of their own volition as she lightly ran her thumb over his broad head, making his body weep a single tear of anticipation.

"Clarinda," he said hoarsely. "I'm not the sultan. You don't need tricks to please me. I'm perfectly happy with . . ."

She bent her head to him, rocking his world to its foundations with nothing more than a teasing swirl of her tongue. Then all he could do was throw back his head, grit his teeth, and tangle his hands in the silky ribbons of her hair as she proceeded to show him just what able teachers the women of Farouk's harem had been.

When Ash woke to find Clarinda snuggled against his side, her slender arm curled trustingly around his waist, he had only one thought — *Dear God, I've done it again*.

The desert sky above them was already beginning to melt from pink to blue. The crisp, golden edge of the sun peeped over the feathery fronds of the palms on the far side of the oasis, giving little warning that it would soon turn the vast sweep of sand and sky into a raging inferno.

Feeling as if its flames were already licking at him, Ash disengaged himself from Clarinda's embrace with painstaking care. He quickly drew on his trousers, boots, and shirt. He had no choice but to leave the shirt hanging halfway open since Clarinda's eager little hands had ripped away several of the buttons in their desperate quest to bare his chest so she could devour him with her luscious lips.

Ash's hands faltered on the front placket of his breeches as he remembered how those same lips had enfolded him with such enthusiasm and generosity. Clarinda had always been a bold and adventurous girl, but last night she had taken him on a journey beyond any he had ever experienced or even imagined. The memory made him hard all over again, tempted him to strip his breeches right back off and bury himself in her warm, sleepy body. It didn't help to know that she would probably welcome him with open arms. And legs.

Ash raked a hand through his hair, trying not to remember how her fingers had felt doing the exact same thing. All he had done last night was prove everything his father had ever believed about him to be true. He was an unscrupulous son of a bitch. He had saved Clarinda from Farouk's bed only to waste no time tumbling her into his own. He had betrayed his own brother without giving one thought as to what was best for Clarinda — or her future. He had sought only to satisfy his own selfish lust.

Just as he had done all those years ago.

Remembering the cost of that mistake, he turned toward the tent, determined to dump Luca out of his bedroll and demand that he escort the women the rest of the way to Max's encampment without him. He obviously couldn't be trusted to do what was best for Clarinda. He had to escape this place, escape *her*, even if he had to walk all the bloody way to the nearest port. He would rather face a poisonous asp, a scorpion's deadly stinger, and a band of desert marauders than face the temptation of another night in her company.

He had barely taken two steps when a voice rang out behind him with the pristine clarity of a bell. "Going somewhere, Captain Burke?"

❖ Chapter Twenty-eight

*A*s soon as Ash turned and Clarinda saw the guarded look on his face, she knew he was leaving her. Again.

And this time he wouldn't be coming back.

She sat up, gathering the robe they had used for a bed in front of her to shield her breasts from his gaze. She no longer wanted to be naked — or vulnerable — in front of him.

Hoping to stave off any awkward excuses he might make, she said, "I suppose it's time to resume your role as the dashing and romantic Captain Sir Ashton Burke. After all, there are adventures to be had, damsels to be rescued . . . rewards to be claimed."

Judging by the look in his eyes, her husky murmur had succeeded in reminding him just how *rewarding* last night had been for the both of them.

"I can't expect you to understand," he said.

Still clutching the robe in front of her, she rose, remembering yet another lesson he had taught her—it was far better to face your adversary while standing on your own two feet. "What's to understand? The legendary Lothario sneaking out the window of his lady love and creeping through the garden at dawn with boots in hand? Why, it's a tale as old—and trite—as time!"

Ash bent to scoop up his own discarded robe from a rock and tossed it to her. "You'd best put this on. I can't very well return you to your fiancé looking like that."

She let her robe drop as she caught his, deliberately standing there for a moment in the waves of sand like Venus rising from the sea in Botticelli's famous painting, before securing the robe around her. Borrowing a gesture from Yasmin's repertoire, she shook back her hair so that it spilled down her back in a waterfall of molten sunlight. "Like what? Like I just spent the night in his brother's bed?"

He couldn't deny that was exactly how she looked. Her hair was tousled, her cheeks flushed, her lips still tender from the kisses they had shared. The scrape of his beard stubble had left lightly abraded areas on her throat . . . and her inner thighs. She had the look of a woman who had been well satisfied by the man she loved.

"I don't expect you to believe anything less than the worst of me at this point in our relationship," he said, "but marrying Max is your only hope of reclaiming the social standing you enjoyed before you were abducted."

"Who said I enjoyed it? I seem to remember suffering through dozens of stifling suppers, incredibly dull tea parties, and boring balls. My only amusement was imagining you strolling through the door at one of those functions just so I could give you the cut direct."

"Without the protection of Max's name, all of society will be giving you the cut direct. Think about it, Clarinda. You've just spent three months imprisoned in a sultan's harem. For anyone who's ever read *The Lustful Turk*—and I can promise you more people have read it than will ever confess to it—a harem is no different from a brothel down on Fleet Street. What do you think every man—every *gentleman*—in London is going to be thinking about every time he looks at you?"

"Probably exactly what you think about every time you look at me."

Ash swore beneath his breath. "This time your father's wealth won't even be able to protect you from their censure. The men will lay wagers at their gaming clubs on which one of them will be the first to bed you, while their wives and daughters publicly shun you. You'll never be welcomed in their homes again but will be forced to live out the rest of your life on the fringes of polite society. You'd have a better chance of restoring your good name if you threw yourself off a bridge or down a well. At least then they could murmur and sigh over the terrible tragedy of it all while secretly admiring you for choosing the most honorable means of dealing with your 'disgrace.'"

"And just how is marrying your brother going to prevent all of this?"

"Not only is Max the heir to a dukedom but he sits on the Court of Directors of the East India Company. Some of the most powerful and influential men in all of England are indebted to him for their living. With the Earl of Dravenwood as your husband, at least their condemnation will be confined to whispers behind closed doors. And once Max becomes chairman of the Company, they won't even dare whisper your name with anything less than respect for fear he would ruin both their reputations and their fortunes."

"Ah! So you're letting me go for my own good. How very noble of you!" Clarinda winked at him. "Don't worry. I won't tell Poppy or the scandal sheets. I'd hate to ruin your reputation when you're so intent upon saving mine."

Resting his hands on his hips, Ash glared at her. "You know, you haven't changed one whit. You're every bit as impossible as you were when you were a girl." Shaking his head, he turned to walk away from her.

Panic swelled in Clarinda's heart. She had nothing left to offer him now. Nothing that might entice him to stay. He had already taken everything.

"It would probably be best if we strove to lay aside all of our past enmity before we reach the earl's encampment," she said. "After all, you're going to be my brother-in-law very soon. Perhaps, in time, you'll even learn to think of me as a sister."

Ash's steps slowed a fraction.

"I do hope you know our home will always be open to you. You can come visit for Christmas and Candlemas. You can stay at our town house in Mayfair during the Season, attend the christenings of our children."

Ash slowed even more.

"I suspect you'll make a very fine uncle, and your nieces and nephews will adore you. Most children can't resist an adult with a naughty streak even greater than their own. You'll be able to entertain them with stories about all of your exotic travels and dashing exploits, leaving out the seedier parts, of course, so as not to corrupt their tender young souls." As the distance between them grew, her words began to tumble out even faster. "Perhaps you would even consider traveling to England with us for our wedding. I'm sure it would please Maximillian more than you could ever know to have his brother stand up for him at the altar."

Ash froze in his tracks, then shook his head and kept walking.

Clarinda had promised herself she would not cry or beg this time, but she had no control over the furious tears that sprang into her eyes. "I suppose it shouldn't surprise me that you're running away again," she called after him. "After all, running away is what you've always done best!"

Ash quickened his pace, each long stride more resolute than the last.

Pride had kept the lid on Clarinda's anguish and fury for almost ten years, but now she didn't have enough left to stop it from boiling over. She had believed she was no longer capable of loving with the same headstrong recklessness that had broken her heart and nearly brought her to ruin, but then he had come sauntering back into her life and proved her wrong.

"I'm such a fool," she shouted, trembling with rage. "I should have known not to trust a single word—or a single kiss—that came from those lying lips of yours because you stood right there in that meadow after you made love to me and promised you'd come back for me. But you never did! You didn't even have the decency to send me a polite letter begging off our engagement. You just left me standing there waiting for all those years while you went off and—"

"I came back!" Ash roared, wheeling around to face her. His face had been stripped of the devil-may-care mask he wore so well to reveal the face of a man in the throes of a passion strong enough to destroy him. Strong enough to destroy them both. He retraced his steps one by one, stopping less than an arm's length away from her before saying, more softly this time, "I came back."

❧ Chapter Twenty-nine

*C*larinda gazed up at Ash in astonishment, struggling to understand how the boy she had last seen standing beneath the sturdy boughs of an English oak could have suddenly materialized in the middle of the Moroccan desert. "I don't understand. What are you saying?"

"I came back a little over four months later on the eve of your wedding to another man."

"Dewey," she whispered. No matter how often she said the name, she couldn't seem to bring the bland, pleasant features that went along with it into focus in her memory.

"Yes, the Honorable Viscount Darby," Ash said with excoriating sarcasm. "A far more suitable mate for a wealthy heiress than I could have ever hoped to be."

She shook her head in disbelief. "How on

earth did you find out I was supposed to marry Dewey?"

"As soon as my ship docked, I rode straight to your father's estate. I was passing through the woods when I overheard the gamekeeper and his son discussing the grand wedding that was to be held there the next day."

"So you just turned your horse around and left? Without saying a word to anyone?"

"That's exactly what I should have done. But I waited at the edge of the woods until nightfall, until you appeared in the window seat of your bedchamber."

He would have known she loved to curl up in that window seat every evening at twilight with a novel by Jane Austen or a book of poems by Lord Byron. He had scaled the rose trellis beneath her window countless times just to steal a good-night kiss from her eager lips.

The hard edge in his voice softened a degree. "You were wearing a cream-colored dressing gown and your hair was pinned up in an untidy knot on top of your head. You had your chin propped on your hand and you were watching the drive with the most wistful expression on your face. I assumed you were waiting for your adoring bridegroom to arrive."

Clarinda briefly pressed her eyes shut. It hadn't been her bridegroom she had been waiting for at all. "Why in the name of heaven didn't you come to me? Why didn't you say anything? Why didn't you try to stop me from marrying him?"

Ash's casual shrug conveyed volumes. "Why would I? You were on the verge of getting everything you ever wanted."

"You were the only thing I ever wanted!" she cried.

"Well, then . . . everything you deserved. You were going to be the wife of a viscount. You were finally going to have a title to go along with your fortune. No one would ever be able to mock you again for not being a lady or make you cry. And most importantly, you were going to be marrying a decent man, something I wasn't sure even then I could ever be." Passion roughened his voice, reminding her of how it had sounded in the night when he had urged her to roll over to her stomach or lift her leg a little bit higher. "If I had been a decent man, I would have never compromised you. I would have been willing to wait until I had more to offer you than just a hasty tumble in the grass."

"If that's what you believed, then why did you come back at all?"

He reached to tuck a strand of hair behind her ear, the tenderness of his touch sending a shiver dancing over her skin. "Because I decided I'd rather live in a garret and eat bread and cheese for the rest of my life than spend another night without you in my arms." His hand fell away from her, curling into a loose fist at his side. "But when I realized you couldn't even wait four bloody months for me, I knew I had been right to leave, knew the best thing I could do was to go away and never darken your door again. So that's what I did. I rode straight back to Portsmouth as if the very devil was on my heels and caught the first ship to India."

Clarinda shook her head, staggered by his revelation. The treacherous joy singing through her heart was tempered by a wealth of regrets. "If only you had come to me . . . if only I had known you were right outside my window that night . . . if only . . ."

She was so caught up in mourning the years they had lost that she didn't see the golden cloud approaching from the east until Ash shaded his eyes against the climbing sun to track it.

"What is it?" Clarinda asked, moving closer to him without realizing it. "Is it a sandstorm?"

The bitter twist of Ash's lips should have warned her. "I do believe, my dear, that the cavalry has arrived. My brother always did have an impeccable sense of timing."

That was when Clarinda realized the sand wasn't being stirred by the wind but by hundreds of hooves pounding their way across the desert.

She stood paralyzed in place, watching the shimmering cloud grow larger and more inescapable right along with the trepidation in her heart.

Their oasis idyll had come to an end. They didn't have three days. They didn't even have three minutes.

Her bridegroom was coming for her.

❧ *Chapter Thirty*

The regiment of East India Company soldiers came bearing down upon the oasis, the hooves of their mounts sending up golden plumes of sand. Many of the men wore native kaffiyehs to protect their heads from the sun's blistering rays along with their handsome scarlet coats and white-and-buff trousers.

As they drew closer, Yasmin ducked out of the tent flap and came tearing around the edge of the pool. Luca emerged right behind her, his chest bare and his breeches undone. He was wearing one boot and clutching the other in his hand.

As they joined Ash and Clarinda, Ash noticed that Luca's olive-skinned chest and back were scored with several scratches, as if he'd spent the night wrestling with an angry cat.

"So many men," Yasmin purred, eyeing the approaching regiment as if it were one of Farouk's exotic buffets.

"Thank God they're coming from the east," Luca said, his shoulders sagging with relief. "For a minute there, I thought the sultan had changed his mind."

"I almost wish he had," Ash muttered. He would have gladly returned to almost any moment in time when he and Clarinda had been shut away from the rest of the world in Farouk's palace of sensual indulgences.

Even among a regiment that large, it wasn't hard for Ash to recognize the tall, dark man riding at their head. Max might not be a military commander, but he still wore the mantle of authority with the grace and ease of one who had been born to it. He was bareheaded, no doubt believing the sun wouldn't have the audacity to burn him.

Ash had never seen Max behave with anything remotely resembling spontaneity, but as the riders approached the copse of palms, his brother flung himself off his horse before it even came to a full halt. Max came striding around the pool, his burning gaze fixed on the woman who stood next to Ash, her long flaxen hair dancing in the wind.

Ash stepped dutifully aside as Max pulled Clarinda into a fierce embrace. Cradling the back of her head in his palm, Max rested his clean-shaven cheek against the softness of her hair, his eyes closed as if he were enduring a pain too sharp and sweet to be borne. Ash recognized the look on his brother's face only too well. He suspected it had been mirrored on his own just a few hours ago.

Clarinda's arms slowly crept around Max's waist. She buried her face in his broad chest, her shoulders hitching in a silent little sob. Ash could hardly blame her for crying after everything she had been through.

Everything he had put her through.

When she tipped back her head to smile up at Max through her tears, Ash's worst fears were realized. He wasn't sure what he had expected to witness between the two of them, but the genuine affection shining in her eyes struck him low in the gut, like a punch he hadn't anticipated.

Clearly, Max hadn't exaggerated his feelings for Clarinda. Although his brother was searching her face with hungry eyes, Ash could tell he wasn't looking for the telltale signs of another man's possession but was simply struggling to convince himself that this wasn't all a dream.

That she was actually alive and well and safe in his arms.

Max tenderly smoothed back her hair with one hand, murmuring something intended for her ears only. Ash was afraid Max was going to kiss her right there in front of them all and Ash was going to end up back in front of a firing squad for murdering his brother in cold blood in front of dozens of witnesses. Fortunately for them all, Max contented himself with pressing a fervent kiss to her brow. Given Max's respect for propriety, he was probably waiting until after they were wed to kiss her on the lips for the first time.

Ash's brother might annoy the hell out of him but he was everything Ash would never be — honest, steady, reliable. Clarinda might want Ash, but it was Max she needed. Ash watched through narrowed eyes as his brother peeled off his impeccably tailored cutaway coat and wrapped it around Clarinda's shoulders to shield her from the curious eyes of his soldiers as if she weren't already wearing a robe that covered her from chin to shin.

Keeping a protective arm close about her, Max turned to face Ash, his grave countenance lit by something akin to happiness.

Before he could speak, Ash steered Yasmin in front of him. "Max, this is Yasmin. She's looking for a husband. Yasmin, this is my brother Max. He's not married, you know. He's an earl and he's going to be a duke someday, which where we come from is almost as good as a sultan."

"A duke, you say?" Yasmin sashayed even closer to Max, raking her luminous dark eyes over his impressive form. "If it is a wife you seek to warm your sleeping couch, my lord, you need look no further. Why, there are things I can do with my tongue that—"

Clearing his throat with a violent bark, Max gave Ash the evil eye. "I'm sure you'll make some man a very fine wife someday, miss, but what my brother neglected to tell you is that I am already betrothed to Miss Cardew."

Yasmin's mouth formed a perfect *O* of disbelieving outrage. "Another one!? Is there any man between Morocco and England who is *not* betrothed to that greedy little ice princess?"

Max slanted Clarinda a puzzled glance. "Would you care to explain that?"

"No," she replied, staring straight ahead.

Throwing her hands up in the air, Yasmin went marching back around the pool, a stream of Arabic curses spewing from her beautiful lips. When she slipped in her haste and almost fell *into* the pool, she nearly incited a riot as the soldiers jostled and shoved to see which one of them could be the first to dismount and rush to her aid.

Luca watched the whole scene with a lopsided grin. "Isn't she spectacular? She's going to make a wonderful mother for my children."

"So what are you doing out here?" Ash asked Max, folding his arms over his chest as he surveyed his brother. "Were you afraid I'd run off with your money? Or your bride?" he added, taking great care not to look at Clarinda.

"When so many days passed without any word from you, I was afraid something might have gone desperately wrong."

Ash couldn't very well tell his brother something had gone desperately right. So right he wasn't sure his heart—or his body—would ever recover from it. "It took longer than I expected to convince the sultan it would be in his best interests to free Miss Cardew."

Max tightened his grip on Clarinda, his face grim. "When I think of all she must have endured . . ."

"The sultan never touched me," Clarinda said simply. "Captain Burke arrived in the nick of time."

Max looked at him sharply then, the unspoken question hanging in the air between them. After a moment's hesitation, Max reached into the pocket of his waistcoat, withdrawing a cheque that could have been a twin to the one Max had given Ash when Ash had been fool enough to accept this job.

Max held the cheque out to him. "This can't even begin to repay the debt I owe you."

Somehow his brother's heartfelt gratitude was more galling to Ash than Max's contempt or his suspicion. Ash wanted nothing more than to tear the cheque into a thousand tiny pieces and hurl them back into Max's earnest face.

Instead, he took it from Max's hand, eyeing the impressive row of zeros with a jaded eye. "I won't bore you with my hollow protests because I can assure you I've earned every halfpenny of this."

"Where will you go now?" Max asked, although Ash could tell it was more out of politeness than genuine interest.

"Oh, I don't know." Ash furrowed his brow thoughtfully. Now that he had finally been given the perfect opportunity to walk out of Clarinda's life for good, he couldn't quite bring himself to do it. "Luca and I have traveled from one end of the world to the other fighting battles that weren't even our own. I was thinking it might be time to pay a visit to merry old England."

"England?" Luca squeaked, dropping his boot.

"England?" Max echoed, starting to look slightly bilious. "Why on earth would you want to come back to England?"

Gratified that he had finally managed to rattle Max's legendary composure, Ash gave him the same innocent look he used to give their mother after she had discovered someone had filched all the lumps of sugar from the sugar bowl. "Haven't you heard the news? My only brother is getting married. Surely you wouldn't expect me to miss such a momentous occasion."

A familiar flicker of annoyance danced over Max's face. "Who invited you?"

Allowing himself to meet Clarinda's startled gaze for the first time since Max had arrived to whisk her from his arms, Ash said, "Why, who else? Your bride, of course."

"He always could turn on the charm when it suited his needs."

Clarinda didn't have to turn around to see Maximillian's face. She recognized the note of mingled contempt and admiration in her fiancé's voice only too well.

"It was a trait that served him well in the sultan's court," she admitted, keeping her face turned away from Max so he wouldn't see just how well it had served her, too.

She had come up to the quarterdeck of the ship to be alone with her thoughts only to end up spying on the kneeling circle of men who had gathered for a dice game on the deck below. As Max joined her at the rail, Ash gave the fist curled around the handful of dice a kiss for luck before sending the dice clattering across the weathered boards. A collective groan went up from the deckhands clustered around him. Ash swept out an arm to collect his winnings, then softened their disappointment by offering them an affable grin and a sip from the flask of rum he tugged from the inside pocket of his coat.

She still couldn't believe he had called her bluff and was traveling to England to attend their wedding. Did he also plan to come for Christmas and Candlemas and the christenings of their children? Was he going to pop in unexpectedly just so he could give his adoring nieces and nephews rides on his shoulders and hold them enraptured with the tale of how he had once rescued their mother from the clutches of a rapacious sultan? The thought made her feel slightly hysterical.

"If they're not careful, he'll scam them out of a week's wages with a single toss," Max said. "I do hope they were bright enough not to let him use his own dice."

Clarinda slanted Max a look of mock censure. "Surely you're not implying your little brother might stoop to cheating?"

Max snorted. "When we used to play mumblety-peg as lads, he always used to say that if you weren't cheating, you weren't trying." Dismissing Ash with far more ease than Clarinda had ever been able to, he said, "I brought you your shawl. You haven't had time to adjust to the change in climate yet. I was afraid you might catch an ague."

As Max draped the cashmere wrap over her shoulders, Clarinda had to fight the urge to shrug off its smothering weight. While the brisk sea air was undeniably an abrupt shock to her system after months of living beneath the sweltering desert sun, she was tired of being treated like an invalid. Every time she turned around aboard the ship, Max was there—pressing a cup of warm tea into her hand, offering to fetch her a fur muff or a sturdier pair of gloves, encouraging her to retreat to her cabin for an afternoon nap. She was starting to feel as if she'd been rescued from a hospital, not a harem.

"You're too kind," she said, summoning up a wan smile. She couldn't very well strangle him with her shawl just for being solicitous of her needs. "I can't believe it's already the first of November. Time seemed to stand still in El Jadida. Sometimes it was impossible to even remember which century I was in."

Time might have stood still in Farouk's harem, but now it was rushing past like the sleek bow of the schooner cutting through the choppy swells. England—and home—lay just beyond the misty gray ribbon of the horizon. As the damp chill wormed its way deeper into her bones, Clarinda hugged the shawl tighter around her, thankful for its sheltering folds after all.

Gazing out over the sea, Max said stiffly, "I hope you understand why I couldn't come after you myself."

Clarinda had to school her features to hide her surprise. Despite the long days and nights they'd spent at sea, it was the first time Max had broached the topic. It was almost as if they'd entered into a silent agreement not to bring up her time in the harem, no difficult feat since they each had their own reasons for not wanting to discuss it.

"Of course I do," she assured him. "You had a responsibility to the shareholders in the Company. You had to protect their interests in the region."

He tugged her around to face him, his cool gray eyes searching her face with unexpected heat. "*You* are my only responsibility, my only interest. I couldn't come barging into the sultan's palace with guns blazing without risking your life. If I had had any other choice—any choice at all—do you think I would have sent *him*?"

Clarinda gazed up into his face, reading its anguish all too well. It was a dear face, one she had learned to rely on many years ago. It was also a devastatingly handsome face, one any woman would be lucky to love.

She reached up to lightly touch his cheek with her gloved hand. "You've always done exactly what was necessary to get the job done. It's not just what you do, it's who you are."

He briefly lowered his eyes, shielding their dark-lashed depths from her gaze. "Speaking of doing what's necessary, I've been thinking that perhaps it would be best for us to wed when we reach your father's estate."

"So soon?" she said weakly. Somehow she had thought there would be more time.

"If you're already my wife when we return to London, it will stave off a great deal of gossip about your months in captivity."

It would also prove to all of England that he still considered her worthy to be his wife.

As if sensing her uncertainty, he gently tipped her chin up with one finger. "You forget how long I've already been waiting." He offered her one of his rare smiles, his eyes crinkling in a most winning way. "Don't stay out in the cold too long. They'll be ringing the supper bell soon."

Clarinda sighed as she listened to the click of his bootheels fade on the planks of the deck. Max had been her dearest friend and staunchest champion for a long time. If not for him, she wouldn't have survived Ash's leaving the first time. But when he touched her, she didn't feel even a ghost of the yearning she felt every time his brother merely glanced at her with those tiger's eyes of his.

Ever since Max had come riding up with his men to whisk her away, Ash had treated her with the cool courtesy of a future brother-in-law. But she was still haunted by his impassioned confession at the oasis.

He hadn't abandoned her all those years ago after all. He had truly loved her. Enough to lay aside all of his pride, all of his ambition, and come back for her.

But he had spent the last nine years believing her as faithless as she had believed him. Believing all of her tender words and passionate promises had been nothing but the meaningless prattle of a fickle girl in the first throes of infatuation.

If she let him walk out of her life now without sacrificing her own pride and telling him the truth, he would never know just how wrong he had been.

She leaned forward, stealing another furtive glance over the rail. The dice game had broken up, but a lone man still stood on the deck below gazing up at her, the tip of his slender cigar glowing in the gathering shadows.

✤ *Chapter Thirty-one*

*S*omehow Ash knew exactly where he would find Clarinda on the morning of her wedding day.

The last time he had seen the meadow it had been draped in the minty green gown of spring with a lacing of mist overlying it. The awakening birds had filled the air with song. When he and Clarinda had rolled into the folds of her cloak, the new leaves unfurling along the spreading boughs of the oak had formed a sheltering canopy above their heads, and they had crushed the fresh clover beneath them, releasing its heady scent.

Now the first snow of the year fell from a leaden sky. The ground was hard, the blades of grass poking out from the snow brown and brittle. The autumn winds had stripped the oak to its bare bones, and instead of birdsong, the only sound that accompanied Ash's steps was the whisper of the falling snow.

Clarinda was kneeling beneath the tree, the burgundy hood of her ermine-trimmed cloak spangled with snowflakes. The cloak was similar to the one she had thrown over her nightdress with such haste on the morning she had raced out to the meadow to try to stop him from leaving. Even as Ash smiled, his throat tightened. That had been just like her, remembering her cloak but forgetting her shoes.

On this day, he was the one coming to say good-bye. He had thought he could stand by and watch her become another man's wife, but he had been wrong. He had no well-wishes to murmur, no brotherly embraces to offer, no blessings to give.

He was a much wiser man than he had been the last time he had stood in this meadow. Now he knew there was nowhere in this world he could go to escape her. She would haunt his every thought—and his every dream—until he whispered her name with his dying breath.

Even though she continued to gaze at the ground as he approached, he knew she was as aware of his presence as he had always been of hers. He didn't have to see her or hear her to recognize when she came within a dozen leagues of him. She was simply . . . *there*.

He leaned one shoulder against the trunk of the tree, crossing his booted feet at the ankles. When Clarinda tipped back her head to look at him, her eyes were dry but her beautiful face was as pale as the snow. Only her eyes held the promise of spring.

Yasmin had called her an ice princess, but Ash knew what a warm, passionate heart beat beneath that cool exterior, knew how her quivering flesh could burn with fever in response to the loving stroke of his hands.

"If you've decided to leave, I won't waste my breath this time begging you to stay," she said softly. "But before you go, there's something you should know. There have been too many secrets and too many lies, not all of them from your own lips." She rose, bracing one hand against the other side of the tree. As she gazed out over the meadow, snowflakes caught in her lashes like frozen tears. "Less than two months after you left, I discovered I was with child."

Ash felt his own face go as bloodless as hers.

She lowered her eyes as if reliving an old shame. "My father was devastated, not so much for himself, but for me. If word got out, he knew what everyone would say—that all the wealth in the world couldn't change the fact that his daughter was nothing but a common bit of baggage who had allowed herself to be seduced by a nobleman's son."

Ash's hands curled into fists. He wanted to travel back in time and beat to a bloody pulp anyone who would dare debase her in that way. Then he remembered that he was the cause of it. He had taken what he wanted and left her to suffer the consequences of his recklessness.

"Why didn't you send word?" he asked hoarsely. "I was at sea during most of that time, but someone could have had me found . . . my father . . . my brother . . . *someone*."

She faced him, her gloved fingers still clutching the tree as if it were her lifeline. "What was I going to do? Demand that you come back? Force you to marry me just because I was carrying your child? Spend the rest of my life wondering if you had ever truly loved me or if you were only wedding me out of some misguided sense of duty?"

Ash closed his eyes against a wave of remorse and regret. Of course she wouldn't have done any of those things. She was far too proud.

When he opened his eyes again, her gaze had returned to the snow-frosted meadow. "Papa wanted to send me away for a few months, ostensibly to visit an aunt at her isolated cottage by the sea in Yarmouth. His plan was that the child would be removed from my arms the minute it was born and shipped off to be raised by some nice family in the country, a family who would be generously compensated for their trouble . . . and their silence. Then I would return and resume my life as if nothing had ever happened."

Ash's voice sounded like the voice of a stranger, even to his own ears. "Your father always was a lot like my brother. He believed the best solution to any problem was to write a hefty cheque."

"Precisely. But I was having none of it. It was going to be my child—*your* child—and no one was ever going to take it away from me. You know exactly how stubborn I could be then."

"Then?" he said before he could stop himself.

Clarinda shot him a reproachful glance. "That's when Maximillian stepped in."

"Max?" Ash was beginning to wonder if his heart could bear any more shocks. If not for the sturdy trunk of the oak beneath his shoulder, he wasn't sure he could have remained on his feet.

"I couldn't very well confide in any of my friends from school, not even dear Poppy. Her father may have only been a humble country squire, but he would have never allowed his daughter to associate with a woman of weak moral character."

Ash started getting angry all over again.

"Max already knew how I felt about you so it wasn't so difficult to tell him the rest. He immediately offered to marry me and claim the child as his own."

"That's my brother," Ash said, unable to disguise the bitter note in his voice. "A hero to the core. So why aren't you already the Countess of Dravenwood?"

She brushed the hood of her cloak from her hair, boldly meeting his gaze. "Because I refused him. I would have done almost anything to keep that baby, but the one thing I couldn't bring myself to do was marry your brother. Max did everything he could to sway me, but when he saw my mind was made up, he and my father came up with the idea of salvaging my reputation by marrying me off to Viscount Darby as quickly as possible. Dewey had already proposed to me at least half a dozen times. He was ever so sweet but none too bright, and Max figured it would be a simple enough matter to convince him the child had been conceived on our wedding night and born early." She sighed. "When I look back, it seems like an impossibly cruel hoax, but we were all so very desperate. And Dewey did adore me so I convinced myself I would make reparations by being a model wife to him." She shook her head ruefully. "The very idea of me as a model wife must make you laugh."

The last thing Ash felt like doing in that moment was laughing.

"I spent that entire endless day before the wedding telling myself that it wasn't too late. That all was not lost yet and you could still come riding up the drive to save the day."

Ash couldn't believe how close he had come to doing just that. Instead he had abandoned her once again, believing she had thrown him over for another man.

"After the sun went down, I realized I couldn't go to Dewey's bed and let him put his hands on me while I was dreaming of you. I decided I would rather give up all claims to my father's fortune and society's good will and live in a humble cottage and raise our child on my own than spend the rest of my life living a lie."

Ash's heart began to beat faster at the thought there might actually be a child somewhere.

"So I sent a footman to the inn where Dewey was staying with a note telling him I was sorry but I couldn't marry him after all. He became so overwrought he jumped right on his horse and started out for my father's estate, hoping to change my mind. Instead of staying on the road, he took a shortcut through the woods. It was a moonless night and unfamiliar terrain, and he wasn't half the rider that you and Max were. He tried to take a jump he shouldn't have and his horse balked. The fall broke his neck." Tears welled up in her eyes as she turned to look at him, melting the snowflakes from her lashes. "I killed him. He was a decent, gentle soul and I broke his heart and then I killed him."

"You didn't kill him," Ash said grimly. "*I* killed him."

"When Max brought me the news, I was stricken with grief and guilt. I felt a terrible pain in my belly, even worse than the one in my heart. I cried out and collapsed in the entrance hall. Max carried me up the stairs, shouting for the doctor."

Ash would have done anything in that moment to silence her. He would have gladly snatched her up in his arms and kissed her forever, if only to stop the next words from spilling from her lips.

"Dewey wasn't the only one who died that night," she said softly. "I took to my bed for weeks after that. Everyone believed I was grieving over the loss of my fiancé, and I suppose I was because I knew that he had died for noth-

ing. Only my father, Maximillian, and a handful of loyal servants knew the whole truth. Max
refused to leave my bedside. He was always
there—spooning broth down my throat, wrapping me in a blanket and carrying me over to
the window seat, urging me to live when all I
wanted to do was die."

For the first time, Ash truly understood the
depths of Clarinda's devotion to his brother.
That understanding was tempered by a savage
surge of regret. It was just like Farouk rescuing
her from the slave traders all over again. Why
couldn't he be there at the right moment? Why
couldn't it be his hands smoothing her tousled
hair or drying her tears when she wept?

He might have done just that if she hadn't
dashed the tears from her cheeks herself. "When
Max carried me up those stairs, I was a girl.
When I walked back down them nearly two
months later, I was a woman. Max still wanted
me to marry him, but with both you and the
baby gone, I didn't see any point in marrying at
all. I was perfectly content being alone."

"The child?" Ash whispered, unable to choke
another word past the raw knot in his throat.

Clarinda knelt again, her knees cushioned by
the rippling folds of her cloak. It was then that
Ash realized she was kneeling in front of a small

stone that hadn't been there the last time he had visited the meadow. It was covered by a thin layer of snow.

"My father wanted to throw the baby away like so much garbage so he could pretend it had never existed. When I wept and screamed and begged him not to take it away from me, he tried to dismiss it as the hysterical ravings of a grief-struck girl. It was Max who intervened and insisted that my wishes be honored. He offered to find a place for the child in the Burke family crypt." A sad little smile curved her lips. "But I knew where he belonged."

Her gloved fingers gently brushed the snow from the simple stone to reveal the single word carved upon it.

CHARLIE.

Not CHARLES or CHARLES CLARENCE BURKE or even a date to mark his passing, but simply CHARLIE.

Their son rested in the exact same spot where he had been conceived in a moment of wild, reckless passion between two young lovers who had let their hearts overrule every vestige of their good sense.

If Charlie had lived, he might be romping through this meadow even now, whooping with delight and catching snowflakes on his tongue.

Instead, he would forever sleep beneath the sheltering arms of the mighty oak, his lullabies the quicksilver voices of the changing seasons and the whisper of the wind through the tree's swaying boughs.

Clarinda rose, tugging the hood of her cloak back up over her hair.

"Before you left, I wanted you to know that if I had had a single word of encouragement from you after Charlie died—a letter, a message, some small token of your affection, anything at all—I would have waited forever."

Ash stood frozen in place as she brushed a kiss over his cheek, her lips as warm as a summer day, then turned and started back across the meadow.

He waited until she had disappeared over the snow-swept rise to drop to his knees in the exact spot where she had knelt. He ran his hand gently over the small stone, his own tears melting the snow where they fell.

Ash couldn't have said how long he knelt there by that tiny grave, saying good-bye to the son he would never know. A son who might have had a sheaf of silvery blond hair and eyes the color of clover.

When he finally rose, the snow had stopped. A pale sun was making a valiant attempt to peek through the low-hanging clouds, its slanting rays transforming the snow-covered vista into a glittering wonderland.

If Ash squinted, he could almost see the fiery orb of the sun blazing down upon a sweep of golden sand; Clarinda standing in the courtyard at Farouk's palace looking as if she'd just stepped out of one of his more torrid dreams; Clarinda reclining on a bed of crimson silk, her smile inviting and her green eyes glittering with desire.

If today had proved anything, it was that she had already suffered enough at his hands. If he had even an ounce of decency left in him, he would accept her kiss for what it was—a final farewell—and leave this place for good.

She had found something in his brother's arms she would never find in his—peace, security, stability. Max had never been foolish enough to go chasing after a dream when the only woman who could ever make it come true was standing right in front of him.

The passion between Clarinda and him had burned too bright from the beginning. If they ended up together, the future would always be fraught with danger. There would be tempers flaring, wills clashing, epic battles of wits that could only be fought in the bedroom, not the drawing room. Neither of them would ever know another moment's peace.

It sounded utterly glorious, Ash's very idea of heaven.

A grin slowly spread across his face.

Their stubborn pride had already robbed them of so many precious years they might have spent in each other's arms. He'd be damned if he would let it cost them so much as another second.

He gave the small gravestone one last lingering look before he started across the meadow, hoping his son would approve of what he was about to do.

Clarinda stood gazing at herself in the tall looking glass that sat in the corner of her bedchamber.

Since there had been no time to visit a modiste and order a fashionable wedding gown, she had chosen to wear the bronze silk taffeta that made the green of her eyes look especially vivid. The gown was one that had always featured prominently in her fantasies about giving Ash the cut direct should he ever dare to darken her door again.

She studied the face of the woman in the mirror as if it were the face of a stranger, but no matter how hard she searched, she couldn't find any trace of the passionate, headstrong girl who had loved Ashton Burke with every fiber of her being.

The creature who stood before her now with the neatly dressed hair and serene expression was the cool, composed woman that girl had become in his absence. The woman who had stepped into her mother's slippers and hosted dozens of suppers and soirees for her father's influential friends. The woman who had opened society's doors so that she and Poppy might stroll through them arm in arm. The woman who had agreed to become the bride of an earl and a future duchess.

A knock sounded on the door. "Miss?" came the timid voice of her maid. "It's time."

Clarinda lifted her chin. The maid was right. The time had come to bid that other girl and her dreams farewell forever.

Maximillian was waiting for her at the makeshift altar that had been set up before the marble hearth in the elegant drawing room of her father's estate. Somehow it seemed that Max had always been waiting for her, as stalwart and dependable as the old oak tree in the meadow.

His thick, dark hair was neatly trimmed so that its ends barely brushed his collar. His short, gray cutaway coat and striped waistcoat were as conservative as he was. His jaw was clean-shaven without so much as a hint of rakish stubble to mar its strong planes. As he watched her walk down the aisle toward him, the look in his fine gray eyes might have taken another bride's breath away. It had always been easy to take his good looks for granted when distracted by Ash's far more unconventional masculine beauty.

A half-dozen chairs had been hastily arranged to accommodate the guests in attendance. Clarinda's father gripped a walking stick topped with the brass head of a lion. He had wept openly upon her return, but now his ruddy face was wreathed in a beaming smile. He had always hoped his little girl would make a match with a man like Maximillian.

Her bridegroom's parents huddled together on the opposite side of the aisle, looking less than overjoyed by the proceedings. Clarinda strongly suspected the tears Max's mother was weeping into her monogrammed handkerchief were *not* tears of joy. The duke and duchess had always hoped their beloved eldest son would marry someone equal to his station in life, not a common heiress whose father had made his fortune in trade. When the duke wasn't giving his wife consoling pats, he kept checking the gold fob of his pocket watch, as if to make sure Luca hadn't pilfered it.

For a Gypsy and a former concubine, Luca and Yasmin had managed to turn themselves out quite nicely. Clarinda had been forced to give Yasmin the pick of her wardrobe just to keep her from showing up in a collection of flimsy veils and a pair of sandals. Yasmin, of course, had chosen a low-cut ball gown utterly unsuited for morning wear that was at least three sizes too small for her. She kept tugging the bodice down until Clarinda was afraid her breasts were going to come spilling out before the ceremony even began, a fear apparently shared by the staid vicar, who appeared to be teetering on the verge of an apoplexy.

Clarinda had already caught Yasmin making eyes at her father. A faint shudder went through her as she imagined what it would be like to have the woman as a stepmother. If Yasmin's transparent attempts to snare a wealthy husband bothered Luca, you couldn't tell it by the wink he gave the pretty little parlor maid hovering in the corner. His shameless flirting brought a simpering blush to the girl's freckled cheeks.

Only one chair in the room was conspicuously empty.

Even now Clarinda couldn't tell if the glow in Maximillian's eyes could be attributed to happiness that their wedding was finally taking place or relief that his wayward brother had decided to behave true to character and exit stage right before it could begin.

Clarinda drew in a deep breath, no easy feat within the confines of her corset. Since the weather had taken such a bitter turn so early in the winter, there was no proper bouquet to be had. One of the gardeners had managed to scrounge up a nosegay of purple pansies for her to carry. She was surprised her hands were so steady. She was beginning to wonder if this was what she would feel for the rest of her life — absolutely nothing.

She truly did love Max and was grateful for everything he had done for her. But she wasn't *in* love with him. Perhaps if she had never met Ash, she wouldn't have known the difference. She could have lived out her life in quiet contentment like so many women of her acquaintance. She couldn't think of a single one of them who was consumed by a grand passion for her husband.

For some reason, Poppy's joyful face drifted through her mind, giving her heart a sharp twinge.

Perhaps she should just embrace the numbness that had enveloped her since she had left Ash at their son's grave. Wasn't it preferable to the mad rush of her pulse every time he walked into a room, the desperate longing for something she had briefly tasted but could never have again? Wasn't it better to feel nothing at all than to risk losing everything?

She had finally reached the altar. As she took her place at Max's side, he folded her hand in his and gave her a solemn smile.

The vicar opened his prayer book and cleared his throat. He had just opened his mouth as well when the double doors at the back of the room came flying open and Ashton Burke came striding into the drawing room.

✥ Chapter Thirty-two

As Max's fingers convulsed around hers in a painful squeeze, Clarinda's blissful numbness vanished in a flash. Her heart leapt in her chest, then lurched into a thundering rhythm. She pressed the hand gripping the bouquet just below her breasts, wishing she hadn't ordered her maid to lace her corset quite so tightly just so she could squeeze into the bronze silk taffeta. Spots began to dance in front of her eyes, and for a minute she thought she might actually do something so ridiculous as swoon.

Ash's coat was unbuttoned and the collar of his shirt laid open to reveal the broad, tanned column of his throat. He was in desperate want of both a shave and a haircut. He couldn't have looked any more disreputable had he just swaggered down the gangplank of a pirate ship.

Clarinda's father rose, brandishing his walking stick. "What in the devil is *he* doing here?"

"That's precisely what I'd like to know," Max said evenly as Ash came to a halt in the middle of the aisle halfway to the altar.

"I can't blame you for being upset, sir," Ash said, lifting a placating hand to Clarinda's father. "After the grief I've caused your daughter, I'm sure you'd like nothing more than to summon your gamekeeper and have me shot. If I were you, I'd feel exactly the same way. Why, I'll probably shoot any man who dares to lay a finger on my Charlotte before she turns five-and-twenty . . . no, make it five-and-thirty."

"Who's Charlotte?" Luca asked, frowning in confusion.

"My daughter," Ash replied. "*Our* daughter. The daughter Clarinda and I are going to have after we're married."

"She's not marrying you," Max said, looking as if he'd be more than happy to shoot Ash himself. "She's marrying me."

"That's right," Clarinda said, drawing herself up to her full height and giving Ash her haughtiest look. "I'm not marrying you. I'm marrying him."

"I was a bloody fool for not trying to stop your last wedding. If you think I'm going to just stand idly by while you marry my brother, then you're a bigger fool than I was."

It was the duke's turn to surge to his feet. "Cease this nonsense immediately, Ashton. You're embarrassing yourself! And your entire family!" He shook his head in disgust. "Not that there's anything new about that."

Ash faced his father. "I'm sorry, Your Grace. I know this will come as a shock to you, but for once I'm trying to do the honorable thing. I'm afraid Miss Cardew has no choice in the matter. I've already compromised her. Twice. Well, actually four times if you count that night in the desert." He turned to give Clarinda a lazy smile that made her toes curl in her slippers. "Or should I say four and a half?"

The duchess gasped aloud.

"Oh, hello, Mother," Ash said fondly. "You're looking quite lovely in your finery."

"Why, you . . . " Max started forward with a growl.

Clarinda grabbed his arm and held on with all of her strength, forcing him to stop or drag her down the aisle behind him.

She barely recognized this Max. His handsome face was set in savage lines, his upper lip curled in a feral snarl. "It took me nine long years to woo her. To convince her she deserved a home, a husband, children of her own. Do you think you can just come marching in here and destroy all of that? The same way you almost destroyed her?"

"I'm sorry, Max," Ash said, all traces of mockery disappearing from his face and voice. "It was never my intention to hurt her. Or you. Believe it or not, I loved you both."

Max raked a hand through his hair, a despairing bark of laughter escaping him. "I suppose I have only myself to blame for this. I was desperate and naïve enough to believe I could bring you back into her life without you smashing it into smithereens. Sometimes I wish like hell your ship had sunk after you came back here the first time!"

As Ash went dangerously still, Clarinda felt her heart go numb all over again. Her hands slid from Max's arm.

If there's anything Max excels at, it's keeping secrets.

You've always done exactly what was necessary to get the job done. It's not what you do, it's who you are.

Secrets and lies. Clarinda had told Ash there had been too many of them. She just hadn't realized how many.

"You saw me that day? The day before Clarinda was supposed to wed Darby? You knew I had returned for her yet you did nothing? Said nothing?" Ash shook his head in stunned disbelief. "Why, you coldhearted son of a—" He started toward Max, his hands balled into fists.

Before he could reach his brother, Clarinda drew back her arm and slapped Max full across the face. The sound echoed like a gunshot in the stunned silence.

Max slowly lifted his hand, touching his fingers to the vivid print she had left on his cheek.

"How could you?" she whispered, trembling with outrage and anguish as she relived all of the wasted years in that one moment. "You knew what he meant to me. You were the only one who *truly* knew."

Max lifted a hand as if to touch her hair, then slowly lowered it. His gray eyes were shadowed with a pain that had nothing to do with her blow. "I did it because I loved you. Because I had loved you long before he had. If he was worthy of you, he would have made you his wife before taking you to his bed. That's what I would have done. Even if you wouldn't marry me because I would always be nothing more to you than a reminder of him, I was convinced you'd be better off with Dewey than with him."

"That wasn't your choice to make!" she shouted. "It was mine!"

"I realize that now. I realized it even then. But by the time I came to my senses, it was too late. Ash was gone and Dewey and the baby were dead. I knew I could never tell you what I'd done or you'd despise me forever. I'd spent my entire life trying to do the right thing, yet in one blinding fit of jealousy, I did something so terribly wrong that it's haunted me ever since then."

"Is that why you turned against me after I came back from Eton?" Ash asked, still breathing hard. "Because you were *jealous*?"

Max's smile held little humor. "Ironic, isn't it? I had the title and our father's favor, but once I saw the two of you together, I knew you would always have the only thing I ever truly wanted— Clarinda's love." Max gazed down at her for a long moment, then slowly turned away, his every movement heavy with regret. Despite his obvious defeat, he still couldn't resist giving his brother a mutinous look. "You'll never be good enough to deserve her, you know."

"God doesn't always give you what you deserve," Ash said quietly. "Sometimes he gives you what you can't live without."

As Ash's words sang through her heart like birdsong in the spring, Clarinda reached up to dash a tear from her cheek.

A gentleman to the bitter end, Max gave them all a stiff bow before turning and striding down the aisle. Although he probably would have liked nothing more than to slam the drawing room door, he gently pulled it shut behind him instead. After waiting a polite moment, Yasmin went slinking out of the room after him, no doubt hoping he would need a shoulder, or perhaps a pair of ample bosoms, to cry upon.

Ash swept his gaze over the room. "Well, we have a vicar, guests, and a bride. It seems all we're lacking is a groom."

"Are you volunteering yourself for the position, Captain?" Clarinda asked primly. "I heard a rumor that you'd recently become unemployed."

Moving closer to her, Ash lifted one shoulder in a nonchalant shrug. "This may be my only chance to catch you between fiancés. And besides, where am I going to find a corpulent sodomite as pretty as you?"

Clarinda lifted her chin. They were standing in front of several witnesses. She was wearing her finest bronze silk taffeta, the one that made her eyes glow like emeralds. This was the perfect chance to give him the cut direct. To tell him to go to the devil and mean it.

Instead she said, "If I marry you, I'll never be a lady, you know."

"Fortunately for you, I happen to prefer bourgeois little hoydens."

With that tender declaration of his undying love, Ash snatched her into his arms and kissed her as if it were both their first and their last kiss. As the kiss went on and on, the vicar nervously cleared his throat, plainly fearing Ash was going to compromise her for the fifth time right there in front of them all.

According to the scandal sheets, after notorious adventurer Captain Sir Ashton Burke rescued wealthy shipping heiress Clarinda Cardew from the lurid depravity of a Moroccan harem, he refused the extravagant fortune her father tried to bestow upon him, insisting the only reward he would accept was her hand in marriage. They were not wed in the drawing room of her father's mansion but in a snow-draped meadow beneath the spreading boughs of an old oak tree. The future Mrs. Burke wore bronze silk taffeta and an ermine-trimmed cloak while the captain wore the biggest grin of his life.

They named their first daughter Charlotte.

Look for Max's story in the next thrilling
historical romance from

Teresa Medeiros

The Temptation of Your Touch

Coming soon from Pocket Books

Turn the page for a preview of
The Temptation of Your Touch . . .

$\mathcal{M}$aximillian Burke was a very bad man.

He watched a tendril of smoke rise from the mouth of the pistol in his hand, trying to figure out exactly when he had embraced the role of villain in the farce his life had become. He had always been the honorable one, the dependable one, the one who chose each step he took with the utmost care to avoid even the possibility of a stumble. He had spent his entire life striving to be the son every father would be proud to claim and the man any mother would want her daughter to marry.

At least that's what everyone believed.

It was his younger brother, Ashton, who had gone around getting into brawls, challenging drunken loudmouths to duels, and facing the occasional firing squad. But now Ash was comfortably settled in their ancestral home of

Dryden Hall with his adoring wife and their chattering moppet of a daughter. A daughter who had her mother's flaxen hair and laughing green eyes.

Maximillian briefly closed his eyes, as if by doing so he could blot out the image.

While Ash enjoyed the domestic bliss that should have been Max's with the woman Max had loved for most of his life, Max stood in a chilly Hyde Park meadow at dawn, his boots coated with wet grass and the man he had just shot groaning on the ground twenty paces away.

He had little doubt Ash would have laughed at his predicament, even if it had been a drunken slur cast on Max's sister-in-law's good name that had prompted it.

Max could not seem to remember that Clarinda's honor was no longer his to defend.

When he opened his gray eyes, they were as steely as flints. "Get up and stop whining, you fool!" he told the man still writhing about on the grass. "The wound isn't mortal. I only winged your shoulder."

Clutching his upper arm in bloodstained fingers, the young swell eyed Max reproachfully, his ragged sniff making Max fear he was about to burst into tears. "You needn't be so unkind, my lord. It still hurts like the devil."

Blowing out an impatient sigh, Max handed the pistol to the East India Company lieutenant he had bullied into being his second and stalked across the grass to help the wounded man to his feet, gentling his grip with tremendous effort. "It's going to hurt more if you lie there whimpering until a constable comes to toss us both into Newgate for the crime of dueling. It will probably fester in that filth and you'll lose the arm altogether."

Max was only too relieved to hand the wounded fellow off to the man's white-faced second and the hovering surgeon. Resting his hands on his hips, Max watched them load the lad into a carriage.

He had to confess, there was something almost liberating about relinquishing his heroic mantle. When you were a villain, no one looked at you askance if you drank too much or neglected to tie your cravat in a flawless bow. No one whispered behind a hand if it had been three days since your last shave. Max ruefully stroked the stubble on his jaw, remembering a time when he would have fired his valet for letting him appear in public in such a disreputable state.

Since resigning from the board of the East India Company, he was no longer forced to make painfully polite conversation with those who sought his favor. Nor did he have to suffer fools graciously, if not gladly. Instead, everyone scurried out of his way to avoid the caustic lash of his tongue and the contempt smoldering in his smoky gray eyes. They had no way of knowing his contempt wasn't for them, but for the man he had become, the man he had always secretly been.

If he hadn't been so deep in his cups when he had overheard his unfortunate dueling opponent loudly tell his friends that legendary adventurer Ashton Burke had married a sultan's whore, he would have never challenged the silly git to a duel. What the boy really needed was a sound thrashing before being sent to bed without supper.

Shaking his head in disgust, Max turned on his heel and went striding toward his own carriage. He needed to get out of London before he killed someone. Most likely himself.

The lieutenant hurried back across the grass to retrieve the pistol and return it to its mahogany case before trotting after him. "M-m-my lord?" he asked, a stammer betraying his nervousness. "W-where are you going?"

"Probably hell," Max snapped without breaking his stride. "All that remains to be seen is how long it will take me to get there."

Hips & Curves.

This romance has ended, but yours doesn't have to.
Hips & Curves is lingerie for curvy women.
Because you should always feel sexy and ravishing.
Be bold in your own life. Create your own story.

**Visit Hips & Curves online at
www.hipsandcurves.com**

FREE SHIPPING
enter code ssba11
at checkout*

Through September 2012*, Hips & Curves is offering
free standard shipping on any purchase at
www.hipsandcurves.com when you use

offer code SSBA11 at checkout.

*After September 2012, call Hips & Curves at
800.220.8878 for current promotions

*Available only to Continental U.S. residents only.

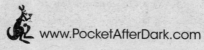